SMALL TOWN STORIES COLLECTION

MERRI MAYWETHER

This book is a work of fiction. The characters, incidents, and dialogue are from the author's imagination and are not to be construed as real. Any resemblance to actual events or persons, living or dead, is entirely coincidental.

ISBN: 979-867-362-0373

PRAISE FOR MERRI MAYWETHER

"Merri Maywether has a way of describing things that makes the reader feel like they are right there with the characters."

Amazon Review *Paradise Hills Thanksgiving*

"Get your tissues ready. This book is absolutely heartbreaking but yet a wonderful journey into love found again

Amazon Review *Home for Good*

"Great writing style. Will read more by Merri Maywether."

Amazon Review *Just a Friend*

"I really enjoyed how the author very credibly grew relationships found in every American small town."

Amazon Review *The Chance to Win Her Heart*

CONTENTS

PART I

PIECE OF CAKE

1

YOU'LL LOVE LIVING IN A SMALL TOWN

"You'll love living in a small town," Paul Sanders promised his younger sister Lacey.

He followed it with, "It's like the programs we watched on television when we were kids." After years of hints, suggestions, and outright challenges, Lacey had finally agreed to give Three Creeks a try.

And, she was happy to admit that he was right. Three Creeks, Montana was the enlarged version of the images people used on puzzles. It had a main street lined with small businesses; a city hall located in a large red brick building in the center of town; and a large park with a picturesque white gazebo that was surrounded by mature trees. The town was named after the three different creeks that met in various areas on the outskirts of the town.

Just as the scenery in and around Three Creeks was beautiful, the people were equally amazing. It took a while for Lacey to figure out that when people waved, they were greeting her. At first, when it happened, she checked to see if they directed the friendly gesture to someone behind her.

On this sunny Saturday afternoon, most of the town had

converged in the high school gym to recognize the success of roughly thirty high school seniors. Balloons people stashed with congratulatory greetings decorated the edge of the high school gym swayed with just as much enthusiasm as the room full of well-wishers. The edges of the rows of chairs were decorated with black and red streamers. In the chairs, well-wishers attentively watched the final moments of the high school experience.

Other than the small class size, the graduation ceremony followed the typical routine. There was a guest speaker followed by the valedictorian. During the reading of the scholarships awarded the soon to be college students, Lacey clapped with pride. They announced that her niece, Noelle, had acquired a little more than fifty-two thousand dollars in scholarships.

There was just enough activity to make them forget that they had already sat in the same space for roughly forty-five minutes. Right when the small children were getting restless, and the older friends and relatives were beginning to notice their joints getting stiff, a montage of photos that captured their school experience signaled nearing the end of the program. People laughed, cried and commented on the memories.

Lacey who loved her life before moving to Three Creeks felt pangs of wistfulness. She wished she belonged to a community like this. With the population being so small, everyone mattered, and their endeavors were acknowledged accordingly. When the graduating class of 2017 gleefully flung their caps into the air, the people who supported them clapped, hooted, and hollered in celebration.

Before the graduates went off to face the world, they had one last celebration. Parents and teachers stood behind tables lined in a row and offered a variety of choices of cakes baked by the local baker. Lacey was talking to Noelle about the irony of their situation. Her niece by marriage was eager to leave her small-town roots, and Lacey was making Three Creeks her home.

She was so engrossed in the conversation that she didn't see the person behind her reach for a fork at the same time as her. As her fingers touched the fork a strong hand came down on top of hers. The touch lasted for less than a second. However, it was long enough to send a spark that began at Lacey's fingertip and shot straight to her heart. It was as though someone briefly turned on a light switch. She turned to apologize to the person behind her and saw the most amazing golden-brown eyes. It looked like a band of gold circled the light brown irises. At a loss for words, Lacey mumbled her apology and hurried to get away from the situation. She felt the eyes on her and turned to get one last look at them. The man offered her one quick smile and having got what he went there for, left the line. With each step further into the crowd, Lacey felt the light from the spark dim. She sighed in admiration and allowed herself to be pulled into the world as it was before she met him.

2

MR. GOLDEN EYES

"You chose the perfect time to move here." Gracie, Paul's wife, handed Lacey a crock pot full of little smokies that had been cooking in a barbecue sauce all morning. "And, I'm not just saying that so I can put you to work."

The bowl of potato salad in Gracie's arms was large enough to feed a small army. Even if the entire army ate until they were full, they'd most likely have left overs. In addition to potato salad, they had a macaroni salad, baked beans, a jello salad, and fruit platters that had almost every color of the rainbow in them. After she had set the potato salad on the table, Gracie took the crock pot of smokies and placed it between a crock pot of miniature meatballs and another crockpot that had a spinach cheese dip. The two of them had spent the better part of two days preparing food for a gathering that would most likely number in the hundreds.

"People pop in, chat for a bit, and go on to the next party," Gracie explained while smoothing a hair on her temple. The waves seemed to have given into the excitement and tried escaping the well-groomed look her sister-in-law favored.

Keeping in line with the conversation, she continued her explanation of the events to come. "We'll have plenty of burgers and dogs. Depending on how many other parties they've been to before they get to ours, our guests might just want to graze on finger foods."

For Gracie's sake, Lacey hoped the wide array of food was necessary. As though her sister-in-law read her mind, she added, "Worst case scenario, we can have the football team for lunch next week." There was so much food, even after the football team came through there was the possibility that Gracie and Paul had the chance to practice creative meal making with the excess hamburgers.

With the distraction of making sure the stacks of plates and cups were full, Lacey hadn't noticed a lot of people had come through the food line. Noelle, Gracie, and Paul bounced from table to table greeting whoever stopped for a visit. From the safety of the food table, Lacey admired the warmth on their faces when they spoke to people. At one point in the day, Lacey caught herself thinking, *"These people genuinely like each other."*

She also found new admiration for Gracie's ability to plan. The second batch of salads was on the table, and the cookies had thinned enough to be consolidated into one plate. The actual number of people who stopped by didn't register until she'd gone through the third package of paper plates. They had easily fed close to one hundred and fifty people.

Lacey noticed they were running low on fruit. The behavior pattern Gracie predicted earlier proved to be true. Toward the end of the evening, people had eaten so much at the parties before this one they were snacking on the finger foods. Rather than disturb Gracie who was in the middle of an animated conversation with Noelle and some of her friends, Lacey made her way to the house to grab another tray of fruit.

Nobody seemed to notice her leaving which was a slight relief to Lacey. She had been peopled to her limit. If someone were to point at a person and say what do you know about them, she could retell their life story. But, if they were to ask the person's name, she was at a loss for words. When things got to this point, she made it a habit of going into the world inside her head and cataloging what she did remember. On the way back to the tables, she made a list and checked it off. Kent works at the hardware store. Zach is the police officer that works with Paul. Mary teaches high school in the town thirty minutes away. Lacey pat herself on the back for the list of names she was able to recall.

At the peak of self-satisfaction, she heard, "Watch out!" But it was too little too late. She didn't know what to watch out for, nor the direction to move to avoid it. Not that it would have mattered because she was in the middle of a collision course with Barkley, the neighbor's Saint Bernard. He nipped her left hip and continued chasing after another neighbor's cat.

Why she was so determined to save a platter of fruit was beyond her ability to argue with the logic. But she was. Lacey grasped the platter and wobbled into the most unceremonious fall ever recorded in Sander's family history. Even worse, through her mind's eye, she saw the sequence of events occur in slow motion. First came the wobble. Then the overcorrection in the movement which was followed by a series of overcorrections. When her body finally surrendered to the law of gravity, everything returned to normal speed, and she fell with such force the fruit escaped from the confines of the plastic wrap. The fall was hard enough to send sliced watermelon, kiwi, pineapple and melons into the air. They eventually complied with the natural course of action and like tiny missiles landed on top of her.

By the time she lifted herself up with her elbows, Gracie and Noelle were at her side fussing over her.

"Are you okay?"

"Colton Hughes, you need to get control of your dog."

Lacey didn't know which was worse, the attention from her sister-in-law or her brother's poorly veiled attempt to hide his laughter. Paul had his back to them with his face turned upward to stifle the laughter. It was the same thing she had seen when they were growing up and she got in trouble for something he did.

"It's my brother's dog. I'm dog sitting while he's on his honeymoon." Lacey's eyes followed the sound of the voice until she found the person that went along with it. When she found it, she didn't know whether to faint from joy or die from horror. The voice belonged to the one and only Mr. Golden Eyes.

3

I LIKE THE SOUND OF THAT

"I don't believe we've been properly introduced." Mr. Golden Eyes extended his hand for her to shake it.

Lacey held out her hand, felt the stickiness from the fruit, and withdrew it. "Sorry, it's better if we skipped the handshake." Instead, she waved at him and tried to slowly back away from the conversation.

She could tell he was conflicted. He alternated glances from her to the direction where the dog had run. "I would love to chat, but I have a runaway dog to find. I'll come back to talk to you later." He didn't wait for her to answer. The man Lacey presumed to be Colton Hughes whistled sharply and hurried away.

When he disappeared completely from her field of vision, Lacey sighed wistfully. She was still staring at the spot where she had last seen him when Gracie brought her back to reality. "You go on and get cleaned up. Noelle and I will take care of this."

"Are you sure?"

Gracie fished a chunk of melon out of Lacey's hair and held it out for her to see. "Really, it's about time to shut down the party anyway." She spoke louder for emphasis, "Paul and Grady are more than happy to help me get things back in the house."

Her brother offered no argument or smart comeback. He simply said, "Sure, no problem." Lacey couldn't hear what he said to Grady, but the next thing she knew both men had grabbed a platter and an oversized bowl and headed for the house.

Being married to Gracie had changed him. Growing up, Paul didn't like to help at all. In the short amount of time he'd been with her, he'd transformed into the kind of man that Lacey wished she could find. Paul got into enough trouble to keep things interesting and was quick to apologize if things got out of hand. Whenever Gracie asked for any kind of help, he was quick to respond. It took a while, but her brother Paul grew up to be a man like her father.

Which is how she ended up in Three Creeks. After he had married Gracie who was a single mother with a high school student, Paul moved into her house. Rather than sell his house, he suggested that Lacey move in and remodel it. Instead of paying rent, she'd help him upgrade the house. In one of their conversations over coffee, Gracie told her that he hoped that after Lacey made improvements, she'd like the house too much to want to leave it.

"Let me help clean up the fruit, and then I'll gladly go home and get showered." She bent down and picked up pieces of fruit and dropped them into the platter. She crawled around on her hands and knees and returned to the platter when her hands were full.

Jeans and boots that had to have belonged to a man greeted her. Lacey's eyes traversed the legs, to the waist and went straight to the face that belonged to them. It was none other than Mr. Golden Eyes. He bent down to pick up the platter of fruit.

She couldn't be certain because the sound of the air leaving her lungs stifled what he was saying. Interpreting the message from the apologetic look on his face, Lacey guessed he said something to the effect of, "I should be the one cleaning this mess."

Wiping her hands on the front of her shirt, she said, "No harm no foul. It's all cleaned up now. By the way, do you know anybody that has a guinea pig?"

"A guinea pig?" he echoed her question.

"Yes, they like to eat fruits and vegetables. We could freeze it and make it into pet frozen pops or something else useful."

As if his eyes weren't enough to captivate a woman, Lacey thought she died, went to heaven and was talking to some sort of an angel when Mr. Golden Eyes smiled. He answered her question with a slow shake of his head. "I don't know anyone with a guinea pig."

"Oh, that's too bad."

"But I do need to repay my debt. What if I took you out for dinner? Would that make it easier for you to forgive me for not being as diligent with the dog?"

Red flares went off in her head. "First, I'm not angry with you, so there's no debt to repay. Second, I don't know your name. I don't go anywhere with strangers."

"Well, let me introduce myself properly. My name is Colton Hughes. I live in the house next door. Nice to meet you." He shook her hand. "Now that we have the formalities out of the way you can say yes to that dinner invitation."

"Just because I know your name doesn't mean I know you."

"Do you have a boyfriend, husband, significant other? I suppose I should have asked those questions first."

"No, I am not attached to anyone at the present time."

"Paul! Can you tell your sister that it's okay to go out to dinner with me? She seems to think we're strangers."

Her brother and Grady joined the conversation. "When are you planning on going?" Paul asked.

"How's next Friday sound?" Colton answered.

Paul called out to Gracie, "Do we have anything we're supposed to be doing next Friday?"

She peeked her head out from the kitchen window. "Not that I can recall."

"Good, we're going to dinner with Paul and Lacey."

"Aww, that'll be nice. Can we go to the Prairie House? We haven't been there in a while," Gracie asked and then added, "Or is it too pricey for a first date?"

"We're married," Paul flirted with his wife.

"I meant for Colton and Lacey," Gracie sassed playfully.

It was time for Lacey to speak up. Her brother was supposed to help her out of the date. Instead, he was one step short of telling her what she was going to eat. "I never said I was going to dinner."

"What else are you going to do?"

His question caught her off guard. She had been in town for a little more than two weeks. She didn't know what she was doing from one day to the next, let alone what she was doing next weekend. "I don't know?"

Paul spoke to Lacey first, "There you have it." He addressed Colton, "How's seven sound?"

"It works for me." Colton flashed Lacey a grin and said, "I'll see you then." He strolled in the direction of his house leaving Lacey to stand there, stunned.

"Why did you do that?"

Her brother responded with the oblivious "What?"

"You were supposed to say I couldn't go out on a date."

"That's not going to happen. I need you to get a boyfriend, so you'll decide to stick around for a while."

"Are you serious?"

"I sure am." The smug smile on Paul's face was more than Lacey wanted to handle.

She harrumphed and growled, "I'm going home."

Instead of saying something like "Aww don't be mad," Paul called out behind her. "I like the sound of that."

4

THE HOUSE IS HAUNTED

After ten minutes of being under the warm water, Lacey started feeling like a normal person. A shower was exactly what she needed to right her world that had been tipped by none other than Mr. Golden Eyes. She was used to finding men attractive and liking them from afar. Usually, the routine went something in the manner of her finding him attractive; him thinking she was a sweet person, and then growing bored with her. That was the story of her life. The whole idea of one of them asking her on a date was more than her mind allowed her to process. It didn't help that her mind was obsessed with one topic: the attractive man whose touch set off a world of emotions. The entire package, the eyes, the smile, the smooth voice, brought an irrepressible smile to her face.

She shut off the water, stepped out of the claw foot tub, and wrapped a towel around her. Of all the rooms in the house, the bathroom was her favorite. Paul had remodeled it before she arrived. Lacey had to give her brother credit. He knew how to take something boring and change it into something that made people say, "Wow!"

Lacey was in the middle of applying lotion to her legs and trying to ignore her thoughts about Colton when she heard a sound in the other room. She froze as soon she heard the sound. Of course, as soon as she was listening it stopped. Slowly, Lacey applied the lotion to her legs as though how quickly she progressed through her routine affected the sound on the other side of the door. When she finished with her legs, and nothing happened, she made fun of herself. "It was probably just the wind."

In the middle of rubbing lotion on her right arm, it happened again. It sounded like someone was moving in the kitchen. This time who or whatever it was didn't seem to care about how quickly she applied the lotion. A dragging sound was followed by a loud bang.

The first thing she did was lock the bathroom door. Then she used speed dial on her phone to call Paul. He was a police officer. He'd know what to do.

"What's up?" His voice blared through the speaker.

"Shhh, don't talk so loud," Lacey whispered.

His voice changed from friendly to concerned. "What's going on over there?"

"Does this house have ghosts or anything like that?"

"No, why?"

"Either the house is haunted, or someone is in the kitchen."

"Where are you?"

"Hiding in the bathroom," she answered and realized her small towel was not a sufficient cover-up. Lacey pinned the phone to her shoulder and slid into her pajama bottoms and a tank top.

"I'll be right over." she heard him tell Gracie that he needed to check on something at the house. Then she heard him tell her that it might be a good idea if she went along. Fearing the ghost or intruder would hear him too, Lacey lowered the volume on the phone and tried to listen to the background noise when the call suddenly ended.

All was quiet in the house. Thinking it was most likely a ghost, Lacey's level of concern changed from fear to worry. How was she going to explain to her brother what she heard with no evidence to support it?

She called back her brother. Before he had time to speak, she whispered, "I don't hear anything anymore. Don't bother with coming over."

"It's too late I'm already here."

Through the door, she heard the key turn in the lock. Just in case someone was in the house, she remained in the bathroom.

The lights for the kitchen clicked when Paul turned them on. "It's safe to come out of hiding."

Through the door, she called out, "Aren't you going to check the other rooms?"

"You said the ghost was in the kitchen," Paul answered her question and taunted her at the same time.

Lacey was right to be worried. He'd never let her live this down. She opened the door to the bathroom and went to the living room to explain what happened. Her mouth fell open when she saw Colton standing there beside him.

Colton's mouth fell agape, and his eyes widened before he quickly averted his attention to Paul.

"I should have told you I brought him along. Sorry about that."

The horror at Colton seeing her dressed in close to nothing was worse than thinking the house was haunted. Lacey wasn't a prude. However, she wasn't comfortable with people outside the family, especially the man who hijacked her thinking processes, seeing her in clothing that covered only a little more than a bathing suit.

She scurried to the bedroom, threw on a hoodie and some

sweats, and returned to the living room where her brother and Colton obviously were in the middle of laughing at her expense. Colton's eyes greeted her with renewed interest.

"I thought I'd bring him along," Paul explained. "Colton grew up in this house."

"He did?"

Colton pointed with his head. "Underneath the paint on that part of the frame is notches that'll tell you how many inches I grew from year to year."

As soon as he pointed it out, Lacey saw a slight indentation beneath the paint. It wasn't enough to catch someone's eye if they weren't looking, but could easily be discerned by someone who knew what they were looking for.

"He says he has an explanation for your ghost."

Lacey looked at him with renewed interest. "He does?"

"I do. Follow me." Colton led them outside. While they walked around to the side, he said, "I like what you've done with the house so far."

Other than clean out the garden, they hadn't done much for anyone to notice the difference. Still, Lacey said, "Thank you."

Colton pointed at a tree beside the house. His finger led them on a path up the trunk toward a window in the attic. From where they stood it was cracked less than six inches.

Paul explained the opening. "Gracie must have forgotten to close it. She opened it to let some fresh air in the attic a couple weeks ago."

"How does that explain the noise I heard in the kitchen?"

"You do have an intruder. Just not the kind that'll bring you any harm," Colton explained. "That's how squirrels get in the house."

All the worry and fear she had felt over the past hour turned to indignation. "You're saying a squirrel is in the house with me."

"I'd say that is a better answer than a ghost," Paul said.

"How do we get it out?"

"That's easy enough," Colton explained. "Since this if the first time you've heard the noise, it probably got lost in the house. You close the window and set a live trap."

"What am I supposed to do when I catch it?"

"Set it free, of course."

Colton was so confident with his answer Lacey didn't want to admit that she didn't know how to set a trap, nor how to set a squirrel free once she caught it. The whole idea gave her the hebejebes.

He must have read something in her reaction, because he added, "How about this. I'll help you out. I have a trap at the house. When we catch the squirrel, I'll set it free."

With the solution to the problem in front of her, the vice grip that had taken hold of Lacey's head slowly released its grasp. Lacey smiled with the sense of relief that came to her. "You have no idea how much I'd appreciate that."

In that instant, all the concerns about him asking her out on a date vanished. Who cared if he was the hottest thing she had seen in quite some time and she was not. Colton Hughes became her knight in shining armor, and nothing could dim the growing admiration Lacey held for him.

5

I'LL GET HIM BACK ONE DAY

Lacey sat on the porch and waited for Colton and Paul to return with the trap. While it didn't seem logical, the thought of being in the house with an animal made her uncomfortable. Maybe it was one too many horror movies. In the quiet of the evening, she related the discomfort with her lack of roots. There she was competing for space in a house that didn't belong to her in a town she could barely navigate.

To anyone driving through, it was a small town with one grocery store, a main street with shops, and a courthouse. After moving there, it was a complex system with inner workings that made living there easier than a larger city. For instance, in the back of the dress shop, a tailor fixed and fitted clothing for people in the community. Unless someone asked, people didn't know the owner of the novelty store had connections to get shoes repaired. There were restaurants, but a large portion of the community met for lunch at the senior center where the young gladly connected with the older citizens.

As far as Lacey was concerned, she and the squirrel had a lot in common. Both of them got caught in a house and didn't know what to do about it.

Paul and Colton returned with a cage that could fit a small animal. Colton pushed on the sides with his fingers. "The gaps between the wires are smaller. You figure a squirrel can get into the house with an opening that is the size of a fist. It'll probably try to go back the way it came in. We'll place this in the attic with some peanut butter, and we'll catch you a squirrel in no time."

Colton and Paul worked together to set the trap. "Do you think we ought to use peanuts with the peanut butter?"

"Only if they're unsalted?"

"What kind of animal would eat unsalted peanuts?"

"One that doesn't have a beer to wash it down."

The affability they shared charmed Lacey. Their conversation lacked the bite of sarcasm she had grown accustomed to hearing in the larger cities. One asked a question or made a suggestion, and the other answered the question or gave a statement of affirmation. The tone set her at ease with both Colton and the situation.

Her brother and Colton worked so well together, Lacey, who began to feel unnecessary, was growing bored with the situation. Her mind drifted towards plans for the evening. Maybe it would be better if she slept on the couch. If she gave the squirrel the freedom to roam around the house, it might feel better about being caught in the trap.

At first, it barely registered that Colton was talking to Lacey when he said, "If you don't mind my company I can stay a while and see if we can catch him."

"That might be a good idea," Paul answered for her. "Do you want me to take you back to the house to get your pickup?"

Both waited for Lacey to approve the suggestion.

"You don't have to go to so much fuss for me. I appreciate

all you've done already. I'm sure you need to get up early for work in the morning."

"Tomorrow is Sunday," Paul spoke first.

"Who wouldn't want to spend time without..." Colton paused at Paul's reaction of interest and picked up where he left off. "I mean it won't take that much time for the squirrel to get in the trap. I'd be able to take care of it, and you'd have the rest of the weekend to relax."

"Yeah, I don't see her sleeping in the house with a squirrel making all kinds of noise once it gets trapped in that cage. They're cute animals, but they can make quite the sounds when they're trapped. It's horrible."

Just thinking about it made Lacey's shoulders tighten. "Yes," she blurted. "If it won't take that much time. I think it's a great idea for you to be here."

"Then let's skedaddle, and he'll be back in no time." Paul tapped Lacey on the shoulder, said, "Make sure to let me know what happens," and turned to leave.

Colton flashed her a smile that melted all of Lacey's concerns and left with the parting words of, "I'll be right back."

She sighed in contentment as she stood in front of the picture window and watched them pull away. They hadn't driven out of her field of vision when she heard the door on the trap fall closed.

Lacey prepared herself for a howl or scream. Instead, she heard nothing. It was so quiet she thought she was mistaken. Just in case she remained still in the living room and waited for a sign that the squirrel was in the trap. Sure enough, it came, but not in the way Paul made her believe it would happen. The sound of movement against the trap was all that she heard.

She had the door open before Colton ever reached it.

Pointing in the direction of the attic she said, "It's in there, but it hasn't started screaming yet."

She noticed the eyebrows raise and the head turn. Colton was trying to hide that he wanted to laugh. Connecting the dots in the situation, she groaned, "Paul was messing with me?"

"Yeah," Colton smiled. "But isn't that what brothers are for."

The smile erased what little indignation Lacey had mustered against her brother. She silently laughed. "I'll get him back one day."

LACEY DIDN'T AGREE with Colton's decision to release the squirrel in the yard. "How do we know he isn't going to try to come back in the house?" Making sure the window to the attic was closed, Colton explained that releasing the squirrel in the yard was the best option for both the animal and Lacey. "Squirrels are territorial creatures. This one will keep others out of the yard. As for getting back in the house. We'll use a spray that mimics the urine of a larger animal to keep the squirrel away from the window."

"It's that easy?"

"Yes, that easy."

With his job done, pangs of disappointment poked at Lacey's heart. She enjoyed spending time with him. Now that he had no reason to stay he'd go home. He placed the cage in the bed of his pickup and to her surprise sat on the top stair of her porch. "Now that we have that taken care of, I have time to get to know you. I'd like to know what brought Lacey Sanders to Three Creeks, Montana."

She sat beside him and began her story. "Ever since my

divorce, Paul has been trying to get me to come here. He thinks I belong closer to family." She smiled at the protective stance her brother had taken since their parents moved to Arizona.

"He mentioned that you were divorced but didn't say why." Colton dug for information.

While she appreciated the sentiment, it didn't make sense to Lacey. People asked questions to get to know the other person. Experience had taught her that people like to pass tests. So they'll give the answer they think will bring them approval. The way to gauge a person's character is to see how they act when they don't know they're being watched. He was better off getting to know her when she was with her brother or Gracie in a natural setting.

Regardless, she told Colton what he wanted to know. "My husband was having an affair with somebody at his job. I walked in on them in the middle of a special meeting." She shuddered with the recollection. "I went through all the emotions. You know anger, resentment, feeling betrayed and what not. But when it came down to the truth of the matter, I got it. While she was unscrupulous and lacked morals, she was the kind of woman any man would have a tough time resisting."

"So you let him off the hook?" Colton seemed incredulous.

"No, I called his mother and told her what he did and then I got a better attorney than him." She grinned, "I'm understanding, but not stupid."

Colton laughed. "I need more friends like you in my life. My ex left me with a mountain of debt that took years to dig my way out of."

"I'm sorry to hear that."

"Don't be. It taught me to not be as trusting."

Lacey caught a hint of bitterness in his voice.

Just as quickly as she heard it, Colton tried masking it with an explanation, "I'm sure you know what I mean. They tell you one thing, but then do another." He turned to face her, "By the way your brother thinks the world of you. He talked about you a lot before you got here. It got to where I was feeling like a horrible brother for not saying as many nice things about my sister."

"We're pretty close," Lacey answered. "He kept me safe when we were growing up. I'm glad to be able to do something kind for him."

"What do you mean?" Colton asked.

"Helping him with the house. I'm here to help him get ready to sell it."

"What'll you do after that?"

"Probably move to Helena," Lacey mused. Not that she wanted to go. But what else was there to do but to go back and pick up where she left off. This time she was going to do things right. Think about herself more, and worry about what others thought less.

Her answer was greeted with silence. With his attention directed at the stars, Colton said, "I wouldn't get too comfortable with that idea if I were you. Life has a way of showing us that our plans are simply something to help us face our problems. Usually, the answer comes to us when we're in the middle of them—and it's something we'd never thought of on our own."

6

THE DATE

They were supposed to be on a date. Not that the seating arrangements gave any indication of their relationships. Gracie and Lacey sat companionably in the back seat of Paul's king cab pickup. Paul and Colton sat in the front seat and discussed the upcoming rodeo days. Gracie piped in occasionally. Lacey who knew little about the annual event sat in silence and absorbed the information. Midway to the restaurant where they were supposed to have dinner, Gracie said, "It's quite a distance from where we live, but the food is totally worth it."

"I wish I took you here for our first date," Paul said.

"Aw c'mon you know chaperoning the prom was a way better idea," Gracie beamed. "At first Noelle wasn't comfortable with having a police officer at the dance. So I told her I'd go along to distract him a little." She winked at her husband. "Your brother has some moves. He knew the steps to all the dances. It turns out Noelle had nothing to worry about. The kids loved him. As for me--do you know what it's like competing with an eighteen-year-old girl for attention? And, my daughter of all people."

Everyone in the car chuckled at the thought. "I fell in love with him then and there."

"Then why'd you make things so difficult?" Paul asked. Without giving Gracie time to answer, he added. "She wouldn't go out with me on a date for months after that. It about drove me crazy."

"I didn't believe any man would really want to have anything to do with a single mother with a teenage daughter. I was trying to wait until she grew up and then think about giving love another chance."

"Love is not as complicated as people make it out to be," Paul answered. "Besides who wants to be attached to someone who isn't going to be there for the rough seasons?"

"I know, I know." The warmth in their tone hinted at the number of times Paul reminded Gracie that his interest in her was beyond the superficial.

Nestled in the middle of the Montana grasslands, the Prairie House could easily have been mistaken for a high-end log cabin someone built for decadent privacy. In the distance, the silhouette of mountains formed the perfect backdrop. Completely awed by what she was seeing, Lacey gushed, "How did you learn about this place?"

"Him." Paul pointed at Colton.

Colton fidgeted with the air conditioning vent, and said, "My father helped build it." His chest rose with the onus being given to someone else. "He could make anything out of wood."

"Wait until you see the inside," Paul stepped out of the pickup and opened the door for Gracie to get out beside him. Since Colton had already walked around the front of the pickup and met them, Lacey scooted across the cab and got out behind her.

It turned out that Paul had not given them a strong enough

impression of what they were about to see. Everything was made of wood. The interior of the restaurant looked more like a sculpture than a place for people to go on a date. Lacey found herself reaching out to caress the scroll work on the edge of the bar when they passed by it. She was so focused on the woodwork that Paul had to snap in front of her face to grab her attention. Determined to make a good impression she hurried to follow the group to the table.

"You might want to run some of your ideas about the house for Colton. He's too humble to tell you he inherited his father's woodworking talent. The inside of his house is amazing."

"He's not kidding," Gracie piped in. "I am in love with the kitchen table. He spent half of last summer making it." Gracie, who was as equally impressed with the layout of the restaurant, gawked every once in a while or sighed softly in appreciation at a new facet of the woodwork.

"I thought you owned a pest control business," Lacey didn't see the connection between craftsman and controller of invasive bugs and animals.

Shrugging at the lack of connection, Colton replied, "It pays the bills, and I get to be outdoors."

The conversation came to a temporary halt when the hostess stopped in front of their table. Paul took the seat beside Colton and Gracie chose the seat across from him. Lacey looked twice before resigning herself to the seat diagonally across from the person who was supposed to be her date. Taking it as a sign that perhaps his impression of her changed after the post squirrel discussion, she guessed this was their way of saying that the three of them came up with alternative dinner plans. Preparing herself for the disappointing we should be friends talk; Lacey forced herself to find a way to dim the attraction she felt towards Colton.

Paul and Colton, united in their message, exchanged stories about things they had seen at their day jobs. Occasionally Gracie leaned in to quietly add her two cents to the conversation. To get Paul to talk more, Colton asked, "Were you the one who answered the call about the lady who said a man was walking around in a Speedo at her apartment complex?" Gracie leaned in again to explain the source of the discussion. "Every police call is registered and listed in the Wednesday newspaper."

"You have got to be kidding." Usually, Lacey focused on the headlines and the home and garden section of the paper.

"I've been in there a couple times myself," Colton sheepishly admitted.

"What for?"

"When I was eighteen, I toilet papered Bernard's house."

Paul and Gracie snorted their laughter. "Back in the day, he was the town crank." Through giggles, Gracie said, "I wish I could have been there to help."

"And the second time," Colton continued, "Was for getting into a fight with…"

"I was there for that call," Paul interrupted. "After I figured out why he was beating friendly Floyd Fletcher to a pulp I felt bad for cutting the whooping short."

The conversation continued to tamer topics. When the men were talking about a fish another friend had caught, Gracie whispered an explanation for the Floyd story. "Floyd was extra friendly with Colton's ex-wife, Barb."

AT FIRST, it was charming to hear the stories of life before Lacey moved to Three Creeks. Through their stories, she learned about friends she was sure to meet and like. The occasional smile or nod of recognition was all the three of them needed to continue the friendly banter. They got through appetizers and dinner without her having to offer much in the way of conversation. By dessert, she was ready to go home. If she was going to be quiet, she wanted to be in her pajamas under a blanket on the couch.

Promising to return before the dessert arrived, Lacey excused herself to go to the restroom. Gracie stood to join her. "I need to freshen up my makeup too." She retrieved her makeup bag from her purse and accompanied Lacey to the women's restroom.

Lacey had been to many places. Nothing prepared her for the lavishly designed bathroom. The stalls separated by lacquered walls that went from floor to ceiling were more like individual powder rooms. It was obvious the owner considered every small detail down to the toilet paper dispenser that had lace scrolling carved around the edges. "They almost made it too nice," Lacey's eyes wandered from one detail to the next. "I'd be happy sitting in here with a good book."

Gracie stopped mid lipstick swipe to talk to Lacey. "You are so good for Colton. He is back to being the person he was when we were growing up. Do you like him?"

From what Lacey observed over dinner, Colton seemed to be a nice enough guy. He held up his end of a conversation which was more than he'd be able to say about her. Lacey said what she knew Gracie wanted to hear, "He seems like a really nice guy."

"Do you think you'll go out with him again?"

One of the benefits of having a quiet personality is people interpreted silence for thoughtfulness. That was the only way Lacey was able to successfully suppress what she really thought. Which was: This was not a date. A date is where you go out with someone, and you both feel awkward as you try to figure out the nuances of the other person. She was looking forward to the back and forth of discomfort of confusion and relief that comes from receiving approval from the other person. She had no idea whatsoever of what Colton Hughes thought of her. This was three friends getting together for a meal and inviting Lacey along, most likely because they didn't want her to be alone on a Friday night.

The emerging pattern of what was to come was as bright as Gracie's lipstick, and Lacey did not see a way to avoid it. Rather than get into a lengthy discussion in the women's restroom, she kept her answer to the question simple. "I can see us going out together again."

When Gracie gave her a beaming smile in response, Lacey knew she had given the correct answer.

With the help of her brother, any interest Lacey may have had in Colton Hughes got pushed to the wayside. There was no way she'd ever be able to compete with their bromance. The ride home was a mirror image of how the date began. Colton sat in the front seat while Lacey and Gracie sat in the back. She hoped nobody was going to quiz her about what they discussed because she had no idea. Feeling like a spare tire on a tricycle she went off in her own mind and considered moving to Arizona to be closer to her parents. Sure, it was hot, but it couldn't be any more uncomfortable than the situation she was in. By the time they pulled up to the house, she was trying to decide whether or not she wanted to wear one-piece bathing suits or a bikini.

Lacey didn't wait for Paul to shift the pickup into park. Going with the group of friends vibe she picked up from them, she opened the door and jumped out of the back of the cab. She tapped the door like she had seen people do in the movies and said, "That was a lot of fun. Thanks for bringing me along." She backed away to see three confused faces watch her head to the house. For a brief moment, she thought *maybe I played the group of friends card too hard*. Before the situation grew any more awkward, she turned and headed for the door. She refused to look back until she walked through and gave her biggest happy smile and waved.

Standing against the door firmly closed behind her, Lacey exhaled the breath she hadn't realized she was holding. She spoke to the empty room. "I need to google excuses for not going on outings with my brother."

7

A DO OVER

Lacey should have known making the decision to not have anything to do with someone and following through with the unspoken decision are two different sides of the same coin. Things could change with a simple flip. She was hunkered down on the corner of her couch scrolling through books on her tablet when the first phone call came.

It was her father. She checked the time and immediately began to worry. Her parents never stayed up past ten, and it was after eleven p.m. Skipping the usual courtesies she answered, "Is everything okay?"

"Does something have to be wrong for a man to call his only daughter?" Lacey could only hope to meet someone like her father. He knew exactly what to say to allay her worries.

"When it's way past your bedtime it might?" she sweetly replied.

"It is so hot out here we take naps during the day and stay up later. Just yesterday we saw a man fry an egg on the hood of his car."

"Are you calling to say you're ready to come home?" Lacey silently pleaded for the answer to be yes.

"No, a little heat isn't going to scare us away. Besides we can go swimming or visit the mall when it's hot. There's no way to get around shoveling snow," he joked. "Your mother just got off the phone with your brother. He said he thought you might be missing us. Something about you going out to dinner and not talking."

It was a classic Paul move. Whenever he got in trouble, he called his mother to soften the aftermath.

"Oh, you know how he gets. Once he starts talking, it's best to take a seat and let him have his audience."

"That's true. I always thought he was going to be an actor or a standup comedian," her father agreed. He pressed into the reason for the call. "So you two aren't at odds?"

"No, not at all."

Having received the information he called to get, her father asked a couple more questions, and they ended the call. Lacey put down the phone and picked up the tablet. She had just logged into her wish list when the phone rang again. She silently moaned about the inability to enjoy some peace and quiet. The grumbling grew louder when she saw it was Colton calling.

"I just called to tell you were a breath of fresh air tonight."

She was not giving him a chance to sweet talk her. She sassed, "Did you get that from a country song?"

He chuckled at her comment, and replied, "I don't think so. But you never know. Sometimes we hear something so often it becomes a part of our regular conversation."

"Hmmm, I can see that happening. By the way, dinner was delicious." She felt better about not having to lie about having fun and offering him a token of politeness.

"I was wondering if you'd want to come with me to a family picnic."

When she googled ways to get out of something, the most

common solution was to make other plans. "I'm already doing something, but thank you for inviting me."

"I never told you when it was happening. I told your brother you weren't having fun tonight.

The last thing she needed was for Colton to contradict what she told her father. "I never said…"

"Let me make it up to you," he insisted.

"There's nothing to make up for."

"We were trying to get you to know as much about me as possible in a short amount of time because you made a comment about not going out with strangers. Paul and I may have gone overboard with our intentions."

"Oh, for heavens to Betsy," she exclaimed.

"Did you get that from a country song?" Her heart swooned. He used her own words against her, and it worked.

"I may have." She felt the grin taking over her face.

"Would you mind if I stopped by?"

As much as she wanted him to logic told her it was a bad idea. "It's kind of late."

"I know, but we didn't end the date right. I'd like a do over."

"Can we do it another night?"

Lacey heard the knock on the door, and it slowly registered to her senses that Colton was on the other side. She gasped in surprise.

He coached her on what to do next, "This is the part where you say who is it, then I'll say, baby, it's me I just came to give you a goodnight kiss."

Her heart started floating around her chest, and her stomach disappeared to give it room to wander. Lacey didn't know what she should do when she opened the door. The anticipation urged her to get there as quickly as possible to find out. She turned the lock and opened the door to see

Colton leaning against the post on her front porch. His thumbs were in his pocket, and his hands rested casually on his upper thigh. He was the picture of the hunky country boy next door.

She forgot she was wearing her pajamas until she saw his eyes widen and retract in surprise. Lacey blushed three shades of pink, and tried to hide behind the door, "Oh, I should go change."

"No, what you're wearing is perfect." He grinned and said, "I just caught a vision of our future, and I'm not ashamed to say I liked it."

Nobody had ever said anything like that about Lacey when she was in her pajamas. Her body said she was over forty. Her head felt like it was the first time she was really in love. The man standing in front of her had frustrated her into considering a move to a place where they fry eggs on their cars. In less than a couple minutes he had her eating out of the palm of his hand. She bet if the squirrel knew he was the trapper it would have happily walked into the cage.

Colton took two steps to stand in front of her and placed his hand on the small of her back. He used the thumb of his other hand to raise her chin toward him and gently kissed her on the lips. His lips turned up to form a satisfied grin. He said, "That's how a date is supposed to end," and he left Lacey standing on the front stoop wearing a silly smile that she couldn't push away if she tried.

8

MORE THAN FINE

Lacey was at the counter of the hardware store waiting for Kent to bring out an order of mini blinds for her bedroom when her eye caught Colton walking toward the lumber department. She wished for a lot of things. Seeing Colton Hughes in a t-shirt and jeans at ten a.m. in the hardware store hadn't been one of them. The loose fit of his clothing did little to hide the well-defined muscles beneath them. As she was checking out the back pockets, she made a mental note, "thank the good Lord for bringing us unexpected gifts."

"These will go well with the paint you've chosen." Kent's voice startled her back into reality. Her cheeks burned at the slight grin he gave her as she forced herself to remember why she was there. "I have some prints coming in that will blend the colors."

"C'mon I'll introduce you two." Kent's playful smile said he'd keep her secret.

"We've already met," Lacey pressed her lips together to try and hide how much she really liked Colton. She didn't want to jinx things.

Kent walked with her to the register. "I'll let you off the hook this time."

Colton came to the register with a large chunk of wood. His smile brightened when he saw Lacey. Kent alternated glances between the two of them. "Is there something I should know about you two?"

They were in the hardware store, but the rest of the world faded into background noise. As far as Lacey was concerned, there were only two people in the world. She held up the blinds for Colton to see. "I'm here to make some finishing touches on a room. What brings you here?"

"Remind me to never babysit a Saint Bernard." Colton held up the plank of wood. "I'm here to make some minor repairs to a chair leg."

Lacey grimaced. "I'm afraid to ask."

"If you like I can show you the damage."

A snapping sound pulled Lacey from the conversation. Kent joked with the cashier, "This happens every time the weather warms."

It was the second time in a short amount of time she had experienced a Colton induced amnesia. She completely forgot that she was in a hardware store full of people. She inhaled a breath and pulled out her wallet to pay for her purchase.

"I can help you install the blinds and then you can come by the house." Colton added, "You can see the table. Thankfully, the dog stayed away from it."

"We can say we were here when it all began," Kent cajoled. At Lacey's blush, he said, "I have to give old Colt a hard time here."

"Old Colt? Who are you calling old?" Colton's indignation at the jab drew chuckles from the people in line behind them.

"He isn't talking to me," a woman who had to have been in her sixties answered.

Considering his alternatives, Colton laughed and took his receipt from the cashier. He walked out of the store with Lacey to where their vehicles were parked. His pickup was parked beside hers. "I'll follow you to the house, and we can decide what to do from there."

When they got to the house, Lacey felt better about making the bed before she left the house. Her mother's wisdom echoed in her mind. "You never know when you're going to have a surprise visitor."

They had the blinds changed in a matter of minutes. The original off white blinds slid out of the clips and they replaced them with the charcoal grey blinds Lacey purchased to match the paint she chose for the room.

She stood with her hands on her hips and proudly assessed her work. "It is coming together nicely. I think Paul will be pleased with the results."

Standing beside Lacey, Colton held his arm folded in front of his chest. "I wondered why you chose a masculine color scheme."

"Well, it is Paul's house."

"That he wants you to live in."

"I am," she answered.

"And like it."

"I do."

He eyed her soft pink hoodie and boots with pink scrolls stitched on the top. His brow wrinkled before he said, "I'd have taken you for the type of person that likes softer colors."

She followed his eyes to look down at her outfit. "Well, yes. But let's just say it's easier to go along with what Paul wants."

"I've noticed you do that a lot."

"Do what?"

"You let other people have their way."

He wasn't wrong. "Like I said—it's easier. I see people fight over things that aren't important. Then when it comes to fighting for something that's of value their bark doesn't have any bite."

"What if they haven't tested their voice? And when the time comes, nobody hears them because it's too soft."

"How did we go from paint color to having to fight with my brother?"

"You're in a new town and trying to feel your way through situations. From the short amount of time we've spent together I can tell your brother calls the shots. What happens when you feel strongly about something, and he disagrees? The way you are now, you'll get steamrolled into bowing to his will."

Lacey didn't like where the conversation was headed. She turned to leave the room. Maybe a change in environment was enough to change the topic. She hadn't got too far away when Colton reached for her hand and pulled her back into him. "Running from the truth isn't going to make it go away."

"I wasn't running."

The already present wrinkle deepened when he squinted to contradict her. His chin dropped, and a smile warned her that the course of the conversation was about to take a turn.

Colton wrapped both of his arms around her. His voice took on a husky tone when he said, "What would you say if I told you that I'm about to kiss you?

"I'd say what took you so long?"

Obviously pleased with her answer, Colton laughed. While she was happy that her answer delighted him, it wasn't exactly the reaction she wanted. She wanted to feel his lips on hers and the connection that followed. She spoke what she wanted and still didn't get it.

"Aww, I wasn't laughing at you." His answer calmed her frustration. Apparently, he heard her thoughts. Colton leaned in to kiss her when a loud knock on the door that could only belong to her brother interrupted it. Lacey turned to go get the door. In a swift move, Colton pulled her into him and pressed his lips to hers. It claimed her and spoke loudly. In a contest for attention against her brother, he refused to lose. Lacey moaned and gladly surrendered to it. He glided his tongue across her bottom lip, softly nibbled on it and slowly pulled out of the kiss.

When Paul knocked on the door again, Colton regarded her with a Cheshire cat grin. "Your brother is persistent."

Lacey hurried down the stairs and opened the door to let Paul in. He opened his mouth to speak and stopped to get a better look at her. "Are you okay you look flushed?"

"Yes, I'm fine," Lacey answered. She was more than fine. She was fantastic.

"We thought we'd come by the house and help with whatever you need."

Colton came up from behind her and said, "I think we got it all taken care of."

9

BATTLE OF THE WILLS

"We were about to head to my house," Colton stepped outside the door. He dangled his keys in front of him. "If you want you can join us."

She watched the unspoken conversation between Paul and Gracie that begged to know the answer to the question: what happened between last night and this morning? Paul nudged his head for Gracie to ask. She peeked into the house behind Lacey while asking, "How long have you been here?"

"Less than an hour," Lacey answered. "We met up at the hardware store, and Colton helped me…"

He cut her off. "Replace some blinds. We should get to heading out."

"You got new blinds." Gracie perked. "In what room?"

"The bedroom. Do you want to see it real quick?" Lacey moved to let them in the house.

"You replaced the blinds in the bedroom?"

As Paul slowly released the words to his question, Lacey figured out why Colton suggested they leave. His logical conclusion ticked her off. What kind of a person did he think she was? He raced up the stairs, probably to look for evidence of what hadn't happened. When everyone caught up to him, he said, "Oh, you replaced the blinds."

"That's what I said," Lacey bit back the sarcasm.

"They're grey," Gracie said to him.

Colton leaned against the door frame, crossed his arms, and observed the ensuing discussion with an I told you so smile.

Lacey paid him no mind. "I know you like the neutral tones, and the colors can go with a variety of themes."

"It's nice," Gracie said the words. However, her voice said something entirely different.

Paul used the same expression as Colton in the conversation they had prior to her brother's arrival. "I always thought you were a pastel colored person."

"I am. But this is your house."

He looked over at Colton who gave him a head tilt that said, "I told you so."

"Yes, but I want you to make it into a place where you would like to live."

There was no it's nice or anything else of that nature coming out of the conversation. She examined the blinds through different eyes. "You don't like them. I can try to exchange them for a different color."

"No. I think you misunderstood me." With his eyes, Paul pleaded with Gracie to take over.

Colton stepped in, "Right before you got here, I was telling Lacey that the color scheme is great, but doesn't reflect HER personality, or that she plans on staying with us for any amount of time."

They all scanned the room. The walls were blank, and all her belongings were stuffed in drawers. She saw what they were saying. Her blush goose down comforter that was accented with mint green and mauve pillows was a direct contrast to the entire room.

"That's it exactly," Gracie said. "We were hoping you'd make this house your home."

"I'd like to think you were staying around for a while," Paul added.

Colton's eyes softened to show he shared the sentiment with her brother and sister-in-law.

"I'll add some plants and pictures and make it work." With her suggestion, the tension left the room.

"Now that we have that out of the way, we should go to lunch. What would you like to have, Lacey?"

"Chinese sounds really good," Paul answered.

"Is that what you want?" Colton directed the question to Lacey.

"Why wouldn't she?" Paul answered the question with a question, and the tension returned to the room.

"Or, we could go to the house. We have a boat load of left overs."

"I vote for left overs and have a picnic," Lacey said. "And, we can hang out. You men can do whatever it is that men do when they hang out." Prompted by Paul's lack of enthusiasm at the idea, she added, "And Gracie and I can do some online shopping for ideas to personalize the room."

10

PEACEKEEPER

Lacey and Colton may have been in the same book, but he was on a different page. The increase of attention cast in her direction heightened Lacey's awareness of relationships on several levels. The first being the rekindled brother-sister bond created by her moving to Three Creeks. She figured out quickly that the way to keep peace with her brother was to act like she only had a cursory interest in Colton.

Paul, who had been the driving force that brought them together, underestimated the interest Colton and Lacey had taken in each other. To express his displeasure at the changes between his sister and good friend, he frowned, made a snide remark, and even rolled his eyes once at a comment of appreciation one made toward the other.

To keep the peace, Lacey forced herself to give Paul the attention he obviously felt he deserved. Lacey and Colton were at the beginning of their story, and all the good stuff would come soon enough. Paul was there with her through all the rises and falls of her life. He was there from her first day in the world, and she wanted him to know that he held a special place in her heart.

Colton, on the other hand, must have thought they were somewhere near the middle of the story. Set on asserting his intentions, he antagonized Paul mercilessly. When they made their plates for lunch, Colton added some fruit to Lacey's plate. He answered her confused reaction saying, "The last time we were together in the presence of fruit you were wearing it. I'm teaching you not to fear it."

As she rolled her eyes in reaction, he pulled her into a side hug. "Denial is the first stage of growth. You're making progress."

The joke was so silly Lacey only had a giggle to offer in response. Colton warmly said, "See and now you're at acceptance."

Paul stoically interrupted the joke. "You're using the stages of grief with fruit?"

"Hey, lighten up. It's a sunny Saturday afternoon. We left college years ago."

Right about then Lacey stared at her plate of food. There was no way for her to walk away from the situation, so she quietly endured it.

Gracie saved her. She opened the door from the kitchen to the deck and said, "Let's go eat and leave the men to fight over the stages of grief as it relates to fruit." She threw Paul a dirty look before walking out the door.

"What?" Paul half asked, half whined. "I was just trying to explain that he used the wrong analogy."

Colton whispered, "It'll get better," and kissed Lacey on her cheek. He motioned to move toward the door. When Lacey didn't follow, he waited patiently for her to fall into step with him.

Out of the corner of her eye, she saw Paul's brows wrinkle in confusion at the change in dynamics between them.

After lunch, the two friends went off in the yard and played a game of ladder ball while Lacey and Gracie navigated online stores. She had already decided on some prints to hang over her bed, and they were looking for some lighting to add a feminine touch to Lacey's bedroom.

In the absence of the women, the tension the best friends held seemed like it was something Lacey imagined. Paul and Colton bantered back and forth and laughed at what each other said. It was as though the power struggle earlier in the day had never happened. The picture of friendship they painted through their camaraderie touched Lacey's heart. Paul made a good life for himself. She hoped that the stress her presence brought their friendship was temporary.

11

TIME TO CHOOSE

True to what Colton predicted, Lacey found herself engaged in a tricky dance of wills with her brother. Every night for the week after "sunny Saturday," Paul called to see what she was doing for dinner. Regardless of how long she waited, the call always came thirty minutes after she had already eaten. On Thursday night she promised herself, she'd wait until he called. At 8:15 she gave up and ate. By Friday she was beside herself with frustration with the situation with her brother.

Staying up late talking and texting with Colton added to the frustration. Lacey had been in Three Creeks a little more than four months. Her idea of working part-time at the community center to become familiar with the town and set a routine had only added to her fatigue. It was nothing like when she lived in Helena where her weekdays were so structured clocks were an unnecessary accessory. For the first time in her life, she needed an alarm clock and had joined the ranks of people who used the snooze button more than once.

When Lacey walked in the door from work, she loosened

her bra strap and pulled the bra out through the sleeve of her blouse. Before anyone called to disturb her hiatus from humanity, she turned off her phone and collapsed onto the couch while exhaling a sigh of relief. She drifted off to sleep while trying to choose between microwave popcorn or baked French fries for dinner.

A firm knock on the door woke her from her nap. Lacey was rubbing the sleep from her eyes when she opened the door to greet Colton holding a pizza in one hand a bouquet of daisies in the other hand. He held out the daisies and drawled, "Happy three-month anniversary, Darling."

Lacey accepted the flowers. "They are beautiful, thank you.

He crossed through the doorway and said, "I figured I'd kept you up too late and you'd be too tired to go anywhere. I thought we'd celebrate like normal couples. We can watch Netflix and chill."

Like normal couples? Until he said it, she hadn't realized they had fallen into a routine together. They were deep enough for him to know without her saying anything that she was exhausted. He set the pizza box on the table and opened it for her to see a large half supreme and half meat lover's pizza. It was half of what he liked and half of what she liked.

Colton's eyes drifted toward the edge of the couch. Just as they fell on her bra hanging over the arm of the chair, Lacey realized what he saw. Colton wagged his eyebrows and nodded toward the bra she had flung on the couch. "I see you got an early start without me." With her response of an eye roll and a surreptitious swipe to hide her wayward undergarment under the throw pillow, Lacey knew things between them had changed more than she'd ever expected.

SITTING on the couch beside Colton with his arms wrapped around her, Lacey recalled a memory of her parents. One night when she came home from a party, she walked in to see her father and mother in the same position. Except her mother had fallen asleep with her chin in the crook of her father's arm. Not wanting to disturb his wife, he quietly regarded Lacey. "Did you have fun?"

"As much as a girl can have when her older brother is at the same party," Lacey joked.

Her father whispered, "Then he's doing his job."

Lacey groaned and made her way to the room, and her father called behind her, "Sweet dreams."

Thinking, *"This is what they were feeling,"* Lacey practically purred.

"You know, I've been thinking."

From the tone he used, she thought Colton was about to propose an idea for a date. "About?"

"I have never felt about anyone the way I feel about you. I can spend hours with you and still not be bored."

"You're one of the few people who get me," she replied. "It's easy to sit in the corner and be quiet. Not so with you."

"What do you think about taking things to the next level?"

Her first conclusion was sex. He was asking her about having sex. They had been affectionate, but Colton had made it clear there was a line he refused to cross. As a result, he became more of a best friend that kissed really well. Although Lacey was more than eager to consider the option, she hadn't prepared herself. "That's kind of tricky. I don't have any birth control."

"Silly girl, that won't come until after marriage. Not that I'd want to do it any time soon. I was just trying to get a feel for your opinion on the matter."

Her heart beat so hard, Lacey thought it was going to fall out of her chest. "I'd been so focused on the house and trying to get roots established."

"So your answer is not yet."

He did get her. "Exactly. I mean Paul wanted me to stay in the house." As soon as she said it, Lacey knew it was the wrong thing to say. Colton's back stiffened so quickly it made her own body hurt.

"So, your answer is no because you want to keep your brother happy?"

It sounded like that was what she said, but that wasn't what she meant. Lacey tried to plead her case. "He had me decorate the house to be something I wanted because he wanted me to stay in it. If I moved out…"

"Let me stop you," Colton cut her off. "I asked your opinion on the matter, and you gave me an answer. Just because I don't like your answer doesn't mean it was the wrong one." He pulled his arm from around her shoulder and moved to create distance between them. Lacey didn't like the chilling effect it had on her when he added, "I respect you for your honesty."

Lacey didn't know what to say or do to fix things, so she went with her stand by response—silence. By the end of the movie, she had no idea what it was about. She passed the time trying to think of a way to fix things and coming up with nothing.

As the closing credits scrolled down the screen, Colton rose to leave. "I should get going. I know you've had a long week."

Lacey glanced quickly at his eyes. A cold edge had taken over, and they looked more like rocks. She quickly turned away and thanked him for bringing the pizza.

"Yeah, no problem." He shoved his one hand in his pocket

and walked out the door without as much as a backwards glance.

She crumpled on the couch as her heart crumbled into a million pieces inside her chest.

12

LIFE GOES ON

To prevent herself from calling Colton and making a fool of herself, Lacey left her phone on the kitchen counter where she laid it when she got home from work. A couple of times she took hesitant steps toward it and corrected the course. Until she had a resolution they both liked, there was no point in discussing the matter. With that being said, she had hoped she'd receive a couple you need to rethink your decision texts from him. His simple acceptance of her refusal was honorable and frustrating at the same time.

She went to bed and tried to sleep. The small plants on the edge of the dresser taunted her. Colton had accompanied her to the store to choose the pots and make sure she chose something she couldn't kill. The string of lights on her headboard that usually delighted her were just a little too bright. Colton found some adhesive hooks that didn't require nails to keep the lights up. Everything reminded her of the person she wanted to forget—if only for eight hours so she could sleep.

Inspiration struck after three trips to the bathroom. A fresh gallon of paint in the garage called out to Lacey. She was waiting for the new shower curtain to arrive to make sure the colors worked together. But insomnia was stronger and convinced her to go ahead and give it a try.

Struck by inspiration, Lacey changed into an old t-shirt and leggings. She brought her cell phone in the bathroom to listen to a podcast. She told herself that in the amount of time it took to listen to one story she'd have a new outlook. Granted it was only in the bathroom, but she had to keep things on a positive track.

The intro music had just come to an end when her phone vibrated from an incoming call. As she turned to see who it was, Lacey watched her phone plummet into the toilet. Her connection to reality swayed in the water, and her heart sank with it.

Trying to keep a positive focus she thanked the heavens that she purchased the insurance protection plan. All she had to do was take a trip to the cell phone store in Ashbrook, and she'd have a new cell phone. It was an inconvenience, not a tragedy.

Out of nowhere unstoppable tears leaked out of her eyes. Her attempts to wipe them away proved to be useless. For every tear, she brushed aside two more were right behind it. Knowing there were no witnesses to judge her for her meltdown, Lacey gave in to her sadness. She sobbed for herself. She cried for being stupid enough to love a man who would have an affair with his secretary when his wife worked in the same office. She cried for being stupid enough to think that moving to a small town would be easy.

Then she cried because Colton just left. He didn't try to convince her that their relationship was worth a little grief from her brother. He just left. Then she cried because she didn't have any chocolate ice cream. When she purged her soul of her sadness, Lacey washed her face and finished painting the bathroom. Because whether or not she liked it—she knew that life goes on.

13

PLACES TO GO AND PEOPLE TO SEE

After several hours of begging sleep to stay with her for more than a thirty minute burst, relief came with the last one eyed peek at the alarm clock at five in the morning.

Lacey woke in confusion to a loud banging sound. At first, she thought it was just a dream. Then she looked over at the clock. It was 12:40 in the afternoon! The second time she heard the pounding on her front door she recognized the sound as being her brother's knock. She stumbled down the stairs to the front door. The brightness of the sun almost blinded her when she opened the door.

She stepped away to make room for Paul to come inside the house. He sternly asked, "What is going on?"

"I had a rough week and needed some sleep." For the life of her, Lacey did not understand, nor care to know why he was angry with her.

"So you don't answer your phone."

In light of the previous day's events, Lacey didn't have the energy for her brother's gruff tone. She was miserable because she put his expectations above her happiness. He needed to go away for a day or two. The attitude came out in her voice. "I dropped it in the toilet. Are you happy? I am stuck in the middle of small town Montana disconnected from a world where I could go buy some ice cream at midnight if I wanted."

Paul took a step back. "You had a rough night too?"

"What do you need?" Yes, she was good and cranky.

"What in the name of all that's good happened last night?"

"I don't know," Lacey threw her hands in the air. "One minute he was talking marriage and I told him that I had to take care of the house for you; and the next minute you're here mad at me for not picking up my phone. I know I said I'd help you remodel, but I did not sign up for all this other mess. This was supposed to be easy." Her voice rose toward hysteria with each job she had accomplished, "Paint some walls. Change some curtains. Add some flowers and bushes to make the landscape more appealing. Maybe you should have got someone else to do the job."

She expected Paul to tell her to settle down. That's what she would have told herself. Instead, his voice softened with concern. "But I didn't want anyone else. I wanted you to make a home here in Three Creeks. Look, most siblings don't get along the way we do. They get jealous of each other, or they're too busy knocking each other off a high horse. I like you as a person and want you to feel like you're a part of my family. That's why I had you move here. I figured if you had a home you'd want to stick around. It wasn't meant to be a prison."

It made so much sense Lacey didn't have a response. So she said, "Oh. Why didn't you tell me that in the first place?"

"I thought it was obvious."

"Well, I'm feeling kind of stupid right now. I just ruined a perfectly good relationship for a house."

"Which explains how I ended up trying to convince a drunk Colton that I did not tell you that you couldn't marry him." He rubbed the back of his neck, "If it'll make you feel any better, he isn't talking to me either."

"I'm so sorry." Lacey didn't know what to do. If she left, things would smooth over between the friends, but then it went against her brother's will to have family around him. "Things moved so quickly. I almost couldn't believe that he'd propose after a short amount of time."

Paul stepped in the house and closed the door behind him. "The best way to explain it is to say that's how it is with men around here. Once we get an idea in our head, it's solid. I knew by the way he looked at you that first day at the graduation party, it was a matter of time."

"Why didn't you say something to me?" she grumbled. The Colton that left the night prior didn't seem as hooked as her brother made him out to be. Her rejection of him may have been more than their budding relationship was able to withstand.

"Gracie did." He waited for her to figure out when the enlightening event supposedly happened.

She tilted her head and focused on the ceiling as though the writing would appear on the wall. Over the many discussions they shared, not once had Gracie mentioned that Colton was in love with her. In fairness, fearing that things were moving too quickly, Lacey never shared the depth of her feelings for him.

"On our double date," Paul began. When nothing registered, he added, "In the bathroom... I know you talked about more than lipstick color."

It registered and hindsight altered the memory. When they were on the date, Lacey thought they were trying to keep Colton away from her; when in fact, the three of them were testing the waters. Gracie had said as much when she asked if Lacey liked Colton and wanted to see him again.

Using her newly acquired writing on the wall skill, she saw

the future, and it wasn't very bright. It was more of a dark haze of loneliness. The night prior, Colton never argued. He hadn't declared his undying love. It only took her saying no, and he accepted it. Her head hurt all over again. If she had known then what she knew now, her response would have been completely different. She'd have asked questions and tested his feelings for her. Yet, she knew she didn't have to; his actions spoke louder than any answer he'd have given her.

Lacey sighed in resignation to the situation. "It's a mess. I'm sorry Paul."

"It'll blow over soon enough," Paul chuckled. "I have Colton's riding mower in my garage. He'll have to talk to me sooner or later, and we'll get things fixed."

Taking in to account her history with men, Lacey figured it would be too late for her. A pint of ice cream was what she needed to help clear her mind. Then she'd figure out how to approach the situation with Colton.

Even though the matter wasn't fixed to her liking, Paul had made her feel better about what happened. Lacy smiled her thanks to her brother, and said, "I have to go to the store."

Paul placed his hands on Lacey's shoulders and pointed her in the direction of the stairs leading to her room. "You. Go get dressed. We have people to see and places to be. Then you can get your ice cream." When Lacey groaned, he added, "You didn't think you'd get out of the annual small-town family football showdown. Did you?"

Truth be told, she had forgot about the community game. Lacey never answered her brother's question, but if she had, her answer would have been, "Yes, I did."

14

DÉJÀ VU

"You will love it!" She could tell that Paul, in light of the previous night's events, was trying to convince her that the day would not be as horrible as she felt. "They have tables and booths with crafts. There's all kinds of food." When he said, "I know there's ice cream," she forced herself to smile. How could she not love her brother who may have fumbled occasionally but always tried to make things better.

"This is where I met Gracie."

"I thought you met at a dance."

"No, that was our first real date. We met at the football game."

"I'm too tired to play football," Lacey complained. She just wanted to go off in some corner and eat a vat of chocolate ice cream.

" It's a one point for crossing the goal line version of flag football, not the NFL. This is more about getting together with your neighbors and having fun." Paul parked his pickup at the end of a long row of cars. "C'mon you'll have fun. And, Colton will be there."

If she didn't know better, Lacey would have accused her brother of summoning the man into existence. He appeared from another row of pickups. With another woman. Already?

It made sense Colton would also be there. When you live in a town of fewer than two thousand people, the likelihood of seeing somebody you didn't want to see was bound to happen. Lacey just wished it was later than sooner. She stiffened her shoulders and prepared herself for the worst. Through her sunglasses, she glared at her brother and said, "That ice cream better be good."

Paul and Lacey met up with Gracie's family who had chairs set up at the corner of the football field. Every person, including Paul, wore navy blue t-shirts with black sleeves. Lacey stuck out like a sore thumb in her pink v-neck t-shirt. Twice in one day, she glared at Paul, "You could have told me to wear something different."

He ignored her anger and continued with the explanation. "This is a process of elimination situation. Each team must have four women and six men. We play for twenty minutes. The team that wins moves on." With Gracie, her sisters and nieces, and Noelle on the team, Lacey understood why what she wore didn't matter. The odds of her sitting on the sidelines to watch were very high. She sat down to smooth her ruffled feathers and focused on the intention of the gathering. They were there to have some family fun.

The first teams to play were Paul's family versus Parker's Hardware. With the first play, Lacey felt the small-town feel Paul tried to get her to embrace. There were no stars on either team. And, Paul failed to mention the rule that stipulated a woman must touch the ball on every other play. As a result, plays intended to dominate a game were waylaid by a situation like the town librarian zig zagging in a formation that was almost professional to avoid having her flag taken. When she reached the end zone, she reverted back to her normal personality and clapped with delight at making some points for her team. There was no way to know which team was going to win.

Paul's team won their first game and stayed on the edge of the field to watch the next teams play. It turned out that the second game was the Hughes family vs. the Cahill family. The sight of Colton in knee length loose fitting cargo shorts, his fitted v-neck t-shirt, and Oakley sunglasses set back the progress Lacey had made in trying to forget she had feelings for him. She rose from her chair and said, "I'm going for ice cream."

Gracie's mother asked, "Weren't you just eating some before the game?"

"Yes, and it was so delicious I think I'll have more."

She overheard Gracie's mother say, "Does she know that Nikki's ice cream shop is at the edge of town?"

With everyone watching the football game, the line for the ice cream was short enough for Lacey to buy it and return to see Colton catch the pass that won the game for his family. He ran to the side and hugged an older woman that had to be related to his mother. "That's his grandmother," Gracie came up alongside to answer the questions Lacey kept in her head. She pointed at the woman Lacey saw with Colton in the parking lot—and that's his sister-in-law Taryn. Lacey recognized the name from the stories he told about his brother's family. She was glad she kept her first impression of what she thought about Taryn and Colton to herself.

They were so engrossed in their conversation about the Hughes family, neither Lacey nor Gracie saw the football headed in their direction until it knocked Lacey's ice cream out of her hands. She jumped back more from the quick turn of events than any pain. Luckily the ice cream fell away from, not toward her into a clump of the grass in front of her.

As her eyes perceived a handsome man running towards her a feeling of deja vu came over her. When he was close enough to be heard, he offered a breathy apology. "Sorry about that. My son thinks he's still the quarterback for the Bobcats.

Lacey had never been so glad to be wearing sunglasses. Otherwise, he'd have seen her eyes pop out of her head. She assured him that she would be fine, but he wouldn't believe her until she agreed to allow him to buy a replacement bowl of ice cream after the game he was playing. Lacey turned to Gracie who was beside her the whole time and said, "Is that how attractive men introduce themselves in this town."

Gracie's eyes followed him onto the field. "No, you seem to have cornered that market." Her face brightened at something she saw behind Lacey. "Speaking of the devil." She directed her attention to Colton who was now standing beside Lacey. "How's your head feeling?"

"It's better." He spoke to Lacey, "Can I talk to you for a minute?"

"I need to go check on something." Gracie moved faster than Lacey had time to ask her to stick around.

In the absence of her ice cream and cell phone, she didn't have anything to fiddle with. As a last resort, she stuffed them in her back pocket.

Colton followed suit and shoved his thumbs into his front pockets. "How are you doing?"

Lacey scraped the grass with the front of her sneaker. She said the only thing that didn't sound needy, angry or lame. "Fine."

"I was worried when you didn't respond to my texts."

She hadn't received the texts. She didn't know whether to be happy because he wanted to make peace or concerned because he was severing the ties between them. Her eyes welled with tears. Her sunglasses were the only thing she had to shield them from Colton. If she spoke, he'd know by her voice fine was the last thing she was. Lacey turned her head toward the sun. Maybe gravity had the power to keep her tears in place. When it didn't work, she turned her back to Colton.

"Hey." He snatched at her hand and leaned forward to make his face level with hers. "What's going on? You can talk to me."

She took a deep breath to control her voice. "I'm okay. Really. I just feel stupid. You were perfect, and I blew it."

He wrapped his arms around her and kissed her on the forehead. "Aww, baby. You're just a bad liar. I told you I could handle the truth and you lied to me and then gave the lamest reason for not wanting to get married. I expected we should wait. I'm not ready. You're ugly. But you're really going to let your brother come between you and happiness?"

A man's voice called out to them, "What are you doing to make Lacey cry?"

Colton yelled over his shoulder, "I'm asking her to marry me!"

"That makes sense." Lacey recognized the voice as belonging to her brother.

"What do you say?" He bent on one knee, reached deep into the pocket of his shorts and pulled out a ring. "Lacey Sanders, I am in love with you. The past three months have been the happiest I've ever had. In all honesty, I cannot see my future without you in it. I tried last night and failed miserably. I promise to love you for the rest of my life. In front of the entire town of Three Creeks, Montana, I am asking you to marry me. Please, say yes."

The world in Lacey's head swirled in the dramatic shift in

the situation. She quietly considered his question. If she said yes, would it be to make Colton happy or was it something she wanted for herself? He liked to go out, and she was a homebody. He liked attention, and she was happy blending in with the curtains.

Lacey asked herself if she saw herself happy in twenty years with Colton by her side. The clouds in her head cleared and she knew it wasn't the ice cream influencing her. Then she felt the warmth that came to her heart whenever she was with him. A vision of the smile they shared that day when they reached for the same fork and their hands touched accompanied the feeling. It matched the one she saw from the man patiently waiting for her answer to his question. She slowly nodded her response.

Colton's smile grew wider, but he didn't move. He was waiting for something. Most likely a definitive answer to his question.

Her words finally came back to Lacey and she whispered, "Yes." Hearing it emboldened her, and she spoke a little louder, "I said yes."

"You said yes! You're going to marry me." Colton jumped up from his kneeling position and pulled Lacey into a hug. He spoke to himself as well as the crowd. "She said yes."

People around them erupted in hoots and hollers of joy. With steady hands, Colton placed the ring on her finger. When the ring was firmly in place, he took her cheeks into his hands and kissed her so strongly it took Lacey's breath away.

Paul's big brother tone of voice pulled them back to reality. "Don't get too caught up in the kissy kissy smoochy smoochy. We've got a game to play."

15

NEED NEW SOCKS

Paul waved for Lacey to join him. "C'mon Lace. We're meeting on the other end of the field."

"Wait? What teams are playing?"

"It's us versus the Hughes' team."

Did he really think she was going to play against Colton? She wanted the rest of the world to go away and be alone with the man she was going to marry. But things were never that simple with her brother. She'd have to take baby steps to walk away from the situation. "Um, how about I sit this one out? You have enough women on your team."

"She's playing on our team," Colton insisted.

His answer stunned her. Last night he walked away from a proposal. In less than twenty-four hours he had not one, but two arguments with her brother. The mixed signals confused Lacey.

"What makes you say that?" Paul argued.

"The ring on her finger."

Then it made sense. Colton was trying to prove to Paul that he was strong enough to take care of his sister.

Paul who had taken the older brother role seriously, even into adulthood, replied, "Her last name is still Sanders."

Colton pointed at the rest of the team who wore matching shirts. "Really, you didn't even get her a shirt."

"Guys. It's okay. I can sit this one out." Lacey pointed towards the booths. "I can go get some more ice cream."

The look on Colton's face said there was no going to get any ice cream. At least not in the next twenty minutes. He took hold of her hand and guided her towards his end of the field. Lacey grimaced her apology at her brother and followed Colton.

Instead of being angry like she expected, Paul watched them walk away with a smile of approval. Her heart settled and soared at the same time, and the words her brother and Gracie had said so many times came back to her. Except this time the pronoun had changed. Lacey thought to herself, *"I love living in a small town."*

They joined the huddle, and Colton's brother nodded his hello to Lacey. His team had enough women without her playing, so they sent her to the sideline. Colton walked her to sit beside his mother, and it clicked. The argument between Colton and Paul was for her benefit. He may not fight with her, but he would fight for her.

Colton's mother leaned in and said, "You sure you don't need some new socks?"

Lacey wrinkled her face in confusion.

Colton's mother explained, "That was an interesting display of ownership over there. I thought for sure both of them were getting ready to mark their territory the way a dog claims its tree." She pat Lacey's hand. "You went with the right team."

They sat companionably in silence while taking in the

game. Taryn pulled Paul's flag ten yard short of making a touchdown. Lacey didn't know whether to cheer Taryn or encourage her brother. Uncertain of what to do she sighed heavily.

Most likely in response to the sigh, Colton's mother said, "This is nice, the last time we met we didn't get much of a chance to talk. Otherwise, I'd have thanked you for being such a good influence on my son. I haven't seen him this happy in a long time."

Unsure of what to say, Lacey smiled in response. "Thank you. He makes me happy too."

They both watched the game. After every play, Lacey made sure Colton saw her clap for him. Her brother couldn't fault her for doing that. Fifteen minutes into the game the score was still 0-0. If neither team scored a point, they had to play a ten-minute overtime game.

Colton's brother, Brian, called a time out and pointed to Taryn who was bent over on the field. Across from the field, it was easy to see that she was having a hard time breathing. Her husband ran to the side of the field and grabbed an inhaler out of a bag and brought it to Taryn. She sucked in two puffs of medicine and signaled with a wave of her hand that she was going to be okay.

"It looks like you're in," Colton's mother said.

Lacey's face fell. "What?"

"The rule is they have to have four women on the field. Taryn isn't playing so you'll have to play, or they'll forfeit."

Lacey hesitantly stood. She was good at cheering for other people. Being in the middle of the action was not her comfort zone. *"It'll be fine,"* she told herself. From what she saw, the men did most of the work. When she got to the huddle, Brian, who had taken on the role of team captain, said, "Okay some of us will go short, and one of us will go long. Just get the ball to one of us, and we'll pass it to each other."

"Who's the quarterback?"

"It was Taryn's turn. If you don't quarterback, we lose."

"Oh, no," Lacey's mouth fell open.

"One of us will be close to you. Just get the ball to us," Brian commanded.

In an attempt to make her feel better Colton's other brother, Darryl, said, "Nobody's scored yet, so don't feel bad about how things turn out."

Lacey nodded and took her position.

The hiker passed the ball to her. The movement on the field was so quick it was hard for her to find who was on her team. From across the field, she heard Colton call her name. She looked to see that everybody had swarmed close and left the far end of the field open. Lacey hooked her elbow and threw the ball in his direction. It spiraled perfectly. Colton followed the arc and took a couple steps back to catch it. With nobody around him, he had a free course to the end zone.

Everyone froze for a second. The Hughes team erupted in yells of joy. Colton ran with his arms in the air to Lacey. He picked her up and swirled her in a circle.

Her cousin said, "Who told us to go for a short pass?"

Gracie's brother-in-law asked, "Who taught her to throw like that?"

"I did, you nimrod," Paul grumbled. He used his pointer and index finger to point at his eyes and then back at Lacey to say, "I'm watching you." Then he smiled and said, "Nice play. Now you know why I wanted you on my team."

He jogged away to join the huddle on the other side of the field.

Nobody scored in the last two minutes remaining, and the

game ended with the Hughes team winning with a score of 1-0. The teams lined up to shake hands. When Colton and Paul met, Colton said, "Next year we'll be able to merge teams." Paul smirked and raised his right eyebrow. "We'd be a force to reckon with."

16

PIECE OF CAKE

Lacey gazed into her husband's eyes. The band of gold that circled the light brown irises glowed. His eyes were so beautiful it almost hurt her to look at them. They drew her to him, and she moved to be closer to him. Colton wrapped his arm around her waist and kissed her. He released her with a smile that said just a little more time. She reached for the knife, and she placed it on the cake. He placed his hand on top of hers and a spark shot through Lacey's arm and went straight to her heart. With it, the vision of their first touch at the high school graduation came to her. Her mind returned to the reason for the touch this time. She smiled, and the camera flashed once, twice and a third time. Colton counted to three, and they pressed into the knife to make the first cut into their wedding cake.

17

AUTHOR NOTES

AUGUST 2020

The entire story of Lacey and Paul came to me in a flash. I was serving cake after a graduation. Two people reached for the same plate and the vision came to me. As soon as I went home, I wrote the outline.

Lacey and Paul would also be my personal introduction to Three Creeks, Montana. I'll give you a little hint. Two men from the other teams Lacey sees on the field are unaware that love is about to come their way. Kent Parker is the first novel in the Ashbrook, Montana series. The second guy she meets is Keane Barnesworth. At the writing of this book, I didn't know that was his name.

Three Creeks, Montana is renowned for their family fun activities. It is also the home of romance for people that are a little more established in life. Translation, they are all in their late thirties to mid forties. I hope their stories bring you some light hearted, feel good, small town fun.

And this is where I'll ask you to leave a review of *Piece of Cake*. You can share what you like about the characters, plot, or the friends of Three Creeks, Montana. I read reviews to see if

I'll like a story. So it would help others decide if they'd like this one.

Lastly, because I live in such a remote area, I am active on social media. I have a newsletter where I send out blog style stories every two weeks. My podcast Small Town Stories is available on anchor, the Google Store, Spotify, and the Apple Store. I also love to share on Facebook, Instagram, and Pinterest. All of the links are on the next page. So grab a cup of coffee or a glass of sweet tea and whichever way you choose you can get a huge dose of small town fun.

xoxoxo

Merri

PART II

GET WELL SOON

18

JUST WONDERING

Becca was on the lake with the sun on her back and her best friend, Donovan Garrison beside her. That alone made it the perfect summer day. The warm sun that hung high above them just made it that much better.

"I'll give you a thirty second head start. "Ready, set, go!"

"Wait!" Becca held her oar in front of her. "I want at least a minute head start." Donovan had always been stronger and faster than her. With a minute lead, she had a chance at tying him in a race.

"Alright. A minute."

Becca paddled before he started the count.

He yelled out, "Cheaters never prosper."

She didn't let that deter her. Instead, she dug deep and focused on what she could control: her breathing. *In two, three, four. Out two three four.* Becca trained her eyes on the water. It splashed enough for her to know her oar had made the right level of contact. She couldn't afford to waste energy or momentum when she raced against Donovan. Pushing the oar to propel the kayak, she kept her eye on the prize.

Ahead of them, trees dotted the edge of the lake. The haphazard pattern, distinct enough to mark the shoreline came into focus as she approached their destination. *I might beat him this time.*

The tip of Donovan's kayak came into her field of vision. Her biceps burned, but that didn't discourage her from pushing forward. They only had twenty feet left to go. Becca gave it all she had. The loser had to buy the winner dinner. Rather than focus on the outcome, Becca kept her eye on the finish.

When she crossed the line, she raised her oar in the air. In an unusual turn of events, Donovan was half a boat length behind her. He lost?

"It looks like I'm buying dinner."

Becca may have been mistaken, but if pressed, she'd have said there was a twinkle in those chocolate brown eyes of his. He was smiling like he won.

"Did you have double shots of protein in your drink today?" Donovan crawled out of his kayak onto the dock and stooped down to help Becca out of hers.

He was a gracious loser too? Becca suspected something was off but couldn't identify it. "Are you sure you didn't let me win?"

She never got her answer. Somewhere between mid-stand and her straightened posture, Donovan lost control of the kayak. Her arms flailed to help her catch her balance, but there was none to be found. The boat rocked side to side. And, the next thing she knew, a cold rush of water had shocked Becca senseless. Like an ice cube in a glass of water, she rose to the surface and sputtered. "You did that on purpose."

Donovan covered his mouth with his hand to hold back the laughter. It didn't work. Wearing a grin wider than he should have had, given the circumstances, Donovan held out his hand to pull her onto the dock. "I don't know what happened."

Becca splashed water at Donovan. "I can get out on my own. Fool me once shame on you. Fool me twice, and I'm one of your ex-girlfriends."

"I'm sorry, honestly." Donovan extended his hand further out.

"I bet you are." Becca took his hand and pulled him into the water. He had to have expected payback.

But he hadn't. Donovan waved his arms as though they had the power to propel him to flight. When they failed, he landed with a cannonball size splash beside her.

She tried swimming to the dock before he rebounded from the surprise attack. This time he was faster than her, and he arrived at the steps of the dock before her. Instead of climbing up the stairs as she expected, he turned around in just enough time for her to glide into him.

Bracing herself for the collision she squinted. Donovan wrapped his arms around her. His hold softened the effect of the crashing of their two bodies. Becca relaxed in his arms. The contest was over. They were back to being friends.

The only thing preventing direct body contact was the two bulky life vest around their chests. Floating in the water face to face, they alternated between laughing and trying to catch their breath. It had been a common occurrence between them lately. They'd be in the unlikeliest circumstance and end up a little too close. When they settled, Donovan's eyes searched hers for something. "Why haven't you got married yet?"

He knew the answer. Donovan was the one who protected her from rebound romances after she broke up with every single one of the cheating boyfriends she had.

"Because men are a species of animals that cannot control

their urge to plant their seed in the first garden that comes along."

He flinched at her answer.

"Too bitter?" He didn't deserve her wrath. If anything, she should be the one paying for Donovan's gym membership. He was the one who joined her in the potato chip, chocolate milk-shake binges she used to soothe her aching ego.

"Just a little."

"Sorry about that." It had been two years since the last boyfriend. Maybe it was the frustration from arguing with her biological clock. Unlike her friends, it wasn't buying the *I'm happy being single* story. Lately, it was screaming at her to take a good look at Donovan. She was thankful for the life vest because she didn't know if she could hold herself responsible if they had made actual body to body contact.

Out of nowhere, something rubbed up against her leg. If she hadn't seen a video about snakes that swam she might have been okay. But, she had seen the video, and her imagination took over and decided some sort of prehistoric water snake had come to make her its next meal. Becca squirmed to get away and squealed, "Something rubbed up against me!"

Donovan's grip around her remained firm. "Contrary to what half the women in this county would say, it wasn't me."

She was in heaven. Being in Donovan's arm was perfect and wrong. They were best friends. "I know it wasn't you, silly. It was around my knee."

With the joke, the moment passed, and Donovan loosened his grip and guided her to the ladder. For a minute there, she thought he was going to kiss her; and if she were honest with herself, she wouldn't have minded.

By the time they loaded the boats into the bed of his pickup, Becca had talked herself down. Their friendship was far more important than a brief fling. The we're just friends talks she'd been having with herself were happening more frequently and were beginning to disturb her. Perhaps it was time to create a little distance between Donovan and herself. It wouldn't be for a long period of time; maybe just enough time for her to get to a place where she would relearn perspective when she was around him.

SHE WAS CONSIDERED A "TOWNIE" and Donovan, who lived in the house his father built on his family farm, was a "farm boy." When they were younger, the geography made it hard to nurture their friendship. They depended on family or friends to drive them to each other's houses.

Even then their fathers' vigilance set the tone of their relationship. Becca thought she was going to die every time her father said, "Leave room for Jesus and the disciples to sit between the two of you."

Granted, it wasn't as bad as the time when Donovan's grandfather invited her to help one calving season. With his hand elbow deep in a cow's nether regions, he said, "This is what birthing is like."

Here they were well into their adulthood, and Becca found herself still respecting the edict handed to them over thirty years ago. She sighed at what never was, and what she wished could happen and let the idea float away.

In the close quarters of the pickup, Donovan grew quiet. Quieter than usual. Perhaps losing bothered him more than she realized. As though he felt her gaze upon him, he turned to meet her focus. Having nothing to say, Becca quickly returned her attention to admire the landscape.

No two days were the same where they lived. One day the road from the lake to the sleepy town of Three Creeks was brown with dry grass; and the next, an array of sweet clover had blossomed and covered the landscape with a golden flowered carpet. She loved when the flowers bloomed. It meant a season had passed and a nicer one was approaching.

Donovan's silence lasted until he guided the pickup into a parking space. He shifted the gear into park but left the engine running. "I was wondering."

Becca blinked away the beginnings of her recurring daydream. The one where she and Donovan were more than friends. "About?"

He hesitated. "It can wait." He pulled the keys out of the ignition and moved to open the door.

"No, tell me," Becca pressed. When he didn't say anything, she added, "Please."

"Do you think you'd be up for a game of golf tomorrow? I know it's short notice. But, if you don't have anything better to do. I'd love to spend more time with you."

The only thing she had planned was washing a load of laundry. Golf with Donovan or laundry? It wasn't that difficult to decide. "Do you want us to meet somewhere or drive separate vehicles?" If she drove her own car, she could stop at the grocery store on her way home. If she rode with Donovan she'd use the leftovers from wherever they ate afterwards for lunch.

"I'll come by the house and pick you up. I don't want you leaving in the middle if I get too far ahead."

"Sure. I'll buy lunch," Becca offered.

The smile from earlier returned. If Becca didn't know any better, she'd have sworn Donovan had read her intention. Maybe she'd start the plan of spending less time with him on Monday when they went back to work.

She made a mental note to pop in the cooperative extension office down the hall from the office where she worked. They kept a list of activities around the community. She only needed one or two of them to keep her mind occupied on a topic of something other than Donovan.

When Donovan opened the door to the Keane's pub, Becca felt her mood change. Her troubles remained out on the side-walk. If she was lucky, they'd be gone by the time she finished dinner. Inside the door was a world where Becca called most of the people who passed through the door a friend. Even if they didn't talk on a day to day basis, or know the person passing by their table, everyone smiled a greeting.

They had been going to Keane's ever since the doors opened when they were in their early twenties. For weeks that seemed like they would never end, Donovan, Keane, and their best friend Kent worked on making Keane's teenage dream a reality.

The three friends transformed the floor level of what used to be a downtown hotel into the pub. Wanting to keep the integrity of the building, Keane preserved the chandelier lighting and polished the all-wood surface until it gleamed. Built with a lighter shade of hickory wood than the flooring, the beams, ceiling, and the tables became a part of the architec-ture. Keane managed to create a classy environment that said, "Welcome home," to everyone who passed through the doors.

Standing behind the taps, Keane greeted them, "You're here earlier than usual." His eyes assessed them as though he were looking for something.

Becca guessed that Keane had sensed the difference in Donovan as well. She offered what she hoped was the answer to the unspoken question. "I finally beat Donovan at a kayak race. So, the score is D- four hundred and fifty-one and Becca one." She exaggerated the numbers to let them know her winning wasn't that big of a deal. If Donovan wasn't so distracted, he would have easily won.

Keane threw Donovan a quick glance. The only other way his thoughts would have been any clearer was if someone had written a large question mark in the middle of his forehead. She hadn't answered his question.

"What's going on?" Becca knew the friends had secrets between each other. For some reason, this secret had something to do with her, and she had a bad feeling about it. "Is he still mad about the surprise fortieth party I threw for him?"

"Nah, payback will come soon enough," Donovan picked up his pint of beer. "I have two years to get you back."

Keane rolled his eyes and went to the other end of the bar to help another patron with an order.

Becca turned to go to one of the tables set away from the bar. She and Donovan had barely sat when Kent strolled in through the door. His eyes scanned the room and stopped on Becca and Donovan. He continued his course to the table and pulled a chair over to join them. His broad smile bordered on enthusiastic. That was the second flag that something was up. Kent was never enthusiastic. His smile was still wide when he asked, "How's it going?"

Donovan cleared his throat before answering. "Not much. We're just stopping for a bite after kayaking."

"Just kayaking?" Kent seemed disappointed by the answer.

"We're golfing tomorrow." The delivery was another hint that the men were up to something. It sounded more like an explanation than a statement.

"You can join us if you want," Becca offered. It had been a while since Kent and Donovan had played.

Kent and Donovan had a silent conversation that mirrored the one she had seen between Donovan and Keane. The feeling that they were in on something and had left her out took the fun out of the meal. It was then that it dawned on her that Donovan might have the same idea as her. He wanted to create a little distance between them and was trying to find a way to break it to her. Maybe that's why he let her win in the kayak race. To be fair, not that it would be that hard, she'd let him win the golf game tomorrow.

19

ONLY FIVE HOLES

The weather was perfect for their weekend plans. Sunday afternoon was just as sunny as the day before, and Becca was not going to complain. However, her weather app predicted high winds and an inch of rain for Sunday evening.

For the time being, she and Donovan were the only people on the nine-hole golf course. However, when they left the driving range, she peeked over at the parking lot. The increase in the number of cars in the parking lot told her they would have a course full of people soon enough.

Donovan noticed as well and pressed her to get going. Because he lost at the kayak race, Becca thought it was only fair that he was the first to tee off. He swung the club using perfect form. Of course, his drive was perfect. His fluorescent yellow ball landed on the edge of the green.

While Becca liked to golf, she wasn't as proficient at the sport as her best friend. She rehearsed her swing in her mind and set the ball on the tee. Eyeing where she wanted the ball to land, she stepped forward to position herself. If she did everything right, her ball might land in the middle of the fairway.

"You're going to hit that tree if you don't shift a little," Donovan coached.

Becca turned her head to see what he was talking about and sure enough, Donovan was right. She pivoted less than an inch and swung to hit the ball. It made it to the green and landed a couple inches away from Donovan's ball.

Pleased with the result, she smiled but refused to allow herself to get too caught up in the feeling. Golf was a long game, and the simplest of mistakes could ruin a person's score. She thanked Donovan, "You're a good coach."

He smiled, "You mean partner. I just told you what to do. You're the one who swung at the ball."

Donovan didn't gloat that he was right? Becca kept her comment to herself and walked alongside Donovan with her clubs to the green.

They parked their clubs at the far end of the green and set up to putt their balls into the hole. Donovan missed the hole with his first putt. His miss pushed at the edge of Becca's confidence. Usually, his short game was stronger than hers. If he missed, she surely was going to have a problem. To her surprise, she made it in one putt, which gave her the lead over Donovan at the first hole.

After he made the putt, Donovan went to the hole to retrieve the balls. However, instead of giving Becca her ball, he shoved it in his pocket.

"That might be my lucky ball," she joked.

Donovan pulled his hand out of his pocket held out a small black velvet box for her to accept. "Remember the agreement we made when we graduated from college?"

Becca thought she knew what he was talking about. But she wasn't forty yet. He couldn't be talking about that one.

"And we made the deal that if neither of us was married when you turned forty, we'd think about getting together."

This was going to be the part where he told her that she was off the hook. He had to be showing her the ring that he wanted to give one of his girlfriends. Light bulbs clicked in her mind. The looks at Keane's made sense. Both Keane and Kent knew that Donovan was going to let her down and they probably suspected that given the amount of time they spent together that she wouldn't take it well.

Another light bulb clicked. *That's why he suggested they forgo the cart and walk with their clubs.* They had eighteen holes of golf to bring closure to the forthcoming changes between them.

It was almost as if the universe had prepared Becca for the situation. She had been planning to do things alone. While spending less time with her best friend might be difficult at first, she'd be happy for him.

Donovan opened the box to show her the ring. "I know you're not quite forty yet. Is there any way we could move up the time line? You know to where I'm forty, and you're thirty-eight?"

Two and two were not making four. Out of nowhere, the man who consistently drew the line of friendship to make sure they honored it was proposing? Becca threw out the first logical reason that came to her mind. "Is this some sort of a midlife crisis thing? Like the male version of your biological clock is ticking?"

"Oh. No. It's nothing like that." Donovan grinned sheepishly, "I'll just come clean. You see, my grandfather had a trust fund for me. If I am not married before turning forty-one half the money goes to charity. It's quite a bit of money too. Since we were close to the ages in that agreement, I thought you might want to help me out."

Secretly she always dreamed of Donovan proposing to her. It was the agreement with him that got her to where she was now. Every time she was in a relationship that went south, in the back of her mind she knew Donovan was on the other side of things. But her mind had a more romantic image. Dinner, warm gazes over candlelight, cuddling while watching television. Let's get married so I can make a lot of money was the farthest thing from her mind.

"If that isn't the most romantic proposal I have ever heard," Becca rolled her eyes.

"I know. I'm sorry. You were the first person that came to my mind in the meeting with my grandmother and her lawyer, Bill."

Hearing that warmed her a little. But not enough to say yes.

"If I were going to spend six months with someone I'd prefer it being you. We spend so much time together anyway. It would just be under one roof."

There was the cold glass of water to bring things back to reality. He only wanted to be married for six months. Becca cursed her fate. She thought Donovan was different. Actually, he was. The men she dated in the past acted like they were serious about her. Time proved otherwise. At least Donovan was truthful. She had to give him points for integrity. Not enough to agree with his idea, but enough to appreciate his character.

She must have made a face because Donovan added, "I mean it. I thought it would be fun. We already do everything together. This would just make it a little more exclusive."

"Thank you for thinking of me." Becca held back the disappointment rising within her. She knew that she wasn't as pretty as the other women Donovan dated. For as long as she'd known him, which was for all of their lives, he had spent the majority of his dating life with women who looked like they needed to eat an entire Thanksgiving dinner. Her love of food was one of the reasons why Becca was so physically active. As long as she was healthy, she allowed herself to eat whatever she wanted, which meant she had curves where Donovan's previous girlfriends lacked them.

Becca waved at the people at the tee box waiting for their turn on the course. "Don't get me wrong. I am flattered that you thought of me as a solution to your problem. But I don't think I'm what you need." She walked to the edge of the green to return her putter to the golf bag.

All of a sudden, playing golf didn't appeal to Becca. She didn't want to disappoint Donovan, but being a consolation prize did little to help her self-esteem. "I probably should get going so you can go find your future Mrs. Garrison." She placed her club back into the bag and circled around to push it in the direction of the clubhouse.

"I already found her." Donovan placed himself in front of Becca and blocked her way. "Becca. Please. Don't be like this." He tenderly pried her hand off the clubs and pulled her off the course to the grass.

There were a thousand other places Becca wanted to be. At this point in time, she would volunteer for a root canal. Her mind scrambled for the right words to help him understand why his suggestion was the worst thing she'd ever heard.

"I don't want it to be anyone else but you. It's only two years short of what we agreed. I know you're not seeing anyone else right now. This is perfect for the both of us."

She searched Donovan's chocolate brown eyes for something to tell her he cared for her. All she saw was he needed her. Logic said leave. Then reality joined the conversation. They used Donovan's pickup to get to the course.

"I bet after eighteen holes I can convince you that us being together is a good idea."

Her heart wasn't in it. Becca had eighteen holes to help him find an alternative solution. Before she had time to say it,

Donovan had cupped her chin in his hand and gently tilted her face to make eye contact. Then he did the last thing Becca ever expected. He kissed her. Right there on the edge of the first hole of the golf course.

Her eyes blinked as her mind processed what had just happened. Donovan had kissed her, and she liked it. This was not good. Not good at all.

Becca heard of people who married for convenience or were in arranged marriages. Every time she felt sorry for them and wondered what were they thinking. Now she knew. It was something along the lines of *"Oh Em Gee! What am I doing?"*

Donovan repeated his challenge. "I bet that after eighteen holes of golf I can get you to agree to be my wife."

If he hadn't stunned her with the kiss, she might have told him no. Not only was his idea crazy. It wouldn't work. But his kiss muffled her logical side. The part of her that liked the kiss was curious. What could this man do to convince her to give up her independence for six months?

His interesting attempt at persuasion began immediately. At the second hole, he placed his hands on her hips and rubbed the area on her back to show her how to straighten her posture. On the fourth hole, he caressed the area between her shoulders to show her how to improve her swing. Suggestion by suggestion, her score improved. But her mind was lost.

At the fifth hole, she waved her finger in caution. "Just let me do it by myself."

"Is that defeat I hear in your voice?" His purr woke something in her gut.

"No," Becca grumbled. He had turned her body into an ally for his cause, and she wasn't sure how she felt about it.

"Does it bother you that I know your body better than you?" He flirted.

"Oh, for the love of Jack Nicklaus!" Becca exclaimed, "Let me hit the ball."

He grinned, "By all means. Go right ahead."

She swung, and the ball flew farther than she'd ever been able to hit it. A wind took hold of the ball and carried it beyond the hole and over the bank into the creek that ran along the edge of the green. It seemed that nature was on Donovan's side.

"I have a solution to all that pent-up energy." He handed her another ball to tee off.

"I do too." Becca barked. She added, "A five-mile run." But, she suspected it might have required a couple more miles.

A golf cart full of gray haired golfers had arrived. Donovan told them to go ahead, and he took Becca to a bench that was a short distance from the tee box. "Becca, you know that once I set my mind to something it happens. My mind is set, and my grandmother approves. I want you. I want to be the one that gets you flustered and is the one responsible for the contented smile. I want to be the first thing you see in the morning and your last thought before you fall asleep."

He almost sounded sincere. If a trust fund wasn't involved, Becca would have believed him. "If it doesn't work out after six months we'll go back to being friends?"

His touch was making her crazy. It took everything in her to stay on her logical side.

Donovan caressed her forearm and lowered his voice. "I wouldn't be lying if I said, I hope it's for the long term."

And logic got up and admitted defeat. "We'd have a prenup. I don't want people thinking that I'm in it for the money. Because I'm not."

"Of course." Donovan's lips slowly formed a smile that declared victory. "We get along so well together I bet we'll wish we'd have done it sooner."

The enormity of the decision pounded into Becca's chest. How would she explain the situation to her parents if it didn't work out? Donovan stood in front of Becca and pulled her into a hug. The warmth returned to his voice. "I promise you won't regret this decision."

"I didn't say yes."

Donovan placed his hands on each of her shoulders and looked her in the eye. His voice took on a sexy growl that made her world fall apart. Maybe if she had looked away, she'd have had a chance. But she didn't. He leaned in to kiss her and like a moth to the flame, her reflexes followed, and their lips met. The kiss tasted like honey tinted with a hint of pepper. She'd always suspected, and the kiss confirmed her secret interpretation of Donovan Garrison. He was sweet and spicy at the same time. At the end of the kiss, Becca released a sigh and Donovan smiled. She recognized the smile. It was the smile that Donovan saved for when he won. He was right. Donovan knew her better than she thought he did.

He called out to the four players at the tee box. "She just said she'd marry me! And it only took me five holes to get her to say it."

20

SOME GUYS HAVE ALL THE LUCK

He couldn't wait until Monday to let his best friends know the news. As soon as Donovan dropped Becca off at her house, he texted Kent. "Meet me at the pub. Drinks are on me."

Kent sat on the bar stool furthest away from the door in front of the large screen television, and Keane was stationed in his spot behind the beer taps. His friends knew him so well he didn't have to say a word. They knew.

Keane set the first mug of beer in front of Donovan. "Let me get this straight. You just said remember that crazy idea we had twenty years ago? Let's do it? And, she said yes?"

Donovan answered candidly, "I did mention a significant loss of money was in the works if I didn't get married." He took a swig of beer and swallowed. When he said it aloud, it sounded rather cold. "There was a kiss after she agreed to help me." He might as well get all of it out there. If there was a kink in his plan, they'd see it and help him make the necessary adjustments.

"There was no date per say, or hanky panky, that we don't know about." Keane placed the second mug of beer in front of

Kent. "You told her that you were marrying her for money and she went along with it?"

"I know it sounds harsh." Even if it was true, Donovan didn't like the hint of sarcasm he heard in Keane's voice. Then again Keane had said proposing without a courtship was a bad idea. Donovan knew Becca. If he turned romantic out of nowhere, Becca would have grown suspicious. Then when he told her the truth she'd have been hurt. No, it was better to tell her the truth from the get go.

"I'm not judging," Keane waved away the miscommunication. "I didn't know we had that sort of a woman in our town. Do you think there are more like her?" He quickly added, "I'm just asking for a friend."

Donovan and Kent guffawed at their friend's solicitation. After his wife's death, Keane had been a committed bachelor. He was friendly enough and talked to the women in town, but that was as far as it went. Even after her death, he was still married to his first wife. The wedding band on his left hand was evidence of it.

"It took me five holes of golf to get her to say yes and four more to convince her it was a good idea."

"You proposed on the golf course? How did you manage that?"

"I let her beat me at the first hole. After I made it, I pretended to put her ball in my pocket. When she accused me of stealing her ball, I pulled the ring box out of my pocket and handed it to her." Donovan's voice retold the story with more confidence than he felt. He had worried that she'd notice the bulky box in his pocket. Or worse, what if the box fell out before he was ready to give it to her? He'd lose the element of surprise.

"And she said yes?"

"She said no," he admitted. However, he expected no. One

of the things he loved about Becca was her level-headed approach to situations. Donovan waved his finger to indicate he had a counter plan. "Of course, she said that she didn't want to ruin our friendship. That was when I brought up the agreement we made in our twenties."

"And that worked?" Kent, who had been listening silently since he sat on the stool beside Donovan, joined the conversation.

"No. But I knew I had seventeen holes to wear her down."

"How exactly did you do that?"

Donovan felt the chemistry between them in the water the day before. If he hadn't had a bigger prize in mind, he'd have done something about it. Not being one to kiss and tell, he lied, "I explained that marriage is not hearts and flowers. It's two people coming together to form a team to make it through life. Since we were already a team, it was only right that we made it official."

Kent shook his head. "You're not telling us something."

One of the benefits of being friends for a lifetime was the ability to see hints of emotions people would rather hide. Donovan saw it in Becca all the time. She'd pretend to be confident, but something in her voice always gave it away. Now, it was working against him. Kent and Keane had probably picked up on something he didn't want them to know. Donovan had every intention of marrying Becca when they were in their twenties. He had never admitted it to either Keane or Kent because he didn't want them to call him out for not following through. Love was complicated. Loving a best friend was that much more difficult.

To shake them off the trail that was too close for Donovan's comfort, he tinted the truth by giving only half the information. "I told her if she didn't like it after six months we'd go back to how it was before we got married." Of course, it wouldn't be an issue. As soon as Becca saw how well they got along, she'd stay with him. The proposal wasn't under ideal circumstances, but the intent behind it was sincere.

Donovan had spent most of their adult life on the outskirts of Becca's life watching her choose men that weren't right for her. He'd helped her see a couple times that the guys she dated were dirt bags. Because of the way the truth came about, he couldn't exactly press the issue. He waited for a sign that there was some interest beyond friendship from her. None came, so he pretended to be satisfied with them being friends. Thanks to a little prod from his grandfather's will that was about to end.

"Seriously, some guys have all the luck." Kent pushed his empty glass in Keane's direction. "Which is why he's going to buy the next round too."

21

JUST SIX MONTHS

Soggy from the spring showers, Becca and Abigail passed by the front window and headed for the door to the pub. Abigail had returned to Three Creeks and was rebuilding friendships from before she had left town over twenty years ago. Becca was glad that her long lost friend had returned to the roost. Secretly she hoped something would develop between her and Kent. They both were kind people. And, then they could go out on group dates. She had been engaged for a day and was already planning couple's events. Becca thought to herself, *"Maybe Donovan's idea wasn't so crazy after all."*

Without giving it a second thought, Becca went to the edge of the bar where she knew she'd find Donovan sitting with Kent. She guessed from their postures that they were in the middle of an intense discussion about something they saw on the television.

"What can I get you, ladies?" Keane pressed his hands into the bar while waiting for their answer.

"Water is good enough for me," Abigail said.

"Can I have an order of chips to go?" Becca set her bag on

the seat beside her.

"Do you really want to eat chips?" Keane inquired, "Usually brides are trying to watch their weight. You know. So they can still fit in the dress on their wedding day."

The four people on the other side of the bar fell silent. Not understanding their reaction, Keane asked, "What? I'm just repeating what I've heard other brides say."

"Good point," Becca replied. "Forget the chips. I think I'm going to head to the community center and hit the gym." She returned the strap of the bag to her shoulder and said to Donovan, "I'll call you when I get home."

"I didn't mean for you to leave?" Keane tried to apologize.

"Don't worry about it." Becca waved his comment away. "No harm, no foul," Keane's reaction was exactly why she hated relationships. People set expectations that weren't fair. Like all of a sudden, she wasn't going to eat potato chips for a wedding that she had three weeks to plan.

She took out the beginning of her anger on the treadmill. When that didn't work, she lifted weights. All she needed was Keane's smart comment about her arms being flabby. After forty minutes of lifting dumbbells in every way imaginable, her arms were noodles, and her mind had numbed. She'd forego dinner, have a protein drink, and use her exhaustion to help her fall asleep.

As SHE STEPPED into the shower, Becca considered the virtue of the tiff with Keane. Thanks to the workout, she might get in some good REMs. Several times the night before, she disrupted her sleep when she woke in a sweat with the same question. What if she fell too deep in love with Donovan and couldn't recover from the breakup she feared was coming? She promised herself seventy-two hours. If she still felt this way after three days, she'd call off the wedding, or suggest they secretly elope and have alternate living arrangements.

Becca had just finished showering when she heard the familiar knock on the front door. One tap followed by a pause and three successive taps. It was the secret knock she and Donovan made when they were in elementary school. Was it irony or coincidence that he brought back the ritual three weekends before they were to get married.

"One minute," she yelled across the house.

The click of the key turning in the lock was followed by the crack of the front door opening. She slid her top over her head and peeked into the hallway to make sure Donovan was alone.

He called out while making his way to the kitchen. "Hiding your key under the mat isn't exactly what I'd call safe. It's the first place a burglar would look."

"You're probably right. I'll get one of those fake rocks."

She rounded the corner to be greeted by Donovan holding up his gift of a to go box. The scent of freshly made chips wafted in her direction. "I brought you a little something."

"Oh, thanks." Becca took the container into the kitchen and placed it on the counter beside the fridge. She opened the door and took out a lite beer for Donovan and a pink Gatorade for herself. She snapped open the beer and handed it to him before making her way to the living room

Donovan pointed back at the chips. "Aren't you going to eat them? They're fresh."

"Maybe later."

Frowning, Donovan said, "You don't think you're fat. Do you?"

Becca shook her head. "No, I hike two times a week and play league sports for nine of the twelve months of the year. I'm too active to worry about what people think about my body type." There was no reason for him to know her insecurities. Already things were changing between them. If they were to have had the conversation three days ago, her response would have been a resounding *yes*.

Donovan went back for the chips. He opened the container and popped a chip in his mouth. He brought the chips with him to the living room and set them on the coffee table. "Clearly it bothered you. Why didn't you say something?"

She sat on her couch and curled her feet under her legs. "You are absolutely correct. I should have told your friend that my body is not his concern."

He sat across from her in the chair her parents bought her as a present for buying the house. She reserved the chair for quiet reading times, movie marathons, and the nights when she strained her back doing something crazy like diving for a ball that was out of her reach. Donovan's legs were so long the chair was almost too small for him.

"I need to know. What are you thinking?" Donovan leaned forward in the chair.

"It's just six months."

His brow wrinkled. "That's just cold feet talking."

"No," she argued, "it's my sense of independence feeling stifled. Before this week I tried to look nice because I wanted to be attractive. Now I have to worry about what people think. I don't like it."

"I didn't say you were fat."

"When someone hints that another person is fat and you don't disagree, your silence is a vote of agreement. So, I have to be very careful about what I eat for six months."

The wrinkle in Donovan's brow deepened. "When did you get so needy?"

He was the one who put her in the position of being on display for people to make comments. And, he called her needy? Becca stood and made her way to the door. On the way there she declared, "You need to go home so I can get a good night's sleep," and then quickly added, "Nobody wants a bride with dark circles under her eyes." There was some truth to the last part of her statement.

Either he didn't get the hint or didn't care. Donovan closed the door. "Why are you arguing with me?"

Becca had a list of reasons. The first of which being she didn't have a good feeling about them getting married. Six months was a long time to be unhappy.

Donovan never gave her a chance to speak. His face brightened as though he figured out the answer to a question where the answer had been slightly out of reach. "I get it." He wagged his finger at her. "If I break up, it'll be my fault; and then you don't have to feel bad about me losing the money." His smile widened, "Nice try. Okay, I'll give you your space." He circled around and opened the door. "We'll talk tomorrow."

Instead of relieving her concerns, Donovan added one more item to her list of concerns. The way things were right now if they had a disagreement, he went to his house, and she stayed in hers. What would it be like when they were under the same roof? All. The. Time.

Becca hadn't made it to the kitchen with the chips when she heard the front door open. Donovan rushed into the room. "We can't end it like that."

"Like what?"

"The way we went about making this happen isn't the most conventional, but I have this feeling. This is it. You are my last girlfriend, Becca."

She didn't think it was appropriate to remind him that technically they were never boyfriend and girlfriend. They hadn't been on a date nor had they partook in the other boyfriend girlfriend benefits. No cuddling on the couch while watching a movie, or holding hands while walking through the store. Other than them planning a wedding that was to take place in three weeks there was nothing to indicate they were an official couple.

Donovan took the chips from her hand and set them on the counter. With her hands free, he held the both of them to form a visible link. "You are my best friend. I know that you watch American Ninja Warriors on Sundays. And, I know, without you telling me, that you scheduled the wedding five days after your special week so you won't look bloated." Becca's hand instinctively went to her abdomen. He took the hand back and held it gently. "You know the right thing to say when I second guess myself. I could have tricked anyone into marrying me. But I came to you with the truth. And, you accepted me." His eyes bore into hers. "This is our happily ever after, Becca. I'm not promising it'll be easy, but I know we can do this."

Becca had no response. She looked for a rebuttal and found nothing.

"Are you with me?"

She nodded her yes.

He pulled her in for a hug. "Good, then no more talk about just six months. We take life one day at a time, and the worst thing that can happen is we end up having a happy life together." He kissed her on the forehead and gave her hand one last squeeze before offering his parting words, "I'll call you in the morning."

The door closed, and Becca stood in her kitchen in utter shock. Her stomach twisted in knots while her heart fluttered. Donovan said three words she'd never thought would come out of his mouth, "Happily ever after."

22

WHERE WERE YOU?

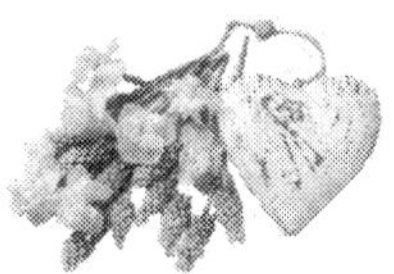

"I'm wondering if we should just elope." Donovan was at his usual Thursday night appointment at Keane's pub with his best man and the man assigned the seat at the furthest table from the bridal party.

It was one week before the wedding. While Becca settled after they talked about the wedding being the beginning of firsts for them, she still presented the signs of being a flight risk.

"What I still don't get is why you threw in the whole we can break up in six months clause." Kent neither agreed nor disagreed with Donovan.

"Because every boyfriend she has had promised her happily ever after and with my help blew it within three months."

"With your help?"

"Only one of them needed my help."

"Please explain."

"Present company excluded, she always chose guys that were tools. It was obvious that they were easily distracted.

Before social media, "I'd coincidentally plan an outing with her where we'd bust the guy with another girl. After social media, it was easy. Pull up pictures where he's tagged on another girl's profile and just drop a subtle hint. Anyway, these guys always presented themselves as Mr. Wonderful. I had to go the opposite direction to keep myself from being in the same category. I said the six months thing to let her know that I know I'm not perfect."

"What about saying something creative like hey I'm not perfect, but I'll try my best," Kent suggested.

"Where were you when it mattered?" Donovan was stressed enough to fall into sarcasm.

"Do you want my help on the honeymoon too," Kent quipped.

"Hahahahaha!" Keane pointed at Kent while he laughed, "At this rate, you'll end up at the back table with me. It'll be the first wedding where the groomsmen are sitting separately from the bridal party."

The door opened, and Becca, Abigail, and Dina walked in wearing smiles that said they had accomplished something. Becca's hair looked different. He was used to seeing it tied back in a ponytail that hung to just above her shoulders. It draped down to between her shoulder blades. Perhaps they got their hair done.

"Say something nice, and you'll get moved back to the front," Donovan coached.

He met Becca midway to the bar and squeezed her hand in a hello greeting. After all the years of holding back, being honest with her about how he felt was a relief.

Her smile held that cautious distance. She still didn't believe his intentions, and that was okay. In a matter of time, she'd see that he loved her.

They returned to his spot at the bar to hear Keane ask,

"Will it be the usual, ladies? If you want to try something different, we have a new low-calorie wine."

Donovan blew up. "Are you trying to get me divorced before I'm married?" He took Becca by the hand and stood to leave. "Don't listen to him."

"What?" Keane asked. "It's my newest best seller. All the ladies love it."

"Is it the Weight Watchers or Skinny Girl brand?" Dina put her purse on the ledge and chose the seat beside it at the bar.

Keane held up his hands as if to say, "I told you so."

The door opened to introduce another group of customers entering the restaurant. Two hulking men entered. They were accompanied by a diminutive woman whose eyes roamed around and stopped on the distinctive features of the restaurant.

Becca brightened and released Donovan's hand. She held out her hands in greeting. "I am so glad you made it."

It had been so long since Donovan had seen Becca's father and brother, Jonathan and John Jr, he forgot how large the ex-professional football players were. When he lived in Three Creeks, Jonathan Cartwright coached the Three Creeks Badgers to winning three titles. Her brother graduated and went on to play for Penn state and the Steelers until he retired five years ago.

Becca ushered her family past the hostess station to the bar. Beginning with Abigail, she reintroduced everyone to her family. Her mother, Gayle, nodded and noted something Becca had said about each of them. Saving the man behind the counter for last, she introduced Keane, "This is Donovan's friend."

Becca's father smiled as he said, "The one who called you fat?"

Keane dropped the cup he had been holding. It took everything in Donovan to resist the urge to point at his friend and laugh.

Her brother John Jr. joined the conversation, "Don't hold it against him. Maybe he isn't used to seeing women with athletic builds."

The statement forced Donovan to check out his fiancée. Because she was his fiancée, he was allowed to smile in appreciation at her curves. Even through her loose-fitting clothes, it was obvious that other than her potato chip addiction, she had been dedicated to a healthy lifestyle.

Keane cleared his throat. "So. You're here for the wedding?"

"Yes. My wife Gayle got the feeling that Becca was feeling the pressures of wedding preparation and insisted we come early and help."

Donovan didn't know whether to thank or fear them. What did Becca say that made them feel like she was being pressured?

"We should go take a table." Becca's mother curled her arm through her husband's elbow. "I know us being here this early is a surprise. Donovan, if you don't have any plans, we'd love to have you join us for dinner."

If two human brick walls weren't standing there, Donovan would have wrapped his arm around Becca's shoulder and gladly accompanied them. Her brother looked like he may have accidentally crushed a couple fingers in a friendly handshake. Donovan shoved his hand into his pocket and said, "I was getting ready to ask Becca what she wanted to do. You've answered the question."

He joined the table to look back at the bar and see four amused faces watching him with Becca's family. Keane's smile was the broadest of them all. His friend was up to something, but Donovan didn't have time to figure it out. Gayle tapped the chair beside her. "Sit by me. We need to catch up on what's been going on since the last time we were here."

On first glance, it seemed like the safest seat at the table. A meal later, Donovan learned otherwise. Gayle was the inquisitor. He wouldn't have been surprised if the other two men handed her a list of questions. The questions began light and easy with "Where are you going for the honeymoon?" and grew progressively heavier. It made sense; they wanted to make sure his intention toward the only daughter in the family was sincere.

"I imagine you'd want to get started on grandchildren right away, with the both of you being older," her mother suggested.

Donovan had no intention of having children. With them getting married at such a late age it should have been obvious that Becca had similar feelings.

"I'm sure Becca's told you that we've taken the more traditional philosophy of marriage and decided to wait until our honeymoon to get to know each other. Let's get past that and then we'll talk children."

Her father, mother, and brother responded with open mouthed, stunned silence. Becca turned fifty shades of red. For the next couple of minutes, they ate their appetizers in relative silence. When her father regained his voice, he said, "I remember things being different in small towns. I'd forgotten how much. Do you still have interesting community events like you used to?"

"As a matter of fact, we do." With things falling into his line of expertise, Donovan was ready to hear Becca's say that they were a good match.

They were in the middle of talking about a chili cook off scheduled in October when Keane stopped by the table with two bowls brimming with freshly fried potato chips. He waved the bowls in the direction of the bar. "I get the feeling that we had a poor first impression over there. I thought I'd stop by with this sampling of your daughter's favorite item on the menu to smooth things over."

Becca's eyes pleaded with Donovan to stop whatever it was Keane planned on doing. Donovan had no idea of what to expect, so he grimaced in anticipation of his friend's well intended but poorly worded attempts of offering an olive branch to the father of the bride.

Jonathon and Gayle sampled a chip and smiled. "These are good."

Keane beamed at their approval and began the explanation of his intention. "Food brings everything together." He scooted into the booth beside Gayle. Just as Becca began chewing on a chip, he said, "With that being said, would you mind asking your daughter if I can come back to the groom's table. I promise I won't say anything offensive until after she's Mrs. Garrison."

Becca choked on the chip. Her father tapped her back and offered Becca a glass of water. When her cough settled, he replied, "How about this. If you stay away from my daughter long enough for her to make it to the altar. We have a deal."

Keane held out his hand for a shake and said, "Deal."

23

YOU MAY KISS THE BRIDE

The weather was perfect for a July wedding. "This is a good sign," Gayle Cartwright said. "The sun is a sign of how your hearts will be toward each other for your marriage."

"What does it mean if it is snowing?" Becca joked about her mother's weather related comparison.

Without skipping a beat, she responded with, "You'll be close to keep each other warm."

Her mother was the eternal romantic. According to Gayle Cartwright, problems were simply life's way of applying adhesive to a relationship. Becca saw it over and over again through her parent's marriage. Something came up, and her mother would lovingly touch her father's forearm and say, "Are we ready to tackle this one coach?"

They had been doing it so long Becca wished she were there to witness what prompted the habit in the first place. When she was married for real, she'd use it with her husband.

Donovan said he was in it for the long term, but she suspected he said it to keep her from fleeing before the ceremony.

The bridesmaids were off sneaking peeks at the wedding guests when Becca spotted Keane from the reflection in the mirror. His eyes panned back and forth to make sure the coast was clear. From there he half tiptoed into the room as though a faster walk would give away his presence. She couldn't help noticing how the vest and tie he wore changed his appearance. At the pub, he was all business. The man standing in front of her was the friendly person she remembered from high school.

Becca turned around to see what he wanted. Guessing his intent, she said, "Hannah isn't here."

Keane blushed and recovered quickly. His eyes darted back toward the door as though it would reveal how much time he had to talk with Becca. He rushed his words, "Look I came to tell you a couple things. First, I am so happy for both you and Donovan. You're good for each other."

Becca opened her mouth to thank him, but he cut her off.

"I also want you to know his love is the real thing. Don't let him trick you into thinking it's because you two made a deal about getting together at forty. That was all an act. He's been in love with you for as long as I can remember. We've been trying to get him to act on it for years. You probably already know this. The man does not understand subtle."

Becca waited in anticipation of a but. In response, Keane's face wrinkled, and his voice raised in discomfort, "What?"

"I'm waiting for you to tell me something like I have a curl out of place, or a smudge in my makeup."

"Awww, c'mon you had to know I was joking with you all those other times."

Becca responded with a blank stare.

Keane shrugged. "No? okay. I'll work on my delivery."

To which, Becca smiled.

They were silent, and it was the most comfortable Becca had ever been with Keane. He quickly said, "You're a beautiful bride," kissed her on the cheek and made his way to the door. Right before opening the door he winked and said his parting words, "Don't tell Donovan I kissed you. He gets jealous when it comes to you."

At her response of laughter, he added, "I finally got the delivery right," and slowly closed the door behind him.

Appropriately, Donovan was the one who tipped the scale in favor of her believing the fairy tale. When she first walked down the aisle with her father, Donovan was in the middle of a conversation with Keane. As he turned to watch her come to him, the softening of his facial expression was enough to capture Becca's full attention. At first, Becca had to ask herself if those were tears in his eyes. When he wiped one away, it was as if he simultaneously pushed her worries to the side as well.

Her father leaned in and whispered, "If that isn't a look of love, I don't know what to tell you."

All the other faces in the room faded, and his became the only one that mattered to her. She kissed her father who passed her hand from his to Donovan's. Through the nervous chatter inside her head, she heard the prompting from the pastor and said the right words.

When Donovan finished saying "till death do us part," he leaned in to kiss Becca.

The pastor stopped him before his lips connected with Becca's. "We're not at that part yet."

Donovan's cheeks turned pink, and he said, "Sorry, I'm kind of excited to be married." Their friends and family laughed at his apology.

The swirl of butterflies dancing around Becca's belly calmed when they kissed. The touch silenced all the concerns she had about being a fraud. A gentle voice within her whispered, "This is real," and her heart sighed as if it had been relieved of a burden almost too heavy to bear. The tenderness of the kiss traveled to a place—a place deep within her nobody else had ever reached, and she never wanted the feeling to end. Donovan was the first to break the kiss. He kept his eyes on hers as he grinned in response to the hoots and hollers from their small-town family.

They walked hand in hand down the aisle. Beaming with joy, Donovan kissed her again at the end of the aisle and then whispered, "We did it. We really did it."

THEY WERE ONLY STAYING at the hotel for the evening and then they were headed on a plane for their honeymoon to Hawaii. After Donovan's confession of them waiting to get married to experience the more intimate side of marriage, her father insisted on paying for the room. Becca wanted to die when Donovan told her father the truth, and she was sure she was going to collapse from the loss of blood to her brain when her father said it again.

The verity of situations hits people at different times. For Becca, it was when they stepped into the honeymoon suite. They were married. Pretty soon, married people things were going to happen. What if he saw her undressed and was repulsed by her? What if the reality of being with him was nowhere near what she imagined? Like the complete opposite of pleasant. She glanced at the door. There was no turning back now.

Donovan sat on the end of the bed. The only bed in the room.

She must have made a face because he asked, "What's wrong. You don't like it?"

"No, I like it. It's just. There's only one bed." Prior to the wedding, Donovan made sure to keep any signs of affection between them to a minimum. She justified the distance as evidence of their marriage being in name only. This one bed situation was not in line with anything they'd experienced before the wedding.

He joined her where she stood paralyzed with nervousness and wrapped his arm around her shoulder to guide her further into the room. "It would be bad for business if they had two beds in the honeymoon suite. We are married after all."

"I. It's just." Becca stammered. "I didn't know what to expect."

"I know it's awkward." His arm went from her shoulder to her hand. "In normal circumstances, I would have done things differently. You know go out on dates, and hold your hand, and push my luck. We'll go slow."

What could she say? They were married. Based on what she experienced at the wedding and reception, there was no doubting his feelings for her.

Becca loved Donovan. She had for quite some time. However, the discussions over the three weeks preceding the wedding centered around the ceremony and not how she and Donovan actually felt about each other. She came to the safe conclusion that he wanted the ceremony to provide the validation the lawyer required. Consequently, she buried her feelings of love or any expectations of reciprocity. Now she had an even larger problem. What if she buried her feelings so deep they never came to the surface? Or worse, they came back not liking him.

Either he was oblivious of her hesitance, or he expected it and read some "How To Be A Newlywed," blogs. His response was perfect. "We can just take it easy. It's been a long day. You know hang out on the deck, play a game of cards, go for a walk. Whatever you like."

To her relief, he didn't say anything about consummating their marriage. "Is it okay if we just put on some pajamas and hang out in the room? After being around people all day, I want to relax."

Donovan exhaled a deep breath. "I'm with you there." He unbuckled his belt, sat on the edge of the bed and removed his shoes. After setting them neatly at the foot of the bed, he slid out of his pants to reveal his athletic boxer briefs. Across the band, it read, "Just married." If pressed, she'd have guessed that he lost a bet.

Becca wanted to ask what he was doing, but it was obvious. Part of her wanted to object to the strip tease; the other part was too busy peeking at the striations in his leg muscles. She slipped and asked, "Have you been working out more?"

"No, I walk a lot. But thank you for noticing." His smile showed he was just as nervous as her.

Donovan began unbuttoning his shirt and stopped on the third button down from the top. "Aren't you going to get into something more comfortable?"

"Oh, yes." Becca shook her head to bring her back to reality and went to roll her travel case into the bathroom.

She didn't get too far when Donovan objected, "Wait a minute. I gave you a show. Don't you think it's fair that you do the same?"

"Maybe, next time." Becca hurried to the bathroom and slammed the door behind her. Through the door, Donovan called, "I'm going to hold you to that."

For the remainder of the night, they lounged around the room. He in his boxers and t-shirt and her in a feminine version of the same outfit. Her bottoms were pink tartan plaid.

"Did you see Keane with Hannah?" Becca asked.

"No, to be honest, you were the only person I really paid any attention to."

It was a lie. But it was one she appreciated him making. He had spent half the night with his groomsmen playing drinking games. It was no wonder he was able to stay awake as long as he had.

His eyes drooped to give away the effects of the excitement. Becca stood on what she'd say was her side of the bed and pulled back the covers. Donovan moved enough on his side of the bed to pull back the covers. He crawled beneath them and waited for her to do the same. Becca got in on her side of the bed and turned off the light. The next thing she knew, Donovan wrapped his body around hers. He kissed her on the neck and whispered, "This is our first night as a married couple."

Becca hadn't taken him for a cuddler. Sure, he liked to hug, and he was friendly. The affectionate man laying beside her was a complete and pleasant surprise. She relaxed into him and tried to sleep. It didn't work.

In another attempt to calm her nerves, she listened to his steady breathing and tried using the rhythm to settle down. His cologne worked her senses into overdrive. After years of convincing herself that dreaming of Donovan was not right; actually being with him was more than her mind was able to reconcile.

As his sleep deepened, Donovan's arm grew heavy. Becca, on the other hand, was still as alert as if it were the first thing in the morning. Her mind refused to be comfortable with the idea that not only was she married to Donovan Garrison, but she was also sleeping in his arms.

After laying there for what felt like hours, she carefully extricated herself from his grip. He sighed, rolled over to his other side and fell back into a comfortable sleep.

Remembering that she packed her favorite blanket, Becca got it from the suitcase and made herself comfortable on the couch that was on the wall facing the bed. From there, with the help of the moonlight, she watched Donovan sleep until her mind drifted into its own state of slumber.

She slept fitfully until the sun shone in her eyes compelling them to open. Her eyes traveled to the bed to find it empty. Becca sat up to search the room for Donovan's whereabouts. The open bathroom door told her he wasn't in there. Her next guess was that he went to the buffet for coffee. She looked down to step onto the floor and found him there, beside the couch, sleeping with a pillow and the comforter from the bed. Not wanting to disturb him, she laid back down and placed her hand on his back.

A subtle softness joined the stirrings within her. With them, she relaxed and allowed herself to consider Donovan's vision of this being their happily ever after before drifting back to sleep.

24

MY WIFE

Now that they were married, Donovan regretted not doing so sooner. They had the paper to validate what he'd felt about her all along, and the intensity of pride filled his chest. His only regret was waiting so long. All those years ago when he made the pact with her, he should have proposed. It would have saved the both of them years of frustration.

What was worse--she had no idea how long he had pined for her. If she did, Becca would understand the depth of his love. Time would prove it, and Donovan was fully prepared for the day to day, test by test approach. In the end, she would understand they were meant for each other.

Donovan feigned interest in an alert from the weather channel when he was really watching her dress. Becca was prettier than she realized and until she was comfortable with their situation, he allowed her some space. Intent on being comfortable for the six hour flight to their honeymoon, his wife chose loose fitting capris, a long sleeve t-shirt, and a light jacket. The outfit emphasized how comfortable she was in her own skin.

It took everything for him to hold back the exhilaration that came from knowing that she was his wife. Now that he had her, nothing would come between them. He'd make sure of it.

His first test came quickly at the airport coffee shop. In one-minute, Donovan was perusing through a magazine at the novelty store. The next minute, from across the walkway, he watched a complete stranger approach his wife. A surge of anger rushed through him. Can't the man see she's wearing a wedding ring? Oblivious of the man's attraction to her, Becca, his wife, entertained a conversation with the stranger. It took everything in Donovan to not walk over there and snatch her away from the man. Instead, he casually approached them. By this time Becca had her coffee.

"Do you know that man?"

"Yes. We were in the same economics classes in college."

That wasn't the answer Donovan wanted. "Oh. How well did you know each other?"

"He dated a girl from my dorm named Jenny."

Her answer settled him.

She stopped to study his face. "Are you mad at me?"

The problem with them having such a strong friendship was her ability to hear the moods in his voice. "No." He began his lie and corrected course. There was no point in lying. She was his wife, and it was better if she knew his feelings for her. "I'm not mad. I just don't like it when it's obvious that you're married and men talk to you. They need to get on with their business and leave you alone."

"You're jealous?"

"No."

Her eyes scrunched and asked the question, "What was that about?"

An uncomfortable feeling came with the look. He couldn't pull off acting cool. "Okay. Fine. Yes. Are you happy?"

She replied with a pleased smile that extended to her eyes.

"What?" For some reason, the smile added to his discomfort.

"I wish I could go back and tell my fifteen-year-old self about this. She would never believe me."

"Why fifteen?"

"She was madly in love with you and swore she'd never have a chance."

This he liked hearing. "You were in love with me when you were fifteen?"

"C'mon. Who wasn't? Running back with the most points. Scoring triple doubles during basketball season. And, you wrapped up the year by being the anchor for the four by four hundred relay."

All this time he thought she hadn't noticed. It wasn't like she said much about it when they went to school. He targeted on one specific point she made. "So. This is a dream come true for you?"

In that instance, he saw it in her eyes. She withdrew in anticipation of something. He had no clue what it was.

Donovan redirected to comfort her. "Just so you know, it is for me too. It killed me all those years seeing you with those losers."

Her brow wrinkled as though this was news to her.

"None of that matters now. I have you, and you have me." He leaned in to kiss her.

"Look at the newlyweds!"

Both of them startled in reaction to the interruption. Lloyd, one of the extension agency officers in the community affairs office where he worked, tapped Donovan on the back. "How are they going to function with two of us being out of the office at the same time?"

"You're on vacation too?"

"Sure am. I planned this trip five months ago. I'm on my way to Hawaii. Where are you going?"

Donovan apologized to Becca with his eyes. He already saw where things were going and there was no way to stop the horse once it got out of the barn. He answered, "Hawaii."

"Nice," Lloyd exclaimed. "I'm meeting my girlfriend over there. Maybe we can go on some excursions together. Having you along will give her a chance to get to know people from where we live. You know, convince her to make a move farther north."

Donovan nodded. In his head, he imagined himself honey-mooning with his wife, not convincing some woman to spend more time with Lloyd.

25

WHAT ARE THE ODDS?

The wedding demanded more energy than a week of CrossFit training. While the occasion was one that went off without a hitch and brought her more joy than she ever imagined, it tapped into Becca's reserves. She was in a constant state of vacillation. In one moment, overstimulation from the excitement made it difficult for her to stay on any one topic. Within the next, exhaustion implored her to just sit down and allow sleep to do its magic.

With the constraint of being refined to one seat for six hours, Becca gladly surrendered to the fatigue. However, her first attempt to lean on the head rest offered her comfort one degree short of being able to sleep. She tried twisting to her side. That didn't work. Her body clashed with the armrest between Donovan and herself.

A thought struck her. The boundary lines had changed. They were more than friends. She could raise the bar and rest on Donovan's shoulder. It wasn't an invasion of boundaries. Better yet, without the bar, they both had more space and no hips were injured in the process of getting comfortable.

At first, Becca leaned into Donovan's shoulder, but something was off, so she loosened the seat belt to reduce the space between them. No matter how she moved her neck to make an adjustment, she found that his shoulder was too high for her. Resigning to herself that the first position wasn't going to work, she raised his arm and rested her head on his chest. Sighing in relief, she nestled into him.

Donovan's chest rumbled to mirror the purring of a cat. He sank into his seat and set his cheek on the top of her head.

Being this close to him woke parts of Becca that had remained dormant for so long she forgot they had influence over her decisions. Her eyes popped open with the new awareness. She laid still while taking an inventory of the rest her body. It followed her heart and was open to the possibilities of being married.

"Becca," he whispered.

"Am I too heavy?" She hoped the answer was no. Granted, the closeness made it difficult to sleep. Regardless, Becca preferred the current arrangement to sitting in her seat alone.

"No," he tucked his head to speak directly in her ear. "In less than half a day we'll be at the hotel and can play husband and wife games."

Being with him alone in close quarters erased the shyness. The time had come to tear down the boundary she had used to keep him at arm's length. Becca wrapped her arm around to reach his other side. "I know I have to, but I cannot wait."

He kissed the top of her head and whispered. "I love you."

She smiled and whispered back, "I love you too." It was the first time they said it, and she believed it to be true.

THEY MET Lloyd again at the baggage carousel. In the crowd of tourists, he wasn't too hard to miss. The man was at least six-foot-tall and wore his typical Montana wear: a short sleeve button down plaid shirt tucked in to show his massive belt buckle. His sometimes overly truthful, yet affable nature, combined with how he presented himself made it easy for Becca to find herself in agreement with the women who took a liking to him. In his own way, Lloyd was an attractive man, but he couldn't hold a candle to Donovan.

Rested from her five-hour nap, her conversations skills returned. So, when Lloyd raised his hand in greeting from across the carousel, she wandered in his direction. "How was your flight?"

Lloyd cricked his back. "Long. The seating doesn't work well with my size."

Donovan stood rather close to Becca. "Lifting the arm rest gives both people more room to move."

"If I play my cards right, I might be as lucky," Lloyd pulled out his cell phone, looked at the face, and rejoined the conversation. "What hotel are you staying at?"

"The Hyatt on the beach."

"What are the odds of that?" Lloyd marveled. "We are too. That will make it easier for us to get together."

"What are the odds?" Donovan replied with a false enthusiasm he had used on occasion with Becca. Like the time she had invited him to the cooking class at the community center. He said he'd attend with her and then conveniently caught a stomach bug a half hour before they were supposed to leave. She wondered what kind of a "stomach bug" he'd get this time.

The alarm went off alerting them to the arrival of their baggage. "You taking a cab?" Lloyd asked. "If so we can ride over together."

"Yes, we're using the cab system," Donovan said. "The last time I was here…" he cut himself off and threw a quick glance in Becca's direction before picking up where he left off, "it's cheaper and easier to take a cab or a shuttle bus to the excursions."

Becca remained silent as she tried to work out when Donovan was in Hawaii. He'd never mentioned it before. She shrugged off the question by deciding it must have happened during one of those seasons in their lives where they weren't talking. Not because they were at odds. At the time they were focusing on making their respective relationships work. Over the years, their boyfriends and girlfriends had been jealous of the friendship between Donovan and Becca. Now that they were together and married in Hawaii she understood why ex-boyfriends were suspicious of Donovan's intent.

Donovan parked both bags in front of Becca and waited for Lloyd to join them. He kissed her on the cheek and slowly pulled her to his side for a hug. When she was close enough to be the only person to hear what he said, Donovan whispered. "I cannot wait to get to the hotel and show you the difference between friends and lovers." Her honeymoon concerns drifted away with the Hawaiian breeze and the newlywed bliss she heard other people talk about settled happily into the newly opened space in her heart.

26

BENEFIT OF BEING GOOD FRIENDS

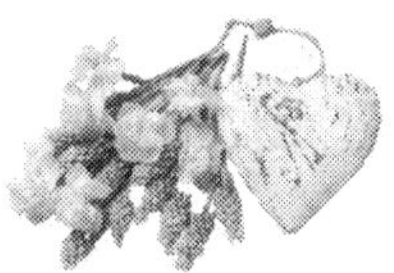

They had been together for so long Donovan could read Becca's facial expressions better than a book. She didn't know he'd been to Hawaii. He'd visited with his then girlfriend, Mindy. The trip didn't go so well. Mindy expected a romantic beach proposal. When it didn't happen, things cooled between them rather quickly. Of course, Kent and Keane were privy to the information about the trip. Other than them, few people were aware the trip even happened.

There was no way Donovan was going to let that nugget of information come between Becca and him. He answered the unspoken question about the previous trip by making it a nonissue. That meant going on the offensive in what he called operation overt affection. It was time for Becca to see the more romantic side of him. Beginning with tame cuddles, hand holding, and bag carrying, he set out to prove to Becca that their relationship had gone to the next level.

It was time that she learned the wedding planning conversations masked his true feelings. He did not care about steak or chicken. The only thing Donovan cared about was being alone with his wife away from the distractions of friends, family, and their jobs.

For weeks, he'd imagined what it would be like to make love to Becca. He'd have his answer in a matter of hours. If it mirrored the magnification of his feelings for her since they had been married, leaving the room would be a huge difficulty.

Lloyd was as dense as a box of rocks. What newlywed wanted to share a cab with his coworker? Donovan wanted to be as close to his wife as possible when she got her first glimpses of the island paradise. But what could they do? Ditch him.

As Lloyd took his place in the back seat of the cab between Donovan and Becca, Donovan questioned the wisdom of treating his friend with politeness.

Oblivious to what he'd done, Lloyd chattered away about the excursions he planned for his date. "Of course, there is the pig roasting. It seems so cliché, but it is so much fun. These Hawaiians have done their research when it comes to what people like."

Donovan hoped that Lloyd got lost at the excursion. Not long enough to cause an uproar. But, for just enough time for him to enjoy his honeymoon with Becca. Then they'd find him in a hut without a television or a cell signal surrounded by beautiful women. He covered his mouth with his hand to hide a chuckle at the news report. "Montana man stranded with a harem of women."

As soon as their bags were on the curb, Donovan approached Becca and planted a quick kiss on her lips. "Are you ready to honeymoon?"

She nodded in response. Her half smile told more of the truth. His wife was nervous.

"I hope I'll be doing the same thing in the near future," Lloyd commented.

After they were all checked in, Lloyd said, "I'll head to my room and give you a call after I pick up Monica from the airport. She won't be here for another three hours."

Donovan said to Lloyd, "It sounds like a plan to me." He thought to himself, "I'm not answering the phone for the next three hours. If I'm lucky, it might not be for the next three days."

27

TRAVEL BROCHURE

Becca was familiar with green. Three Creeks was surrounded by creeks and a various assortment of trees ranging from cottonwood to pine. The green in Hawaii was like nothing she had seen outside of pictures. Some of the vibrant leaves were longer than her arm. She half expected a fairy or nymph to appear from behind a leaf and wave a greeting of some sort.

Her mind expected the island to resemble more of a jungle and less of a thriving city that hosted thousands of people on a daily basis. One time she went with some friends from college to California. For some reason, Hawaii seemed like the cooler sibling from across the ocean. It had the expensive stores, nice cars, and beautiful scenery. However, the bustle had a flow. Then again, the groups of people with wandering eyes most likely contributed to slowing the movement.

"What do you think about it so far?" Donovan tilted forward to speak to Becca.

In his finite understanding of relationships, Lloyd chose to sit between them for the cab ride. Becca had to press against her door to make room for his hulking body.

"It's different than Montana." She smiled her approval. "They have a lot of tall buildings."

"Wait until we get to the honeymoon suite. It has a spectacular view of the beach."

At the time Becca laughed to herself. Donovan sounded like a brochure. Now that they were standing in front of the window looking out at the beach she understood his word choice. The place looked like a post card.

Donovan wrapped his arms around her and clasped his hands in front of her waist. He nuzzled his chin into the crook of her neck and kissed her behind her ear. "I wouldn't want to be here with anyone else but you."

She wanted to challenge him. He had been there with someone else. His touch made it close to impossible. Becca found herself melting into him and her concerns drifting to a place far off in the back of her mind.

He held out his watch for both of them to see. "We have been married for twenty-four hours." The tone of his voice had all but undressed her. His voice compelled her to turn around and face him.

Becca's body complied. She wrapped her arms around his neck. The awkward awareness of being close was gone. Being like this with him was so natural to her. It was as if they were meant to be together all along and the stars finally aligned to make it happen.

With his hands still on her waist, he pulled her closer to him and kissed her. The intensity of the kiss caught Becca by surprise. For all their lives, he had been low key. Donovan Garrison never got too excited about anything. This was a different variation of the Donovan she knew. He demanded all of her and expressed it in a way that gave her no options. Becca was his to claim. He had her in name, and he was about to have her in body as well.

She yielded to his demands while making some of her own. Donovan smirked and said, "I have been waiting for this day my entire life."

Wrapped in each other's arms, they made their way to the bed. Donovan was in the process of lifting his shirt over his head when his cell phone rang. He kept his eyes on Becca, and said, "If we ignore it, he will go away." His shirt came off, and he tossed it aside. The phone stopped ringing, to which he said, "See, I know what I'm talking about."

He went in to kiss Becca when the ringing started again. Groaning his annoyance, Donovan said, "Let me turn that off." He crawled to the nightstand where he had set his phone. After an eye roll, he pressed the button to silence the ring.

Instead of returning to Becca, he hurried to the door and opened it. Becca watched in curious confusion. Her question was immediately answered when he took the do not disturb door hanger and placed it on the other side of the door. Satisfied that the message had been sent, he returned to his place beside Becca. "It's time to show you one of the perks of being married."

28

IF ONLY LIFE WERE THAT SIMPLE

Donovan didn't turn on his phone until noon the next day. And, that was because his grandmother sent messages on Becca's phone to have him call her. He rolled his eyes at the series of dings from messages waiting for a response. While he read aloud the congratulatory messages, Becca ran the water for a bath. Somewhere in the middle, he found the message from his grandmother asking if they had arrived safely.

The tub, large enough for her to lay in it without having to bend her knees, enticed Becca to step in and unwind. She couldn't wait to see what it felt like to lay completely flat in the warm water.

From the room, Becca heard, "Kent wants to know why we haven't posted any pictures of the beach." The message was followed by the sound of the cell phone camera click. After capturing the image of the beach on his cell phone, Donovan closed the deck door behind him.

Becca relished in the florally scented bubbles. The situation lobbied in favor of the feeling of contentment. For the time being she embraced it in hopes that the mistrust of her happiness would finally go away. Several times she woke in the middle of the night in Donovan's arms reliving his proposal. He told her several times the trust fund had provoked him to follow through with his intention, but she still struggled with believing something this good would happen to her.

The bubbles eased her to a place where the conflicting emotions resided side by side and began a constructive conversation. Becca had endured breakups in the past, and if it were a part of her future, she'd survive. It would hurt like hell, but it wouldn't kill her. When the voice in her head reminded her that none of the previous breakups were with her best friend, Becca ducked her head under the bubbles to silence them.

When she came to the surface, she met Donovan standing at the edge of the tub. His eyes relished the scene. "You have one of the most beautiful bodies I have ever seen."

"Its under the bubbles," Becca corrected his assessment.

He came back saying, "Not when you move. They swirl to the sides, and I get a peep show."

It was enough for Becca to swish the water with her hand and see what he was talking about. When she saw that he was right, she giggled.

"Do you mind if we meet Lloyd and his girlfriend Monica for lunch? I got something like five texts from him." He scrolled through his screen. "Make that six. Who knows? It might be fun."

Before Becca knew what was happening, Donovan set the phone on the bathroom counter and took off his shorts. Her eyes blinked in response to the change in him since they were married. Donovan, her on and off best friend since childhood, kept a safe distance. Donovan, her husband, wouldn't leave her alone for more than a couple minutes.

He motioned with his head for her to move over. "I know

this tub is large enough for the both of us. How many chances are we going to get to do something like this?"

Becca slid to the side, and he stepped into the warm water. The added weight made the water level rise to the top of her chest. She sat up straight, and Donovan sat with his back on the other side of the tub. "Wow, you like the water warm."

"I have to start it hot. Otherwise, the water gets cold too fast," she responded.

"We should go to the hot springs in Fairmont," he suggested. "The water stays at a constant temperature."

Donovan caressed Becca's leg, and she silently released a sigh of relief. She remembered to shave her legs before she got in the tub. He continued to rub her leg. "I like this," he said. "This being friend and married thing. I feel like we can do anything together and it wouldn't matter. If I were to give anyone advice, I'd tell them to marry their best friend."

"I'd have to agree," Becca replied.

"With that being said," Donovan added. "Don't put the jelly knife in the peanut butter. That's just gross." He wrinkled his face for emphasis.

He stopped caressing her leg, and Becca pulled it toward her. She didn't know if the coolness was from the temperature change in the water, or from the absence of his touch. Regardless, it was enough to make her want to get out of the tub. Becca reached for the towel and stood to dry herself. In response to his statement, she said, "How about you make the sandwiches, and I'll wash the dishes. Then it won't ever be a problem."

"Look at us making married people decisions." He accepted the towel she handed him. "In a tub in Hawaii. If I'd have known marrying you was going to be this good, I'd have done it a lot sooner."

Becca chuckled at his assessment. "If only life were that simple."

❦

DONOVAN AND BECCA waited for Lloyd and Monica at the table of a small restaurant just outside the hotel. They had waited fifteen minutes, and there was no sight nor sound coming from Lloyd. Donovan checked the time on his cell phone screen. "Now that his girlfriend is here, I don't think Lloyd will be too much of a distraction."

Becca flexed her jaw. "For the record, doing what we did in the bathtub was not relaxing."

At the time faking a cramp to trick her back into going back into the tub seemed like a good idea. Ergo the water in her ears. "That's not how I remember your reaction," Donovan punctuated his reply with a sly grin. He rubbed her cheek with the back of his fingers and kissed her.

"If you two need a moment we can go to the bar." Once again Lloyd had startled them out of their world made up of only the two of them. A woman that looked like she was a yoga teacher stood beside him. Her long, lean stature contrasted Lloyd's muscular build.

"No, we're good," Donovan gave Becca's knee a gentle squeeze.

Lloyd and Monica took a seat across the table from them. Monica arched a brow to give her face a curious look. "I feel like I know you."

"I am a community liaison. Perhaps we worked on a project together." Donovan dismissed the comment and reached for the beverage menu.

"I live in Billings. That's not it." She shrugged to dismiss the conversation. "It'll come out sooner or later."

All eyes were reading through menus when the server dressed in a Hawaiian shirt and shorts came to the table. "How's everything going today?"

"Couldn't be better," Donovan answered for the group.

"I figured it out," Monica exclaimed.

"Good, we'll start with you."

"No," Monica said, "I figured out where I knew you."

"Me?" The server pointed to herself with her notepad.

"No, him." Monica pointed at Donovan. "I have your profile saved to my Meet My Match wall."

Becca looked over her menu at Donovan. Lloyd sat a little straighter. "I'm sure you're mistaken. He's here on his honeymoon."

"No, I'm serious," Monica persisted.

"Did we want to start with appetizers?" The server added an enthusiastic thumb up to her question.

"You think I'm crazy. Don't you?" Monica started digging through her purse.

"We'll start with a fried zucchini platter," Donovan kept his eyes on the menu. "And, do you make homemade chips?"

"No, but we have some killer fries and sauce."

"We'll take it," Donovan replied. "Add a beer and an umbrella drink to it."

"Really," Monica flipped through screens on her phone. Having found what she sought after, she held up the screen to reveal a picture of Donovan in hiking clothes with a mountain landscape behind him.

If lasers could have come out of Donovan's eyes, Lloyd and Monica would have been incinerated on the spot.

"Did I mention he's here on his honeymoon," Lloyd side whispered.

Donovan squirmed in his seat and positioned himself closer to Becca. He cleared his throat before explaining the situation. "Before we got engaged I met women on Meet My Match." He placed his hand over hers and gave it a reassuring squeeze. "It's been a while since I visited the site."

LIKE A DOG WITH A BONE, Monica stuck with her point. "It says here you visited the end of May."

Becca started doing the math in her head. They had a four week engagement. He was on the site the week before he proposed to her? It shouldn't have mattered. But it did.

"Okay, we get the point. You know me from the Meet My Match site." Donovan's voice chilled the atmosphere around the table.

Out of the corner of her eye, Becca saw the people at the table beside them turn away quickly. Before things got out of hand, she thought it best to leave the situation. The table and the food would be there when things settled. She reached for her purse and stood to leave the table. "I think I need to go to the restroom." Her intention was to go to the bathroom and pull her act together. Regardless of what Monica had divulged, Becca and Donovan were married, and that was all that mattered. One minute of talking to herself in the mirror would fix everything.

She heard Donovan from behind her. "Great idea Lloyd."

Telling herself to pretend that she hadn't heard, Becca hurried into the bathroom to avoid the conversation she didn't want to have. Once she was in there the major flaw in her plan came to light. Monica's truth sharing bothered Becca, and it was written all over her face. The questions came faster than her mind could answer them.

Making use of the little time she had, Becca paced in the bathroom. She had no right being upset. It was before they were married. She had no right being upset. It wasn't like he said he was in love with her when he proposed. She had no right being upset. He married her. She had no right being upset. The phrase, "six months" came back to haunt her. She whispered, "Stupid, stupid, stupid." This is how it always happened. She'd let a guy get close to her and then it all fell to pieces. Donovan was there with her for every one of them. If she could trust anyone she'd have picked him. She did pick him.

A conversation outside the door had her scrambling to the sink. Just as she began applying her lipstick, Monica walked into the bathroom. Playing the part of the ignorant wife, Becca faked a smile and gave the best lie she had. "The tropical food is wreaking havoc on my digestive system."

Monica's expression changed from wearing tight lined lips to exhaling in relief. "I was afraid you were in here because of what I said. Sometimes I don't know when to keep quiet. It isn't like you husband knew I tagged him on the site."

Becca agreed with Monica's self-assessment. Then again, Monica probably saved her a lot of heart ache. What if she found out about Donovan's online dating profile after she grew attached to the idea of being married to him? She turned off the water and said, "I appreciate your honesty. It's better knowing I married a philander than to go through life obliviously unaware."

She used her forearm to move the handle of the paper towel holder. Monica waited for Becca to throw the paper in the trash and opened the door to reveal Donovan who had been waiting on the other side the entire time. Monica spoke to him as though Becca weren't right behind her. "It's alright. She wasn't mad."

It took everything in Becca not to respond. Instead, she faked a smile and returned to her seat. The server brought the appetizers to the table. "Are you ready to order?" She heard them ask for food but was too distracted to hear what it was they requested. When it came to her, Becca was at a loss. She had no appetite. "I'll just have a salad."

"I don't think that's a good idea," Monica spoke up. "With your stomach being upset with the new food. You should try eating something with substance."

"It could be morning sickness," Lloyd suggested. "They have been honeymooning."

"Impossible," Donovan answered. "I made sure of it."

"There have been exceptions to birth control." Lloyd elbowed Monica and winked. "Who knows? We might be the ones to say we were there with the first changes in their marriage."

For their sake, Becca hoped it wasn't true.

29

MALE TO FEMALE RATIO

When Keane's wife was alive, he'd occasionally say, "A quiet woman is a dangerous thing." Donovan wanted to text Keane to find out how to undo the silence.

Becca reached for a slice of fried zucchini. She was mad. When Becca was mad, she didn't eat. Lloyd and Monica, on the other hand, filled their plates with appetizers. Monica, oblivious of the discord she had caused, gushed about their trip. "I've been here for less than a day, and I never want to leave. It is so beautiful here."

"I may be biased, but Three Creeks is beautiful too," Lloyd directed his attention to Becca. "Wouldn't you say there are a lot of things that make it just as nice as here?"

"I'm sorry what were you saying?" Becca sat at the table, but Donovan could tell her mind was elsewhere. Probably rehearsing the conversation she planned to have with Abigail when she was free of the constraints of an audience.

Lloyd didn't get the hint. "I was trying to tell Monica some of the nicer things about where we live."

"Yeah, it's so great you have to go to a dating site to meet women."

Donovan who was just as guilty as Lloyd didn't know whether to cringe or laugh at his wife's comment. Self-preservation advised him to go with the latter.

"What is the male to female ratio where you live?" Poor Monica probably said it to help Lloyd. Becca wasn't having it.

"No. The ratio is fine. I imagine the men are looking for a different kind of companion. The ones they have been around all their lives know what they're getting. Or at least they should."

At this point in the conversation, Donovan knew better than to eat anything. Lloyd, in his lack of perception, had taken a huge swig of beer and choked on it. Monica rubbed his back and offered him a drink of her water.

"Could you two excuse us for a minute?" Donovan didn't give Becca a chance to refuse his request. He tugged at her elbow to follow him. She offered Lloyd and Monica her biggest fake smile and scooted out of her chair to join him.

In the waiting area closer to the entrance, the restaurant had chairs in front of an aquarium full of live fish. Donovan brought Becca there in hopes that the lack of an audience, but being in a public place would foster a healthy discussion. In other words, he wanted witnesses if she tried to kill him.

"Let me explain."

"There is no need to explain anything. What you did before we were married is none of my business." Sadness tinted her voice.

Donovan was prepared for anger or hostility. Sadness was an emotion he had difficulty decoding. He went for the safest word he knew. "I'm sorry."

She turned to face him. "What are you sorry about?"

"I'm sorry that you are upset."

"Thank you for your honesty," she replied. "I'll be fine after a while."

After a while? "Does that mean you accept my apology?"

"There is nothing to accept." She shrugged her shoulders, "It isn't like we had a real engagement. One minute you were single and the next we had to plan a wedding. We never said anything about dating other people. I just assumed."

She didn't have to say it for him to know what she was thinking. His hands-off engagement policy was working against him. "I wasn't seeing anybody else. What we have is real, Becca."

Keane was right. As soon as Monica dropped that bomb of information, Donovan should have followed Becca into the bathroom and straightened things out.

Instead, he allowed the giver of the message go in and take care of things for him. In doing so, Becca had at least a good twenty minutes to forge a wall. A wall he taught her to build. He used to say to her, "Look for the signs. Infidelity has a way of making itself known if you know what to see." He never expected to be on the receiving end of his wisdom.

"We should get back to the table. We're being rude." Becca motioned to stand but never made it because Donovan pulled her back to sit.

"After I made my decision to propose to you, I went on Meet My Match to delete my profile. While I was on there, I got a call and went on to do something else. Until Monica mentioned it, I forgot about it. In my mind, I deleted my information." He pulled her hands into his and leaned forward to force her to look into his eyes. "You have to believe me."

"I do."

"You do?"

"Yes."

She said yes with her words, but her face lacked the small

barely perceptible smile of reconciliation. Her eyes were distant, and her jaw was slack.

"Good," Donovan stood. "I'm going back there to tell Lloyd and Monica that we're ditching them to go make up."

Becca stood and gasped. "You can't say that."

Her desire to be discreet charmed him. "I can and will. Are you joining me?"

She scanned the area. Other than the woman at the hostess stand, they were alone. Becca half whispered, "I don't want to go and make up."

"Trust me you will." He stopped to offer a sly grin. "Unless of course, you want me to go back there and spend an entire meal helping Lloyd convince Monica that Three Creeks is the place to be."

Donovan's wife said the three words that proved he knew her better than she thought he did. "We're making up."

30

EVER SINCE

The waves crashed onto the shore. Oddly, the collision of land and water made a sound that soothed Becca's heart. She watched the crash and retreat. The ebb and flow of water meeting the land and returning from wherever it came from. Donovan walked alongside her in silence.

"When I was sixteen, I got sacked so hard I was unconscious for a couple minutes. And somehow. My ankle took the impact of the fall, and I couldn't walk off the field. At first, everyone thought I had a concussion and a broken ankle."

Becca remembered it well. It was all her father talked about for days. If Donovan were benched for any considerable amount of time, their chances of going to state were gone. The team had other players to fill in his position, but none of them had reached the level of maturity of their starting player.

"You brought me a get well soon card and wrote the sweetest note." He took her hand in his, and they continued traversing the shoreline.

The train of thought eluded her. "It's funny that you'd remember that."

"It was the only one."

"I doubt that. You had girls carrying your books. One went so far as to get your lunch and bring it to the table for you. It was almost ridiculous."

"Don't get me wrong. That was nice. What guy wouldn't want girls fawning all over him? But they were public displays of affection. They were getting as much out of it as I was." He looked off into the horizon. The sun had fallen low enough to look like it was melting in the water. Slivers of orange changed the color of the coastline. "But you dropped the card off with my grandmother and left. You do that all the time you know."

She didn't know.

"You do something to get someone's attention, and then you shrink away."

Pinpricks touched her cheeks, and the urge to be anyplace else struck her. "What does this have to do with anything?"

"Nothing. I just remembered wanting to thank you. But every time I got the chance you'd vanish. It was a game of cat and mouse, but there were a lot of other mice there to pull away my attention."

She pulled her hand away from him to push a hair away from her eye. "This is a crappy way to make up with a person."

"No, it isn't. Because I won. You hid, and I still found you and made you mine. We can both pretend that what Monica said matters. But it doesn't. What matters is those little gestures of kindness over the years stuck. What matters is you trusted me enough to say yes. What really matters is you are here with me. I want you to know this Rebecca Garrison. When I promised to love you, I meant for it to be forever. I will build a bridge over every divide. I will climb mountains to find you." He placed his hands on her cheeks and kissed her. "And when you stop running, you'll see that us being together was worth it." He took her hand in his and resumed walking.

They walked hand in hand in silence, giving Becca time to consider what he had said. She hoped that Donovan remained her best friend. His ability to stay playful in their adulthood was one of the facets of his personality that kept them together. She didn't want him to think that because they were married that what they had up to this point in their relationship wasn't special.

It was almost like he read her mind when he said, "Let's have a race."

Becca found herself wondering if she said what she was thinking aloud.

Donovan must have taken her silence as acceptance of the challenge. "We can jog. The first one to stop and walk loses."

"I don't know about you and your contests," Becca answered. "The last time we had a contest I ended up engaged. Next thing you know you'll be telling me you want to have a baby."

"That'll never happen," Donovan replied.

She smiled softly. "Says the man who said we'd be married after the both of us were forty. I'm thirty-eight."

"No, I'm serious," Donovan said. "For my thirty-fifth birthday, I got a vasectomy. There will be no children, accidental or intentional in my future."

It was going to take time to process that nugget of information. She thought they talked about everything as friends. Apparently, her bestie had all kinds of secrets. Rather than belabor the issue, Becca opted to focus on his intent to reconcile with her. "Okay, loser gets the shower last." Becca took off jogging before he had time to agree or disagree.

Donovan pulled up alongside her. "That isn't much of a prize. Shower first."

Becca kept her pace steady. Jogging with a pair of shoes in her hand altered her balance and required more attention than usual. "It's the best I had in the current setting."

"You're just saying that because you know you're going to lose," Donovan goaded her.

"Famous last words," Becca wasn't taking his bait. The sun had sunk below the horizon, and the lights from the boardwalk took over for them to see. Even in darkness, the beach had a way of being beautiful. If there wasn't so much for Becca to see, she might have stopped. But there was more.

Scents of grilled meat came from one of the restaurants on the boardwalk. She wanted to run to the restaurant for a fish taco. But that would mean losing to Donovan.

She slowed down just enough for him to think she was tiring. He didn't say anything. His smile illuminated by the moon light was enough for her to know he thought he was winning.

Becca put her hand on her waist to fake that she was massaging a cramp. She slowed to an almost walkable jog.

Donovan stopped to ask, "Are you okay?"

Becca returned to her normal pace and turned to jog backwards. She boasted, "I won. You stopped."

Donovan's mouth fell open, and he charged in her direction. He was running so fast, Becca squealed and ran toward the water. He curved to follow her. When the water got to knee level, she tried to run back to the shoreline. In a yet another unanticipated turn of events, he crouched and ran into her with his shoulder. The next thing she knew, he had picked up Becca and was striding into the waves. She kicked and squealed to get away, but his grip was firm.

When the water reached his waist, Donovan dropped to his knee and released Becca to fall into the water. The water broke her fall, and she was submerged in a matter of seconds.

Sputtering salty water and pushing her hair out of her face, Becca howled, "What was that for?"

"Now getting in the shower first is a prize," Donovan teased.

"That is not funny." Becca splashed water at him.

He flinched. But it was the change in his expression that caught her attention. The next thing she knew, a wave pushed her into Donovan's arms and knocked them both into the water. They both recovered and ambled to the shoreline. Becca alternated between gasping to catch her breath and spitting out more salty water.

Donovan pointed while laughing at her reaction. "Haven't you heard? Cheaters never prosper."

She leaned back to give him a hard look. The salt had given her a bitter stomach.

He approached her and lowered his face to be even with hers, "You can't be mad. We're married."

"What does that have to do with anything?" she grumbled.

"It means we get to do this," Donovan pulled her to him and quickly kissed her. Then he stepped closer to her, so their bodies were touching. His voice was ragged with desire when he furthered his explanation. "It means, wife of mine, we get to kiss and make up."

31

I LOVE IT WHEN YOU USE BIG WORDS

Best friends went home to their own houses when they grew tired of the other person. Married people somehow learned to endure the barrage of stimulus. The first time she wanted to escape the sound of Donovan's late evening ice cream chewing with no place to go, Becca thought she was going to die. It was rude to complain, but who chewed their ice cream, really?

How he failed to understand that sometimes a long bath without repetitive interruptions from the other side of the door was beyond her. First, it was, "Do you mind if I use the bathroom. I'll be quick?" He closed the curtain and stopped midstream. "You're not peeking, are you?"

Truth be told, Becca had sunk her head under the bubbles to avoid hearing the sound.

No less than two minutes later, he was at the door again. "Do you think you're going to come out any time soon? I want to watch *The Shining* and don't want to start without you."

"Go ahead, Donovan. I don't want to watch *The Shining*. It'll give me nightmares."

"It's okay if you want me to hold you in the middle of the night."

They argued back and forth about whether or not she was going to watch the movie. At the pinnacle of frustration, Becca yelled, "If you do not go away I will leave smidges of jelly behind in the peanut butter jar."

His parting words of, "You're harsh," gave her the false impression that she'd have the chance to enjoy the end of her bath in peace.

A couple minutes later, her husband was at the door. "How about if I go in there and just talk with you until you're done?"

The method to his madness clicked. "You are feeling amorous. Aren't you?"

For their honeymoon, Donovan had been openly affectionate with Becca. Once their plane landed, beginning with allowing her to get her own baggage from the carousel, he had fallen back into the person she'd known all her life. She sighed and reminded herself of the adage that she suspected she'd have to repeat more than once in the near future. Once a best friend always a best friend.

In lieu of affection, the attention he gave her came in the form of texts, phone calls, and randomly appearing in places she wasn't used to him being. It was as if the wedding ring gave him license to sacred places like the bathroom.

"Can't a man spend time with his wife without having his motives questioned?"

"So, you're saying if I were to get out of this tub and tell you I was going to the bedroom completely nude nothing conjugal would take place?"

"I love it when you use big words for sex."

"Distraction is the same as denial," she called through the door.

Taking her response as permission to enter, Donovan

opened the door and made himself comfortable on the commode beside the tub.

"Do you always take baths with candles?"

Becca had candles on two corners of the tub. One of them was vanilla, and the other was a variation of a lavender fragrance that her friend Hannah had bought as a bridal shower present for her. She had been in the tub so long the bubbles that once threatened to seep over the top of the rim barely hid her body.

"Can you pass me the towel please?" She pointed at the mauve colored towel beside Donovan's gray towel. It was one of the few variations in the decorations to indicate that a female resided in the house. Until she was certain they were married for real, Becca did not want to upset the dynamic any more than moving her clothes had caused.

"You're not leaving because of me, are you?"

"No, the water was getting cold."

Donovan wrapped the towel around her back. With the gesture, he spoke barely above a whisper. "I know a way to make things warmer."

The feeling of his hands against her bare skin combined with the temptation in his voice was enough for Becca to acquiesce to the intentions she had suspected all along.

An hour later she woke feeling slightly chilled. Her eyes scanned the room for Donovan. The blankets on his side of the bed were pulled up neatly, making it look as though he was never there. Through the bedroom door, she heard the tinny scream come from the television. Becca pulled an extra blanket from the top of the closet and returned to the bed to enjoy the peaceful slumber that came from living with someone she knew almost better than herself.

32

NOT IT

"You added another beer to the tap." Donovan was in his usual Thursday after work place at the bar in Keane's pub.

"Yeah, this is from the microbrewery in Cut Bank." Keane tilted the handle to pour the gold colored brew into a pint glass for his friends. "This is their oatmeal stout." The foam had settled enough for Donovan and Kent to see the gold make way for the darker hues of the beer.

"Have you two had your first fight yet?" Keane leaned against the bar ready for the juicy details of Donovan's newlywed life.

"Other than the fiasco Lloyd's girlfriend caused? No." He considered the question and couldn't figure out why Keane asked it. "We've known each other for all our lives. What would there be to fight about?"

Keane rubbed his chin in thought. "Hmm, where shall I begin? What colors to use for the bathroom?"

"Or how the deer head belongs in a different room. Usually the garage or the basement," Kent added.

Raising his finger and pointing to address the next issue,

Keane said, "We must remember how we don't know how to organize our kitchen."

"Like I've said all along because we were friends for so long we already knew each other's issues." Donovan took a drink of his beer. The smooth liquid had a deep taste that lingered long after he swallowed it. However, the aftertaste was sweet, not bitter like most beers.

"Issues are hidden until you have to make room for other things." Keane looked apologetically at Donovan. Like he missed something everyone else could see.

Thinking his other friend would take his side, Donovan turned to Kent for support. Before he opened his mouth to say something like, "Tell our friend he is mistaken," he saw the same look of incredulity in Kent's eyes too.

Donovan was getting ready to launch into an explanation of how his engagement and prenuptial agreement set up the parameters of the relationship when he noticed Keane's attention was elsewhere. His eyes followed the invisible trail Keane had made. At the edge of the front window, he saw Hannah and Katie from the County Extension office pass by. He returned his attention to Keane who, in the absence of what had distracted him in the first place, blinked and began wiping the counter.

"What was that?" Donovan used his thumb to draw an imaginary line connecting Keane to Hannah. "Do you have a thing for her?"

"No." It was Keane's turn to exercise the skill of denial. "Can't a guy enjoy an attractive woman when she walks by?"

"For the record, she's been attractive for years. You were acting like it was the first time you saw her." Donovan motioned to stand. "If you want I can go get her and bring her back to talk to you."

"I'm good. Anyway, we're talking about your marital issues. Or the lack of them." Keane replied.

"I don't have any issues."

"And that is a problem," Kent said. "She just moved into the house you have owned for the last fifteen years and settled in with no issues. I hate to say it, but that is an issue."

"It is called a honeymoon period," Donovan defended. However, in the back of his mind, the yellow flag of caution waved its warning signal.

"It is called your dear wife, Becca, is not invested in the relationship. If anyone should know about that it would be me." Kent warned.

Donovan wanted to negate Kent's advice by calling it a lingering bitterness that came from his friend's wife leaving him for another man. Then again, who would know the signs of infidelity better than the man who had survived it? But it didn't make sense. Whenever he called, Becca happily answered the phone. She was never too tired or too busy for sex. Was it possible that her sexual appetite surpassed his ability to match it?

"Has Abigail said anything about her talking to any other men?"

Kent's response was interrupted by the front door opening. Abigail, Dina and Becca walked into the pub. It was as though the mention of her name made Donovan's wife appear.

Becca came up alongside him and gave his hand a squeeze that conveyed a warm hello. Since they'd returned from their honeymoon, the public displays of affection pulled back to subtle touches and eye contact that hinted at the special connection between the two of them. Up until ten minutes ago, he liked that they weren't overtly expressive. Now he was second guessing the behavior. Maybe he should have put it out there a little more that she was his wife.

He loved Becca more than anyone, Becca included, could know. There had been times when he woke in the night and laid in silence and full of awe at her beauty watched her sleep. After all these years, she was in his bed as his wife. It was almost too good to be true. He hoped that she shared the sentiment within the gleam in her eye.

"Do you ladies want to try a sample of our newest beer?" Without waiting for an answer, Keane placed three mugs on the table.

The smile all but disappeared from Becca's face. "No, I'm good. I'll just have water with lemon."

Dina answered, "I'll have my usual wine."

Abigail scrunched her face while considering her choices. "I'm not feeling beer right now. How about a soda?"

"None of you are going to try the beer? What? Is one of you pregnant?"

All three women startled. "Not it," Abigail called out.

"Since when did wine become the pregnant woman's beverage of choice?" Dina's voice dripped with sarcasm.

"And we know that isn't happening anytime soon in our house." Donovan broke his code of being openly affectionate and wrapped his arm around Becca's waist to pull her closer to him.

She choked and tapped on her chest while she coughed to loosen her throat.

Donovan tapped on her back while she took sips from the glass of water that Keane slid in front of her.

"I was just joking around." Keane's explanation was his way of apologizing. After the chip incident, Donovan noticed how he worked to stay on Becca's good side.

When she caught her breath, Becca said, "I'm fine. Something just went down the wrong pipe."

The front door opened, and a family came through the door

signaling the beginning of Keane's dinner rush. The friends had been at his pub for so many years they knew the signs of the ebbs and flows of his business routine. Donovan placed his money on the bar. "It looks like it's time for us to head home." With the gesture, the friends said their goodbyes and promised to call each other tomorrow. As they stepped on the sidewalk outside the pub, Donovan thought to himself, *"It doesn't get any better than this."*

33

BUTTER HIM UP

Dina had been married longer than all of them. That made her the expert on marriage. Abigail's entanglement with Donovan's best friend, Kent, made her the spy. She pumped Kent for information that Donovan might not share with Becca because she was closer to the situation. The only thing Abigail was able to come up with was Donovan was concerned about the five pounds he gained since being married.

But, Dina on the other hand, was a wealth of information. "Honey, I've had to dig my way out of a hole so many times, I should go into construction." Given Donovan's stance on children, with his help, Becca was in a hole. A big hole. The Grand Canyon was small compared to the crater this was going to create in their lives.

At first, Dina wasn't sympathetic to the cause. "Everyone knows the rhyme."

Abigail and Becca shared a confused look.

Dina rolled her eyes. "We sang it all the time in second grade. First comes love, then comes marriage, then comes the baby in the baby carriage."

It was enough to stress Becca to tears. They had done it in reverse. For them, it was marriage and then love. That had to be a sign that things weren't going to end well. She stepped off the stationary bike. "I have to go to the bathroom. I'll be back in a minute."

"Hey, it isn't that bad," Dina rushed to her side. "And this is hormones."

Becca inhaled a breath to pull herself together. "No, this is Donovan never wanted to have children."

"Most men say that. And then when the baby gets here, they fall in love."

"Did most men have a vasectomy?" Maybe it would be easier if Becca ran away from home.

"We'll get you through this." Dina wrapped her arm around Becca's shoulder. "It'll be alright. I promise."

With that, Dina began teaching arguing 101. The three friends pedaled on stationary bikes and discussed the variety of ways Donovan could respond when Becca broke the news to him. First came disbelief. Then came the accusation of sabotaging the birth control, followed by the rant of how she ruined their lives. Then came the suggestion: butter him up.

"The trick is you have to have him in a state of almost bliss with where you are in your lives. You know, nice dinner and a back rub. Maybe bring him some snacks while he is watching the game. This is better if his team wins, but you have to work with the circumstances you're given. Or wait for a really good play, and when they turn to go to a commercial, you break the news to him. That's even better because when the game comes back on, he'll want to go back to watching it. If there ever was an argument, he'll want to drop it."

Through breaths ragged from riding the bike, Abigail asked, "This is how you dig yourself out of holes with Rhett?"

"Every time?"

"And it works?" A fourth voice joined the collaboration. The aerobics instructor who was walking by at the time overheard what they were talking about and stopped to catch the end of the conversation.

By the time they finished their cooling stretches, a small group of women had formed a support system that addressed what to do if everything went right, and a backup plan for just in case it didn't.

As soon as husband and wife walked through the front door of their home, Becca launched into her plan to tell her husband that they were about to enter the next stage in their adult life. Parenthood. The thought made her stomach lurch. They had been single for so long, the idea of a third person alternated between exhilarating and unnerving Abigail. One minute she was thrilled about the possibility and the next she feared not only ruining her life but that of the child she was carrying.

"Are you okay?" It was almost like Donovan could read her mind.

"Yes, I'm fine," she answered and then regretted it. There was her chance to tell him. Then again, she hadn't done anything to prepare him. Pulling the plan to the front of her mind, she added, "I was wondering if you wanted me to make some nachos for you while you watched the game."

"It's a bi week. No game this week." He pulled her into him. "Which means we can play a little contact sport of our own."

Becca placed her hand on his chest and stepped back to loosen his grip on her waist. "A back rub. Do you want a back rub?" Determined to tell him as soon as possible, Becca hurried to get to his back before he turned to face her. She kneaded his shoulders to give him a sample of what was to come. Keeping secrets was not her forte. That, and the sooner he knew what was happening, the quicker they could get on with the next steps.

Her intention was to guide him to the couch where he could lay down and get the full benefit of the back rub.

He placed his hands on hers and rotated. Holding both her hands in his, he cut to the chase. "You want something. There isn't much you could ask for that I'd refuse you. So out with it."

The truth was more than she was able to contain. Becca blurted, "I'm pregnant." She bit her lip and held her breath in anticipation of Donovan's reaction.

It wasn't as immediate as she expected. The process was so slow; she practically saw the gears in his head move. First, the freeze as the information went from his ears to his head. Then the eyes widening and contracting as the impact of the information began sinking in. Finally, he loosened his grip on her hands. Donovan took two steps away from her. "That is impossible."

Her hands, chilled from the absence of his touch, went into her pockets for comfort she instinctively knew he wasn't going to provide. This was the last thing, the only thing Donovan didn't want. He had said it so many times; she almost wondered if she should have got him drunk before telling him. Becca frowned. "I thought the same thing. Then the doctor said that sometimes vasectomies repair themselves."

"You're blaming me."

Becca almost wished they weren't standing so close together. Then she wouldn't have seen the disbelief followed by the shadow in his eyes. He thought she was lying to him about more than the pregnancy. She stepped away in preparation for the barrage of accusations. The doctor said it might happen.

She softened her voice. "No, I was explaining how it was possible."

"What's his name?" Donovan demanded. When she didn't answer, he asked, "How far along are you?"

"Six weeks." Her heart pleaded with him to see that she had been faithful to him.

His eyes went to the ceiling as though he were reading an invisible calendar. "I was in Helena giving a presentation on grizzly migration three weeks ago." He continued with the details of the past, "Five weeks ago it was Missoula. How can you be so certain it's six weeks? What if you're off by a week?"

It pained her, but she knew any effort she attempted to get him to believe the child was his was useless. "You need some time. I get it."

"Time for what? Time to get used to the fact that you're trying to pin me down with some other man's child?"

The accusation stabbed her heart and lodged itself somewhere in the pit of her stomach. Becca expected the insults. She hadn't expected them to cut so deep.

"Don't think crying is going to work on me either."

She motioned to move in the direction of their, his, bedroom. Her heart raced in her chest. They had bickered back and forth over the years, but she and Donovan had never argued. They had lived by the creed *"It is better to be happy than right."* If he was right, it might have made a difference. But he wasn't, and it made the argument that much worse.

Donovan stepped in front of her. "You couldn't make it to six months. Six months was all I asked for."

Becca knew from the advice he'd given her over the years, that Donovan had a severe side to him. The number, six months, was a slap of reality. She had been right all along. He had no intention of being with her for longer than six months. It did little to soften the blow of being the recipient of it. But it didn't hurt as bad as she thought it would. She didn't feel like she was going to die.

Steeling herself for what was to come, Becca made a mental list of what to pack. "Can you step out of the way?"

"Why?"

"Rules to a breakup number one." She held up her finger, "Assert the prepared boundaries. I believe you said 'six months.'" Her index finger joined the pointer to make number two. "In a couple seconds, you will initiate the second rule. Make a clean cut. They heal faster."

Donovan's mouth opened, but it failed to produce any words. She had him.

"Let me say it for you. It's time we took a break. We don't want to say anything we'll regret later."

"Things are done between us," Donovan yelled. "Done."

Becca flinched and quickly recovered. The stress had an adverse effect on her, and she found a calm within herself. It had to be shock.

"Can you move so I can get a bag packed?"

He stepped aside and went into the kitchen. Becca packed enough to get her through the weekend. This was a day by day plan. If he didn't calm down, she'd come by when he wasn't at the house and get more of her clothes.

Donovan kept his gaze on the wall on the far side of the room. When she got to the door, he said, "I might have been able to forgive an affair, but I told you from the beginning I didn't want a child."

Becca replied, "Be careful about what you wish for Donovan. It might come true." She closed the door behind her.

34

TIME FOR A FRIEND

The splash of cold water on her face did little to add some oomph to Becca's attitude. She just wanted to go home, curl on the couch, and sleep until her problems disappeared. Instead, she was in the bathroom of the city hall building where she worked fighting to make it through the day. She tapped on the paper towel dispenser when Hannah joined her in the bathroom. Hannah worked in the office two floors down from the tax assessor's office where Becca worked.

Not one to mince words, Hannah said, "Oh, honey you are a hot mess."

What little bravado Becca had going for her left and she wilted. "It's that obvious?"

"Right about now a raccoon could take some tips on how to have the perfect circles around its eyes."

Becca stepped back to look in the mirror. Hannah was right. There was not enough makeup in the world to cover up her lack of sleep and the general feeling of malaise. Since it was just the two of them in the bathroom, Becca felt comfortable telling Hannah the truth. "Marriage is not all hearts and flowers."

"From what I've heard it can be a test," Hannah agreed. "Not that I'd know. My husband passed away after we were married for six months."

Hannah worked in the same building as Becca for years. She'd seen Hannah's son, a tall and handsome guy, pop in for a visit over the years. If he was fifteen years older, Becca might have made an effort to get to know him more.

"Why didn't you remarry?" Becca wondered.

"I wanted a husband, so we could have been more of a family. But I was so busy with Marcus and my family that there never was time. The next thing I knew he was grown and I had gotten used to having the bed and bathroom to myself."

Hannah's story brought a glimmer of what the future may hold for Becca. While it may not be the best of circumstances, she found herself able to follow suit. Her parents would be glad to have another grandchild. And there would be cousin gatherings over the summers and holidays. She may have to raise her child without a husband, but she wouldn't be alone.

"It may not help solve your problems, but I do have chocolate covered pretzels on my desk. I'd be more than glad to share, and it'll help get you through the last hour of the day.

Becca hadn't been hungry all day. Maybe it was the kind words; maybe it was the idea of sweet combined with the salty flavors. Regardless, chocolate covered pretzels became the equivalent of gastronomical gold to Becca's taste buds. "I would forever be in your favor."

They hadn't got too far from the bathroom when Hannah stopped. "I forgot that I actually went in there for a reason." She rolled her eyes and said, "I'll be right back."

"I can always stop by your desk later," Becca offered.

"Or, you can meet me at my desk. Katie knows where my secret stash is." Hannah hurried to the bathroom and went through the door with one last glance.

Becca considered her options. She could go back to her desk and fight sleep over a stack of property tax files, or she could wander to the Cooperative Extension Office and find out what events were forthcoming in the community. Donovan was out at meetings, so there was no risk of bumping into him at the office. She was going to need things to occupy her time, and there was no better time than the present to get started.

35

I NEVER SAID

Keane's eyes scanned behind Donovan to find Becca. When his search proved fruitless, he asked, "Where is the Mrs.?"

"Turns out that you were right." Donovan took an empty seat at the bar.

"Right about what?" Kent was standing at the bar behind Abigail who sat on the stool. Donovan was so caught up in his thoughts he hadn't noticed her.

Motioning toward the tables of the restaurant, Abigail added. "For the record, we're actually going to eat tonight."

"She's pregnant! I called it," Keane crowed. "Drinks on me."

The curse where his life took a left turn when he wanted to take a right taunted Donovan. "I meant Kent was right. But we can talk about it another time."

Kent held up his beer to make a toast. "Congratulations. It couldn't have happened to two more deserving people."

The bile rose in Donovan's throat. "No, I meant about her seeing someone else." He almost choked on his words. He expected Abigail to offer some sort of apologetic expression.

One that said, "I just found out myself, but hadn't had the chance to tell you."

Again, he got the left turn when things were supposed to go right. Abigail's widened eyes confronted Kent. She gasped, "You accused Becca of cheating?"

He held his hands up in surrender. "I never said she cheated," Kent went on the defensive.

Then she directed her attention to Donovan, "Is that why she hasn't returned my calls?"

There was no way he was getting out of this. Kent was his wingman. "You did." Donovan made a rolling motion with his fingers. "Remember there was something keeping her from being fully invested in the relationship."

At some point, Kent was supposed to say, "Oh, that. Yes." Instead, his expression began to mirror Abigail's. "I said she wasn't fully invested in the relationship. I didn't say she was seeing someone else." He turned and began pleading his case to Abigail. "They've been married five months, and she hadn't moved her things into the house."

Donovan should have seen this one coming. As soon as the pressure began to pinch people, their true nature came out. Impressing Abigail was more important than his friendship with Donovan. Donovan was about to call him on it when Abigail interrupted.

"She left her furniture in the house because she turned it into a seasonal rental. People pay good money to rent houses for a vacation. Some of us want a little more than a tent or a cot for a trip."

Kent held out his hands to point at Donovan. "He never said any of that. He just said they didn't argue about moving in together because they didn't have to make room for her things."

Keane interrupted the conversation. "Is anyone going to

say anything about me being right?" Silent stares from the triangle of controversy silenced him.

Kent, Abigail, and Donovan waited for him to catch up to the argument.

Keane grumbled, "That's what I figured," and turned to go help other patrons.

Free to continue their conversation, Abigail leaned in toward Donovan. "Where is she now?"

"Her house. I guess."

"I guess?"

"She won't answer my calls either." He tried calling her after she left to make sure she made it to the house safely. After what he said, he wouldn't answer his calls either. When she didn't reply, he left a text. He figured if something really was wrong, she knew how to get a hold of him.

After the initial shock of their argument wore away, he still didn't want to talk to her, but he needed to know that she was okay, so he called her office. The receptionist said that she was in the bathroom and Donovan told her not to bother with taking a message. He'd call back later.

Abigail huffed. "I'm going to go check on her."

Kent threw Donovan a dirty look that said thank you for ruining my Friday night. He asked Abigail, "Do you want me to come with you?"

She got out of the seat and put her hand in the crook of her back. "No, I'll call you later."

Donovan didn't care what Abigail thought of him. If the look of disgust she threw in his direction was any indication, it wasn't good. As he watched her walk out the door, Donovan sensed that his three lefts were going to make a right. With Abigail gone, he could tell his side of the story. Becca may have been a cheater, but she wasn't a liar. She'd tell Abigail the truth and thanks to the prenup; they'd quickly wade through the mess she'd created. She had said as much before she left.

He whispered, "There is no way I am the father of the baby. I had a vasectomy over five years ago."

"So you kicked her out?" Kent asked. "No checking to see if perhaps the internal plumber reconnected some pipes?"

"For the record, I did not kick her out. She left. And, what do you mean?"

"You know about Bernard's heart right?"

When was Kent going to get a clue and follow the script? Donovan was familiar with creating an agenda and people gladly following it. These diversions, especially when it pertained to his life bothered him. "What does Bernard's heart have to do with my wife getting pregnant by another man?"

"Fifteen years ago." Kent paused and looked toward the ceiling. "At least I think it was fifteen years ago. Bernard went in to have his heart checked. His brother had just died of a heart attack and our friend wanted to do some preventative maintenance. To get to the end of the story and make my point, he did have a clogged artery. Except it didn't kill him like it did to his brother. His body had made a vein that bypassed the clog. The internal plumber added a pipe to keep things in working order. It happens."

"But this isn't my heart," Donovan argued.

"It's something bigger," Kent answered, "It's your chance to leave an enduring legacy."

The words hit him Donovan like a punch in the gut. Without meaning to. Or maybe he had, Kent had confirmed Donovan's worst fear. He accused Becca, but it was him who may have ruined the one thing he had wanted for his entire adult life.

36

ALL FOUR FOOD GROUPS

Granted it had only been sixty-three hours and twelve minutes, not that she was counting, and Becca's plan to survive without Donovan had proved to be unsuccessful thus far. It was harder than she thought it would be. Usually, when she needed to talk through a serious problem, Donovan was the first person she called. Obviously, that was removed from her list of solutions. She was too embarrassed to call her family, so she struggled through the motions of life while trying to figure out what she was going to do next.

Abigail stopped by the house on Friday night and kept Becca company for a while. She also convinced Becca, who thought that maybe she should move to another country, to wait out Donovan. "He'll come to his senses. I know it," Abigail encouraged. "Besides, I want to share food cravings with you. It will be the closest I ever get to experiencing pregnancy."

The next morning Hannah was at her front door with homemade bread and tea. "Abigail told me what happened. I'm not skilled enough to knock some sense into Donovan, but I can help with morning sickness." Hannah pretty much said the same thing as Abigail. Give Donovan time. If he didn't pull it together, she'd have a community of people to support her through the pregnancy.

In a moment of desperation, Abigail considered calling Donovan's grandmother and telling on him. The moment passed as quickly as it struck, and she found herself reading on Google what she already knew. Men who professed their distaste for fatherhood did not magically change their perspective. In other words, she gained a child but may have lost a husband and a best friend in the process.

There were no ifs, and, or buts about it. Life was about to get rough. And, life set out to remind her, beginning with Jadine Renton, the town crank. A month ago, she proclaimed Becca a disappointment to independent women.

Becca ducked to hide in the cracker aisle. She thought she avoided the confrontation with Jadine when she passed the aisle without saying a word. Engrossed in trying to choose between the rosemary and garlic crackers or cheddar Chex Mix, Becca never saw Jadine coming. As far as Becca's mind was concerned, the woman materialized out of thin air.

When Jadine said, "Have I ever told you how much I appreciate that man you were smart enough to marry?" Becca questioned her reality. She blinked twice to make sure it was Jadine and not an alien that had taken over her body speaking. "Donovan? Donovan Garrison? The one you said I shouldn't have married."

Jadine shooed away Becca's restatement. "I was just hungry at the time. You can't blame a woman for what she says when she needs to eat. Besides, last night I was talking to his grandmother. She says he's a different man since you two married."

Twice, in the time span of two minutes, Jadine stunned Becca to near silence. First for recanting a criticism and the second for half apologizing for something she said. According to Jadine, she never was wrong.

Becca decided on the rosemary garlic crackers. As soon as she finished the conversation with Jadine, she'd go get some provolone cheese and salami to complete the meal. Ever since she'd been pregnant, chips didn't agree with her stomach, but she still craved salty snacks.

She shouldn't have taken Jadine's bait. But she took it: hook, line, and sinker. Instead of saying okay, and agreeing with Jadine, Becca threw Jadine the side eye. "What is going on?"

"I'm sure you know being single can be hard in a small town. While you young couples, and old couples, for that matter, get together, I'm sitting at home watching television, or hating you all for finding the happiness that always seemed to run away from me." The growl from Becca's stomach had little influence over Jadine. She continued with what Becca expected to be a long drawn out explanation. "Anyway, did you know there are classes, so people like me can meet up with other women, married or single, and pass the time talking about cooking or crafts or whatnot?"

Seeing where the conversation was headed, Becca smiled in appreciation. Somehow, Jadine figured out that Donovan was in charge of coordinating activities for the community. Most of the time he worked on collaborations between organizations and the local businesses and farmers. However, he always put aside time for people to find the hidden treasures in their own community.

She expected the explanation to end there and motioned to leave aisle.

Jadine rushed to keep a hold of Becca's attention. "Did you know there is a chef from Austria that has a class tonight? He makes the fancy food for all of us to eat. To make us feel like we accomplished something, he lets us help with the dessert." Jadine grinned. "If you want to know my opinion, the man's not too hard to look at either."

Becca wasn't all that excited about the man's attractiveness. Getting out of the house with a group of people to help her forget that she missed the man who according to the rules of a breakup was going to serve her divorce papers at any time—that was what made the class appealing.

"I'd love to see you in the class," Jadine suggested. "I'm finding myself wanting to connect more in a positive way with people. You should join us."

It was the first time in four days Becca's stomach hadn't fought her. That had to be a sign that perhaps Jadine's suggestion was the beginning of her starting life anew in some state of peacefulness. "I'll think about it," Becca answered.

"Good, I'll tell the chef you are coming." Jadine headed down the aisle for whatever it was she sought after. Her voice drifted as she walked away and continued the one-sided conversation.

The class seemed like a good idea. The immediate plan of adding pickles to the salami, cheese, and crackers lunch seemed like an even better one. Grasping at anything to keep her from falling into a state of depression, Becca found food to be the most effective at taking her mind off Donovan. The distraction of having something to do freed her mind to consider other things—like whether or not the addition of raw carrots and ranch made it a meal that covered all the food groups.

37

LISTEN TO LOVE

Donovan heard through the grapevine that things had gone from bad to worse for Becca. She hadn't said anything about their fight, but couldn't hide that the stress of the situation was getting the best of her. Katie from the office stopped to talk to Donovan in the coffee shop on Saturday morning. "You need to remind your wife that she has sick days."

"She's in one of those moods where she is not listening to me right now," he confessed.

In the days before they dated, both of them expected arguments. Couples do. What never crossed his mind was the possibility of him taking his worst side and giving it all to Becca in one fell swoop. As he explained what happened to his grandmother, Donovan said, "I wouldn't be talking to me either."

He drove by Becca's house a couple times and saw the dim light from her bedroom, but never stopped in. After the third pass by, Jadine Renton waved him down. From there she told him the truth as she saw it. He was acting like a teenager and needed to man up and go apologize to his wife. She was right.

Jadine figured out there was more to the problem when Donovan knocked, and Becca didn't open the door.

"Married people don't have to knock to enter their own houses." She had been watching from the front gate.

"I lost my key," Donovan told her a bold-faced lie.

"Or you didn't know she left a half hour ago with Abigail Cahill to go to Great Falls."

"You could have said something before you watched me make a fool of myself," Donovan griped.

"And miss out on the opportunity to find out what the Sam Hill is happening," Jadine crowed.

Donovan may have growled. His mood darkened. He wanted his wife at home with him where she belonged. She had responded to his text with a polite, "Thank you for checking on me." However, he knew that the longer they were apart, the more time she had to build an argument towards regretting she married him.

Jadine's smile faded into a look of authentic concern. The transformation happened so quickly Donovan felt a little guilty. "It's nothing that won't solve itself."

"Or, it's something I can help you with."

"What do you mean?"

"You're never going to find your wife without some help. She's had an army of women coming in and out of here. Fort Knox needs the support that wife of yours has had this past couple of days."

He never thought it possible, but he was living it, so it had to be true. The same Jadine Renton who had antagonized Donovan for his entire life became an ally.

NOTHING ANYBODY TOLD him prepared him for what he saw when he walked into the community cooking class and saw his wife looking worse than the time she caught the flu and stayed in bed for a week before letting anyone know she was sick. It had only been three days since he'd seen her, and she looked like she easily lost five pounds. Despite her eyes widening in what he at first thought was surprise when she saw him, he saw the haggardness in her face. Fatigue gave way to fear, and she beelined for the bathroom.

This was not good. Not good at all. Nothing his grandmother said to him prepared him for what he had to do. She said, "You need to go and admit why you behaved so poorly to her. And after that, you apologize. And, you apologize every day after that until she believes you."

"Why do I always have to be the one that apologizes," he argued. He knew why. What he really wanted to know was when was it going to be Becca's turn to mess up? It was like the woman was always one step ahead of him. "Son, love is being brave enough to make mistakes and trusting that the other person will forgive you. It grows when you've watered the seed by admitting your faults. If you had listened to your heart years ago, you'd have married Becca because you loved her. This is life's way of teaching you to listen to love and not your fears."

And she was right. He feared that she'd realize that someone out there was better than him. That this stranger would not only admit that he loved her, but he'd also tell her that he loved her without provocation from an inheritance. It only took the pressure of a child to push Donovan to admit his fears in the form of accusations.

The room of women and the chef stared at Donovan as he watched Becca run. In her absence their eyes accused him.

"You did this to her." Then they challenged him, "How are you going to fix this?"

Donovan stood outside the bathroom door and mentally rehearsed his first apology. Before she had time to say anything he'd say, "I came to say I'm sorry. This way she'd know he wasn't angry with her."

However, when Becca opened the door, his mind blanked. Dark circles had formed around her eyes, and her skin tone went from pink to a pale white, and then a shade of green in a matter of seconds.

Becca's parting words, "Maybe the ranch dressing wasn't such a good idea after all," was his first hint that perhaps her silence wasn't anger as much as a retreat.

38

SOME SORT OF FLU

Becca had never felt this bad ever. Her stomach felt worse than that time she drank an entire bottle of champagne at her cousin's wedding. At twenty-five, she should have known better than to drink on an empty stomach. The next day her stomach and head gave her a reminder that she always remembered. Apparently, now it felt the same about something she had eaten for lunch. She hoped to heaven it wasn't the ranch dressing. She silently prayed, *Let it be the carrots. I can live without those.*

The sound of water rushing from the faucet alerted her to the fact that someone else was in the bathroom. Becca grimaced with the light from the stall door opening. In her haste to get to the bowl, she forgot to lock the door behind her.

"Maybe a cool paper towel on the back of your neck will help with the nausea." Donovan's voice had a level of tenderness that was the stark contrast of the vitriol he had given her a taste of three days prior.

"I'll be okay," she flushed the bowl and turned to take the towel. Instead of wrapping it around her neck, she washed her face. It felt hot and sweaty like she'd spent a couple hours in the gym and not five minutes in the bathroom. She waited for the "I told you so," or the "we need to talk," that she knew was coming. Maybe confronting the truth would release the tightness in her stomach.

"Look, about what happened the other night," Donovan began.

Becca held up her hand to stop him. "You don't have to say it. I get it. I just can't believe you came into the women's bathroom to tell me."

"No, this needs to be said, so things are clear between us," Donovan continued.

There was no way to stop him, and she knew it. It was one of the steps he had missed on Thursday. "Do it with kindness. Treat the person with just enough dignity to reduce the sting, but make sure your words are clear."

Becca rested her forehead in her hands and held her breath. If her air was thin, she'd at least have the dignity of not crying when Donovan tried to kindly tell her that he wanted a divorce.

"I could have handled the information better. For that I'm sorry." There was the kindness she never wanted to hear from, of all people, Donovan Garrison.

Becca nodded to let him know she heard him but remained silent. They sat there in an awkward quietness that was probably only a couple of seconds but seemed like a year's amount of time.

His coaching broke the silence. "This is the part where you say something like, 'I get what you're saying, Donovan.' Or 'I agree with you.'"

She kept her hands on her forehead, purely out of self-preservation. If she moved, the waves might take over again. "Okay, I get what you're saying."

A woman's voice came through the door. "Is everything

okay in there?"

"Yes, April May." Donovan replied, "Becca's just having a rough patch of morning sickness."

"Morning sickness?" April May confirmed what she had heard and yelled back to what Becca imagined to be the class. "It's morning sickness." Her voice lowered to a normal register, "We're glad it's just that. All of us were worried that she had some sort of a flu virus."

"Thank you for checking," Donovan replied.

The hinges on the door creaked, and the sound of April May's footsteps entering the room changed the atmosphere. "Here's a piece of gum. It's not as good as mint tea, but it'll help settle her stomach a little."

"Thank you," Donovan passed the gum to Becca.

"You're a good husband to come in here with her. If your mama was here with us, she'd be so proud of you."

Stuck in the stall, Becca followed through with her only choice. She popped the piece of gum in her mouth and waited for the conversation between Donovan and April to reach a natural conclusion.

"Thank you for saying so, but I do mess up on occasion," Donovan crossed his arms in front of him.

When Becca saw his signature long conversation with a friend posture, she began planning a way to gracefully leave while allowing the two of them to go on with their talk.

"All of us do on occasion. How we make up is what matters," she said.

"I have a question," Donovan said. "Do all women's bathrooms have flowers and smell like potpourri?"

"The nice ones do," April answered. "Why?"

"Our bathroom at the house doesn't look like this. I kind of balked at the idea of Becca changing the decorations, but after being in here for as much as I have, I'm beginning to change my mind on the matter."

Becca had had enough. She stood to leave. "I think I'm good now."

April crowed, "It's the gum. I knew it would help."

"I appreciate it." Becca offered a weak smile. She wanted to go home and sleep.

"That's my signal," Donovan began his goodbye. "It's been good talking with you."

Becca hadn't made it to the door when the chef announced, "I hear congratulations are in order."

As if Donovan's presence wasn't making her uncomfortable enough, he had to bring attention to the fact she was pregnant. He was ambitious and driven, but she had no idea he could be vicious too. She already heard the chatter that was sure to follow when people learned of their breakup.

"I'm sure she'll feel better after her stomach gets used to the workload of nourishing two people." Donovan almost sounded proud of their situation.

The chef held up a small white ceramic bowl. "This won't be as good as the beef bourguignon, but it will help settle her stomach."

"Look at that," Donovan spoke to Becca, "the chef made something to help your stomach." He didn't give her a chance to decline the offer. Donovan placed his hand on her lower back and gently guided her back in the direction of the class.

But it didn't make sense to her. Donovan hated cooking classes. His specialty recipe was crunchy peanut butter and jelly sandwiches with barbecue chips in the middle. What had happened to her husband in the time they were apart? The answer hit Becca like a fluorescent yellow ball that should have made it into the hole in one putt. Donovan wasn't there to break up with her; he was there for another eighteen holes.

39

EIGHTEEN HOLES

"You aren't here to break up with me?" Becca half asked half spoke.

Except for one person, the amused grins the women in the class had been wearing fell, and curious stares took their place. Jadine, who had helped Donovan get Becca to the class, nudged the woman next to her. "This is where it gets good. Look at his face. He never saw that one coming."

And she was right. All this time, Donovan thought Becca's distance was anger with his harsh words. After several rounds of beer with three other extension agents that knew Becca, and threats from Lloyd to sabotage their marriage so he could have Becca for himself, Donovan texted his wife. "I'm a jerk. Call me." But she never called. He assumed her silence was the way women punish men. The *"don't talk to him, and he'll miss me"* strategy. He pleaded his case to the women. "I never said anything like that."

"You accused me of sleeping with another man," Becca quickly responded. "You said that we were done."

He felt the blood rush to his face. "I may have been hasty with my words."

Becca's mouth fell open, and she raised her eyebrows in confusion. "You think I'm supposed to come running back to you because you changed your mind. I may be wider than your past girlfriends, but I am not a yo-yo."

One of the women said, "This would be a good time for some popcorn or something,"

Donovan took Becca by the elbow while glancing at the room of eager observers. "Can we talk about this in private?"

She followed without argument while he guided her back toward the corridor that led to the bathroom. She opened her mouth to speak, and he interrupted her, "I know I'm the father."

Her mouth closed, and she eyed him suspiciously.

"Vasectomies can reverse themselves." His tone was matter of fact mixed with *"I'm surprised you didn't know it too."* They had something more pressing to discuss. "And while we're getting everything out in the open, why didn't you call me back?"

"I replied to the text messages I received." She showed him her phone. There were a couple of texts from Abigail, her mother, and her brother. In there was the one from Saturday evening that asked if she was okay. It was followed by her response that she was fine. All the other texts he sent weren't there.

"I swear I called you Friday night and several times Saturday. It went straight to voice mail."

It was her turn to point out the obvious. However, her attitude lacked the zeal of defense. She sounded exhausted. Not angry. "You realize the network booster is at your house. I don't have a cell signal when I'm at my house."

As soon as she said it, he remembered it was true. One of the necessary evils of living in rural Montana was the dodgy cell service. Donovan helped her set up the booster years ago.

Since hers was stronger than the one he had at the house, they brought it with her when she moved in.

"You weren't avoiding me?"

"I've been making myself busy, so I wouldn't be lonely."

"You've been lonely?" he perked. He thought for sure in the absence of his presence she would have created a list of reasons of why she'd be better off without him. It was what he taught her to do after every breakup.

A hesitant voice joined the conversation. "I don't mean to interrupt, but a couple of us needed to use the restroom. We were wondering if you were going to be done arguing soon."

"As a matter of fact, we are." He reached into his pocket and pulled out a folded envelope. "This. This right here will fix everything."

The older woman rolled her eyes and went to the end of the corridor. "It's going to be a while. Maybe we can use the bathroom at the senior center across the street."

Donovan unfolded the envelope and ran it across his thigh to straighten the crease. He held it out for Becca to take. When she refused to touch it, he waved it toward her. "It isn't going to bite you."

Becca accepted the card. When she pulled the card out of the envelope the wrinkle in her brow deepened.

To emphasize the significance, Donovan said, "I got a new envelope. The one that came with the card had a cute picture on it."

Her fingers traced the lettering on the front of the card. She felt herself grin in recognition at the picture of a cat holding a balloon. The text inside the balloon read, "Get Well Soon."

"That was the day I knew I was in love with you. I didn't do anything about it because I didn't think I had a chance."

She made a face that said she didn't believe him. To which

he responded, “Okay. I was afraid your father was going to kill me.”

Her slight grin was the first sign of the possibility of the evening ending with three people in the Garrison household.

“Open it. See what it says inside.” Donovan knew what it said. On the bottom of the card was a note from Becca that read, “I can help you with whatever you need until you have recovered. Just let me know what I can do to help you. Get well soon.” On the side of the card, Donovan wrote, “I'm sorry about the morning sickness. I know it is my fault. I'm sorry about not trusting you. The idea of you being with another man made me crazy. Please come home so I can heal what I have broken."

Tears welled in Becca’s eyes. Donovan knew what she was going to say next.

"It's a beautiful card Donovan, but I cannot be with you. You'll end up resenting both me and the baby. I don't like the way it happened, but us separating is probably for the best."

That was not what he expected. His fear that she figured out that life was better without him came to confront him.

He stammered. "Why? I'd never resent."

Becca's arched eyebrow challenged him. She would accept nothing less than the truth.

He couldn't look her in the eye as he admitted the truth. "I resented the baby.” His grandmother said the truth would forge the cracks he made in the foundation of their relationship. Donovan hoped beyond hope she was right.

Becca’s voice contained the softness of understanding. “I get it. Which is why it’s better for all three of us if we weren’t together.”

He had to interrupt her before she got too attached to the idea of them living apart. “Because it was a baby’s fault I never had a mother.” The words left a bitter taste in his mouth.

"What?"

"My mother died in childbirth."

"No, she died in a car crash when you were ten," Becca corrected.

"That was my step mother. She adopted me when I was four. My real mother died in child birth."

Becca's mouth fell open.

Donovan didn't want her pity. He wanted her to understand his hesitance was a result of his issues. He continued, "I didn't want to be like my father—stuck raising the child that killed his wife. I still don't know how he did it."

"How did I not know this?" She had her hand pressed against her heart, and her eyes darted back and forth like they were trying to find a lost memory.

"It isn't like people go around telling sad stories from their childhood." He shrugged, "Unless they're drunk."

Becca wrapped her arms around his waist and nuzzled her forehead into his chest. He inhaled the fragrance of her shampoo and exhaled in relief. Even though she hadn't said it, Donovan sensed it was a matter of time until he brought his wife and son back into his house where they belonged.

He pulled her toward him. "Best friends forgive each other."

She replied, "Best friends trust each other."

"I will from now on." Not wanting the hug to end, he held her tightly.

When she pulled out of the hug Donovan held out his hand for Becca to accept. "Are you ready to come home?"

He felt like the king of the world when she gave it a little squeeze and said, "Let me tell the chef."

Donovan waited by the door for Becca to join him. When he saw how tired she was, he made a silent promise to do everything in his power to make her feel better. He'd make her some peanut butter toast and a cup of tea when they got home.

With her key fob in her extended hand, she stepped outside the door. Becca pressed the button, but no sound followed. Unfazed by the lack of response she said, "The battery must be dying," and walked in the direction of where she last parked her pickup.

She stopped short when she found Donovan's Chevy in its place. "I could have sworn I parked here."

The grin on his face grew wider. "You did."

"Where is it now?"

"At our house. Kent drove it home for you."

As if she didn't believe Donovan, she backed away from the parking space and searched the parking lot. "You didn't know I was coming home with you."

Donovan looked down and covered his mouth to hide his smile. If things hadn't gone as he planned, he would have driven her to her house. His heart told him that the suggestion wouldn't be necessary.

40

EPILOGUE

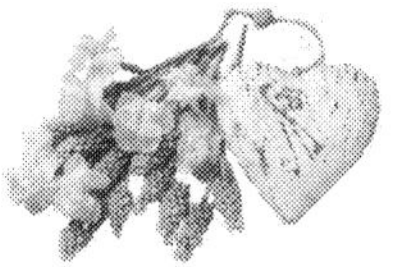

Becca woke feeling refreshed for the first time in a long time. Her mother warned her that things were going to be different with her pregnancy. Knowing lack of sleep and experiencing it were two different realities. A smile warmed her heart. Parker had slept through the night. She turned to tell Donovan only to find his side of the bed empty. Maybe he had gone to the bathroom.

She stepped into her slippers to go to the crib and check on their son. Thinking twice, she grabbed the cell phone on the side of her bed. She'd take a picture to memorialize the milestone. Becca shuffled down the hall to Parker's room to pause. Something in the living room had caught her attention. She altered her course to see something even more heartwarming than their son sleeping through the night. Donovan was in the recliner with Parker sprawled out on his chest. The baby blanket was bunched on Donovan's waist, and his hand was on Parker's back.

The phone clicked when she took the picture, and Donovan's eyes blinked open. He offered his wife a sleepy grin. He whispered, "He was lonely, so I thought I'd keep him company for a while. It worked like a charm. He fell asleep in a matter of seconds."

Ever since the whale of a fight they had when he found out she was pregnant, Donovan had been by her side as much as possible. It didn't surprise her in the least that the mirror image of him that they created would share the same need for companionship. Becca whispered, "Sounds like someone I know," and gently kissed her husband on the cheek.

She could have mouthed the words she knew Donovan was going to say but let him say it without interruption. "We should have done this sooner."

41

AUTHOR NOTE

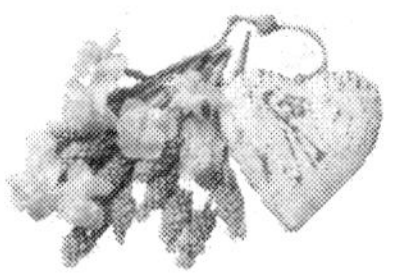

We have come to the end of the story of Becca and Donovan. This was one of the several stories that were inspired by a trip to a restaurant in Great Falls, Montana. I walked in thinking I'd get some Irish food and left full of story ideas. One day, I'll be brave enough to go back and tell them.

Becca and Donovan are special to me because they were friends. One thing I've noticed about couples around here is the unmistakable bond of friendship. I hope I captured that in this story.

With this being said, I invite you to leave a review of Get Well Soon. I am curious to know what you liked about the story.

Here is where I tell you a little about my writing world. The world of happily ever after came to me in the most unusual circumstances. Back in the day when I was young and didn't know much about the world, I was in graduate school to be an English professor. With three weeks remaining in the first semester, my mother passed away. It was my first lesson in grief, and how the brain works. Short version of the story is

I woke up a week later not able to read. I could decode the words, but if you asked what they meant, I couldn't tell you. So, at twenty-six I had to learn how to read again. I taught myself using romance novels. The first book I read was The Gift by Danielle Steele. I have been hooked ever since. To this day, when I am overwhelmed by life, I only need to pick up a romance novel. After twenty to thirty minutes all is well in my world.

If you are interested to see the images I used to help me with the story, they are on my Pinterest Board.

I also have a Facebook Page where I post regularly. If you're looking for a regular dose of a little something to make you smile, like or follow the page.

This is where I thank my husband, Randy. When we were dating, we were rather competitive. I won a lot. Then we got married. I lost at all the games that I used to win. One time I got rather grumpy about losing. He said, "I let you win because I wanted you to like me." Ha! Now you know what inspired the kayaking scenes. Randy is the one who hears the plot lines and fields the questions. Occasionally, he'll tell me I forgot a comma.

I close thanking you for allowing me this brief period of time into your world. I hope it brought you some smiles.

42

WHAT'S NEXT

D*id you like Three Creeks, Montana? The Three Creeks stories pick up with Kent*

Time changes people...and every once in a while it can heal a broken heart.

Against her better judgment, Abigail Cahill is coming home. Abigail's family is set on proving that she belongs in Three Creeks with them. Their childhood best friend, Kent Parker is willing to help them give Abigail a proper welcome.

From the beginning, Kent makes it clear that he has zero interest in a serious relationship. Who cares that every time he is around Abigail he has the urge to punch anyone in the face that looks at her?

Abigail is okay with having the small town hunk as a pal for her mini-adventures. She's not so thrilled that he chases away any guy that takes an interest in her.

In this feel-good, love story, Abigail discovers the beauty of second chances and the meaning behind Welcome Home.

VISIT your favorite online retailer and grab a copy of Welcome Home.

OR

Want to read more of Kent and Abigail's story. There's a couple more chapters on the Small Town Stories website.

PART III

FOR A VISIT

43

LIGHTNING IN FEBRUARY

Annie stopped in front of the portrait of her graduating class on the wall. She couldn't help smiling at the younger version of herself. Close to twenty years of life had passed since the portrait had been taken. Crow's feet accented her amber eyes, and her long brown hair had blond highlights to mask the signs of aging. Otherwise, she remained the same. She still loved deeply and gave all she had. Annie laughed at her lie. During the snowy season, she power walked the halls of the school three times a week to slim down the hips widened by childbirth and her love of apple pie.

Portraits for the all the classes that attended the school lined the hall. The picture of her husband, Jesse, who graduated a year earlier hanged adjacent to hers. It was as if something meant for them to be together from the start. His mischievous smile and long bangs that hid his eyebrows ushered in a rush of fond memories. She remembered helping him choose the tie he wore for the picture. Only the frames from the two graduating years of 1995 and 1996 served as a boundary between them.

Her smile faded as quickly as it appeared. Like the pictures, something beyond her control separated her and Jesse. This time it was life and death. She missed having him there to laugh, cry, and work together through their problems. Annie shook her head to pull herself back to the present. Her brief visit down memory lane pinched less, but it still hurt. She needed to focus on what she could control—getting 10,000 steps before her son finished basketball practice.

She marched to the end of the hall, circled around, and slowed only to check her steps. Pleased with her progress of 8,432 steps she kept her eye on the prize. Jesse Jr.'s basketball practice ended in twenty minutes. She had more than enough time to get the last 1500 steps. Then she wouldn't feel so bad about eating a piece of pie for dessert.

The gym door was open enough to allow Annie to peek through as she made a pass to make sure basketball practice was still in session. The screeching sound of sneakers against laminate answered her question before she watched her son touch the ground with his fingertips and sprint down the court. Annie continued her walk but hadn't got too far.

Al, the school janitor, pushed the cleaning cart in front of him. Annie and Al passed each other in the halls several times in the past three years. She noticed that regardless of the day of the week, Al's short gray hair stood on end and he seemed to have a permanent smile. His face tightened in concern, and he asked, "Is someone bothering you?"

Annie was out of breath and ready to be finished with the activity. She stopped to talk to Al. "I'm walking a little faster in hopes that it will help me lose a little weight." Holding out her arm to show him her Fitbit, she added, "I'm at 9,112."

"I'm sure it'd be easier if the weather were a little more cooperative."

A boom of thunder cracked in the sky.

He rubbed the back of his neck and cast a concerned look

toward the door. "Lightning in February isn't common. My mother always said when you have lightning in the winter, a big change is about to come."

"I could handle a big change right about now," she tapped her thigh and giggled.

Al shook his head and joined in the laugh.

The pounding of feet running in their direction caught both of their attention. They looked up to discover that Annie and Al stood between fifteen tired basketball players and the drinking fountain. They stepped to the side to let them pass. Her son J.R. stopped in front of Annie and swiped at her water bottle. "I've never been gladder to see you than I am now."

Her time to exercise had ended and her time to be mom began. Annie promised herself that she'd get those last nine hundred steps before she went to bed.

Coach Evans approached her while she waited on the bench. The man was tall and lanky and hadn't aged since he took the coaching job over twenty years ago. Several people joked that coaching high school basketball was the fountain of youth and asked where they needed to sign up to be next in line. He fiddled with the whistle that hung from the lanyard around his neck. "J.R. plays just like his father." To eliminate confusion on who they were addressing people got into the habit of calling Jesse Jr. J.R. A tint of sadness mixed in with the pride in his voice. "I'm sure Jesse would be proud if he saw how J.R. turned out."

"I see him more in J.R. as he gets older." Annie offered a warm smile. Thankfully she was past the stage where the mention of Jesse brought tears to her eyes.

J.R. came out of the locker room with his duffel bag hanging off his left shoulder. His wavy brown hair still wet from the shower hung onto his forehead. For that brief moment, time transported Annie back to 1994, and she was outside the locker room waiting for Jesse.

"Does that mean no?" J.R.'s voice interrupted Annie's reverie.

Annie blinked herself back to the present. "I got lost in a thought. I'm sorry what were you saying?"

J.R. frowned, and a crease formed in the middle of Coach Evan's brow. Impatience flicked across J.R.'s face. "I asked if we could eat dinner at the Elderberry Cafe tonight. I could go for a burger."

She wrapped her arm around her son's shoulder. It was getting harder to do. At seventeen he was three inches taller than her. Pretty soon, she'd be holding on to his waist. Like her, J.R. was having as hard a time as her without his father. It had been three long years since a crash on his quad took him away from them. They made it by taking it one day at a time, and when that didn't work, they tackled life by approaching it from one minute to the next. The scent of fabric softener from his clothes combined with the soap he used made her heady. Her life wasn't perfect. But there sure were a lot of things in it to make it worth living.

44

HAPPY TO SEE YOU

They were half a mile from the Elderberry Cafe when Annie turned the corner of Puckett Street and drove straight into a two-foot-deep snowdrift. Her vehicle was high centered and refused to budge. Annie shifted her pickup into reverse. Sometimes it was easier to back out of the situation and add speed to plow through the patch of snow. Her engine revved, the wheels spun, and the pickup remained in the same spot where it had stopped.

"Do you have it in four-wheel drive?" J.R. snapped at Annie.

She sighed in resignation. "We're going to have to get help." They were in front of the mercantile. Someone in there had to have the equipment to tow her out of the drift.

"If you had a boyfriend like normal women your age, we could call him," J.R. grumbled. He shoved the door open and jumped out of the pickup. He craned his neck and peered in the window. "Bob Miller is in there."

Annie didn't want to ask Bob Miller. She already asked him for help more times than she wanted. He lived at the end of their street and made sure to stop by often and check on Annie and J.R. She groaned and prepared herself to go into the store and grovel. "This snow could stop anytime."

It was so cold the door to her pickup resisted opening and Annie had to give it a sharp shove. She jumped out with both feet for a safer landing. She turned around to see the last person she expected.

Noah Flynn, her childhood best friend, knelt beside a tire and searched under the pickup. "I can give you a nudge with my Suburban."

"Holy mother of snow!" Annie exclaimed. On any occasion, she'd have been delighted to see Noah. The last time she heard anything about him he was practicing medicine in some tropical location. His arrival at the exact moment she needed help was a sign from above. The tan from living in a warmer climate gave him a relaxed air. While everyone else was grumpy at this time of the from snow fatigue, Noah had a relaxed smile. Annie realized that everything was going to be okay. "Where did you come from?"

"My mother says heaven," Noah winked. "But my father says I got here a different way altogether."

"I don't care which one is right. I'm just glad to see you." Annie launched herself into Noah and wrapped her arms around his shoulders. The last time they hugged was at Jesse's funeral. It felt good to embrace him in better circumstances.

He wrapped his hands around her waist and gave her a warm squeeze. "It's good to see you too."

Hugging him felt like home. Like he hadn't been gone for the better part of fifteen years. When they were growing up, they saw each other every day, and had dinner at each other's house so often their parents knew to make an extra plate. Then one day it ended. He went to college, then medical school, and on to his job as a traveling doctor. They kept in touch, but it wasn't the same as trading french fries for a couple slices of meat. The way he squeezed her said, "I missed you too." Annie pulled out of the hug and said, "Do you remember how to tow a car out of the snow?"

"It has to be easier than avoiding a mud slide," he stepped away and looked at the underside of her car. "The worst thing that can happen is we can call someone with a plow to get the both of us out."

J.R. trudged through a snowbank to the sidewalk. He clapped his gloved hands together and folded his arms in front of him. Snow accumulated on his cap and glistened on the brown bangs that peeked out from beneath the bottom. He bent down and examined the car. "It's caught by the rear axle."

The three of them worked together. Noah attached the tow rope to the back bumper. J.R. used his right hand to guide Noah and left hand to help Annie. In a matter of moments, Annie was freed from the snowdrift and headed toward the Elderberry Cafe with a teenager who seemed more congenial since Noah agreed to join them.

For a minute, Annie's mind made a trip to the past. A younger Annie, Noah, and Jesse crammed into the front of Jesse's Ford Courier pickup were walking into the cafe. She'd eat her French fries dipped in her chocolate milkshake while listening to Jesse and Noah talk about plays they learned. She never imagined she'd be doing the same thing close to twenty years later.

Before they got out of the pickup to go into the cafe, J.R. reached for Annie's hand. When he wanted her undivided attention, he'd anchor her to him with a touch. His voice held the tenderness from when he was a child and wanted something from her. "About what I said earlier. I'm sorry. That was hunger talking."

Annie offered him a soft grin of conciliation. "Thank you for your apology." She tapped him on the shoulder and gave him a gentle shove. "Otherwise I'd have pushed you out of the vehicle."

"No, you wouldn't." J.R. grinned wide enough to show the blue band on his braces. "I'm your darling boy." He motioned to open the door and turned back to the conversation. "And, the only one who is able to give you grandchildren."

"Not anytime, soon. I hope." Annie scowled.

"Don't worry. I have my eyes on something bigger," he answered. "Right now, it is a double bacon burger with tots." He curved his body to avoid the swipe she made at his arm.

With the air between them cleared they helped each other navigate the icy parking lot to the entrance of the diner. Noah was already there and had saved two seats for them. He greeted them with, "J.R. told me the bacon cheeseburger is good enough to make him clean his room."

J.R. rolled his eyes. "Now she will use it against me." He pulled out the chair across from Noah and took Annie's purse and put it in the seat beside him. "You sit on the other side of the table. This will give me room for all the food I want to eat."

Annie chuckled at Noah's raised brow. "He's joking."

The joke worked at keeping the tone light and opened the door for Noah to get acquainted with J.R.

The last time Annie had seen Noah was at Jesse's funeral. He came back from a hospital in Panama and returned as quickly as he arrived. They had had little time to catch up. Noah entertained J.R. with stories of injuries and illnesses, and he described in detail the ones J.R. had never heard of.

The conversation gave Annie a whole new perspective on life. If she ever thought about complaining about the snow, she'd remind herself that there were people in the world who needed a doctor to extract fly larvae that had been embedded in their backs.

It was getting late, and J.R. still had homework, so Annie

asked for the check. As she signed the credit card slip, she said, "If you're not too pressed for time, we'd love to have you come by the house."

"And take in a game," J.R. added, "We have a chance at taking state this year."

Noah came back to the states for a couple months every three or four years. In the last visit he spent two weeks in Ashbrook and left to go on a cruise with his aunt and uncle who still lived in town. Annie wanted to give him a way out if he was too busy. She knew how visits back home went. People made more plans than they'd ever be able to fulfill. "If you can't we understand."

"Jesse made me promise that if anything happened to him, I'd make sure to check on you." Noah's smile softened. "It's what I've been looking forward to ever since I knew I'd be back in town."

"How long are you going to be here?" J.R. asked. He stole a fry off of Annie's plate and shoved it in his mouth.

Noah cast a quick glance at Annie. "I have a month to decide where I'm going next."

45

CHOCOLATE SILK PIE

Seeing Noah the day before added fuel to Annie's fire to get toned up. While he failed to age, she looked like life had put her through the wringer and forgotten to leave her out to dry. She regarded the tiger stripes around her waist and the laugh lines around her eyes with pride. Both marks of aging represented a mother that loved. When she put her head on her pillow, she felt good about herself. Still, she couldn't help hoping that the 10,000 steps she walked faithfully would magically melt inches from around her waist.

Before J.R. left for school, she reminded him that they had a crock pot meal for supper. She didn't want to be tempted by Hazel's pies. Hazel owned the café and made the best pies in the county. More important her role in the community made her a town matriarch. When you were sad, you could visit Hazel and she'd offer dessert and a listening ear. Annie's foresight to have a meal prepared before she left the house for the day proved prudent when she imagined the cinnamon and brown sugar-coated apples tendered by the baking process melting in her mouth.

Annie rounded the corner of the school hall and pulled up

her wrist to check her steps. It was the same place she always checked her steps. This time the turn surprised her. She thought it was just her, Al, and the high school basketball team at the school. She heard the squeaks of the player's shoes in the gym. Which is why it surprised her when, from out of the blue, a man's body pressed against hers. He wrapped his arms around her and twirled so quickly Annie didn't realize what happened until she landed on top of him and exhaled with an "oof."

She struggled to gather her senses. What had happened? One minute she was walking down the hall and the next she was on the ground in Noah's arms.

A smile spread across his lips, and his eyes sparkled. "I've had women fall for me. But not with as much vigor."

Uncertainty filled Annie. Her heart raced, and her world lost its balance. Annie pushed at his chest to get away from him. She couldn't help noticing that someone replaced his chest muscles with rocks. It was like pushing herself away from a wall. "I am so sorry. I wasn't paying attention..." She rolled away from him and scanned the area around them to see if anyone else had seen the fall.

The sound of balls dribbling on the other side of the gymnasium wall told her the whereabouts of everyone else. Nobody had seen her make a fool of herself.

Noah stood and offered her a hand to help her up. "J.R. told me you'd be here exercising. I thought I'd join you."

Annie accepted his hand and pulled herself up. "When did he tell you..." She never finished the question because the answer sparkled through his copper colored eyes. She also understood the sly smiles the two of them had shared over dinner after she returned from the ladies' room.

She arched an eyebrow in challenge. "Is there anything else I need to know about what you two discussed?"

The dimple in Noah's chin deepened as he tried and failed to suppress his smile. "That's for me to know and you to find out."

Annie swallowed hard to tamper down the fluttering of the butterflies in her stomach. What has my son done? Because she feared the answer, she kept the question to herself.

Noah eyed her Fit Bit. "How many steps do you have to go?"

Annie pressed the button too hard, and it bypassed the steps and displayed the heart rate monitor. Her pulse read at 142 beats per minute. Twenty over her normal walking heart rate. Her eyes widened, and she pressed the button several times to get back to the home screen. When she skipped it again, Annie dropped her wrist to her side and said, "It doesn't matter, I have enough."

His gaze traveled her body, and he smiled his assessment. "Yes, you have enough."

It had been a long time since anyone had flirted with Annie and she didn't know how to respond. Heat flushed through Annie's body, and her face reddened.

Noah cleared his throat and adjusted his tone. "What are you two doing for dinner tonight?"

His inclusion of J.R. in the dinner plans set Annie's mind at ease. Perhaps she had misinterpreted his intention.

"It's crock pot, chicken and rice for us. We have extra if you'd like to join us." Annie always made extra because Jesse's uncle and brother made it a habit to stop by. When they didn't have the company, J.R. brought leftovers to school for lunch the next day.

Noah reached over and fiddled with the hair around the base of her neck. "I'd love to, but I promised my Aunt Peggy I'd eat with them. She's making a chocolate silk pie for dessert.

If you're willing to change your plans, you're welcome to join us for dinner."

Just then Al came around the corner. Noah pulled his hand away, and Annie startled. For the brief time they had talked she forgot they were in a building full of people.

"What are you two crazy kids doing in the hall by yourself?" Al's eyes twinkled through his scowl.

"Pie," she exclaimed, "we were talking about pie."

Al's face changed to reflect his congenial nature when he laughed. "Ha! You should see the look on your face, Annie."

"I can't wait to see what it looks like when she tells J.R. that they're not having pie because she wanted to eat crock pot, chicken and rice casserole," Noah joked.

Later that night Anne smiled quietly as she looked back on how her plans failed to come to fruition. She only walked 8000 steps and J. R. had to help her pack two lunches of chicken and rice casserole for the next day.

46

NACHOS IN A BAG

The stands in the high school gym vibrated with energy from the crowd. On the left side, it was a sea of red and white. Some high school students wore wigs while others used colored hair spray to show their school pride. With every basket scored by the Ashbrook Eagles the frenzy grew. Men hooted and hollered, and women cheered. "Get that basket, Nickerson!" or "Way to go Eagles!"

A mixture of pride and concern filled Annie. J.R. had been in the game for most of the first and second quarter. He was a good athlete and handled the pressure from the crowd well. However, the momentum could change with one timeout session. The other team could go back on the court with a new game plan. Then, cheers of adoration would take the form of harsh rebukes, "Go for the rebound," or "Block your man." J.R. said the criticism didn't bother him, but he always stayed after and threw one hundred free throws for every one he missed when the team lost a game.

When Noah arrived, he headed straight to the scoring stand and took a seat beside the coach's wife. He didn't acknowledge Annie at all. No wave, or head tilt of hello. It was as if she wasn't in the building. She sank. Perhaps she thought more of the two dinners they had shared. Maybe he was just being friendly. Annie shrugged away the rebuff, concluding that her loneliness clouded her interpretation of the situation.

After she and Jesse married, things changed. The best friends whittled down from three to two when Jesse and Noah pushed her out of the triangular relationship. She reminded herself that Noah was Jesse's best friend and was probably making sure the absence of a father didn't hamper J.R.'s progress.

Annie forced herself to adjust her thinking. Was she attracted to Noah? Of course. Only someone who suffered from blindness or oblivion would fail to notice how handsome he was. Annie overheard Lisa from the donut shop joke about adding some extra sprinkles to Noah's pastry. The women who sat beside her snickered while agreeing with her.

A woman that had to be at least ten years younger and twenty pounds lighter than Annie sidled up to Noah and confirmed Annie's conclusion. The smile he offered the young tart, filled Annie with an anger she didn't know existed. Annie muttered to herself, "Could her sweater get any tighter?" She tsked Noah for being too familiar with someone much younger than him. She was also disappointed in her reaction. How could she have thought he had any interest in a single mother who had a pie addiction? It should have been obvious to her that the time they spent together was for J.R.'s benefit.

Hallmark Channel stories about high school friends reconnecting in their later years happened to other people. Annie stood to go visit the concession stands. Surely, they had something to help her take her mind off the relationship that never was. The quarter was almost over, and if she left now, she'd beat the rush. Annie sidestepped down the row and trotted down the stairs.

The buzzer signaling the end of the first half of the game rang just as Annie reached the counter. Allowing the foul mood she developed to guide her decision, she ordered what she wanted. "I'll have a Pepsi, a Snickers bar, some popcorn and..." she paused and added, "I should get something healthy to go with this. I'll also take some nachos in a bag." Normally, a concoction of Doritos topped with taco meat, nacho cheese, cheddar cheese, lettuce, tomato, and sour cream would have given her the worst case of the day after consumption regrets. Annie didn't care. It was her body and her life.

Carly, the new math teacher who often volunteered to cashier for the first half of the games, peered around Annie. "Is anyone here to help you carry all this stuff?"

"I'll shove the candy in my pockets, and it'll be fine." Annie's voice gave off more confidence than she felt. As she paid the $9.50 for the armful of food to drown her sorrows, impulse eater's remorse struck her. She grinned at Carly, "I'm sharing the popcorn with some friends."

"Do you want me to help you carry some of that?" Darryl the auto shop teacher offered.

Annie took one look at the grease under his fingernails and thought better of accepting his help. She placed the nachos in a bag in his hands. "I bought these for you."

Darryl's face brightened. "You didn't have to do that."

"It's the least I could do for your kindness."

"Why, thank you." Darryl took his reward and stepped forward in the line. "Can I get a Pepsi to go with this?" He waved the bag in Annie's direction and nodded a last thank you.

Annie rushed to get into the gymnasium before the second

half of the game started. If she hadn't tried to rush, she might have missed bumping into Noah. This time he stepped back and held his hands in the air to avoid the collision. "You have an interesting way of getting close to people."

"Sorry about that. I was trying to get back to my seat." Annie hid the popcorn behind her back. She didn't want to help Noah see that she was the exact opposite of the woman he chose to sit by at the game.

Noah's eyes searched the basketball court where the team was taking practice shots. Annie knew when he found J.R. because Noah's eyes targeted in on him. His face softened to show his appreciation. "My memory may have distorted facts, but from what I remember about Jesse, I think J.R. plays better than his father." He turned back to focus on Annie. "And Jesse was one helluva player." He pointed at the candy bar in Annie's hand. "You still eat those?"

Smiling at the shared memories Annie held up the chocolate bar and said, "They remind me of Jesse. Most of the time, I give them to J.R. after the game." She glanced toward the basketball court in time to catch J.R. make a layup. She said, "I'll pass the message along to J.R."

"Make sure you do. I want him to know he has the potential to play in college if he wanted." Something behind Annie caught Noah's eye. Annie turned to see that his uncle had come in the door to the building. Noah nodded when he caught his uncle's eye. He kept his focus on his uncle when he spoke to Annie. He said, "I'll catch up with you later," and moved to meet his uncle in front of the concession stand.

She walked back into the gym and stopped before climbing the stairs to her seat in the bleachers.

The logical conclusion came to her. Noah and J.R. had formed a friendship. She was just a conduit. Sadness pinched the edge of her conscience. The last thing she expected when they reconnected was the distance between them would remain. With the mystery of Noah's intention being solved, she went back to her place in the stands and waited for the next half of the game to begin.

47

THE THIRD QUARTER

The start of the third quarter went off with an intensity that made Annie glad she gave the taco in a bag to Darryl. Her gut clenched with the tension. The purple and gold uniformed, Paradise Hills Panthers must have had an interesting pep talk from their coach. They executed more physical plays. From her seat in the middle of the stands, Annie saw elbows jut out a little further. One player backed up and poked out his butt with such an intensity it tripped Andy mid layup. The Ashbrook Eagles, six-foot four center recovered, but it was too late. He missed the shot.

If the strategy was an attempt to intimidate the Ashbrook Eagles into submission, it didn't work. The players took the negative energy and used it to their advantage. After every free throw they made, they threw out a little fist bump and nodded in determination. They intended to beat their rival.

Annie wanted to look away but kept her eyes glued on her son. She watched the Panthers player throw a shoulder into J.R. Both boys were running at full speed, and the action caught J.R. off guard. His arms flailed as he adjusted his body to recover from the shift in momentum. It didn't work. J.R. fell to the ground like a building that crumbled in a detonation. The hush of silence in the stand was almost deafening. Any time an injury presented itself Annie feared the worst. Her heart sank to her stomach. She prayed that her mother's worry was getting the best of her and J.R. would be fine.

One dad who sat in the left row of the bleachers called out, "Shake it off, J.R."

J.R. sat up, and the crowd gasped a collective sigh.

"I think he can't get up." Annie heard the concern in Hazel's voice. When Hazel wasn't baking pies at the Elderberry Cafe, she sat in the same place in the stands and cheered on her favorite team. Rather than turn around and make sure, Annie devoted all her senses to her son as though wishing him better would make it happen. Through her hand that covered her mouth, she whispered, "Get up, son. Please."

J.R. writhed in pain, and her heart sank even deeper. Instinct kicked in, and Annie pushed her way through the people between her and the aisle. She ignored the whispers of, "I hope he's okay," and "That does not look good."

Annie hustled down the stairs. Hoping against hope that J.R. would be fine, she stopped at the boundary line of the basketball court. The last thing her son would want was for the team to get a technical foul because his mother coddled him. She craned her neck to get a better view of him. Officials and his teammates surrounded him and blocked Annie's view. Under her breath, she muttered, "This is not supposed to happen." But she knew injury came with playing athletics.

In her peripheral vision, she saw Noah approach where she stood. He wrapped his arm around her shoulder to offer a quick side hug. "I'll take care of this."

Annie had never been so thankful to have a friend as a doctor. She nodded her assurance in him. As much as things changed, they remained the same. Twenty years ago, Noah was on the court with Jesse. Now he was there in proxy offering support to Jesse's son. Noah marched to the circle the team of boys formed around J.R. They separated to make room for him and reconverged when he bent down to assess the situation.

Murmurs of speculation drifted from the stands. "I'll bet you twenty bucks it's broken," was followed by, "I'm not stupid enough to take that bet. That family has had nothing but bad luck."

Although their comments weren't anything Annie wanted or needed to hear, it was her truth. It began when the doctor diagnosed Jesse with prostate cancer at nineteen. From there, she and J.R. worked through an unfair share of hardship. They didn't have time to complain. As soon as they recovered from one situation, another one they never saw coming presented itself.

Lennie Archer, her neighbor from down the street, approached Annie. The man wore a maroon red, long sleeve t-shirt with "will work for beer" written in black letters across his chest. Annie noted that at least Lennie had the decency to wear a shirt that coordinated with the school colors. He looked Annie in the eye and offered a hopeful smile. "If it'll make you feel better, I can hold your hand."

Annie blinked in shock. "Um, I think I'll be fine." She inched away from Lennie and shoved her hands behind her back just in case he didn't believe her. "Thank you for your support."

"I'll be right over there." Lennie pointed to an empty spot in the middle of the front row. "If you need anything just holler."

She had to give the man credit; he tried to be nice. It wasn't his fault that the thought of holding hands with him made her want to hurl. Annie forced a grin and said, "Thanks, I'll keep that in mind," and turned to face the middle of the basketball court. Two boys had their hands on their chin as they spoke to each other. Their postures confirmed what Annie feared. She would not like what they saw.

Darryl came up alongside Annie and stood with her in silence. The two of them had been a part of each other's lives since elementary school and fluently spoke the silent language of close friendship. He didn't need to say a word for Annie to understand that he worried alongside and for her.

Lisa joined them and stood on the left side of Annie. "Noah's out there taking care of him. Everything will be fine. Just watch."

Just then, Andy's twin brother Rodney trotted to where Annie stood. "The trainer wants to talk to you."

Lisa, Darryl, and Annie exchanged glances of concern. Annie's heart raced faster with each step she took alongside Rodney. Her pulse stopped, and the world spun when Annie saw the lump in the middle of J.R.'s leg. She didn't need to be a doctor to know he had a compound fracture.

Annie knelt on the ground beside J.R. who was laid out flat on the ground. His eyes dilated, and his bangs clung to the sweat on his forehead. His voice croaked, "I don't think I'll be able to take out the trash when I get home." Annie choked back the cry that came with her son's attempt at humor. She took J.R.'s hand in hers and said, "We'll get you fixed up, son."

He groaned, "I know, Mom. Noah's a doctor."

There was the teenage son she remembered. He had to let her know she missed the obvious. In the midst of her eye roll to hide her relief, Annie's esteem of Noah changed. She felt stupid for getting jealous when he flirted with the younger woman. Her interpretation of the relationship shifted, and she thanked God for bringing a man into her son's life to help him through this difficult period.

48

SAUSAGE BISCUITS AND GRAVY

From her post in the kitchen, Annie listened to Noah tell J.R. stories from their childhood. She sipped her cup of coffee while leaning against the kitchen island. A lot of the stories she hadn't known about because they came from a time when it was just Jesse and Noah. While she was off doing the things young teenage girls do, Noah and Jesse tested their wits against life.

"One time your dad and I got this crazy idea that we could move faster than alkali absorbed." He chuckled and added, "Which, now that I think about it, made little sense. On more than one occasion our fathers' tractors got stuck when the soil didn't match their expectations. If something with a wide surface area couldn't make it, it would have been easier for something with a tire this thick to sink."

J.R.'s chuckle at Noah's insight sent rays of warmth through Annie. She leaned against the counter with her cup of coffee in her hand. The further Noah got into the story, Annie remembered how the story ended. Right after the two friends recovered their vehicles from the muck, a cleaned up Jesse stopped by her house to ask her to a barn dance. Noah got grounded. Jesse, in need of another companion, invited Annie instead. That began the story of Jesse and Annie.

She joined the two in the living room. J.R. sat on the couch with his leg perched on a stack of pillows. They reset the bones in his leg and had him in a red cast that went to the bottom of his knee. Noah sat in the recliner he moved to position himself across from J.R.'s head. The pain medication they gave J.R. in the hospital had taken effect, and he blinked to fight off to sleep.

Noah spoke to Annie, "It looks like I'm losing him."

"He does it to me all the time," she joked. Glad that her son was at home and comfortable, Annie brushed a piece of J.R's hair away from his eyebrows. Sure, she loved her mother and sister, but maternal love drove her to keep moving when she thought the world ended. She didn't know what she would do if anything happened to J.R.

"What time is it, anyway?" Noah asked.

They both glanced at the clock she made. Framed pictures of J.R. at different stages of his life made up the different times.

"It is four in the morning," she exclaimed while looking down at the empty cup of coffee in her hands. "Maybe I shouldn't have drunk this."

"I'm glad you did." The corners of Noah's mouth curved to form a mischievous grin. "That means we have the time to make breakfast together."

Annie did a quick mental inventory of the items in the pantry. She didn't feel comfortable offering her staples of oatmeal, Honey Nut Cheerios, and breakfast cookies. Then it came to her. She had biscuit mix. And in the basement, her box freezer full of venison supplied the protein for a quick meal. They had made some into sausage. "If it isn't too small town for you, I could make us some sausage biscuits and gravy?"

Noah groaned his delight. "Sausage biscuits and gravy.

That's what I love about coming home. Eating the food that I grew up with." He wriggled his fingers. "I make a mean biscuit."

Annie pulled out the biscuit mix and gravy mix and handed them to Noah to place on the counter. He followed her to the basement. Annie found the package of sausage and handed it to Noah. "Jesse's dad gives us half of his deer every season." He called her at the hospital and said he'd be by the house in the afternoon to check on his grandson. He'd have more food and stories to share to console J.R.

From out of nowhere Noah said, "You're doing all right, Annie."

While she appreciated his assessment, Annie wrinkled her brow in confusion. She didn't know where it came from, or why he shared his opinion with her.

Noah explained, "I don't know what I expected." He shrugged. "A more fragile version of the person I remembered from when we were growing up?" He gave her hand a reassuring squeeze, "Instead, you seem stronger."

"I have my days," Annie admitted. "I wasn't feeling strong when I was stuck in the snow the other day. Thank you for helping us."

"To be honest, I'm glad you were stuck." Noah played with a strand of hair that rested on Annie's shoulder. "It brought us back together."

"I've been here the whole time," Annie answered.

"That's not what I mean," Noah's voice softened.

Annie's heart fluttered at the change in his tone. The voice in her head reminded her that Noah was there for J.R. Before she made a fool of herself, Annie held up the package of sausage, said, "We should get this in the pot. It'll take a while to cook," and headed for the kitchen.

Noah talked while she browned the sausage. "When I was

in Jinotepe the women brought me fresh tortillas for breakfast every day."

"Was there a special tortilla baker in your life?" Annie pried for more information about his life outside of Ashbrook.

He fiddled with the utensil drawer. She saw a slight blush in his cheeks. "One or two."

She had to give Noah credit. He had the decency to blush. She smiled at the change from the Noah she remembered. When they were in high school, he'd tell Jesse and Annie every detail of his dates. There were still a couple of women she couldn't look in the face because of some things Noah shared.

"What about you? Have you dated since Jesse?" He paused as though he was searching for the correct word, then said, "Left?"

Three years had passed since Jesse died. He died doing what he loved, riding the quad. So while she was sad for herself, she always thought if it was his time to go, that was the best way for it to happen. "No, I didn't have it in me to see anyone else." She admitted. "And, J.R. keeps me busy."

"Jesse said that would happen." A wrinkle formed in the middle of Noah's brow.

"What?" Annie had no idea Jesse and Noah talked about her. Although it made sense. He survived cancer in his twenties. After facing death, he approached life differently. Sometimes when they laid in bed, he'd ask her what she'd do without him. Annie always replied that she didn't want to think about life without him. Now she was living it. If he were to come back and ask how she was doing, Annie would have said that she was right. Life without him was too hard.

"You're too young to stop living." Just as Noah said it, the timer signaling that the biscuits were finished baking went off.

The sound startled Annie into moving. She pulled the oven mitts out of the drawer and opened the door. After the initial wave of heat passed, Annie inhaled the aroma of warm biscuits and her mouth watered. As she set them on the counter, she said, "I need to get your biscuit recipe."

"Some things are best kept secret," Noah's eyes sparkled. "Besides, if I don't tell, you'll invite me back."

Annie wished it were true. That he'd stick around to make biscuits whenever she had a taste for them. But she said nothing because it would be too harsh to remind Noah that he was only in town for a visit and then he'd be off living his life of adventure.

49

THE FULL PACKAGE

Noah sopped up the last bit of his gravy with the last bite of his biscuit. "What would you say if I said your cooking is good enough to make me want to move home?"

"I'd say it was the gravy talking." Annie joked. She had witnessed the coming home pattern enough to identify the first signs. People who wanted to come home talked about what they missed when they were gone. Other than his mentions of Jesse, Noah hadn't made any mention of what made living in small town Montana special. When he inquired about how people found a job or commented on the price people were asking for their houses, she would allow herself to believe he was coming home. Until then he was there for a visit. It was longer than most, but signs of the lack of permanence in his plans warned her to not get attached.

He picked up his plate and took Annie's before walking over to the sink. "Where is your dish soap?"

"Under the sink." Annie rose to wash the dishes. "I can get it."

"No, I can clean a dish." He spoke with a firmness that

warned Annie that if she pressed the issue, she might not like his response.

She retreated and sat on a stool on the other side of the kitchen island. With nothing to do but watch him, she noted how his shirt was still wrinkle-free. The stubble on his face added a measure of attractiveness that made her heart hitch. Everything in her wanted to go up to him and caress his cheek with the back of her hand.

He placed a dish in the drainer and stopped. "What are you thinking about?"

Annie's face reddened as though he had read her thoughts. She cleared her throat and said, "I can dry the dishes and put them away."

A soft smile formed on Noah's lips. "Fine, I'll let you help me a little."

"Thank you," Annie rose to join him. She walked around the island and pulled a clean towel out of a drawer beneath the dish drainer. The first dish was almost dry and didn't need too much wiping, so she set it on the counter and waited for the next dish.

Other than when she was at her mother's house for the holidays, Annie did the dishes alone. The atmosphere around her hummed a peaceful, silent melody. Having someone beside her changed her attitude about washing dishes. It was a time to connect with the person beside her.

"A penny for your thoughts," Noah inquired.

Glad to have a question where she could tell the truth, Annie answered, "This is nice. I could get used to washing the dishes with someone."

"It's nice being the someone to wash the dishes with you." He held onto the dish for a moment longer than he needed to. "Are you ready to have someone in your life?"

"I haven't thought about it," Annie replied.

Noah lowered the biscuit pan in the sudsy water.

"Why didn't you ever get married?" Annie asked. One time she and Jesse talked about it. Jesse told her that some men know what they want and won't settle for less. Noah was that type of person and when he found what he wanted everybody would know it. When a man lived as many places as Noah had, he had to have come across one or two women who met their handsome friend's criteria.

Noah arched his eyebrow to question what she meant.

"I mean you're hot. You're a doctor. You wash dishes. C'mon you're the full package."

"Is that so?" Noah's lips formed a thin lined smile.

"Yes. If I was an available woman, I'd go for you in a heartbeat." She meant it too. Growing up with Noah gave her the benefit of seeing the full picture of the man. Noah was kind, trustworthy, and down to earth. Working on the farm with his father built his character to show a tender tenaciousness that gave him the ability to push through a problem until he saw it resolved.

Noah's chest rose and fell giving away his silent chuckle. "I hate to break it to you like this, Annie, but you are an available woman." He rinsed the biscuit pan and placed it in the drainer. Then he took the towel from Annie's hands and dried his.

Annie stammered, "I meant a single, available woman."

"How do you not meet the definition you're giving me?" He took Annie's hand in his.

The warmth of his hand around hers begged her to consider the possibilities. She wished she was the woman that could meet his needs. "I have a son, and a job, and responsibilities. It isn't like I can pack up and leave everything to go traipsing around the world to exotic places."

His eyes bore into hers as though they were searching for something. "Your son is amazing. My uncle is looking for a partner for his practice, and some men don't care about exotic. They want a place they can call home."

"Are you coming home?" A vision of them being able to see each other every day like when they were younger brightened her heart. It was almost too good to be true.

Noah released her hand and stepped back toward the dishes. He set the frying pan in the suds. "If you're asking about whether I've joined my uncle's practice, the answer is no."

For a moment there, allowed herself to believe Noah was coming home. She grimaced at her misunderstanding and made a mental note to remind herself that his talk of coming home was hypothetical.

Noah interrupted her silent rebuke. "But if you wanted me to, I would." He kept his eyes on the frying pan while he waited for her answer.

She didn't like the direction the discussion had taken. It reminded her she was lonely. If she were younger, Annie would have said you need to come home. The older Annie knew better. Noah had to do what made him happy. Life was too short to live for other people. She touched his elbow to anchor him. "Come home because you want to. Not because I want you here."

His eyes searched hers for something. He leaned in like he intended to kiss her. Annie felt the pull and held her breath. It may not have been right, but she wanted to kiss him too.

J.R.'s groggy voice broke through the moment. "Mom, I need help to get to the bathroom." The doctor told him he couldn't put any weight on his leg for at least three weeks. Annie sighed and told herself to get ready for many late-night trips to the bathroom.

"I'll be right there." She set the towel on the counter and motioned to go to the living room.

"Is Noah here?" he asked.

"Yes, why?"

"No offense, but I'd rather he helped me."

Annie made eye contact with Noah. He nodded and turned to go help J.R. As he walked away, she wished something as easy as sausage biscuits and gravy would be all it took to convince him to stick around.

50

NO GAME

J.R. reclined on the couch with his leg perched on the cushions. It had been two weeks since he broke his leg. He and Annie worked to make the best of the situation by trying to do as much from home as possible. Across the room on the big screen television, they watched the Ashbrook Eagles play against the Three Creeks Elks.

Annie sat in the chair beside him. They both nibbled popcorn from hulk sized bowls of popcorn on their laps "This is almost as good as being there." The popcorn in his mouth muffled J.R.'s voice.

Since the injury, J.R. had a good attitude about being out for the season. She overheard his side of the conversation he had with a friend while playing Ark. "You guys will do fine without me if you rebound like you're supposed to." But, occasionally, when he thought Annie wasn't watching, a forlorn expression took over his face.

After Ashbrook made a basket, Annie broached the topic. "I was wondering..." When he tilted his ear toward her, she continued. "Maybe they'd let you help with the stats or do something in the broadcaster's booth when you're a little more mobile."

He said nothing. But the straight-lined expression combined with the nod was enough of a signal to assure her he'd consider her suggestion.

During the halftime show, Annie refreshed their drinks and met J.R. back in the living room. They still had five minutes until the second half began. When she sat down, J.R. asked, "Do you ever get lonely, Mom?"

She leaned away from the question to consider the source. Was J.R. missing his father? Even though it made her uncomfortable, it was best to tell him the truth. She replied, "Sometimes. But you can be in a room full of people and feel alone. Why?"

"I saw Noah talking to the coach on the camera." There was a spark of encouragement in his voice, "He's your age."

Her son's concern touched her. "Aww, honey, I don't need a man's company to push aside loneliness. Little by little I'll fill the emptiness with things that make me happy."

"Like power walking?" He joked

"Yes, like power walking," Annie agreed.

J.R. rolled his eyes. "With you as a role model, I'll never be able to get a date. I'll just walk away from her fast."

They both giggled at his joke. Their laughter gave way to focus when the second half of the game resumed. Annie tried to find Noah on the screen. J.R. mentioned seeing him, but he didn't say where. Rather than ask and put thoughts in her son's head, she tried finding Noah herself.

In the last minute of the game, during a timeout, J.R. pointed at the screen. "He's over there, at the announcer's table." Noah wrote something and passed it to the announcer. Shortly afterward, the announcer said, "Our Eagles are doing well, but they wanted to mention they're missing their point guard J.R. Duncan."

J.R.'s face brightened like a Christmas tree. "Did you hear that?"

"I sure did." Annie made a note to thank Noah. He had found a profound way of connecting with her son. Sure, J.R. had his grandfather and uncles. With Jesse being gone she believed the more male role models for J.R., the better he'd be able to handle adulthood without his father.

The game ended with the Ashbrook Eagles winning by eight points. "The District Championship is next week. Can we go to the game?"

"We could try," Annie said. "We can talk about it more when I clean up these dishes." She turned on the Play Station system for J.R. Beeps and chimes signaled his entry into different screens. J.R. commented on the progress his friends made while he was away from the game before a dinosaur's roar took the little attention he had given Annie. Just as she placed the last dish in the drainer, loud rapid knocking interrupted their semi-silence. Annie wiped her hand on the dish towel and rushed to the door to find out who was on the other side.

When she opened it, a group of boys yelled, "Surprise!" J.R.'s best friend Andy held out two boxes of pizza. His twin brother Rodney displayed two bottles of soda. Behind the twins' red hair, their friend Owen waved two bags of chips. A fourth head popped in the middle of all the faces. Kris said, "We brought the party to your house." In the back of the group, Annie found Noah's beaming grin. One by one they paraded into the house.

Noah who held a pie in his hand stopped in front of Annie and kissed her on the cheek.

Owen, the tallest of the group of boys, plopped on the

couch at J.R.'s feet. "I hope you don't mind us coming over. It didn't feel right celebrating without J.R."

Annie and J.R.'s eyes met from across the room. In the joy of being with his friends, she saw the source of his earlier question. He was no longer lonely.

Andy rolled the wheelchair from its position in the corner. "Noah taught us this game called Killer Uno. Let's go to the table."

"I'm sorry. It's a rowdy game," Noah half apologized.

The boys corralled into the kitchen and set themselves up at the table. Annie and Noah followed. He got out two plates and cut a slice of pie for the each of them. His smile softened when he handed Annie the plate. "According to my Aunt Peggy, this is your favorite pie."

Annie pressed her fork into the crust that flaked, and her mouth began to water. She could almost taste it melting in her mouth. "She is right. Apple pie is my favorite. I'm curious. What other secrets has she shared about me?"

They made their way to the living room and sat on the couch. "She said you could use a little distraction in your life."

They both chuckled at the comment. His aunt's comment wasn't anything new to Annie. Every time Annie visited the dentist's office to have her teeth cleaned, Peggy said, "You should find yourself someone to have fun with." Apparently, Noah's aunt found someone to do that. She lifted the fork to her lips when she noticed that the room fell silent. Noah and Annie turned to see five teens staring at them. Rodney spoke in a hushed voice. "What we are seeing here is the mating habits of adults when they don't have any game."

The friends behind him roared with laughter.

Noah blushed and responded, "How can you say I have no game? Those are my Uno cards you're using."

Their laughter filled the room. It had been so long since

Annie laughed it hurt like she used a muscle that hadn't been active for quite some time. The pain passed and the air around her lightened. Annie had never been as grateful as she had been in that brief amount of time. People told her the day would come when she would laugh again. Noah proved their statement to be true.

51

HE'S HANGRY

All morning J.R. had been cranky. Nothing on television caught his attention, and video games seemed to aggravate his mood. When he threw his controller across the room, and it hit the picture posted in the seven o'clock spot on her wall clock, Annie knew she had to take control of the situation. How? She wasn't sure, but something had to be done.

"Is the pain medication affecting your mood?" Annie reread the label for the side effects. It said it may cause drowsiness and advised against the use of heavy machinery. "It says nothing here about taking one's frustration out on the family clock."

"You should change the pictures anyway," J.R. grumbled.

Annie waved her finger as she pointed. "You're hungry. I can make a snack to carry you over until dinner."

"I don't want to go to dinner with you and Noah," J.R. shifted his weight.

This came as a surprise because J.R. was the one who initiated the outing. He saw on Facebook that the American Legion's annual chili dinner was on Saturday evening. He asked Annie if she minded if they invited Noah to the dinner. When she gave her consent to the idea, J.R. called Noah and completed the arrangements. There was no way she was reversing the course her son set. He'd resent her for it.

Something else had to have been bothering J.R. The answer came to her. He had never been still for any large amount of time. Being confined to the couch, or a wheelchair was getting to him. "You can't work your lower body, but we could get weights, so you could keep your upper body in shape."

"I don't need exercise, Mom!" he yelled, "I want to be left alone." His voice echoed in the silence that followed.

"Who will help you get around?" Annie hoped her voice sounded concerned and not naggy.

"I am six months away from moving away to go to college. I think I can take care of myself."

"Getting help doesn't make you any less of a man. I helped your father all the time."

"And look at what happened to him," J.R. barked.

J.R.'s words hit her in the middle of the heart. If it were a physical blow, she would have died then and there on the spot where she stood. *I am the adult, and he is the child.* She said, "I don't know how to respond to that. So, I won't." She turned on one foot and forced herself to calm down. Under her breath, she muttered, *"I understand why Dina drinks a lot*." Her friend over in Three Creeks drank every time she had the chance. Annie used to worry about her friend. Now that she was getting a taste of teenage spirit she wanted to call her friend and apologize over a bottle of wine.

Instead, when she got to her room, she sent off a text message to Noah. "Won't be able to make it to dinner."

Before she set the phone on the counter, the phone rang.

Noah skipped the pleasantries and went straight to his question. "Is everything okay?"

"Yes, J.R. doesn't want to go. So I'm stuck staying home with him."

"So." His reply caught Annie off guard. Didn't Noah know he was supposed to complain about J.R.'s moodiness?

"So, who will help him get around?" She stated the obvious. Now he'd see the picture clearer.

"He's a grown kid," Noah answered. "What are you afraid of? That he'll pee on the carpet."

"Don't be ridiculous. He's a boy. Not a dog."

"My point, exactly," Noah said. "A boy who doesn't want his mother coddling him. Give him some space. I'm sure he'll be fine. It isn't like we're going away on a safari. We'll be five miles away and back in a couple hours."

"I'm not sure," Annie faltered. She was torn between taking care of her son or enjoying time with Noah.

"I bet when you get back things will have blown over. We're going out," Noah insisted.

"Maybe another—"

Noah cut off Annie's deferral. "I'll be there in a half hour. And don't try to text and cancel because I'll show up, anyway." He ended the call.

Annie tried calling him back, but he wouldn't pick up the call. She yanked several tops out of the drawer and slammed them on the bed. When that didn't satisfy her anger, she slammed the drawers shut. Then she kicked a shoe under the bed, only to realize it was the shoe she wanted to wear.

As she reached under the bed to retrieve the shoe, the ridiculousness of the situation caught up with her. Noah called her out for being a control freak, and she didn't like it. He treated her the way she handled J.R.

The situation that aggravated her moments prior suddenly struck her as funny. Annie looked at the picture of her and Jesse on her nightstand. The photographer had caught Jesse in the middle of a laugh. She imagined that he was laughing at her right now and agreed with him. With new eyes on the situation, she turned on the radio, set it to the country music station, and went to the bathroom to apply her makeup. It had been awhile since she had been out with adults. She hoped she remembered how to talk like one.

52

ALASKA

Annie applied the last dabs of mascara when Noah knocked on the door. She called out, "I'm coming," as she rushed down the hall to get to the door. She hop-stepped to secure her foot in the shoe. Her foot fell in place just as she opened the door.

Noah scanned her body from head to toe. "You look nice."

It had been a long time since anybody had complimented Annie. Her mind went blank, leaving her to respond with a blush and shy smile. "Thank you." She opened the door to let him in. In a rush to get to the living room, Annie left her purse on the edge of the bed. "I have to get my purse, and I'll be ready to go."

She motioned to go to the back of the house. Out of the corner of her eye, Annie saw J.R.'s face with his mouth ajar. He pressed his hands into the couch to make it easier to sit straighter. Annie remained silent. The boy was so moody, anything she said could and would be used against her.

She hadn't made it to the hall when he said, "You're going to dinner?"

Annie called from her bedroom door, "Yes, that was the plan."

"Without me?"

"You said you didn't want to go." Glad to be out of J.R.'s view, Annie grinned. Noah was smarter than she had given him credit for.

"I don't want to go."

Annie set the purse strap on her shoulder and returned to the living room. "We can bring you some food in a takeout box. I'll have them double up on the corn bread."

"I don't want chili," J.R. wrinkled his face in disgust.

"I'm sure you can make yourself something from what we have here," Annie replied.

"I thought you'd stay home, and we'd have a pizza or Chinese food." His eyes widened in disbelief.

His change in attitude stunned Annie. One minute he didn't want to have anything to do with her, and the next he wanted takeout. "You never said anything about."

"Why should I have to say anything? I'm your only son. You get me." He threw his hands up in the air.

Annie threw her eyes at Noah as if to say this is your fault.

Noah shrugged. "I don't speak teenager."

"You were supposed to say something like." He changed his voice to mock hers, "Okay, son, I'll stay home tonight, and we can play board games." His voice returned to normal. "Not, I'll go out with the first guy who likes me and leave you home alone."

"Hey!" Annie replied. It was a good thing Noah was there. Otherwise, she might say something they both would regret later.

"Hold on a minute." Noah held out his hand in opposite directions and stepped between Anne and J.R.

They both fell silent.

He addressed J.R. "Did you or did you not tell your mother you wanted to stay home alone?"

"No!" J.R. face wrinkled to show the depth of his anger.

Annie's mouth fell open. Not only was her son saying mean things; he was lying. "You said that you didn't want to go to dinner. AND, you could take care of yourself."

"Just because I can doesn't mean I want to!" J.R. yelled.

"Hold on!" Noah yelled. Both Annie and J.R. stopped talking.

J.R.'s chest trembled. Annie could tell that he was waiting to say something and would do it the first chance he got.

"Annie, you decide. Chinese food or pizza? I'll stay here and talk with J.R." Noah said.

She glanced over at J.R. who wrapped his arms in front of his chest. In a matter of minutes, her son transformed from an angry teenager to the pouty child that needed a hug to make things better.

J.R. mumbled, "Get extra cheese on the pizza."

Annie inhaled to swallow her retort and headed for the door. She thought to herself that the worst thing that could happen was Noah would be a witness to J.R. knocking a couple more pictures off the already ruined clock.

Annie returned to the house with two pizzas—one pepperoni with extra cheese, and the other a supreme pizza. She expected to see some evidence of an argument: a video game controller on the floor or a picture turned incorrectly, or at least a red-faced man and teenager. None of those were in the room. She had an empty couch with the pillows plumped, a picture with a cracked frame was in the correct spot on the clock, and no man nor child was to be seen.

Her ears sharpened to find evidence of what the men were doing. A snippet of a conversation coming from the kitchen bled over to where she stood. "Your father was my best friend growing up. There is no way I could fill his shoes."

"I'm not asking that. It's just nice having a man around to balance out mom. You see how crazy she gets."

Annie set her purse on the floor. She couldn't wait to hear Noah's response.

"Raising a teenager is a daunting job." Noah neither confirmed nor denied the crazy.

She heard a cabinet door open and shut. What were they doing in the kitchen? The clattering of dishes being set on the table answered her question.

"If I get a vote, I say you stay."

What did that mean? Before she got busted for eavesdropping, Annie opened the door and closed it louder. "I'm back with two pizzas."

With J.R. wheeled out in front of him, Noah walked through the doorway that separated the living room and kitchen. J.R. said, "You're just in time. We set the table."

Noah's eyes searched Annie's for something. She maintained her ruse of having just arrived and held out the pizzas for him to see she accomplished her task.

WHILE ANNIE CHEWED on her pizza, she tried to piece what Noah and J.R. said over dinner with what she had overheard. Unless she counted the choice between Monopoly, Scrabble or Kerplunk, nothing matched voting or deciding.

At the suggestion of Kerplunk, Noah smiled, and a faraway expression was in his eyes. "One time when your dad and I were…" He paused and resumed the story, "Younger. We got this idea to make Kerplunk into a drinking game. If we had one marble fall, it was a swig of beer. If it was more than one, we had to take a shot."

J.R. laughed with food in his mouth. "You two were crazy."

There's that word again. Annie got up from the table and brought her plate to the sink. She set the empty pepperoni pizza box beneath the box holding the one remaining slice of the supreme pizza. Both Noah and J.R. declined to take it. J.R. handed his mother his plate. "I'm done."

Annie took the plate to the sink. She bent down to get the soap. When she rose, Noah was beside her. "I'll dry this time."

"Why are you doing women's work?" J.R. asked.

"When you don't have one around to help you, you'll learn it's just something that needs to be done."

Annie thanked Noah with a smile.

They washed the dishes. Noah and J.R. talked about the upcoming college basketball games. If someone had asked her about the specific details of their conversation, Annie had no answer. She heard the words but not the meaning behind them.

Noah placed the last dish in the cabinet and set the towel on the counter. The warmth that came to her when she thought about him made her uncomfortable. He fit in her world. When he was around, life flowed smoothly. J.R. was amenable, and Noah hanging out with her in the kitchen was what she imagined married life would be like. She reminded herself that there was no point in getting attached to Noah. He was scheduled to leave in the next couple of weeks. The problem was, she had already fallen for him. She sighed and began to think of ways to cut the ties her heart had formed.

"You're quiet," J.R. mentioned through a sly grin. He cast a furtive glance in Noah's direction.

"I'm tired," Annie said.

"Noah. I mean a friend mentioned that when women are in love, they go through a quiet phase."

"Or she is watching what she says because her teenage son will say mean things to her," Annie snapped.

Noah and J.R. exchanged a glance. "About what I said earlier. I didn't mean it."

Annie didn't know what to do with her hands, so she picked up the towel and wiped the clean counter top.

"I don't want what I said to come between you and Noah."

She didn't know what made her do it. With her brows screaming the question, Annie's eyes darted to Noah. "I wonder where J.R. got this interesting idea?"

Noah held his hands with the palms up and stepped back to say, "I don't know." He turned his face and spoke to J.R. "That wasn't in the script."

J.R.'s voice rose in defense. "I wanted her to know if there was something between you two, I approve."

When did her son go from that sweet kid who only had to have gummy bears to be happy? How long had he been watching out for her wellbeing? Noah witnessing the conversation sent pricks of awkwardness through her. Annie offered him a sheepish grin.

His smile mirrored her sentiment. "J.R. Can I have a moment alone with your mom?"

"Does it get me out of cleaning the kitchen?" J.R. joked.

Both Annie and Noah chuckled. The fact that she had no intention of asking J.R. to take out the trash added to the levity. His mode of movement guaranteed that she'd have an even bigger mess if he helped. Her chest expanded in the absence of the tension between them. "Yes, it will get you out of cleaning the kitchen."

"You don't have to ask me to leave twice." He backed up the wheelchair and rolled out of the room. When he reached the entrance to the hallway, he said, "I'll be in my room listening to an audiobook. Mrs. Vice said I could listen to the book and it will count toward my book report." He rolled away a couple of inches and stopped with his elbows in the air. "That means I won't hear anything." He pushed forward on the wheels, and the squeak of the chair on laminate flooring marked his exit.

Annie reached for a glass they forgot to wash and scrubbed it. When it was cleaned to her satisfaction, she set it back in the dish drainer. Noah reached in front of her and turned off the water. "We need to talk. First, I didn't put J.R. up to saying that. I have no idea where that came from."

She wanted to ask him about the decision he and J.R. were discussing earlier but didn't because it would reveal that she heard more than he may have intended. Something Noah said pressed J.R. into speaking on his behalf.

He took Annie's hand in his and held them in front of her waist. "I have something to tell you."

The seriousness of his tone worried Annie. Did he have to tell her something about J.R?

"They have offered me a job in Alaska." His eyes searched hers.

Disappointment darkened her world. The possibility of him leaving had been tucked away in the back of her mind. It had stepped to the front and demanded she accept the inevitable. Noah was just there for a visit and the time for his departure had come. It shouldn't have surprised her, but it did. The men she allowed into her heart had a way of leaving.

Annie forced herself to smile. "I'm happy for you."

"You are?"

"Isn't it what you wanted?"

"I want you to tell me to stay home."

"I'm not the type of person who holds people back from pursuing their dreams."

"I'm ready to make a change. To have a life where I have someone to come home to. Someone to laugh at my jokes, and someone to talk with while we cook dinner together."

He was talking about what they had done over the past month. "But, that isn't romantic. That's something you can do with a roommate." The things she missed about being married came to her. "What about spending hours talking about everything and anything? What about the emptiness you get when the person isn't in the room? Or, having different touches to tell what you're thinking."

He moved to be closer to her. "Different touches you say?" The husky tone caught her unaware. He had never used it on her, and she struggled against it. For as long as she had known him there was a line of women competing to get his attention. The voice created a charge between them that had Annie ready to get in line for a chance. Annie told herself that there was nothing between them. They were good friends.

The proximity of his body to hers upended a part of her argument. Whichever one it was had been lost. Annie stepped away to clear her head. Noah still had a hold of her hand and squeezed it to stop her. When she did, he leaned in and whispered, "Can we talk about those touches, Annie?"

She struggled to remember what they were discussing. "We were talking about something else before touching."

He caressed the side of her cheek. "I was trying to convince you that being with you is a strong enough argument to not go to Alaska." His finger glided from her cheek to the tip of her chin. Annie felt her body obey his silent command. He wanted her to come to him. She complied, and he pressed his lips to hers.

The last kiss he gave her was sweet and said I'm glad to be

home. This kiss—the depth of this kiss demanded Annie's attention. When she pressed her body into his, a fire ignited in her core. It was such an intense eruption of feeling Annie gasped.

Noah had awakened a sleeping giant in Annie. The spark in his eye told her he knew it. He not only caught, but he also captured a piece of Annie's heart. His grin warned that now that he had it, he wasn't about to give it back anytime soon.

53

THE NOTE

"I have something to show you." Noah set his hands on Annie's shoulder. His lips were swollen from the kiss.

Since she never considered anything like this happening between Noah and herself, she had no idea what show you something entailed. "I don't know if I'm ready for this," she admitted.

He swallowed hard in response and cleared his throat. His eyes traveled to the hallway. "You have no idea how long I have loved you."

Taken back by his declaration, Annie scowled. He had only been home for a little more than a month, and their reconnection was one of those chance meetings. If she hadn't been trapped in the snow, the odds of them meeting were slim.

Noah reached into his pocket and pulled out his wallet. In between the bills, a worn piece of notebook paper protruded. Noah wiggled at the note to separate it from the bills. When he freed it from the wallet, he handed it to Annie.

The first thing she thought was *he wrote a poem*? Careful to honor the tenderness of the moment she gently unfolded the paper. To her surprise, she opened it to see Jesse's handwriting. Annie looked to Noah to explain.

"Read it." His eyes clouded with concern, and he shoved his hands in his pockets.

Annie read the heading. It was a note to Noah. It began with Jesse thanking Noah for his years of friendship. Jesse told Noah that he suspected that his time was short. He apologized for causing Noah pain. The following sentences explained the apology. Jesse wrote that had he realized the situation sooner he would have made different decisions. But by the time he figured it out, it was too late.

Her brow wrinkled. "What decision?" She asked.

"It's in there."

The hesitance in his voice threw up a caution flag. What had Jesse done?

Annie hung on every word as she read the note. "I fell in love with Annie at the barn dance." She remembered the dance. Jesse remained by her side for the entire evening. After that, they were permanently Jesse and Annie. There was peanut butter and jelly, bologna and cheese, and Jesse and Annie. Something in her warned Annie not to get too sentimental about her husband's declaration.

"Had I known how you felt about her, I would not have invited her to come along."

A bowling ball landed in Annie's stomach.

"Your faithfulness as a friend and to my marriage is why I trust you. Take care of my girl."

Her hand trembled when she returned the note to him. "Is this true?"

"Yes." Noah folded the note and returned it to his wallet. The silence between them was almost palpable.

Annie whispered, "Does J.R.?" she stopped herself mid-question. Of course. J.R. was aware. It explained why he pressed for family time. He wanted to prove Jesse's plan worked. Her mind whirled through scenarios in the past couple weeks. Had Noah stayed with her at the hospital when J.R. broke his leg because Jesse told him to—not because he cared for her son?

She pulled away from Noah and whispered, "This is not right." Noah should never have involved her son in the situation.

Noah stepped toward her. Annie held her hand up to say stay away. Her eyes searched the room around her for answers to questions she hadn't asked. Questions she didn't know to ask.

Her response stuck in Annie's throat. She fought to get the words out. "This changes everything."

Her eyes locked in on Noah's. Maybe the answers were there. Except the only thing she saw was deep-seated concern. He gave her the space to work out the truth.

"Why didn't you say something earlier?"

"I was committed to working in Panama. And, you needed time to grieve." His voice laid somewhere between apologetic and pleading that she'd see things from his perspective.

"I need time," Annie answered the silent question.

"I figured." He pressed his lips into a thin line. "I should go."

"Yes, I agree."

"Bye, Annie." Noah kissed her on the cheek.

Annie watched him shut the door behind him. The quiet click of the knob setting in place marked his departure. Still stunned by everything that had transpired, Annie tiptoed to her room, so she wouldn't disrupt J.R. When she reached the edge of her bed, she took off her shoes and hid under the blankets she used to share with the love of her life.

54

COOKIES

Regretting that cup of coffee she drank after three o'clock, Annie forced her mind to topics that would bore her into falling asleep. She started with making a grocery list of things she needed to buy the next time she drove to Great Falls. She soon learned the flaw in her plan when she had to get out of bed to write the list.

Hoping answers she hadn't seen earlier hid within the small details, Annie turned to the picture of Jesse and her on the nightstand. Her arms were wrapped around his shoulders, and their smiles gave away the fact that they laughed just before the photographer captured the shot. Did Jesse remember he wrote the note during the photo shoot?

When Jesse couldn't sleep, they'd get out of bed and make cookies and have tea. She padded her way to the kitchen and rummaged through the cabinets for the ingredients. For years, someone always stood at the edge of the counter and waited for the chance to steal a spoonful of cookie dough. Baking alone still seemed foreign to her. She half expected Jesse to appear from around the corner.

Annie set the ingredients on the counter and sighed to herself. She'd have to get used this. J.R. would go away to college in August and living alone would be her new normal. *Thirty-six is too young to be a widow.*

The phone on the counter buzzed with a notification. She picked up the phone to read a text message from Noah. "Are you awake?"

She replied, "No."

"Can I come over?"

"It's too late. We can talk tomorrow."

"I'm outside. I can see the light."

Annie should have been angry with him, but she didn't have it in her. So she crossed the room to open the door. Noah stood on the porch. He had his phone out in what she assumed was in anticipation of her response.

"C'mon in." She stepped aside to make room for him. "I'm baking cookies."

His lips formed a tight thin line. "We need to talk about what happened earlier."

"I know."

When they were younger, Noah was the negotiator. If Jesse or Annie didn't buy into an idea, Noah would wrap his arm around the objector's shoulder and lay out the logic behind the idea. He'd pepper persuasion with details explaining why it worked to that person's advantage. Talked into playing the role of the damsel in distress, Annie suffered being buried in more snow forts than she cared to remember. On the other end of the spectrum, Jesse used Noah to explain why she couldn't go out on an excursion. Apparently, fifteen-year-old girls weren't supposed to like playing on snowmobiles. Especially when three interested riders had to compete for time on two snowmobiles.

Noah followed her to the kitchen and leaned against the counter where J.R. sat when he was younger. It was almost like someone had whispered in Noah's ear and told him where to stand. "Now that you've had time to process tell me what you're thinking."

Annie pressed into the butter with the wooden spoon. It gave in easier than usual. She checked the refrigerator to make sure she hadn't adjusted the temperature with an accidental bump. It was exactly as she set it. Just in case, Annie set her hand on the milk carton. It still felt cold to the touch. Annie shrugged away her confusion and returned to pressing the butter. "I haven't thought about it."

"Not at all," Noah arched an eyebrow in challenge.

"Not at all," Annie echoed. She added the sugar and the vanilla into the smashed butter. As she stirred the ingredients, she added, "I planned my next shopping trip in Great Falls." There she hadn't lied.

"Really?" Noah inhaled. "So, you didn't think anything like perhaps we lied to you?"

"Not until you mentioned it." Annie thought it was one of their setups. Jesse made a plan, and Noah was there to talk her into it. There was one problem. Neither considered the most important detail: being in love. Sure, she loved Noah. But not the happily ever after, I'll take care of you when you are sick kind of love. She did that once and failed. Despite her efforts, her begging him to stay with her, Jesse died anyway.

"Or, maybe we aren't playing fair?" Noah talked like Jesse stood beside him in the room.

Annie pointed with the wooden spoon. "Stop it, Noah. Just stop it. Your logic will not work on me this time."

Noah tilted his face away from her and covered his smile with his hand.

"This is not funny." Annie cracked the first egg. She hit the bowl too hard, and the egg slid down the side of the bowl and oozed onto the countertop.

Noah placed his hands on her hip and eased her to the side. "Let me help you with this." He tapped the egg on the bowl, pressed his finger on the weak spot, and separated the shell. The egg plopped into the mixture. His eyes searched the kitchen and focused when he found what he was looking for. He opened the lid of the trash and deposited the empty shell.

Annie grabbed a paper towel and wiped up the mess she made.

"You were saying," Noah pressed.

"Did you know the first time Jesse and I were together, I got pregnant? The first time." Her eyes widened in shock. First at the outcome of an awkward encounter that was in no way romantic; and then for the subsequent understanding of it being their miracle. "In less time than it takes to bake a cake, the course of my life had been decided." They say things happen in threes. Shortly after J.R.'s birth, Jesse visited the doctor for what he thought was a urinary tract infection. He went in for an antibiotic and left with an appointment for a biopsy to test for prostate cancer. If they hadn't got pregnant when they did, Jesse and Annie wouldn't have been able to have children. Once again in a matter of minutes, the course of their life had been changed. The third time, they nicked a nerve. In less than a fraction of a second, Jesse has been rendered impotent.

"Jesse expressed mixed feelings about marriage too," Noah recalled. "Especially after the surgery."

"That didn't matter."

Except for the intimate sense of the word, Jesse and Annie were married in every way. Before everything happened, she promised Jesse in front of God and the world that she'd cherish him in all circumstances, and she held true to her word. It was hard, but it worked.

Noah's eyes widened. "That's what this is about."

Annie had mixed the dry ingredients and blended them with the butter, sugar, and egg mixture. She chose to ignore the correlation.

"We used to talk about everything. What changed, Annie?"

"Everything changed." She plopped a pile of a cookie on the pan. "You moved." She dug the spoon into the cookie dough and slapped another cookie into the pan. "Jesse moved on to a better place." She dropped the third lump with a little more force than may have been necessary. "I was the one who got left behind to deal with reality." She dipped the spoon into the bowl. Noah put his hands over hers to stop her.

"I would stay if you told me to."

"Only if I told you to. Only if I surrendered to the setup you and Jesse decided without me. Face it, Noah. You are here to test the waters. If they get too rough, you can go on to the next exciting place."

He poked at the cookie misshapen from the way Annie dropped it on the pan. "I'm here to tell you that you will blow it, Annie." Noah took a butter knife from the drawer and smoothed the edges of the cookie to make it round. "If you don't open yourself to love, you will wind up hardened and alone."

"What you mean is I will lose you?" Her heart pounded in her chest. Sure, they were at odds right now. But better times had to be on the horizon. Good always followed the bad. That was their rule.

"You'll never lose me," Noah admitted. "Things just won't be the same."

"I don't know what to tell you."

"How about this." He pulled her close and kissed her on

the forehead. "When you figure out what you want, give me a call. You know how to reach me." He turned and left her standing in the kitchen with three well-shaped cookies on a baking pan ready to be baked. Annie sighed and set the pan in the oven. She decided since she was awake, she might as well throw a load of laundry in the wash too.

55

WERE YOUR EARS BURNING?

Remnants of snow blocked her path in some places. Otherwise, the snow melt cleared Annie's path around the neighborhood enough for her to enjoy the outdoors. The chilly air burned her cheeks and invigorated her. The deeper into her walk, Annie committed herself to forgetting about Noah. If she focused on breathing and the burning in her thighs, she couldn't focus on the man that made her check her cell phone every fifteen minutes.

He hadn't called or texted to check on her. Sure, people needed space to think. But space wasn't fun unless you asserted that you needed it. She never got the chance. He just gave it to her.

Annie passed Lisa's donut shop and resisted the temptation to go inside and warm up with a cup of decaf. She had steps to make and a son to go home to. Darryl's pickup, parked behind Lisa's, beckoned her to join them in the warmth. By the time Annie reached the end of the block, she had lost her breath and motivation. She looked over at her shoulder. Darryl's pickup was still there, and the light from the window whispered for her to join them in the shop.

Annie looked down at her Fitbit. It read 9,800 steps. The walk back would help her reach her goal. Better yet, the friend time would distract her from what bothered her. She circled around at the stop sign and headed for the shop.

Darryl opened the door before Annie reached it. He greeted her with a friendly grin. "We wondered if you were coming back."

"This is the last maple bar," Lisa held it out for Annie to accept.

"I don't think I could eat," Annie admitted. Ever since her disagreement with Noah food didn't taste as good.

"That's the first thing that happens when people are in love." Darryl took the donut before Annie changed her mind. He bit into it and grinned. "Mm mm good."

"I am not in love," Annie argued.

The air in the room changed. Darryl stopped chewing. He and Lisa exchanged a glance that told Annie that she had been a recent topic of conversation. "You're not?"

"But, we saw Noah's Suburban outside your house," Lisa argued.

"That doesn't mean we're in love," Annie defended her statement.

"Yes, it does. It means Noah is courting you," Darryl replied. He said it like he was explaining how to turn on a John Deere tractor. "First, he visits you at the house with your family. After he gets their blessing, he'll take the next steps to let you know he's serious about things between you."

Annie did not like Darryl's explanation. It may have been stupid for someone her age to want hearts, and flowers, and sweet words, but that's what she had hoped for. "What happened to going on dates? You know dressing up and going to a nice place?" If Noah had been serious about her, he'd have worked to make her like him. He just passed her a permission slip from her deceased husband and expected Annie to go along with the idea. She was right to pull out of the relationship.

"Not when you have kids," Darryl explained. "He had to prove that he was there for J.R. too."

“I deserved a date. Some flowers. Something to say I was special.” In Annie’s eyes, Darryl became the proxy for Noah.

“She has a point there,” Lisa conceded.

There! Annie had someone to agree with her. She and Noah weren’t on the road to happily ever after. He came to town for a visit—albeit a long one, and she was something to distract him until he moved onto his next adventure.

Lisa poured a cup of water with cleaner into the coffee machine and pressed the button. The pot gurgled, and Lisa wiped down the counter. Darryl sat at the table in front of the counter. They resolved the argument, and they’d resume their usual positions of talking about other people’s problems.

“Doctor Flynn said Noah decided to stick around.” Darryl reached for a napkin and wiped the frosting off of his fingertips. He grinned, “I wonder what we’ll call Noah, so people will know the difference.” Like she didn’t know the man he added, “They both have the same last name.”

Usually, Annie and Darryl got along well. Today, everything the man said provoked her anger. She wished that he hadn’t eaten the donut, so she could shove it down his throat. It wasn’t bad enough that he contradicted what she said, he had to argue with her thoughts. She looked down at her Fitbit and faked horror. “Wow, I need to get more steps in.” She rose to leave and hurried before Darryl and Lisa had time to offer a valid reason for her to change her mind.

She opened the door and rushed out. In her eagerness to avoid the conversation she didn’t look before she rushed. If she had, Annie would have seen someone approaching the shop from the other side of the door.

The collision with Noah knocked her back a couple of steps. He reached out and grabbed her hand.

Darryl said, "Look at that. Of all the people who walked through the doors, it's none other than Dr. Noah Flynn. Were your ears burning?"

56

FLOWERS

Noah began the two-block walk with Annie to her house. Mrs. Peterson waved at him before she walked into the house. To the rest of the world, Noah had been there all along. They called out comments like, "You need to stop by for a beer," or "You should try my peach pie. I plan on entering it in the fair this summer." Annie thought, *Am I the only one who remembers that Noah has been gone for over fifteen years?* Even worse, he would leave again in a couple more weeks.

He walked close to Annie. Every time she tried creating space between them, he drifted closer to her until only inches separated them. He waved at Mrs. Maycomb and reached for Annie's hand. She pulled it away and scowled at him. Noah kept his eyes ahead of them when he asked, "Do you remember Emmett Taylor?"

She searched through her memories to match the face to the name.

Noah filled the silence, "He was in our class for a year in second grade. I met up with him again in medical school. We talked about coming back here and opening a practice together. The night after our graduation he met this girl. I declared it a fling... That he wanted to celebrate the years of hard work."

Annie kept silent. So far, his story failed to impress her.

"Six months later Emmett married her, and they moved to her hometown. They have three kids, a bulldog and spend their weekends barbecuing and going to athletic events."

The plot twist caught Annie by surprise. Guilt poked at her shoulder for considering a fling when Noah first arrived. When they reached her front yard, she saw Noah's Suburban parked in front of the house. Annie thought about what Darryl said and groaned. At this rate, nobody would believe her if she said that they were friends who platonically reconnected.

"Thanks for walking with me." She took the first step. "I should get dinner ready."

Noah nodded okay and waved to her as she walked into the house. She opened the door and made her way to the kitchen. Annie pulled off her coat and mittens and set them on the back of the couch. She made it halfway to the kitchen when she rebuked her laziness. *How are you going to yell at J.R. about tidiness if you can't follow your own rules?* She picked up her coat and headed for the closet. J.R hanged his red letterman jacket. Annie added her coat to the rows of winter gear and headed for J.R.'s room. She peeked around the corner and saw her son wearing a pair of headphones and typing on his laptop. Annie avoided noticing the socks on the floor and kissed him on the top of his head.

J.R. pulled off the headphones. “Hey, Mom!” For someone in the middle of a pile of homework, he was in a pleasant mood.

“We need chaperones for the school dance. I told Mrs. Smith to call you. I'm letting you know so you wouldn't be surprised when the call came.”

Ahhh, he was trying to butter her up. "How are you going to dance?"

"I talked to Noah. He told me people's lives change when they don't go to dances." J.R.'s eyes widened as though he recalled a horror story. "I'm not living a life of regret. I'm going to that dance."

Annie held in her chuckle. "Thanks for letting me know about the call. What do you want for dinner?"

"Noah brought chili and rolls by earlier."

"He what?" Hearing that Noah brought food to the house angered Annie. He and J.R. formed an alliance against her too. While she should have been surprised she wasn't. The low key conversations and laughs from inside jokes were beginning to make sense.

"I called to talk to him about the prom. He brought the food when we talked."

She planned to call Noah as soon as she finished her conversation with J.R. She needed to set boundaries for Noah and her son.

"Don't be mad at him, Mom. I called him." J.R. was so in tune with her emotions she didn't have to say a word. It astounded her. Sometimes they were on opposite poles, yet he could detect the slightest shift in her emotions.

"I'm not angry," she said. She touched her hair to make sure none of it had loosened from her top bun. Her hair went wild when her emotions were left unchecked. Annie corrected her lie. "Yes, I am. But I'll get over it."

"Why are you giving him such a hard time, Mom? It's obvious he is into you. You should give the guy a chance."

"I wish it were that easy, son."

"I don't mean to sound like one of those mushy novels. It should be simple. He digs you. You think he's nice. You think his jokes are funny and he likes doing things for you. How complicated does it have to get?" He shook his head, "I thought old people had things like love and family figured out."

His assessment of love and relationships beyond thirty tickled Annie. "Are you saying I'm old?"

He shrugged. "You're closer to old than me."

Annie tousled J.R.'s hair. His straightforward approach to problems mirrored how she would have talked to him. Hearing her wisdom echoed back softened her foul mood. "I'll keep that in mind, son."

J.R. put the headphones back on and read through the document on his laptop screen. With the conversation coming to a comfortable close, Annie made her way to the kitchen. The bouquet of yellow roses on her table stopped her in her tracks. She wanted to go back and ask J.R. about them. She found the card and read the message. "Flowers for our first fight. I Love You. Noah."

She tried hardening her heart toward him. Instead, her heart replayed them kissing in front of the kitchen sink. It was a losing battle. Her feelings for him overpowered her will to maintain a safe distance from him. Annie wished Noah were there. If he were, she'd run into his arms and hug him and kiss him the way a woman kisses a man when she is happy to not be angry with him anymore. But, he wasn't there, and she was left alone to replay the scene in her mind. Her indignation had burned away, and all that remained was the sense of loss and loneliness.

A gentle knock on the door pulled her out of the moment. Annie guessed that it was Darryl stopping by to check on her. She prepared what she would say to threaten him if he told Noah anything she said. Instead, she saw Noah on the other side of the opened door. Annie rushed to him; wrapped her arms around his shoulders; and snuggled into his neck.

He pulled out of the hug and gazed into Annie's eyes. His voice sounded hoarse from the mixture of remorse and regret. "I learn from my mistakes, Annie. I won't be quiet about how I feel about you anymore. Everyone will know that I am in love with you. If I have to, I will hire a plane, and have it written in the sky."

Annie raised her face to him. Noah pressed his lips to hers with such force there were no misunderstandings about how he felt about her. He wrapped his arms around her waist and pulled her closer to him.

The need to be as close to Noah as possible replaced the tension Annie used to fight him. She committed every sensation, every taste, every sound to memory. This was a moment she intended to embrace and burn into her soul. Noah softened the kiss. He caressed her bottom lip with his thumb as he pulled away from Annie.

He rested his forehead against hers, and they relished each being in each other's presence. The sound of Darryl honking the horn on his pickup and yelling "I told you so," out his window brought them back to reality. With reality, the cold Annie ignored brought goosebumps to her arm. "Let's get you into where it's warm." Noah ushered Annie into the house.

They hadn't made it to the kitchen when J.R. wheeled his way into the hallway. When he saw Noah, a broad smile took over his face. He sounded half surprised when he said, "You were right, flowers get them every time."

57

TRUTH OR DARE

"I have something else for you." Noah left the door open as he made his way to his pickup. Annie threw J.R. a questioning glance that asked if he knew what was going on. J.R. shrugged his ignorance. Entranced by curiosity, the both of them watched and waited.

Smiles of recognition replaced their confusion when Noah appeared from the back of his pickup with a pie in his hand. "I hope it's my favorite flavor," Annie gushed.

"I'd be happy with any flavor of Peggy's pie," J.R. replied.

Noah crossed through the door opening and said, "Let the record show, I also cooked dinner."

"Mom, can you start an argument with him by lunch tomorrow?" J.R. wheeled ahead of Noah and Annie into the kitchen.

"Your mom doesn't like to argue," Noah answered J.R.'s question.

J.R. stopped so abruptly Annie almost ran into him. "How do you know that?"

"When we were kids, she'd run away if your dad or I said anything mean to her."

"It that why Dad talk talked like that?" J.R. asked Annie.

"Like what?"

"His voice would get soft like he didn't want to scare a kitten."

"He did not," Annie objected.

"Another thing about your mother. Don't tell her she's sensitive. She doesn't like it."

"I am not." Annie's mouth fell open.

"I wish you'd have come around sooner." J.R. waited by the cabinet so Annie could pass him the bowls to set on the table. After Noah talked to him about helping out, J.R. sought out ways to help her.

When everything was on the table, he set a deck of cards by his plate. "We should play a game of truth or dare. Hearts and spades are truth. Clubs and diamonds are dares."

"This sounds like we're asking for trouble." Annie frowned.

"I have a broken leg. How much trouble can we get into? J.R. held out his hands facing up.

"It'll be rated G," Noah added.

"Definitely," J.R. admitted.

"Okay, a couple rounds and then we have to get ready for tomorrow," Annie agreed.

"Good, you go first." J.R. held out a card for her to choose.

She grimaced as she displayed the two of diamonds. Annie could already guess the dare. He was going to dare her to let him use the car or something crazy like that.

J.R. face beamed with his cat that ate the canary grin. "I dare you to go out on a date with Noah. One without me."

"Ooh, that is good," Noah answered. "I like this game."

Annie glared at Noah who held his hands up in surrender.

"I just said I like it. I didn't put him up to it."

Her voice tightened when she acknowledged the dare. "I can do that."

Her son's smirk said, "You're welcome," to the unspoken thank you from Noah.

It was Noah's turn. He pulled out the ten of hearts. Truth.

"What's the scariest thing you've ever done?"

Why does he get the easy questions? Annie's mind drifted to figure out ways to get out of the game.

"Come home," Noah admitted.

Annie didn't understand his answer. Home was supposed to be the safest place to go, not the heart of a person's fears.

"You were right, Annie. I had to come home because I wanted to be here. Not because of anything you said. I begin working in my uncle's office next week."

J.R.'s mouth fell open. His mouth formed the word, wow, but it didn't produce any sound.

Her heart raced. Noah was coming home because he wanted to be there. She wasn't the anchor that held him from what he wanted.

She worked for an accountant's office that was in the same building as his uncle's practice. "If you have time, we can meet up for lunch sometimes."

His face, tightened in anticipation of her response, softened with her answer. He reached over and squeezed Annie's hand. "I'd like that."

She tightened her hand to hold his for a moment longer. "We can plan what we'll bring to share."

A vision of them sitting at the park across the street from the building came to her. Rays of sun poked through the trees created a soft light for them. Noah was talking about something, and Annie smiled in amusement at whatever it was he said. She blinked away the vision and took a hard look at Noah and J.R. to identify which one had cast the spell on her.

"Your turn," Noah took the deck from J.R. and displayed the card for him to choose one.

J.R. picked up and revealed the card. It was a joker. "It's a bye."

"A what?"

"He gets to skip this round." Noah examined the card for any distinguishing marks. He passed it to Annie. "It looks like all the other cards." She rubbed the edge and compared it to the other cards to determine if there were any difference. It felt like all the other cards.

"We should get a handle on these dishes." J.R. swiped at the card and returned it to the deck.

Annie threw her son a suspicious glare. He stacked three bowls on his lap and headed for the sink before a rebuke came to her. The concerned expression remained for a moment longer. Somewhere along the way she was at the beginning stages of admitting to herself that she might be in love with Noah Flynn. Even worse, she didn't know what to do about it.

58

BARN DANCE

The stack of clothes on Annie's bed grew by the minute. Her blouse was too pink. Why did the jeans she used to love make her hips appear too wide? She cast aside a top that made her pooch stick out too much. J.R. who had been fitted for a walking cast limped by her doorway. He raised his eyebrow to question the mess. Pointing at the shirt at the bottom of the stack he said, "Wear your favorite shirt."

"I wear it too many times." Annie pulled a beige plaid shirt out of the closet. "Maybe this will blend better with whatever Noah's wearing?" Lace eyelet was sown over the buttonholes and the edges of the pocket. Before J.R. replied she said, "It's too summery," and put it back in the closet.

"Guys just pick clothes that are clean and match. I did not understand what women went through." A knock on the door pulled at his attention. "I'll go get it." He turned to leave and peeked back in through the door. "You look good in what you have on right now. Trust me. I know what men like." He disappeared from her field of vision, but she heard his clunky steps down the hall to the door.

Annie sighed and resigned herself to the blue chambray

top and jeans with lace stitching on the pockets. She could only hope that she didn't spill anything on her outfit.

When Noah's eyes brightened in appreciation of her outfit, she released the breath she had been holding in. J.R. was right about her choice of attire.

"There are rules," J.R.'s voice took on a mock serious tone. "No coming home before 11 p.m." He held up two fingers. "If a guy checks out your date you have my permission to take care of him. And last but not least, don't do anything I wouldn't do." He grinned. "I got that last one from an episode of Star Trek. I've been dying to use it."

Noah chuckled and pat J.R. on the back. "We're going to the Prairie House."

"In that case," J.R. added, "Bring home leftovers." He pointed at his mother. "I don't care what happens between the two of you. I still get dibs on half your plate."

Noah held the door open for Annie. She was about to comment on the change in the way he treated her when he smiled and said, "J.R. is watching, I need to make a good impression." He also fastened her seat belt and waved at J.R. who stood in front of the picture window until they pulled away.

When they were on the highway, Noah handed Annie a thin spiral notebook and a pen. "The Prairie House is an hour away. You'll have time to work on this."

"You want me to write an essay?" Annie opened to the first page of the book

"I want you to write your bucket list in there."

"Bucket list?"

"Things you want to do before you're too old to try them." Noah pointed out the page he dog-eared. "There's mine."

Annie flipped the page back. "Kiss Annie like I mean it," had been crossed out. Beneath it he had written: go to a country dance, hike to many glaciers, have dinner on a train, go skydiving. See Machu Picchu, have a glass of wine near the Eiffel tower, and tell a woman you love her had also been crossed off. The worn edges of the page hinted at the age of the list. Noah had had it for quite some time. Annie wondered who the woman was. Even more unnerving was the jealousy that struck her.

The sun, in the beginning stages of setting, cast colors as a backdrop for the restaurant. The rows of trees around the restaurant glowed with white led lights. Annie caught her breath in awe at the fleeting beauty they were lucky enough to capture.

Noah took her by the hand and guided her to the door of the restaurant. He released her hand to hold the door open for her. When she looked back, she noticed how dashing he looked in his button-down shirt accented with a leather vest. The paisley pattern on his shirt pulled at her eyes. Like her, he chose clothes in the blue color scheme.

After they ordered their food, he flipped the book open to Annie's bucket list. He wrote the heading at the top of the page. "Annie's To Do's"

Annie wondered if there were lists from other women in front of Noah's list. She sat silently and watched for his reaction as he read through her list.

"Both of us want to visit Glacier. That's a trip we can combine." He grinned in satisfaction. "I never thought of the Hot Springs. I might add that to my list."

"Add it?" Annie asked.

"Yes, add it." Noah said, "The adventures don't end because you crossed one off." He flipped two pages back to show a list of ten items he crossed through and marked as completed.

Dread filled Annie's chest. Maybe it wasn't a good idea for

Noah to come home.

"What was that?" he inquired.

"What?"

"Your face. It changed. Like something bad happened."

"What if you regret coming home? Most people are content with living in one place. It's like this world isn't big enough to hold you."

The world is big enough to make me appreciate being home, Annie." He took her hand in his, "Sure Paris is beautiful, but the people aren't as friendly as home. They don't wave at each other as they pass each other on the road. And they'll yell at someone for getting stuck on the road before they stop to help him." He caressed her hand, "Home is where you go, and people tell you in little ways that you belong."

His touch soothed her, and all her concerns drifted. Country music played in the background. "We're here to accomplish one item on the list." Noah kept his eyes on hers. "It's country dance night."

"You've been to a country dance," Annie flushed. They had several barn dances every summer.

"But not with the woman on the next line."

Annie remembered the jealousy she felt earlier and blushed. "Oh,"

"We can sneak one dance in before dinner gets to the table." He held his hand out for her to accept.

"Sure." There was no reason for Annie to be flustered. She'd been to country dances, and she'd known Noah all her life. The combination of the two familiarities changed the experience to being something new.

They stood at the edge of the dance floor and watched other people. The next thing Annie knew, Lennie Archer was at her side. She noticed that he was dressed better than the last time she saw him.

Noah caressed her arm and whispered in her ear, "We should get out there before I have to follow through with J.R.'s second rule for dating his mother." His voice sent shivers of anticipation through Annie. The change in her must have sent a signal because Lennie slid a few steps away from Annie.

The tempo changed to a slow song. Noah's left hand rested on Annie's waist, and he held out her hand with his right. They moved in rhythm with the music. His right foot stepped back signaling that he was getting ready to twirl Annie. She fell into step with him. She laughed mid-twirl and the chain that had bound her heart broke. When the twirl completed, he pulled her closer to him, and his hand dropped to her lower back.

Somewhere between the twirl and her landing in his arms, Annie changed. She was in love with Noah Flynn.

Annie swam in the sound of Noah's voice. "I know those eyes. Someone is happy."

Her body hummed with the happiness she thought she'd never feel again.

"I am too," he added.

She rested her head on Noah's chest, and he sighed in contentment. Noah whispered, "You know what would make me happier."

"What?" Annie asked.

"If you'd promise to dance with me for the rest of our lives."

Annie stiffened in surprise.

The sincerity of his request changed his voice. "I'd make every wish on your list come true."

"Why do I believe you, Noah?"

"Because it's true."

Her loudest objection came to mind. She was set up by all

the men in her life: Jesse, Noah, and J.R. Where was her say in the matter?

You can be right, or you can be happy. She said it more than once to Jesse when he worried about their marriage. Most of the times he was right about the limitations of their relationship. But they didn't damper Annie's love for Jesse. They chose happy and embraced it.

Sure, Annie was right. Jesse and Noah had set her up. And, J.R. joined the bandwagon. All of them worked to bend her heart in Noah's direction. But what would she gain by sticking to her stance on being right?

"We can take it slow," Noah's whisper sent warm shivers down her spine. "I'll wait for you to love me."

Their plan worked. She saw a future with Noah. Her mind's eye saw an older version of him smiling at her after sharing a funny story. She saw him handing her an iced tea as he sat beside her in the stands at the rodeo. The wisdom of choosing happiness changed her. She chuckled. "I already love you, Noah."

He purred, "I mean the way a woman loves a man when she's willing to take his name."

With the awareness of the change within her, a smile spread across Annie's face. "I love you, Noah."

Noah stiffened and froze. He pulled away, set his hands on Annie's shoulders, and searched her eyes. "I'm talking spend the rest of your life with me love, Annie."

Annie nibbled on her bottom lip and shrugged. "That's what I thought I was saying."

Noah straightened and cupped Annie's cheeks with his hands before leaning in to kiss her. The people around them hooted, hollered, and clapped. Noah ended the kiss and wrapped his arms around Annie's shoulders. He called out loud enough for everyone to hear, "I finally got myself a wife."

59

EPILOGUE

The softness in J.R.'s voice woke Annie from her nap. Her eyes cracked open to see her teenage son, holding her newborn child. "Remember you wear blue and gray when you are in the stands. When I make a basket, we'll do something like an air high five." J.R. held up his hand like he was high fiving. The baby nestled in his other arm didn't move. J.R. said, "We'll have time to practice."

Annie held in the chuckle, and it warmed her. If someone would have told her four years ago that she'd be happy again, she'd have laughed. But here she was in a hospital bed recuperating from childbirth.

J.R. looked up at her and grinned softly. "I hope you don't mind. After watching that little show, it'll be a while before I decide to have a kid."

"Speaking from someone who has seen the after, I can say it was worth it."

Annie couldn't be sure, but she though J.R. teared up. He quickly averted his gaze to his little brother. "I have to warn you. Our mother is worse than professional paparazzi. I can say with confidence she will save and share all your embarrassing moments."

"Embarrassing and cute are in the eye of the beholder." Annie pushed on her elbow to get into a sitting position.

"And, then she'll say something like that to make you feel better. Pretend it works. It'll make life easier." Annie and J.R. giggled at his comment.

"You're going to be a great older brother."

J.R. nodded, "You're a great mom."

Noah's voice bled in the door. "Who would have thought both of our kids would be in the same class."

The other voice sounded just as proud. "Their teachers are going to have their hands full." She recognized it was Jorgen Backman. His wife, Pam, came in shortly after Annie to deliver their baby.

"Oh, the stories we'll have to share when you come home to visit," Annie said in response to the conversation outside the door.

J.R. kept his eyes on his brother, but Annie could tell by the tone of his voice he was talking to her. "I love small-town stories. When I hear one I know I'm home."

Noah stepped into the room. "I know exactly what you mean."

60

AUTHOR'S NOTE 4.20.2020

This story started as a dare. I was on a running down our dirt road and the song "Jesse's Girl" was in the play list. Forty years after I heard Jesse's Girl, I had a rude awakening. Jesse and his girl were, ahem, intimate. When the song released, my naive twelve year old mind did not process the meaning behind, "She's loving him with that body."

I took my discovery to Facebook. A friend challenged me to write a short story inspired by the song. The theme, two friends are in love with the same girl, isn't anything new. But I had a twist. I wrote the story and shared it with my readers. I told them it was a challenge. I told them it was a short story. They sent me emails. "I looked on Amazon for the book. Where is the rest of the story?"

The original short story was added to my *Small Town Spring* Compilation, and here is a novella expanding on the relationship of Noah and Annie.

There is something I can relate to in all my characters. With Annie it was her love of pie (and of course raising teenagers). Many times, in our small town, hurt feelings have been soothed by a baked good. It is hard to hold on to hurt feelings when you're munching on a fresh baked cookie or pastry.

As I write this note, I thought I'd add we are in the throes of isolation caused by the COVID-19 virus. A trend that we don't brag about but is happening is the drive by baked good giving. A friend will send a message, or a text, or a post on Facebook about being sad. Several of us do this thing where we fill a Tupperware container with baked goods and leave it on the front door. As the recipient of cookies (that my husband ate while I wasn't looking) I can say it reiterates that love always finds a way to touch the heart.

Lastly, because of my remote style, I am active on social media. Visit me on Facebook, or my website. If you'd like a biweekly dose of sweet stories, sign up for my reader list. The places you can find me will be on the back of the book.

I'll close this note thanking you for your review. A few words about what you liked helps other people decide if this story would suit their tastes.

Okay, I spoke too soon. This is the real last thought/message. I send you off with warm wishes. Wishes for smiles, positive affirmations, and lots of baked goods.

Until the next note,

xoxo

Merri

PART IV

JUST A FRIEND

61

IN LOVE WITH A PERFECT STRANGER

Nancy linked her elbow with Pam's in anticipation of what they'd encounter on the other side of the doors of the Forty-Ninth Parallel. The state's newest micro-brewery had been open for less than a month. They'd heard about it and planned to go several times. Now, it was really happening.

Pam threw a cursory glance at the parking lot. Rows of pickups and cars parked neatly in the gravel area around the entrance promised that the excursion was sure to meet her expectations. The business that brewed beer from local barley had won the unofficial vote of approval from the community. In a matter of minutes, she'd be able to tell why.

As soon they passed through the front door, Pam sensed it was more than a place to go for good beer. It had a home away from home vibe. The cement floor was painted a soft brown and everything was made of wood and accented with tempered steel. A glass wall separated the people from vats of beer in the back corner that held the golden mixtures. Pam counted three and guessed there were three behind the ones she could see.

She craned her neck to get a better look at what was going on. Groups of people gathered around tables either cheered or groaned at something or someone out of Pam's field of vision. Other people rolled their eyes while others held their hands up as if to say, "I should have known."

Nancy stopped at a popcorn machine and scooped out two bags of the snack for each of them. "It's almost as good as the stuff they sell in the movie theaters." She passed a bag to Pam. "Go ahead try a bite." Nancy threw a couple of kernels of popcorn into her mouth and waited for Pam to do the same.

Pam tossed a couple of kernels in her mouth. The light salt and hints of butter complemented the airy taste. "You're right."

"I always am," Nancy responded in a playful tone.

Another round of commotion caught their attention. Both women stepped deeper into the room. As soon as she saw the images projected on the big screen, Nancy smiled in recognition. "I forgot it is Trivia Pursuit night. Noah mentioned something about it."

Their friend Noah, who mentioned the outing, bailed out of the excursion. Determined to have some fun before the winter weather kept them homebound for the season, Pam and Nancy went without him.

From the size of the crowd, Pam sensed it was a wise choice. With little publicity the place was packed. She scanned the room and noticed the vats behind a glass wall. Her eyes returned to the general seating area. There wasn't an empty table in the room. She noticed the thickness of the wood that made the tables. Noah mentioned the furniture was made from recycled materials from around the community. A heavy lacquer glossed over the tables added to the rustic vibe.

Nancy and Pam made their way to the only two empty seats at a table at the far end of the room. Three men who looked like they were related took up the other seats at the long bench style table. Two of them looked down at their cell phones. If anyone were to ask, Pam would have guessed that they were father and sons. The older of the three commented on the question projected on the big screen. "How many counties do we have in Montana?" Beneath the question, four shapes had a different answer. Without having to think, Pam answered, "Fifty-six." She had read about it in the newspaper earlier in the day.

The guy sitting beside her looked like a model for the men of Montana magazine. He was rugged with a hint of I'd like to fix your flat tire if you'd let me. Pam couldn't help liking him. When he said, "Are you sure about that?" her impression of him changed. He was too full of himself to get attached.

"Why do men second guess women when it comes to geography? If the question was something like where the closest shopping mall is, you'd take my answer without any argument."

He arched his eyebrows in amusement. "Okay, fifty-six it is."

After she said it, Pam wished she could have taken back the attitude behind the words. If given a do over, she would have removed some of the why are men shallow from the tone in her voice and replace it with some sass.

When the answer of fifty-six came up on the screen, he grinned as though he were proud of her. "You know your Montana history." When his response lacked the unspoken, "for a woman." Pam found herself liking him again.

That was all the time he had to make an impression because the next question came up on the screen. "How long were Gilligan and his friends supposed to be on the boat?" The four possible answers appeared beneath the question. Just as

Pam was about to lean forward to see what answer he chose, the waitress approached her for her order. Pam temporarily pushed away the decision saying, "You go first Nancy, I want to know the answer."

"It's three hours," the man replied and pressed a square on his cell phone.

"Who is Gilligan?"

"The guy from Gilligan's Island. This group took an ocean tour and ended up stranded on a tropical island for years."

The story was new to Pam. She got lost in his ocean blue eyes and wished that she was stranded with the man who made her heart race every time he spoke.

"I ordered a flight, so you can sample all the flavors," Nancy's voice interrupted the conversation. Something in her tone chilled the warm feeling in Pam's chest.

"I'm sorry what did you say?" Pam directed her attention back to her friend. With the shift of attention, the sound, and colors of the room around her returned. For the couple of minutes, she and the man chatted, the rest of the world disappeared. Oddly, Pam felt at ease with the sensation.

"Since you didn't know what you wanted, I got you a little of everything," Nancy replied. She stopped talking and wrinkled her brow in concern. "Are you okay?"

"Yeah, sure. Why do you ask?"

"You seem a little out of it." Nancy shifted her glance, and recognition of something crossed her face. "Oh"

Pam never had the chance to ask her what "oh" meant. The man, who with each ticking of the second hands on the clock was transforming into her future husband, tapped her on the shoulder. "Okay, the goddess of geography, what is the area of Montana?"

She didn't have to think hard. The numbers in the other

choices were too large or too small. "147,040 miles," she answered.

His blue eyes sparkled and took on the shine of sapphire as he tapped the answer. "No wonder it's been so hard for me to find a wife. The state's too big!"

Pam knew then and there she was in love with a perfect stranger, and there was nothing anybody could do about it.

62

THE LADIES ROOM

The game was too fun not to play. From one question to the next the participant's rankings changed. Apparently, the timing of the response mattered as well.

During one of the pauses between the questions, the handsome hunk who remained by her side during the game introduced himself. "My name is Jorgen. I live on a farm outside of Ashbrook. What's your name?"

"A farmer?" Pam matched his body structure with his proclaimed profession. He had to have thrown a lot of hay bales to get a chest that broad.

"Yes. And you are?"

"I am?" Maybe it was something in his voice, or the rich blue in his eyes that threw her off. Intrigued to figure out what it was, Pam had forgotten the question.

"This is the part where you tell me your name. Or you make up one, so I can't find you on social media." He grinned.

"Pam. My name is Pam. I'm a nurse at the senior living center."

"So that's where they hide all the pretty women." He nodded his approval, and they were on to the next question.

The chatting went back and forth between the people at the table who Pam learned also lived in or around Ashbrook. William, the older gentleman who she guessed was Jorgen's father, joked cordially with Jorgen and another man named Sam. Like Jorgen, Sam's eyes caught Pam's attention, but his salty personality made it difficult for her to admire him or them.

From their conversation, she learned the three men worked together but lived on separate farms. And, contrary to her initial impression, William was not Jorgen's actual father. But, something deeper than they cared to reveal forged the paternal like bond between them. When they weren't playing the game, all three men bantered back and forth about stories they had lived together in the past.

Unfamiliar with the people, Pam felt more at ease experiencing the stories as an observer. When they included Nancy, she presented her way of avoiding situations. "I have to go to the bathroom." She stood to leave and waited for Pam to join her. Pam checked on her glass to find that both of their glasses were empty. It wasn't until she rose to her feet that Pam's bladder forced her to admit that she too shared the need to use the ladies' room.

She politely excused herself, wrapped her purse around her shoulder, and motioned to speak.

Nancy pulled on Pam's elbow and practically dragged her to the bathroom. As soon as the door closed behind them, she wagged her finger at Pam. "You can look at the pretty man, but you cannot touch."

"What are you talking about?" Pam tried to hide the obvious by taking an interest in the paper towel dispenser. The man who had kept her attention for most of the evening was even more tempting than one of those dark chocolate squares that came wrapped in gold foil.

"Jorgen Backman is known as Jorgy Porgy in three counties."

"Jorgy Porgy?" She scrunched her face. The nickname made no sense.

"The nursery rhyme. Georgie Porgy pudding and pie. Kissed the girls and made them cry." Nancy tilted her hand and waved her fingers towards Pam as though she were trying to summon the ending of the poem out of Pam's mouth.

"She isn't kidding." A woman closed the stall door behind her. "He broke my best friend's heart."

Pam's mouth fell open.

The woman added. "What made it worse was Jorgen knew another guy wanted to go out with her."

Pam had heard about small towns being hotbeds for drama, but never in a million years did she imagine she'd witness it firsthand. "This sounds like an episode of *As the Wheat Spins*."

Just as Pam turned to walk away from the conversation, the woman added, "Oh, Jorgen's been different ever since. But my theory is a tiger doesn't ever really lose its stripes. Jorgen knows how to catch a woman but doesn't know what to do once he gets her."

Pam had no idea on how to handle the dump of information from a stranger. What was her motive for trashing a man's reputation?

"By the way, this is Amanda," Nancy introduced the woman who was quick to join the conversation. "She is cousins with Marianna who works in the intensive living unit of the senior center."

If things weren't confusing enough, the women just added a layer to the tapestry of small town life. Pam was friendly with Marianna which meant the odds of her running into Amanda were inevitable. Whether or not she liked it, she was friends by association with the hot guy's enemies. "Everyone is related here." Pam was still learning the ins and outs of small town living. How it was possible for any of them to not marry a cousin eluded her.

"Pretty much," Amanda nodded to confirm her statement.

"So, Jorgen is a no go?" Her heart hurt when she said it. Before she was aware his background, he seemed like a guy she'd want to spend more time with.

Both women nodded.

"Okay, I won't talk to him anymore." It felt like someone pinched her in the middle of her chest. She motioned to go into the stall.

"Whoa, whoa, whoa, whoa." Both Nancy and Amanda rushed to stop her.

"You can't be rude to him," Nancy corrected.

"Well, you can," Amanda added. She raised her left eyebrow in amusement of the imagined situation. Her facial expression relaxed, and Amanda returned to the position of a neutral person in the matter. "But, you'll find yourself regretting it the first time he has to help you with something. And, that definitely will happen at some point in time."

Pam had grown tired of the conversation. She wanted. No, she needed to move on to a more constructive topic.

"Jorgen and I have never been fond of each other, but we respect each other. It goes back to when we were on the playground in elementary school." Amanda held up her hands like they were scale balances. "Yet, if there is a fire, Jorgen will be at my house with all the other volunteer firefighters trying to save my belongings." She tilted her hands to demonstrate the shift in power, "And every couple of years, I'll have one of his cousins in my high school English class."

It made sense to Pam. Jorgen and Amanda hadn't seen eye to eye on a lot of things. Jorgen probably had something about

Amanda's history that she knew would come out. So, Amanda was getting her side of the story in first. Pam wouldn't have approached the situation that way, but she wasn't the type to judge a person until a situation tested them and proved what they were made of. "Okay, be nice, but not too nice." It was going to be how she handled both Jorgen and Amanda.

"Yes," both women nodded.

"Now, can I go to the bathroom?"

Nancy and Amanda startled as though they had just been reminded why they went to the restroom in the first place.

"Sure. I'll wait out here for you," Nancy offered.

Less than ten minutes ago, she was close to falling in love with the man. It didn't make sense, but she felt connected to Jorgen. In the short time they had been together, she felt at ease with him. For once, she hadn't had to try to be funny or impressive. She also admired the way he revered his friends, especially William. However, she also believed in heeding warnings. A great amount of heartache came her way because she ignored her family's concerns about her ex-boyfriend Mark.

In the short amount of time she had been in the ladies' room Pam had changed her mind. There was nothing that could make her want to have anything to do with Jorgen or his troublesome group of friends.

63

JUST A FRIEND

After the conversation in the ladies' room, Pam and Nancy opted for a change of scenery. Rather than go back to the table with Jorgen and his friends, the two women headed outdoors. They found a place to sit around the stone fire pit built in the middle of an open area behind the brewery.

The stars above them shimmered, but the absence of stars in the distance warned of the chance of change. The weather system they had a twenty percent chance of seeing might make an appearance.

Pam and Nancy relaxed in lawn chairs and blended in with the activity around them. On the other side of the fire, a local musician played his guitar and encouraged people to sing along with the song he played. Pam, who didn't know the words to the song, enjoyed listening to Nancy cut loose. Her friend belted out the lyrics like she had been the original performer of the song.

Off in the corner of the fenced clearing, a group of people played a game of bags. From where Pam sat, it looked like an easy game. The concept was simple enough: throw bean bag twenty-five feet away and try to make it into a small hole carved out of a piece of board propped at a twenty-degree angle. If the bag landed on the board, the person who threw it earned a point. If the bag landed in the hole, the person earned three points. Either the people had a microbrew beer induced loss of perception, or the game was harder than the concept. They needed to get to twenty-one points to win. Neither team was anywhere near that number.

Just as she was commenting to Nancy about the game, Jorgen approached her. "We need a fourth. Want to join us?" William, Michael, and Sam waited behind him. Sam's eye roll said what he was thinking. "This one has it bad."

Pam's head whispered the warning, "You're supposed to say no." Her heart, however, jumped into action. The next thing she knew, Pam rose to join them. "Yes, that sounds like fun." She shifted her attention toward the unused game setup to avoid the "I warned you" look, Nancy, tried to throw her way.

In Pam's defense, it was too easy to ignore Nancy in Jorgen's presence. The man didn't have to say a word. Something about him demanded all of Pam's attention. Perhaps it was the easy grin. Or, it could have been the pleasant fragrance of his cologne. Whatever it was she felt compelled to move closer to him.

Jorgen wrapped his arm around Pam's shoulder as he guided her their side of the game. "We don't have much to worry about. Sam can't throw to save his life. And, odds are William will get bored and fake throwing out his back when they start losing."

She learned quickly. Playing bags was harder than it looked. They had stopped drinking beer and moved on to the root beer and ginger ale that was also made by the microbrewery. It didn't matter. Alcohol or the lack thereof had little influence on Pam's throwing skills. Her bags either fell short of the board or off to the side of it. One time when she tossed the bag, Sam had to jump to dodge her throw. Jorgen and William burst out laughing. Even Nancy thought it was funny. Through laughter, she said, "I didn't know you could move that fast, Sam."

As though to prove his sour attitude, Sam showed Nancy that he thought she was number one with the wrong finger. That just made her laugh even harder. "You better hope you don't ever have to come to me to get that hand fixed."

Sam hid his hand behind his back, and Nancy stuck her tongue out at him. It was obvious to Pam that the two of them were longtime friends. If anyone else had been that rude, Nancy would have given them a different kind of scolding.

When the game ended, as Jorgen predicted, with a bad back complaint, Nancy suggested they leave. "I don't want to ruin your fun, but I have to go in for my shift in the morning."

Jorgen, William, and Sam began the goodbyes that took them to the door. Ten minutes after they started to leave, Pam and Nancy found themselves in the parking lot separating to go to their cars. The door opened abruptly behind them, and Jorgen appeared.

He called out, "Pam, can I talk to you for a quick second."

Nancy raised her eyebrow in warning.

"I had a good time hanging out with you tonight. I was wondering if you wanted to go out for dinner or something like that."

Pam grimaced. She wanted to say yes. He was attractive and funny and charming. However, Nancy who positioned herself out of his field of vision shook her head. To make her point known she mouthed the word, "No," several times and waved her hand to say cut him off.

Fighting to resist her friend's disapproval of Jorgen, Pam replied, "I had a lot of fun with you."

Nancy waved both of her arms to say stop.

Pam fought to keep the struggle hidden. She did want to go out with Jorgen. He was sweet, and funny, and didn't seem to mind that Pam was her own person. Carefully measuring her words to leave room for a second request later, she said, "It's just that I'm not looking for a boyfriend right now. I think it would be better if we were just friends."

Nancy released a giant sigh of relief. Pam felt like she just walked away from a cookie jar with a carrot stick in her hand. While her decision may have been healthy in her friend's eyes, it didn't bring Pam any satisfaction. She just turned down the only man who had ever had the power to make time and space fade into background noise.

Jorgen shrugged his resignation, "If that's the way you want it, that's the way it'll be."

"That's the way I want it," Pam said it more for herself than him. It wasn't the way she wanted it, but her friend knew more about who they were dealing with.

Just then a flake of snow landed on Pam's cheek. She touched the spot where it landed and looked up at the sky. The diamonds that decorated their evening were hidden behind the clouds. Apparently, the forecaster's prediction of the weather system bypassing their small town needed some revising.

Looking up at the sky, Jorgen said, "That's the thing about Montana. You never know what life is going to be like from one minute to the next."

"Isn't that the truth?" A cloud of unhappiness formed over Pam's head.

"Are you sure you're able to handle the drive home?" Jorgen asked.

"Yes, I've been in harsh conditions," Pam answered.

The cloud above her head loomed heavier. Perhaps because it was the second time in less than two minutes, she had lied.

64

ONLY IN MONTANA

At first, Pam didn't have time to regret rejecting Jorgen's offer. The further she drove away from the microbrewery the stronger the wind blew. She had to drive with both hands on the steering wheel to prevent the wind from altering her course. It was as though the brewery were protected from the elements and once she left the safety of the parking lot, nature took charge of the night.

To maintain some level of confidence, Pam spoke aloud her encouragement to herself. "You are ten minutes away from home. You can make it."

As though it responded to her statement, the wind hissed louder than the radio and taunted her. "You should have said yes to Jorgen."

Pam strained to hear the words to the song playing on the radio. The wind's deep tones beat on the windows and muffled the words. She wasn't sure, if it was "If Tomorrow Never Comes," by Garth Brooks or "Don't Blink" by Kenny Chesney. She hunched to listen to the speaker in the door. A woman's voice broke through the rattling. "Talk about not knowing your music," Pam joked at how far her guess was from what the radio played. For the moment she felt better about her situation. If she could joke, she could make it home in one piece.

A gust of wind pushed against the side of her car and forced it into the next lane. Pam gripped the steering wheel and corrected the course. Her eyes widened at what was in front of her. The back of a semi swayed in the wind. She couldn't be certain, but if she were forced to guess, Pam would have sworn she saw the lights rise an inch in the air and fall. Since the radio was no help, Pam talked to herself. "Did that semi just take to the air?"

Her shoulders tensed as she gripped the wheel to stay between the lines. "This is ridiculous," she continued the conversation with herself. Pam considered pulling off at the next exit. It was better if she created distance between her and the semi. The last thing she wanted was to end up alone in a ditch.

Across the highway, two lanes and a grassy divider away, the back of another semi-truck toppled on its side. Time came to a standstill as she watched the events unfold in slow motion. She saw flakes of snow drifting in the light from the side of the highway. Then she saw the light from the semi curve away from her. In the absence of illumination from the headlights, darkness filled the space. Within the darkness, the sound of metal sliding against the asphalt took over her senses. Pam cringed as the sound made everything down to her teeth jolt. The sound amplified a warning to Pam. The back of the semi was sliding in her direction. Instinct kicked in, and Pam pressed the brake pedal and swerved right. Her intention was to swerve, straighten out and then stop parallel to the highway. The slick road condition made it an impossible feat. The laws of gravity and force exceeded Pam's ability to control her vehicle.

Time returned to normal, and her face met the airbag. It was the first time she experienced it in real life. The videos made an airbag deployment seem less violent. Then again, they were in slow motion. In comparison to the jostling she had just endured, the world fell silent. The wind still blew, but it didn't have any effect on her pickup.

Pam reached for her cell phone. Her hand roamed around the empty console and returned with nothing. Not as much as a pen was in the tray that held her easy to reach items.

It fell in line with her luck since leaving the brewery. Her mama said life would teach her right when Pam did wrong. If she had known it included lying to attractive men, Pam would have told Nancy and that Amanda woman to keep their opinions about Jorgen to themselves.

Obviously, the cell phone had fallen with all the motion. It couldn't be too far from where Pam laid it. She loosened her seat belt and felt around the passenger seat of her pickup to find it.

Beginning with those lies she told Jorgen, her night went from bad to worse. She wished she could go back in time and undo what she had done and told Jorgen that she didn't like driving in inclement weather. Maybe then on the ride home, she would have asked him about what Amanda said. Then he'd convince her that it was just like the programs she watched on the Hallmark Channel. Small towns have a way of holding on to the past. Perhaps since making his mistake, he became a new person. Then he'd say something like they should go out on that date to prove his change of heart.

If she told the truth, she'd have a date. And, she wouldn't be on the side of a road in a ditch.

A knock on the window and the glow of a flashlight changed her stream of thoughts. Someone cared enough to stop and help her. To whoever it was she was eternally grateful. Pam pressed the button to lower the window. The papers in her car shuffled with the introduction of the wind. She squinted to see who was on the other side of the light. Then she recognized the familiar voice.

"Are you okay?"

The first thing that came to her mind was "M*aybe I died, and I'm just dreaming*." Pam cautiously asked, "Jorgen?"

"Pam," he exclaimed, "I knew I should have driven you home."

A prick of light broke through the cloud that followed her since she lied. Her world was about to be righted. It was only a matter of time before reality matched what was in her head. She smiled and thought of the stories she'd tell her children—like the one about how she was able to find the love that she almost lost when she got stuck in a ditch.

65

WHEN YOUR WORDS COME BACK TO HAUNT YOU

From the way her headlights reflected off the snow coated grass on the side of the road, Pam had a hunch that her pickup was stuck. Beyond stuck. Years of driving in the Oklahoma back roads taught her how to get out of the worst of situations. This was not one of them. If that wasn't bad enough, she could tell by the big chunks of snow sticking to her window that the storm was closer.

Jorgen opened the door of her pickup. With the light from the overhead cab, Pam found her cell phone. It fell in the space between the gas and brake pedal on the floor. She reached for the phone and her cheek collided with the deflating airbag. Pam rolled her eyes to hide her embarrassment. She shifted her position and tried again. This time she reached the phone. Brandishing it like a prize, she said, "Now I can call for help."

"That's what I'm here for." Jorgen held out his hand in encouragement. "It is slippery out here."

Pam scooched out of the seat intending to land on the steady ground. Except, two inches lower than her mind calculated, the ground failed to meet her. When her feet finally made contact, her ankle turned. She wobbled like a deer taking its first steps. Her arms flailed in front of her. As if to add insult to injury, the cell phone flew into the ditch. An indentation in the snow marked the spot where it landed. A sharp pain shot up the right side of Pam's ankle and stopped somewhere in the middle of her calf. Somehow, Jorgen caught her before she completely fell to the ground.

His arms around her weren't enough to distract her from the pain and embarrassment from the near fall. She hissed to soften the pain coming from her ankle. In her head, Pam prayed, *"Mother of Mercy, please transport me to a different place."* She added, *"if it is all possible can it have a huge warm tub filled with bubbles and a plate of fudge on the counter?"* To Jorgen, she offered a forced grin. "I am so sorry. I hope I didn't hurt you." The pain was not enough to distract her from realizing that being in Jorgen's arms felt good. Like being in a hot tub after a long day at work good. At least part of her prayer had been answered.

"I'm fine," she said.

He eyed Pam with a hint of suspicion. The wrinkle in his brow was almost cute. "That was quite the fall. How are you doing?"

Pam stood a little taller. "Other than my ego being a little dented, I'm alright." She might have pulled it off if she just stood still. But mid-sentence she took a step away from him to demonstrate her stability. This time her lips puckered in response to the shooting pain and her leg gave in to the weight.

The next thing she knew, he swooped his arms beneath her legs, and Pam was in Jorgen's arms. As he carried her up the side of the ditch, she weakly argued, "I can do it by myself." Secretly, she was thankful for the help. It would have taken her much longer, and a couple more near falls, to get to the sturdier ground on her own.

If her ex-boyfriend Mark were there, he would have let her try to get out of the situation on her own and then made fun of her every time she toppled. She tried to push away the comparison, but it was too late. It had been made and solidified her assessment of both men. Her mother was right when she said Mark was not good enough. It took being treated right by another man to make Pam understand her mother's admonitions.

Jorgen set Pam down on two legs but hadn't fully released her. He held her against him as her body slid to the ground and she readjusted the weight to regain a sense of balance. At this point, the adrenaline from the situation clouded Pam's mind. Dizzy from all that happened, she kept a tight hold on Jorgen. She didn't want to fall. But in a sense, she had. Her heart had fallen into his hands to do whatever he chose.

They stood there with her wrapped in his arms and gazing into each other's eyes. The feeling that everything was going to be okay warmed her. Her mind perceived it the same way an astronomer knows the specific stars in the galaxy that she had found her one. Not the perfect one, but the one who was perfect for her.

A hint of a smile tilted the corner of his mouth. It encouraged her to remain in the safety of his hold. His lips beckoned her. "Why don't you come a little closer?"

Pam held her breath and followed the invisible magnet that drew her to him. Their lips were a breath's distance away when her heart exclaimed, "We are going to kiss!"

An authoritative voice broke in. "I hope I'm not interrupting anything."

Pam startled, and Jorgen loosened his grip on her lower back. Their eyes traveled toward the voice. With his flashlight beaming directly into their face, the person said, "I should have known it was you, Backman." Not only had the voice lacked condemnation, Pam thought she heard a hint of admiration from the man.

Jorgen shielded his eyes with his hand. "Can you please get the light out of my face, Zach?"

The man lowered the light to the ground in front of them. "Only you can find a woman on the side of the road and end up with her being all cozy in your arms."

With the absence of light, Pam made out the bulky gear around Zach's chest. He was the police officer on duty.

"She hurt herself trying to get out of the ditch," Jorgen replied. Pam noted that he hadn't defended himself against the implicit accusation. Jorgen's reputation for being a Romeo was common knowledge to everyone including himself.

"I need to ask her some questions."

"How about we walk her to my pickup, and you can ask your questions there?" Jorgen offered.

Zach pointed his flashlight in the direction of Pam's pickup that remained catawampus on the edge of the ditch. It looked like it wanted to fall in and a well-placed rock was the only thing holding it in place. He nodded his agreement and Jorgen held out his arm to guide Pam in the direction of his vehicle.

The snow continued to drift around them, and the temperature dropped. The change in the atmosphere was enough to form a mental thermometer. With every passing moment, Pam imagined the fluid dropping closer to the zero mark.

Every once in a while, she pushed aside a flake that landed on her while she slowly recalled the details that had her pickup stuck in the ditch. Zach echoed back what she said before writing anything and had her read through the report before having her sign it. As he ripped off her copy for her to submit to her insurance company, Jorgen returned.

Pam thought Jorgen left them alone to give her privacy. His grim face when he returned said otherwise. "It looks like your axle is busted. We're not going to be able to drive your pickup out of that ditch."

"I can call Nancy to come get me." She didn't want to make assumptions on how much help Jorgen had to offer. "I'll have a tow truck pick it up in the morning."

"Good luck with that," Zach said. "This weather system is supposed to drop eight to ten inches of snow tonight. I imagine yours is the first of many cars that'll get stuck on the side of the road tonight." Zach pointed at the semi, "The department of transportation is more concerned about hazards than people's folly." He spoke to Jorgen, "When are people going to learn to stay home when a severe storm is on the horizon?"

"When the weather coordinates with the Weather Channel App," Jorgen smarted. "They're only right about half the time."

Zach was quick to retort, "Half is better than none."

The driver of the semi who had been on the phone beside the cab of his truck piped into the conversation. "My boss said the tow truck should be here in about five minutes to get this mess off the road."

He stuck his hands in his pocket, "Speaking of. I'm sorry about all this ma'am." He nodded

"Thank you for your apology." It struck Pam as being odd that a person would apologize for causing a collision. Usually, people were so worried about being sued they avoided conversation. She saw it many times when she worked in the emergency room. Both parties to a collision laid in beds beside each other with only a curtain separating them. Neither party peeked through to make sure the other person wasn't severely injured let alone apologize. It seemed that legal boundaries had taken precedence over courtesy.

"I overheard the officer say you couldn't get a tow. If you

need a ride to the hospital to get your injuries checked out, I'd be more than glad to help you get there." He punctuated his offer with an apologetic smile.

She replied, "Thank you for the offer. From what I can tell, some ibuprofen and a good night's sleep should take care of them." Pam pat her pocket to find her phone. Once, I find my phone I'll have my friend...." Pam cut herself off as she remembered that her phone had fallen out of her hands with her tumble. Her eyes scanned over the ditch that had to have at least a half inch of snow in it. They widened in horror with the realization that her phone had most likely been soaked with the moisture and was no longer usable.

"I might have to take you up on the offer," she groaned. "My house isn't far from here. If you wouldn't mind."

"I can take you home," Jorgen interjected.

"Oh, I'm sorry I didn't realize that you two were together." The driver stepped back making more room between himself and Pam.

"We're not," Jorgen cleared his throat and stepped away from her. Pam's body whimpered at the absence of his touch. That was nothing compared to how deeply her heart sank when he threw back the words Pam had said earlier that night. "We're just friends."

66

FASTER THAN A NEW YORK MINUTE

It rolled off his tongue so easily. Pam thanked the good Lord that it was too dark for the men to see her cheeks redden. Her eyes darted to where she imagined Jorgen was going to kiss her. Had her mind played tricks on her?

What if the stress tricked her, and she misinterpreted his kindness as interest? Pam didn't have a good reason for the sense of loss that weighed on her heart, but it was there. For the entire drive home, she held two conversations. In one she gave Jorgen the directions to her house. The other took place between the lines. Earlier, she believed there was something between them. But, it came straight from the man's mouth. There was nothing between them. Weary from the stress of the collision she gave up the argument. There was no point in worrying about what never was.

They had one more turn until they reached the block she lived on. Pam sighed in relief. She was minutes away from a warm shower and a cozy blanket.

"This is your house?" Jorgen asked.

Pam blinked to make sure what she saw was not a figment

of her imagination. If she hadn't seen it with her own eyes, she wouldn't have believed it possible. A humongous cottonwood tree rested in the middle of her roof. She motioned to speak, but the only sound she produced was a squeak. Pam set her hand on her chest, took a deep breath and tried again. "Tell me I'm having a hallucination," she pleaded. This had to be a bad dream.

"I'm sorry to say Gary Turner's tree is on your roof."

Before she rented the house, Glenn, the homeowner boasted the history of the tree. "My grandfather, Gary, planted the tree when my father was born seventy-five years ago." Glenn tapped the trunk with his weathered hands as though the gesture validated the landmark's longevity. "This tree, right here, is an official Ashbrook, Montana landmark. They even added it to the map painted on the old mill."

And it was true. When people gave directions, they referenced the tree. "You want to turn two blocks after Gary Turner's tree," or, "if you reach Gary Turner's tree, you've gone too far."

Her first explanation of where she lived to Jorgen only proved the point further. She said, "I live on the corner of March Street and First Avenue."

Like everyone else, Jorgen responded to her description with a wrinkled brow. When she clarified by saying, "I live in the house that has Gary Turner's tree in the front yard," he nodded in recognition of what she had said the first time.

The tree was not supposed to topple. But there it was. The trunk inclined up against the front of the house, and the leaves had to have been hanging down the other side.

Jorgen barely had time to shift the pickup into park when her next-door neighbor, Claire, opened her door. She clutched her plaid housecoat close to her body. The snow in the yard between the two houses was deep enough to alter her walk into a mini march. Claire's pink paisley Muck boots rose and fell in an awkward yet familiar cadence.

She approached the passenger side of the vehicle and waited for Pam to open the door. Somehow Jorgen had run around the front of the pickup and opened the door before Pam had a chance to find the handle. He offered her a hand to help her step down from the cab. Inwardly she sighed at what she lost before having the chance to find it.

"I tried calling you about a half hour ago to tell you what happened." Claire's voice was breathy. She held her hands on her hips as she inhaled to recover from the march across the yard. "We had a really bad windstorm that started up about an hour ago. I thought for sure it was a tornado. The weather stations said it was a microburst." She paused for a second. "Anyway, one minute the wind was howling like a coyote looking for its partner. The next minute we heard a creak that was almost like a scream, followed by a crunch. When we came out to see what happened the old tree was perched up against the house."

All three of them, Claire, Jorgen, and Pam processed the events as Claire had told them. Their eyes started the journey with the roots that hung from the upended tree, traveled the trunk to the roof, and the returned to the roots.

Claire shook her head. "And this had to happen when Glenn decided to take a trip to San Diego. We called and told him. Either he was in shock or had too much sauce with his clam chowder. It was hard to tell. But he took it better than I thought he would."

She searched for what to say, but nothing came to mind. Shock had rendered Pam speechless. Her now dead phone laid somewhere on the side of the road under inches of snow. Now, this had happened. Pam fell back, and Jorgen caught her.

"I'd offer to let you stay with us, but my son is here with

his wife and two kids." Claire turned to the window and waved at the faces peeking out.

Pam had no pickup, no phone, and she wasn't sure if the house was sturdy enough for her to stay. "That is okay," Pam said it because that is what she was supposed to say. But it wasn't. Her ankle was screaming in pain, and her head throbbed from a tension headache that lobbied for her attention.

She wondered if the house was safe enough to enter to get her toiletries. "I hate to be a bother since you already have done so much for me. But, would you mind taking me to the motel?"

"How about this?" Jorgen said, "I have a guest room. You can stay at my place for the night. It would give you time to figure out what you're doing."

"I don't want to intrude…" she began her objection to get cut off first by Claire and then Jorgen.

"You don't want to go to a motel alone," Claire gasped, "that is what ladies of the night do."

"I have an empty guest bedroom ready for a visitor. Unless you want me to take you to Nancy's house."

Nancy was at her house with her husband and teenage son. The last thing she needed was for Pam to crash on her couch. And, her friend was scheduled to be at the hospital in the morning. Odds were Nancy had already gone to bed.

"Are you sure?" Pam asked.

"Let me talk to her a minute," Claire sided up to Pam and shooed Jorgen away. She half whispered, half hissed. "Are you kidding me? The town's most eligible bachelor invites you to stay at his house." She threw a smile in Jorgen's direction. "If I didn't have my children in my house, I'd be in the seat of that pickup faster than New York minute."

The smirk on Jorgen's face gave away that he heard more

than Claire intended. Pam could tell that he was pretending to be interested in something off in the distance.

"Now, go tell him you'd be happy to stay with him."

Pam never had a chance.

Using her matronly voice of authority, Claire called out, "She's going to stay with you."

The street light shone enough for Pam to see the amusement from Jorgen's smile extended to his eyes. The effect of the smile jarred Pam's heart. If she didn't know any better, he won a bet she didn't know about.

67

SAFE WITH ME

Old ladies on a Sunday drive were faster than Jorgen who carefully navigated his pickup down the country road. Pam didn't say anything, but it did surprise her a little. Usually, playboys loved hard and drove fast. So far, Jorgen proved to be guilty of neither.

"Bad weather blurs the lines between safe and tricky terrain," he explained. "I know most of this area like the back of my hand, but a simple distraction like a beautiful woman in the passenger seat is enough for me to forget where I am."

How could she find fault with that argument? Pam sat still and listened to the sound of the windshield wipers going back and forth as they pushed aside the falling snow. One minute the skies were clear and the next it seemed like nature dumped a bucket of the flurry white over their heads.

Her head pounded hinting at an impending migraine. She forced herself to focus on what he was saying. "Another thing," Jorgen interrupted her thoughts. "You are safe with me. Nothing is going to happen when you're at my house. Contrary to what people say about me, I know how to treat a woman."

She appreciated how he didn't let what other people said about him get in the way of how he conducted himself. Pam wished she could be more like him.

After a couple of minutes of silence, Jorgen continued his explanation. "I had this friend Gina. She came by the house for dinner one time. Things got hot and heavy. I liked her. She felt the same about me. And, one thing led to another. While we were getting to know each other a little better, William. He's her father. Was in a rollover accident. I wondered if it was life's way of saying that it was my turn to take care of her. Anyway, this other guy was interested in her too, and we found out at the hospital that William and his dad had some sort of agreement that his family would take care of her."

Her eyes darted to the dashboard, and she noticed their speed had dropped to ten miles per hour. She looked out the window and noticed the visibility was worse than before. Sasquatch could have been in front of them and they would have been none the wiser.

"So, I told her that we should take a break. You know, give us time to sort out the issues. As soon as I said it, I knew it was wrong. But she stopped returning my calls. Stopped talking to me. I found out through the 'he said—she said line' that Gina was pregnant. It got complicated. William told me that it was better for Gina if I let her go."

Jorgen sighed. Pam felt his eyes watch for her reaction. When she remained silent, he continued where he left off. "After that, I promised myself that the next time I bring a woman to my house for anything hot and heavy, it's for a long-term living situation. If you know what I mean."

"That's a lot of truth," Pam said. "Thank you for sharing it with me."

She was humbled by how genuine he was with her. He hadn't tried to present himself as a knight in shining armor.

And, her earlier assessment of him was right. There was more to the story, and after hearing Jorgen's side of the story, it made sense. He was trying to figure out life and messing up like every other person. Perhaps them being friends might have been the right decision after all. Would he have been quick to divulge his truth if they were going to date? She watched the road ahead of them to see where they were going and allowed the silence to absorb the cab of the pickup. Like a thin blanket, it surrounded them and provided just the right degree of comfort.

Jorgen was the first to interrupt the silence. "Why aren't you married, or at least hooked up with someone?"

"I was," she admitted. "In a relationship. That is. It's how I ended up here. My boyfriend, Mark, and I moved here to make a clean start. I got a job, and he didn't. After two months, he left. He said I was too good for him."

"Where'd he go?"

"Idaho. I think." She shrugged and added, "Nancy helped me pull it together. She's been like a sister to me." When the nurse known for her no nonsense bedside manner heard about the breakup, she refused Pam the time to wallow in her misery. For the first two weeks, ranging from invites to dinner to outings at the high school sports events, Nancy kept Pam distracted from her loneliness.

"Your family is okay with you being out here by yourself?" He turned the car down a road. The snow drifted in swirls around them. How he knew where they were headed eluded Pam. Then a solitary beam of light broke through the flurries. She imagined that Jorgen's house was attached to the light.

"I never told them. They didn't think I should have moved in the first place. I didn't want to hear I told you so."

"Sometimes 'I told you so' is a family's way of saying they love you enough to see the future for you," Jorgen replied.

He spoke the truth. She nodded to acknowledge what he said and promised herself that she'd call them when she got a phone. With that being the end of their conversation, they rode in companionable silence for a couple more minutes. Jorgen pressed on the remote control attached to his visor. At the same time, Pam noticed the house in front of them. The garage door opened, and the pickup crawled into the haven. When Jorgen shifted the gear to park, he pressed the button, and the door closed behind them.

The first thing Pam saw when they walked in the house was a brown plush sectional. Directly across the room, a large screen television hung on a wall made of wood paneling from the 1970's. Pictures of farm equipment and people she assumed were Jorgen's parents dotted the top of a shelf beneath the television. In front of the pictures, he had the controller for the satellite television, a DVD player, and three gaming systems. The room screamed single man without the intention of changing anytime soon—yet it was clean.

"I can show you the guest room, and you can go to sleep. Or, I can make some coffee, and we can play a game."

Before she had time to respond, Jorgen walked to a door at the edge of the room. He opened it to reveal shelves of board games. His eyes traveled the shelves and stopped when they found what they were looking for. He reached in and pulled out a wooden board a little larger than his hand and a deck of cards. "A game of cribbage would get us through this frigid winter night."

He set the game on the coffee table and crossed the room to grab one of the remote controls beneath the television. He pressed the button, and an in-wall fireplace lit to show the LED flames. The fan blew coziness into the otherwise coolly furnished room. It took everything in Pam to not fall in love with Jorgen Backman then and there.

The last time she played cribbage was when her grandmother was alive. They stayed up until all hours of the night scoring the fifteens and runs. Pam loved the times when she lived them; she missed them even more now that they were gone.

One time after her grandmother had passed, Pam invited her ex Mark to play a hand of crib. Rather than accommodate her request to share a memory, he added the app to her phone. As an explanation, he said, "Now Gigi," which was her nickname for her grandmother, "is with you all the time."

Without provocation on her part, Jorgen recreated her warmest memories. As they sat down on the couch and played, she found herself miserably failing at keeping Jorgen an arm's distance away from her heart. Other than having an unfairly earned a bad reputation there wasn't much for her to find him disagreeable. Also, fighting the feelings had grown tiresome; like she was carrying an armful of groceries, she'd never use. Pam relented and embraced the fact. She had it bad for Jorgen Backman. The only thing she could do was hope that when the snow cleared, and she went home, he'd feel the same way about her.

68

I DON'T BELIEVE YOU

The pulsing pain from her ankle throbbed and demanded that Pam give it the attention it deserved. She ignored the pain for too long. Finally, her ankle gave out on her while she walked down the hall to the shower. Pam caught herself by placing her hand on the wall and gasped to mask the pain. Through the sharpness, she heard her nurse's voice in her mind. *"Discomfort is a temporary and natural response to distress."* In this instance, her ankle was not happy with her for landing on it incorrectly. Her head wasn't pleased with all the discombobulation that occurred in such a short period of time. She told herself what she hoped. In a couple of days, everything will be back to normal.

If she were in her house or near her pickup, Pam would have access to the supplies she needed. Simple things like a cold pack and an ace bandage to keep things stabilized always worked with sprains and minor muscle injuries. Pam promised herself she'd ask Jorgen for both when she finished her shower and took the next steps to the bathroom.

"I saw that," Jorgen placed one hand under her elbow and

the other one around her waist for support. "We can try to get you do the doctor."

It took them an hour to drive the five miles to Jorgen's house. She imagined the drive to the hospital ten miles away. Zach's warning of other drivers being stuck in ditches because of the poor visibility peppered the vision. She wasn't going to die. "Going through all that trouble for a sprained ankle. They'd tell me to ice it and take it easy. I'm not paying someone to tell me what I already know." Pam replied.

"Okay, at best, I'm sitting outside the shower. That way I'll be right there if you need me."

"That just isn't right," she complained.

"What isn't right is you being the poster girl for I've fallen, and I can't get up."

There was the smirk. The one that said he had her right where he wanted her. If she said no, he'd call her out for being intimidated.

She was a bundle of nerves, but she didn't want him to know it. "If you promise not to look." She kept her voice light to let him know she was joking.

Jorgen chuckled in response.

A sense of relief came over her. He got her jokes. Trying to keep up the humor she suggested, "I have a better idea. You go first."

"What if I catch you looking?" He taunted with the same tone she used on him.

"I'm a nurse there isn't anything I haven't seen on anybody else."

"If that's the argument, I can say the same thing."

The red crawled up Pam's cheeks so fast she didn't know if there was a way to tamper the fire. He was downright attractive. She was normal at best. Sure, she looked good with a touch of makeup and the right clothes to accent the better qualities. Jorgen needed no corrective attire or cosmetics to make him appealing. The last thing she wanted was him seeing her undressed.

"Gotcha," he joked. He pulled out two towels and a washcloth and passed them to her. "I'll stay outside the door. If you need me holler."

She thought she'd be fine. It was a typical bathroom with a typical shower. Shampoo and conditioner were placed precariously on the edge of the tub lotion and toiletries on the counter. Pam moved the shampoo and conditioner to the floor, so they wouldn't fall and stepped into the shower. The water warmed quickly and soothed her muscles. The tension she refused to acknowledge melted away.

Another bottle of shampoo and conditioner were on the shelf of the tub. "How many bottles of shampoo does one guy need?" she called out the door. As soon as she asked, she regretted it. What if he had a secret girlfriend?"My cousin sells those fancy cosmetics." He answered through the door. "She asked me to try it and tell her what I thought. I liked it, so she let me keep it."

Pam shrugged. It made sense. Just last week she ordered some Perfectly Posh body wash from one of the patient's daughters. She took a better look at the bottle so she could remember to buy some for Jorgen as a thank you for his kindness. After committing the green paisley pattern to memory, she squirted a dollop of shampoo in her hand and massaged her scalp with it. With the recognition of a tingling sensation, she stopped working the lather. Pam smelled a hint of mint. "What's in this..." The room turned dark and the water pressure decreased to a drip. "That is not funny Jorgen Backman."

He opened the bathroom door. "It isn't me. We lost power. There must be too much snow on the electrical lines."

"I don't believe you," she snapped. She was standing naked in a dark shower with shampoo in her hair.

"You don't have to believe me for it to be true. Stay here, and I'll get a flashlight."

She heard him move, and the uneasiness formed a knot in her stomach. "Can't you just stay here with me until they come back on?"

"That could be in ten minutes or ten hours." She heard him shuffling around the cabinets. "I have something around here somewhere." The sound of bottles falling and Jorgen talking to himself about knowing what he was looking for being in the back did little to comfort Pam. The suds grew heavier in her head. She knew it was her imagination, but the fear that the soap would make her hair fall out forced her to rethink the situation. The instructions on the bottle said lather then rinse.

A catalog of videos they watched in college rushed to the front of her mind. She mentally searched for the doctor's recordings of people who hurt themselves in situations that seemed harmless until the person had to visit the emergency room. Had anyone gone in for a shampoo related scalp burn?

"Jorgen is there anything in your shampoo that would negatively affect my scalp. Like you don't have Rogaine or anything like that in there?"

"Do I look like the kind of man that uses Rogaine?"

"Maybe you don't look like it because it works for you," she suggested. A flash of light pierced her eyes. "What are you doing?"

"Not looking at a beautiful woman who is unclothed," he answered. Her hand went from shielding her eyes to pulling the shower curtain in front of her to hide from him.

Jorgen held out the flashlight, "Hold onto this."

Pam accepted it without question. Jorgen bent down and

reached under the sink again. "Can you shine that a little further?"

She obliged his request.

"There's what I was looking for." He pulled his hand out from the cabinet and displayed a two-liter bottle of water. "We can use this to get the shampoo out of your hair."

In that instance, she forgave him for peeking at her.

"It's going to be cold, but it's enough to rinse it clean."

"I swear to God you are my hero." She reached for the water.

She heard the pleased grin in his voice. "Let's hold off on the judgment until the morning. You may think differently when we have to eat jerky and canned fruit for breakfast."

69

PERFECT GENTLEMAN

With the last of the soap being rinsed out of Pam's hair, Jorgen passed her a towel and handed her the flashlight. "I think I have some candles in the basement. I'll be right back." Quicker than a wisp of steam, he was gone leaving Pam chilled, half-naked, and alone in the darkened bathroom.

Somewhere outside the bathroom, she heard Jorgen's footsteps descend what she imagined was some wooden stairs. What was she going to do in the meantime? Sit on the commode and wait for him to return? Make herself a dress out of the towels he had given her? She heard the footsteps mark his return, but Jorgen did not appear as Pam expected. Filling in the silence with a logical conclusion, Pam surmised that he most likely didn't have them in the first place and was scrambling to figure out what he was going to do to save himself some embarrassment. She sighed, *this is going to be awhile.*

Pam scanned the room with the flashlight to get her bearings and found the lotion on the far edge of the sink. Because it was a brand she hadn't recognized, she assumed it was cheap and would pump out thin. Although it lacked any definable fragrance, the moisturizer proved her assumptions wrong. It was thick and creamy. When she applied it to her arms, they quickly absorbed the liquid and felt smooth. She was not sorry to be wrong. Just as she allowed herself to be impressed with his knowledge of beauty products, she heard the changes in the house.

A loud humming, followed by a series of clicks, preceded the lights coming back on. Her eyes had grown accustomed to the dark and Pam had to blink a couple of times before they adjusted to the new settings. In no time, Jorgen was outside the bathroom door. "Is everything okay in there?"

"That was lucky," Pam answered, "I thought it was going to take hours for the electricity to return."

"It might," Jorgen replied. "I just turned on the backup generator."

He said he was going to get a candle. Offense fought with her sense of relief. Jorgen cracked open the door just wide enough to pass some of his clothes through the gap. Pam decided that life was too short to get upset over the little things and gladly accepted the t-shirt and sweats he handed through a small opening in the door.

She limped to the hall. Jorgen, who was slanted against the wall, with his arms crossed in front of him, greeted her with a smile of appreciation. "My clothes look good on you." He straightened, and his normal composure returned. He held out his hand to offer her support. The old Pam would have pushed away his kindness and told him that she could do it herself. Ever since she met him, he had been the kind of man her mother wanted her to bring home. There was no reason to close herself away from him. Pam placed her hand over his and said, "Thank you."

Jorgen grinned and remained close beside her. "Just to

warn you the generator isn't enough to run the main heater." He guided her down the hall to what she guessed was the guest bedroom.

When they turned into the room, a small LED lit stove oven blew warm air into the room. It contradicted what Jorgen had just said. Pam tilted her face toward him. "I thought you said there wasn't enough electricity to heat the house."

"There isn't. But there is enough to power this and the electric fireplace in the living room." And it clicked. He most likely took the heater out of his room and placed it there for her. To verify her suspicions, she asked, "Do you have one of these in your room?"

"I'll be sleeping on the couch." He pressed forward to get her to the side of the bed.

"Alone?"

"Unless there's someone out there that I don't know about- yes, alone."

His playful grin offered nothing in the way of remorse. Pam assessed the situation. His couch was a sectional that took up the entire wall. Her parents had the same couch when she was a teenager. Every once in a while, her family spent hours on the couch for movie marathons. Mid viewing her father and mother fell asleep on different sides of the couch. There was always still enough room for Pam and her brother to lounge comfortably. Convention was the only thing keeping her from joining Jorgen. Quickly, she weighed the pros and cons. Pros: they'd have more time to get better acquainted. Cons: her back looked forward to the mattress. Her heart told her back to shut up.

"What if I joined you," she suggested. "The couch is big enough for the both of us. I could take one end, and you would have the other.

A devious sparkle in Jorgen's eyes changed his facial

expression. He rubbed his chin as though he were considering the situation. Through the sweetest crooked smile, she had ever seen, he asked, "What if your invitation is just a clever ploy to seduce me?"

If Pam wasn't so banged up, it might have been.

70

GOOD MORNING

Jorgen and Pam nestled under the covers on opposite ends of the couch. She watched him sleep with his hand still tucked under his head and wondered who nodded off first. The last thing she remembered was him explaining how he blew it with Gina. "We were friends, and I took for granted that she'd always be there." He seemed more remorseful about losing her friendship than seeing her with another man. His honesty with himself and her touched Pam.

The quiet rhythm of Jorgen's breathing ushered a flow of memories from home. What were her parents doing? They'd freak out when she told them she ruined her pickup. Her father pressed for her return in the last conversation they shared. He insisted that it was time for her to go back to Oklahoma where she belonged. Something in her gut argued otherwise. She needed to be in Ashbrook for something important. Until last night she had no idea why.

Jorgen's eyes flickered before fully opening. A slight curve on the edges of his lips formed a smile. He turned to see her watching him. "Good morning, sunshine."

His voice, rich with sleep, sent a jolt of electricity to Pam's heart. She was in love with the small town bad boy. Except, he wasn't the villain Nancy and Amanda warned her about. He was a man who tried and failed, who thought the best of people and missed his father who died when Jorgen was ten.

"I didn't say anything to embarrass myself?" He pushed the covers aside and set his feet on the floor. His eyes wandered toward the window.

They couldn't see through the blinds. If the absence of wind was any indication, the storm had passed. Pam watched him shuffle toward the window. He whistled. "That's quite a bit of snow."

She shoved the covers aside and hurried to get off the couch to join him. When she stood, sharpness radiated through her ankle. Pam's breath hitched.

Jorgen turned around to face her. "You okay?"

"Yes, it's just a little sore." She wasn't looking forward to the day after aches that were sure to come from being jostled in the pickup. The spot on her shoulder where the seat belt held her down was tender too.

Satisfied by her answer, Jorgen returned to the window. "I need to get out there to plow the road."

"How are you going to do that?" Pam asked.

"With my tractor of course."

A white carpet of snow covered everything for as far as the eye could see. Pam wished she had her cell phone to capture the image. The landscape was a winter wonderland.

"As soon as we get the road plowed, we can check on your house," Jorgen promised. "Glenn called and said it was safer if you use the back door."

"Glenn talked to you? How did he know to call you?" She had slept so hard she didn't hear the phone ring or Jorgen's conversation with Glenn.

"Claire called Glenn and told him that you were here with me. He and I have done some projects together, so he had my number. I meant to tell you, but I fell back to sleep."

Another call interrupted their conversation. Pam tried to not listen. Sam's voice was so loud on the other end; it was like he was in the room with them. Jorgen and Sam planned out which roads to plow. After that, another call came through, and he was talking with someone else about pretty much the same thing. Somewhere between the calls, she used his phone to call Nancy at the hospital to let her know that she was okay.

"I drove by your house on the way to work." Nancy didn't sound pleased, "Claire told me where you were." Through the phone lines, Pam heard her friend's disapproval. "Why didn't you stop by the hospital to get yourself checked out."

"So, I could pull Noah out of bed to tell me to take some ibuprofen and ice." Nancy tried every trick in the book to convince Pam there was a love connection in the works for Pam and Noah. More than once her well-intentioned friend mentioned, "I don't think it's a coincidence that Mark broke up with you the same day Noah arrived in town."

"That's exactly why you should have come here," Nancy replied. "I bet after a little TLC you two would get along fine."

Pam rolled her eyes. Her friend was among the list of nurses who were terrible patients. "How about this, I'll have Jorgen bring me by later this afternoon, and you'll see that I'm okay."

"Where are you staying tonight?" Nancy pressed for information.

"Glenn called Jorgen and said the house was okay. So, I'll be home tonight."

"Alone?"

"Can we talk about this when I get there?" Up until now, Pam appreciated Nancy's protective tone. She smiled awkwardly at Jorgen who feigned ignorance of the conversation by acting like she pulled him out of a thought. Pam handed him his phone.

Jorgen placed the phone in his shirt pocket. "I suspected Nancy was one of my biggest fans. She and I go back a long way too. I remember her before she was married to Ron."

"Was she different?" Pam was intrigued.

"Sadly, no," Jorgen chuckled. "She's always been a little uptight."

Agreeing with Jorgen's assessment, Pam joined in the chuckle. Her friend meant well. But sometimes, she took things a little too far. Pam was forty-two years old for Pete's sake. If she spent the night doing adult things, which she hadn't, that was her business. She had half a mind to not visit the hospital. However, the other half thought of how Nancy's feelings would be more hurt than angry if Pam didn't stop by. She wanted to be independent, not spiteful. So, it was off to the hospital when they were done plowing.

For the remainder of the ride, Jorgen mentioned things she'd never remember. He'd point at something on the dashboard of the tractor and say, "This keeps track of the miles on the GPS system. If I wanted a record of what I plowed today, it would send the map with details like how much fuel I used and how long it took me to cover the distance."

After that, Pam vaguely understood that he used it to track his progress during the farming season. Jorgen was so proud of his equipment she didn't bother asking him to explain what he meant. She just smiled and hoped her appreciation for what he said came through.

If anyone were to ask, she would have complained that the time it took to plow the roads passed faster than she preferred. The ride to the hospital was even quicker. She watched Jorgen walk around the front of the pickup. Pam feared that this was going to be the last time she saw him for a while. She didn't have a phone to be able to exchange numbers. And, if Nancy had her way, Pam's free time would be taken up on miscellaneous projects and community activities.

Jorgen opened the door and held it securely for Pam to step out into the snow-crusted parking lot. He held out another hand for her to keep her balance. "It's slippery out here." She looked down at her running shoes. They had some tread, but not enough to catch her balance if she slipped in the snow.

Pam took ahold of his hand and tested each step before committing to the next. When she was five steps away from the pickup, she stopped to face Jorgen. "Thank you so much for your help. I don't know what I would have done if you weren't there to help me."

People said the same thing to her several times. Pam gracefully received the appreciation. Until now, she didn't understand the depth of the statement. While she knew there were other alternatives to resolving the issues from the night prior, none came to mind.

Before Pam lost her confidence, she stood on her tiptoes and quickly kissed Jorgen on the lips. Feeling proud for doing something out of her comfort zone, she released his hand and motioned to go to the hospital entrance.

Jorgen gripped her hand and gently pulled on her arm. Pam's body seemed to work on pure instinct. She rotated and pressed her body against his. Jorgen cupped her cheeks with his hand and kissed her.

A surge of energy traveled through Pam's body. If she weren't in the snow-covered parking lot, she would have sworn she had been struck by lightning.

At the same time, he softened the kiss, Jorgen caressed

Pam's cheek with the back of his hand. The gentle touch removed some of the harshness of being separated. "You're going to go in there to Nancy. And, she's going to try to talk you out of seeing me again."

Pam swallowed and nodded. She had to hand it to him; he knew what he was up against.

"I hope I've changed your opinion on the matter." He offered her a gentle grin.

Her heart threw out a little high five with her head that pictured a future with them walking hand in hand through the fields of wheat. She said, "It does."

"Good answer."

Pam straightened and braced herself for the discussion she was about to have with Nancy. In her mind, she was going to walk toward the hospital with a little pep in her step. When she reached the door, she'd turn around and wave her goodbye.

However, Pam's vision hadn't taken the snowy conditions into consideration. On the first step away from Jorgen, her foot slid. It wasn't one of those safe slides either. Her foot traveled in a forward direction. Even worse, it didn't care that her body wasn't in agreement. Before she had the time to recover, Pam's legs split apart, and her trajectory shifted in a downward direction that exceeded the law of gravity. Her body tried to recover. Arms flailed, her back contorted, and her knees buckled. In a feeble attempt to save herself she reached out for Jorgen's extended hand. But it was too late. She was too far into the fall. The next thing that came into her field of vision was the grey sky above them.

Jorgen's concerned face appeared. "Are you alright?"

"Other than my dignity being smashed somewhere in that fall, I'm fine." Pam rolled over to stand, and her body set out to prove her a liar. Her wrist couldn't hold the weight of her body. A throbbing sensation began in her shoulder, and she could only imagine the words her ankle would use if it could talk. She groaned and offered a feeble smile. "One day this will be funny."

71

YOU LOOK DIFFERENT

Except for the humming from all the equipment, the emergency room was quiet. It was as if the residents of Larkspur County had a gauge that determined when it would be a good time to have a traumatic injury.

Pam refused to trust her eyes. They had tricked her into thinking she could walk across a parking lot with some sense of dignity. She was not about to make the same mistake twice in such a short amount of time. Her eyes scanned the quiet and empty waiting room suspiciously. The magazines and newspapers stacked neatly on the table beside the faux leather lounge chairs confirmed her prior assessment. The E.R. was empty.

Nancy came out from around the nurses' station and stopped when she saw Pam leaning on Jorgen for support. With a voice full of accusation, Nancy launched into the tirade Pam fully expected. "You told me you were okay."

Slightly annoyed with what had just happened, Pam pointed toward the door with her head. "I was until I got to the parking lot."

Nancy's attention shifted as she peeked out the window. "John's getting ready to plow as we speak."

Rachel, the other nurse on duty, stepped around the counter and disappeared into the triage room across the hall. Pam figured that she was getting things ready for her visit. She returned to the conversation with Nancy. "I bet they caught the fall on the security cameras."

Nancy's didn't fall for Pam's attempt at diversion. Her eyes searched Pam's body for signs of injury.

"What hurts?"

"My ego," Pam grinned shyly. She quickly added, "I better not see footage of that fall on Facebook."

Jorgen guffawed.

Nancy rolled her eyes at the joke and motioned for Pam to walk in the direction of the triage room.

The idea of the searing pain coming back to life momentarily paralyzed Pam. Nancy had nearly reached the entrance to the room when she turned to see Pam hadn't followed. She issued a disapproving eye raise that begged to know what it was about Jorgen that kept her friend pinned to him. Pam exhaled slowly to control her nerves and stepped away from Jorgen who she had been using as an anchor.

Nancy's facial expression changed with the additional information. She held up her hand in a stop motion. "Let me get a wheelchair for you." Before Pam had a chance to respond, Nancy disappeared through the door and returned with the rolling chair. "And, I don't want an argument." She tapped the arm of the chair. "This will make moving around much easier."

Pam held onto Jorgen's arm and stepped away from him with her strong leg. She cringed inside. The last thing she wanted was for Jorgen to see her like this. She was the type of person who helped people through their pain. Receiving help did not feel as good as giving it.

Nancy circled to help Pam into the seat. When she was

directly behind her, she locked the chair in place. Pam had barely settled into the seat when Nancy stepped on the lever to loosen the lock. With Jorgen's parting words, "I know you'll take good care of her," as a cue, Nancy wheeled Pam to the triage room for the initial examination.

They barely crossed through the triage room door when the interrogation began. "What in the name of all that's good have you gotten yourself into?" Nancy wagged her finger at Pam. "I told you he was nothing but bad news."

"Nothing happened." To Nancy's suspicious glare she replied, "Really." Pam tried to step out of the chair to make her way to the scale. The look in Nancy's eyes said, "don't bother," so Pam returned to sitting in the chair.

Nancy wrapped the blue blood pressure cuff around the middle of Pam's arm. She tested the Velcro to make sure it stuck. "I wouldn't blame you if it did. There's something about these Montana men that makes a woman lose her mind. I should know. I married one." She pressed on the bulb to add pressure. "Nothing happened, my foot. I can tell by the way the man is looking at you something happened." Nancy scowled, "Your blood pressure is a little high."

Pam rolled her eyes.

"What?" Nancy pleaded for an explanation.

"Is there anything else I need to know about my poor character?" Her clothes were soaked and muddy from the fall. She was cold, and the throbbing in her ankle and shoulder were getting the best of her. "You just assumed that something happened."

"Describe your symptoms." It was a classic Nancy move. Whenever she was losing an argument, she changed the subject.

"I think I broke my ankle when I stepped out of the pickup."

"So, you two didn't meet up after the brewery for some adult time?"

"You think I'm the type of person that adult times with a person she just met?" It was more of an accusation than a question.

Nancy shrunk. "Give a woman a break. Half the women in the next three counties would have played adult time with him." She lowered her voice to a whisper. "If I weren't happily married, I'd be one of them."

"You would?" Pam's mouth fell open, and she quickly closed it. Nancy had been so vehement in her dissuasion, hearing that she thought Jorgen was attractive was the last thing Pam expected.

"If my Clark wasn't such a cutie, definitely." A sly grin punctuated Nancy's nod.

"Oh," Pam didn't have a retort. Instead, she offered a grin to show she accepted the peace offering from her friend. "Well, I didn't."

"Too bad for you." Nancy giggled.

Pam joined in the laugh. It was moments like these that reminded her why they were such good friends. They didn't have to be perfect; they just needed to be real.

The moment passed, and Nancy returned to the examination. She poked the Pam's shoulder and asked, "On a scale of one to ten how much did that hurt?"

"A two." She'd been in worse pain before. So, it wasn't like she was lying.

Nancy took a deep breath. "Okay. With ten being the highest, and one being you could walk out of here without any medical attention, how would you score the pain?" She took on a stoical expression that said, "I will ask the question a different way until you tell the truth."

Sighing in resignation, Pam grumbled, "A seven. It hurts like a seven. Are you happy now?"

"Yes," Nancy gave her an I got you grin. She tapped Pam on the hand and added, "Noah should be here any second."

Pam knew Nancy was happy he was the doctor on call. Her friend had been trying to get Pam to talk to him ever since he agreed to work with the hospital. "You mean Doctor Flynn?" Pam corrected.

"Yes, Doctor Flynn." Nancy winked. "I heard he has a nice bedside manner too."

With the air cleared between the two friends, Nancy happily wheeled Pam to Jorgen, so she could say goodbye and thank him. The two friends were so enmeshed in their conversation they didn't realize what they were walking into until it was too late.

Jorgen had his arms folded and rested on the nurse's station counter. He was talking about something with Rachel. His smile connoted a familiarity that struck a jealous nerve in Pam. The friends didn't know what led up to this point in the conversation. And it didn't matter to Pam. She heard the dismissive tone and saw the flirty smile when he said to Rachel, "No, we are just friends. I got involved when she obviously did not know how to handle the situation."

A buzzing sound in her head cut off the rest of the conversation. Not once in the time they were together had Pam felt like his kindness was mercy. Hospitality, yes. Like he felt sorry for her no.

They slept in the same couch and talked for hours. He told her all about his childhood and asked her questions about hers. She didn't know whether to be offended at his dismissal of their time together or hurt by his perception of her. The last time a man talked about her in that tone of voice, he left her.

She didn't expect an engagement ring, but she hoped Jorgen

would have spoken about her with a minor degree of fondness. Like she was a friend he enjoyed passing the time with. Similar to Mark, Jorgen had deemed her unnecessary to his future. She had no words. They left her.

At this point, Jorgen and Rachel pulled away from their conversation to acknowledge Pam and Nancy.

Nancy maintained her neutral nurse demeanor when she said, "We need to take her for some x-rays. I'll get her taken care of from here."

Pam forced herself to smile. "Once again, thank you for helping me. I appreciate it."

She almost got motion sickness from how quickly Nancy rolled the chair to get away from Jorgen.

When they were far enough away to be out of ear shot, Nancy leaned in and whispered, "I'm sorry I doubted you."

72

THE PERFECT GIFT

A broken ankle, a dislocated shoulder, and a sprained wrist won Pam a "short stay" at the hospital. At least that was what she thought the doctor said between the objections like "I'm a nurse" and "I know how to take care of myself."

Nancy, on the other hand, was beside herself. Behind closed curtains, she whispered her elation. "This is better than the game night I was planning. You two can get to know each other without the distraction of other people."

"Sure. Me. No makeup. In this lovely teal blue hospital gown." Pam flicked at the tie that held the gown pinned at her waist. "This is the perfect situation to get to know someone."

"You never know." Through a sideways glance accompanied with an elbow nudge, Nancy added, "If you saw the conversation between Noah and Jorgen earlier." She peeked out the door and hurried back to the side of Pam's bed. "Jorgen tried coming to the room after visiting hours. Noah told him only family and close relations were allowed past the doors."

Pam gasped. Did Noah overhear what Jorgen said to the nurse at the station too? The last thing she needed was the kind doctor's pity.

Her voice lowered so Pam had to lean in to catch what she said. "Jorgen called Noah a control freak. Noah said it didn't matter. Jorgen had to wait until morning." Nancy slapped the air. "I'd never seen the man that flustered. We thought we were going to have to call security to get him to leave."

Horror. If there were one word to describe what Pam felt it would have to be horror. She lived a life that was dull in other people's eyes. She spent her days working with people in their later years. Her evenings consisted of watching a cooking show on television or cute cat videos on Facebook. She had received more attention from Jorgen in the past twenty-four hours than she had from any man in the past six months. Even worse, it wasn't the hearts and flowers attention. It was the damsel in distress message. Pam was a lot of things, but a damsel was not one of them.

The pain medication Rachel had given her a while ago started taking effect, and Pam found it difficult to push away the sleepy feeling.

"You know I think it is more than a coincidence that Noah showed up the same week that doofus of an ex-boyfriend of yours left." Nancy rubbed Pam's good arm. The last thing Pam heard before nodding off was, "Life has a funny way of making things work out better than we ever expected."

PAM POKED at the pale toast in front of her. It lacked the warmth to soften the margarine square. She had been in the hospital a little under two days, and her home beckoned for her return. The home where her own toaster faithfully gave her slightly burned toast that she enjoyed in front of the news. Perhaps it was the Styrofoam bowl they used to serve the oatmeal, or maybe it was her all around attitude—Pam's world was gray.

"You need to eat to keep up your strength," Nancy who had just come in for her shift was a little more than enthusiastic to suit Pam's mood.

"If you were a real friend, you would have slipped me one of those donuts I know you have hidden by the ice machine," Pam grumped.

"Ha," Nancy pulled a napkin wrapped around something out of her pocket and placed it on the tray in front of Pam.

Pam's disposition brightened a little. She pinched off a piece of the donut and threw it in her mouth. "I'm sorry I doubted you."

"Knock, knock, knock." The masculine voice came through the door before the face appeared. "Is it safe for me to come in?" He didn't wait for an answer.

Pam noticed the button-down shirt tucked in enough to accentuate the lean abs before assigning the name to the voice. The gray Percocet induced haze she had been in for almost two days lifted. Her world wasn't brighter, but it certainly was clearer.

"How did I not notice how healthy you looked before?" The pain medication got the better of her, and she spoke without knowing what she said until it was too late. Her impulsive behavior ruined her chance of creating some distance between them.

Taking her compliment as a welcome, Jorgen held out a bouquet of carnations in front of him and strode closer to her bedside. "I came bearing gifts."

Pam sat taller and straightened the blanket to hide as much of the hospital gown as possible. Out of the corner of her eye, she saw that Nancy scrunched her nose like she picked up a scent that aggravated it.

Undeterred by her cool response, Jorgen offered Nancy a fake smile, "Is there someplace I can put these?"

"Do you want my answer to that question?" Nancy sassed.

"C'mon now. Bedside manners." Jorgen stepped around Nancy and set the flowers on a shelf set beneath the window. He turned to talk to Pam, "This place is harder than Fort Knox to get into." His eyes sparkled, "How are you doing, Sunshine?"

Pam smoothed any stray hairs that may have escaped from her ponytail. While she was happy to see him, she was also completely unprepared. Her thought strayed from the course of cooling things between them to what to do to impress Jorgen. If she knew he was visiting, she would have put on some lip balm and mascara. Something. Anything to look fresher than she felt. "What are you doing here?"

"Isn't it obvious?" Jorgen pushed the bag toward her. "I come bearing gifts that will make you feel better."

"You didn't have to do that," Pam gushed. Her curiosity pushed forward as she strained to see through the tissue paper.

"You kissed me and fell on your keister. I should be doing a lot more than this."

A friendly voice came from the doorway. "I heard your kisses were deadly. This is the first time someone is here to prove it true." Pam was so engrossed in Jorgen's presence she hadn't noticed Rachel had stepped into the room with a manila folder in her hand.

Rachel waved away Jorgen's response of laughter. "Don't

let him fool you." She gestured toward Jorgen with the file. "This one's a heartbreaker."

The conversation in front of her made no sense to Pam. The last time she saw Jorgen and Rachel together, he was flirting with her.

Jorgen wagged his finger in warning at Rachel. "Family is supposed to keep secrets. Wait until Easter. I have a couple of stories to tell on you."

Rachel and Jorgen were not siblings? At the mention of it, she noticed the resemblances between them. Their hair had the same auburn streaks mixed in with the brown, and their eyes had flecks of silver that caught the light.

Nancy cleared her throat. "I have to check on a couple of other patients."

"That's why I came in here," Rachel explained. She held out the file. "I had a question."

Pam and Jorgen watched both women walk out of the room. When they were out of sight, he pushed the present closer to Pam, "Open it."

She ran her fingers along the top of the bag with letters written in faux glitter. "I'm afraid to."

"It's nothing racy," Jorgen encouraged. "Rachel helped me. She's my closest cousin."

His voice took on a softer tone. "I explained to her how you wanted to be just friends and I was having a hard time with it." His eyes were soft with unsure wanting. "I still want to be more than friends."

Pam hoped beyond hope that she wasn't in the middle of a prescription drug induced hallucination.

He continued, "You see, I'm good at catching a woman's attention. Keeping it is where I struggle." His eyes glanced back to the spot where Rachel had been standing. "I hope you like what we chose."

Knowing that Rachel was his cousin was a gift in itself. Here she thought Jorgen had cast her aside when he was talking to his cousin for advice. She was never so happy to be wrong. Pam teased the paper out of the bag. Beneath the layers of tissue, something pink and textured caught her eye. Pam reached into the bag and pulled out the garment.

Jorgen's eyes brightened in anticipation.

Pam unfolded the fabric. He had brought her fleece pajamas! Soft pajamas that covered her in all the right places. "How did you know?"

"Rachel said warm pajamas say cozy."

Pam thought to herself, *How did Nancy not know they were cousins?* She said, "Rachel was right. This is exactly what I wanted." Pam caressed the fabric. She wanted to be comfortable.

"About the pajamas?"

Was that uncertainty in his voice? "Yes, they are the perfect size, and they send the perfect message."

He sat a little taller, and his shoulders lowered. Until she saw him relax, Pam had no idea he was on edge. She reached for his hand and squeezed it. "Thank you very much. This means more to me than you can ever understand." And it did. Instead of unicorns, rainbows, and broken promises, he offered her his heart, warmth, and a message of stability.

Nancy whisked into the room. "It's time to get you to your physical therapy appointment. Up and at em, my gimpy friend." When Pam didn't reply she said, "Do you need me to get a wheelchair or do you want to practice with your new walker?"

"Neither." Pam's heart raced, and her eyes widened in horror. The last thing she needed was for Jorgen to see her looking like she belonged in a nursing home. He'd change his mind about her.

Jorgen covered his mouth with his hand in a poor attempt to veil his chuckle.

"I'm glad you think this is funny," Pam grumbled.

"It is so funny I may never kiss another woman ever again." He winked. "I mean look at what happens when I do."

73

HOME WHERE SHE BELONGS

When she returned from therapy, there was a cell phone on the tray beside her bed. A screenshot of a text message from Jorgen was on the home screen. It read, "Had to go take care of some business. Be back soon." Her heart soared. He was coming back.

Then she received a call from Glenn Turner. He said that the house was livable, but it wouldn't be in the near future. At the first signs of a snowmelt, the moisture would seep through the roof compromised by the tree damage. Until he repaired the roof, it was better for her to find more suitable accommodations. Glenn offered to help her move her belongings into an apartment. "I can have a crew of people when you tell us where you want it moved."

Pam had hoped physical therapy was a sign of things taking a turn for the better. That what was happening in her body would materialize in the real world. Those woo woo people on the talk shows claimed it happened all the time. Apparently, it wasn't her turn.

It was time for her to consider her options. There were some apartments close to the senior center. She wouldn't mind staying there for a while. A familiar pattern of footsteps pulled her mind to the present.

At first, she thought she was mistaken. There was no way anyone from her family would be in the hospital in Montana. She blamed anxiety for getting the best of her. It was tricking her into thinking the moment she dreaded was about to make an entrance.

Nancy's "She'll be happy to see you," added to the rising tension in Pam's gut. Ready or not confrontation was about to make its way through the door.

All smiles, Nancy walked through the door. "You have a guest." She stepped to the side and held her hand out Vanna White style to make room for Pam's older brother Curtis.

"Hello, stranger." The tight smile on her half-brother's face gave no hints of why he chose to visit or how he knew to find Pam in the hospital.

She searched his eyes hoping there was something to help her determine his mood. His steel gray eyes only conveyed concern. "You're looking cozy in those cute pajamas. I didn't know hospitals had things like that." He held out a vase of flowers. The leaves on one side were darker from being crushed. "I got these for you."

"We can set them on the shelf." Nancy took the vase from Curtis. He watched her set the flowers beside the bouquet Jorgen brought the day before. She made her way to the door. "I'll let you have your privacy. If you need anything buzz."

She loved her brother, but she hadn't called anyone from home to tell them that she was in the hospital. How did he know she was there? "I am surprised to see you." And she was. He was not happy about her leaving Oklahoma. When she said that he'd like Montana when he visited, her brother said that wasn't happening, "in this lifetime or the next."

His lips formed a crooked smile. "You're not half as

surprised as me."

"Why are you here?"

His brows dropped, and the gray in his eyes darkened. "Isn't it obvious? You're in the hospital."

"But I didn't call. How did you know?"

"The hospital called your next of kin. But we knew something was up long before this." Curtis moved the chair, so it was closer to Pam. He tested it with his hand before sitting. "Mark's been back in town for three months. He told us you two broke up."

So, her family knew. She could imagine the things they had been saying about her. *"Poor Pam doesn't want to come home with her tail between her legs. We told her this was going to happen."* Pam didn't want to look her brother in the eye and see the confirmation of her family's disapproval.

"He also said it was his fault. Why didn't you tell us?"

The disappointment in his voice stabbed her in the gut. Avoidance fueled her intentions. She wanted to escape their judgment, not pass it on to them. Yet, she understood that silence leaves room for misinterpretation. She looked down at her hands. "You all knew it was going to happen. What was the point in telling you that you were right? Being the recipient of I told you so is not fun."

"I can't imagine it being any worse than our mother finding out when Mark came to the house to apologize."

"He did what?" Indignation gave her the confidence to look her brother in the eye. Not only had the snake come between Pam and her family, but he also set out to drive a wedge between them. He accomplished the mission.

"Mark said that coming to Montana opened his eyes to how things were between you."

Pam tried to keep her cool. She bit her tongue. She forced herself to make a pleasant expression.

"It was nothing like that," Curtis explained. "Mark said he hadn't done enough to prove himself to you. So, when things got rough, he didn't have a leg to stand on."

She waited for it. The part where Mark said she forced him away.

"He asked for Mom's help to get you to give him another chance."

There it was. If Pam said no, it was her fault that they fell apart. Then her family would hold it against her. "Why isn't he here instead of you?"

"He's getting things ready for when you come home."

"I'm not going home." Someone had taken Pam's life and shaken everything out of place. Two days ago, she sought after excitement. Now she had her fill of it. In the recesses of her mind, she heard her mother's voice, "Be careful of what you wish for because it always surprises you when it comes true."

Three strong knocks preceded the door opening. "How's my favorite girl doing?" Jorgen's rich voice filled the empty spaces in the room and made them a little brighter. He halted and remained in place when he saw Curtis sitting in the seat beside the bed. A stoical expression replaced his smile. "Am I interrupting something?"

"No," Pam scooched to sit taller. "This is my brother Curtis. Curtis—Jorgen."

Nancy came up behind Jorgen, "Good news, the doctor is releasing you to go home."

"Did you hear that?" Curtis replied, "I got here just in time."

"Time for what?" Jorgen asked.

Curtis stood to shake Jorgen's hand. "I'm taking Pam where she belongs. Back home with her family in Oklahoma."

"I think there's been a mistake," Jorgen replied. "I'm here to take her home with me."

74

WE HAVE A RUNNER

"Is he why you haven't called home as much?" Her brother's mouth fell open as he asked the question. Standing beside Jorgen, her brother did not seem as tall or big. Curtis's eyes traveled the length of Jorgen's body. He was sizing him up too.

"I am an adult. Why does it have to be a man? Couldn't I have just stayed out here because I like it?"

She wasn't lying. Pam loved her community. People waved at each other as they passed on the road. The clerk at the local store knew she loved salt and vinegar potato chips. She looked at the empty bag on the side of the bed and nodded to herself. That was why she chose to stay. The little day-to-day ways people showed they cared that made her love small town living. Not a man.

"Because you are going to need help getting around. How is that going to happen here?"

"I'll let you two talk. I'll be back in a minute," Jorgen said. He handed Nancy a small bag he had been holding and left the room.

Curtis watched Jorgen leave. When he was out of sight, he spoke to Nancy, "You can help me talk some sense into her."

Pam couldn't tell if Nancy's scowl came from dislike or confusion or a mixture of both. Nancy was the typical mama bear personality. Once she took to someone, it was her job to make sure they were taken care of. Curtis used family relations to assert his rank. He not only put Nancy in her place, but he also tried soliciting her support without asking her first.

The gunslinger music played its first notes, and the duel of the strong personalities was about to begin. Pam grimaced as she thought, "*Bad move big brother*."

Nancy's eyes went straight to Pam. Pam frowned and shook her head no.

When Curtis turned to decipher the silent conversation, Pam's face went straight. "I have a job. I have friends. I have responsibilities. I cannot just walk away because you think it's a good idea."

"You're in as bad shape as the geriatric people you're supposed to care for," Curtis scoffed. "Pam, you're coming home. Where you belong."

A siren went off and blared through the overhead speakers. "Code blue in the emergency room. We have a code blue in the emergency room."

"I have to go." Nancy turned to join the shuffle of doctors and nurses that passed by the door of Pam's room. Hearing Claire's name in the communication system kicked Pam into action.

"Pass me the scooter," Pam commanded.

"What are you doing?" Curtis asked.

"Claire is my neighbor. I need to go help."

Curtis folded his arms in front of him. "You're not fit to help."

"Never mind." Pam threw the covers aside. She landed on her good foot and hopped to the scooter parked in the corner of the room. "I cannot help the doctors, but I can be there for her family." She planted her leg on the scooter and gripped the handlebars. "Excuse me."

When Curtis didn't budge, Pam pushed off with her good leg. She knew he'd step aside when the scooter threatened to run into him. Curtis hadn't anticipated her tenacity until it was too late. He leaped to get out of the way a moment too late. The wheel of the scooter walker ran over his foot. "Hey, be careful with that thing," he yelled.

Driven to get to the waiting room to meet Claire's family, Pam called behind her, "Or, you can move a little faster when I tell you to."

With the doctors and nurses being preoccupied in the emergency room, Pam had free reign of the halls. At that moment she was not the feeble woman who has been spanked by life, she was a friend with a purpose. Pam would make sure that Claire's family knew their mother was well cared for. She passed Jorgen in the hall. He called after her, "We got a runner."

Pam turned the corner a little too quickly, and she temporarily lost control of her walker. It tilted and rolled on two of the three wheels. She over corrected and aimed the scooter to head straight into the wall.

Jorgen caught hold of the handle and stopped her inches away from the crash. Speaking with a breathy voice, he asked, "Where in God's green acres are you going?"

She looked up to see Claire's family walk through the emergency room doors. There was no mistaking them. All four of them were bundled in coats and scarves. Their hair glistened where the snow had landed. The man's hair waved in the same pattern as Claire. His son looked like a miniature version of him. The wife had her hair pulled back in a ponytail, and the daughter's hair was up in a messy bun. Their eyes scanned the area around the entrance as though they were trying to make sense of the hospital. Pam pointed. "To see them."

75

SOUNDS LIKE HER

Claire's son took one good look at Pam and clutched his teenage daughter to his side. His wife's mouth dropped open. Their son held up his cell phone like it was a weapon. "I can catch it on video."

The image of Claire's frightened family brought Pam back to her senses. "I'm your mother's neighbor, Pam."

Seeing their faces tighten in disbelief, she added, "I live in the house with the tree that fell on the roof."

"Oh! We didn't realize anyone got hurt." The man loosened his grip on his daughter. "My name is Darius, and this is my wife, Madison. He swiped at his son's arm. "Put that away, Randy."

Randy scrunched his mouth toward his right cheek. "There wasn't anything worth adding to YouTube, anyway."

"I'll go with you to the waiting room," Pam offered.

"She knows the nurses," Jorgen added. He offered his hand for a shake, "I'm Jorgen, by the way."

In the middle of the slow walk to the waiting room, Pam fell into nurse mode, "What was your mother complaining about before you called the ambulance?" She made eye contact with Rachel and signaled that she'd sit with the family in the waiting room.

"She was trying to shovel snow off the back deck." Darius ran his fingers through his hair. "I sent Randy out to take over. She wouldn't let him."

"That sounds like Claire," Pam agreed. Her neighbor was always doing something active. Claire said it kept her young.

"Then out of the blue, she handed Randy the shovel, went into the house, and sat in a chair." His brow wrinkled as he relived the memory. She was out of breath." Darius sat in one of the seats and Madison sat beside him.

"She rested her head on her forearm." His eyes darted back and forth like he was searching his mind for a detail he had missed. It was like she was a little kid trying to sneak in a nap."

"We knew right away something was wrong." Madison set her hand on her husband's forearm. "And, here we are."

By this time, Rachel joined them. "Right now, the doctors are taking care of your mother. As soon as they know anything they'll come out and give you an update."

"When will we be able to see her?" Darius asked.

"The doctor will give you the information you need to know." Pam had to give Rachel credit. Her facial expression never changed.

Darius turned to Pam to translate. "What does that mean?" Pam noticed he had his mother's dark brown eyes. They conveyed every thought that passed through his mind. At the moment, worry mixed with fear shaded them.

"It means she isn't working directly with your mother. Rather than give misinformation, she'd rather wait for someone who is more involved to speak with the family." She wished there was more to say to assuage his concerns.

Darius shook his head. "Why did we believe her when she said she could live alone over the winter?"

Noah came out through the doors that separated the patient's rooms from the waiting room. "I'm here to see Claire Gibson's family."

Darius stood. Madison took ahold of his arm, and his daughter took a position on the other side of him. Randy went to his mother's other side.

Pam remained in the back to give Noah the freedom to do his job. She noticed the moisture at his hairline. Whatever had happened had taxed him.

"I'm here to say that for now, your mother is fine. On the ride, her heart gave her some trouble, and we had to treat her for a heart attack. We have her stabilized, but she is not out of the woods completely."

Darius exhaled a sigh of relief and wrapped his arm around his wife's shoulder, and she fell into his hold. "When can we see her?"

Their son Randy placed his phone in his pocket and straightened his posture. His sister joined him. She spoke softly into her brother's ear, "Gram's going to be okay." Randy raised his brow in acknowledgement and made eye contact with his father. His lips formed a thin line of determination.

Noah, who had been observing the interaction between the family, said, "If you like, we can take you back now."

"We'd like that." Darius nodded his goodbye to Pam, "Thank you for talking with us." They headed through the doors with Noah leaving Pam and Jorgen alone in the waiting room.

Jorgen pushed his right hand into his front pocket. "That was kind of you to come out here and be with them."

Until Jorgen mentioned it, Pam didn't think of it as being kind. She replied, "Claire would do the same for me." And, it was true. Claire was outside the door ready to greet Pam when she pulled up to the house. "I hope she's going to be okay. I like her spunky personality."

"We should get you back to the room." Jorgen tilted his head to signal that they should go. "Your brother is waiting for you."

At the mentioning of his name, Curtis appeared in the hall. He did not look happy. Pam was trying to decide if it was because she ran over him when she left to meet Claire's family or if it was because Jorgen was there. "I'm going to the hotel to make some calls. I'll be back in a bit to pick you up."

Pam opened her mouth to speak but didn't get the chance to say anything because her brother cut her off. "We can talk about this later. Now that I know you're strong enough to break my toe, I can tell mom what to expect. Come give me a hug."

He pulled his classic older brother move. When they were younger, Curtis asserted that he was acting on Pam's best interest by delivering an edict and asking for a hug. It was his way of saying I'm doing this because I love you. In the past, she relented and gave in to whatever he said.

"I'll hug you, but I'm not moving home." She slowly wheeled the scooter in his direction.

Curtis chuckled and wrapped his arms around her to give her a hug. "We'll see about that." He pulled his keys out of his pocket and made his way to the door.

He hadn't reached the door when Jorgen said, "We may want to make our way to your room."

A tone of urgency mixed with a hint of humor made Pam pause. Something was up. She grinned. "I'm afraid to ask."

"You'll find out soon enough." Jorgen walked a couple of steps ahead of her and encouraged her to follow him.

They weren't halfway down the hall when they heard the

doors open followed by Curtis's angry accusation. "Did you do that?"

Jorgen grinned at Pam. "We almost made a clean getaway."

She couldn't imagine what he did. If his grin was any indication, she couldn't wait to find out.

76

AUNT SUNNY'S ROCK PILE

"For the record, it isn't anything that'll cause permanent damage," Jorgen said through his hands that covered his mouth. "I don't want him holding anything like that over my head for eternity."

Curtis had caught up to them just as they reached the door to her room. Jorgen ushered Pam into the room and followed behind her. She looked behind her to see a broad smile on his face. There was no remorse for whatever it was that he had done.

Her brother Curtis, on the other hand, was red faced angry. He gestured toward Jorgen, "This guy is worse than Mark!"

From the first time she brought Mark home, Curtis declared him unworthy of Pam's time. For Jorgen to be worse than him, it had to be bad. "What did you do to my brother?"

Curtis didn't give Jorgen time to answer the question. "There is a mountain of snow behind my car. And by mountain, I mean a pile bigger than Aunt Sunny's rock pile."

Pam gasped. Their Aunt Sunny believed in discipline. Whenever the kids were unruly, she made them relocate a pile of rocks she used for decoration. The pile was taller than a ten-year-old child and about the size of one of those kiddy plastic pools. Pam and Curtis got in trouble for fighting when they were younger. It took the both of them working together two days to move the rocks. When the pile was moved, Aunt Sunny added snippets of silk flowers. She said, "Beauty stems from hardship. Watch. You two will get along better because of what you've done."

It only took moving the pile once for the kids to know to settle down when she said, "It looks like I'm going to have to get new flowers for the pile."

Pam gasped at Jorgen. First in horror for her brother. Then in confusion. How did he manage to move that much snow in such a short amount of time? He was gone for less than a half hour.

Jorgen held his hands in the air the way a child shows a parent that they are clean. "Technically I didn't do it." The sparkle in his eyes said otherwise.

At the time, Pam only focused Amanda's advice to avoid Jorgen. But there was a second admonition. Amanda also said, "You'll find yourself regretting it the first time he has to help you with something. And, that definitely will happen at some point in time."

The rule was to be nice. Because of the way the relationships are woven, everyone in the small community was connected one way or another. Pam thought the familiar tone Jorgen used with Rachel was flirty when in fact he was conspiring with her to win Pam's favor. The nurse was his cousin, not a potential relationship.

Pam arched her brow in accusation, "Are you related to anyone else at the hospital?"

He gave her the answer she didn't want to hear. "Of course."

Pam cringed at the complication. Her brother hadn't had

time to be acquainted with a small community. They came from a larger city. He had no idea of the connections in rural towns.

"What does that mean?" Curtis's face said it all. The angry wrinkle in his brow straightened as he tried to connect the pieces of the puzzle. His eyes darted back and forth in search of the one he knew he was missing. He had stepped into a situation far more complicated than he imagined.

"It means he is worse than Mark." Pam pressed her palm against her forehead. "Jorgen knows what he's doing. Mark was just playing games."

Jorgen's brow wrinkled, "I don't know if that is a compliment or an insult."

Pam ignored the request for an explanation. She cut to the chase, "Why did you do it?"

"I didn't…"

"Okay, let me rephrase the question. Why is my brother's vehicle barricaded into one parking space?" Pam hadn't stood for a couple of days. Exhausted from the excitement, she leaned against the bed.

Jorgen rushed to her side to help her get seated. "I figured we needed some time for your brother to hear you out. This bought you some."

"We?" The part of her that was defending her brother struggled against the part of her that took notice of how hard Jorgen was fighting for her. Two days ago, he was satisfied with her just being friends. What changed?

"Yes, we." He said. "I told you I wanted to be more than just friends and you agreed."

"But, we haven't dated," she objected. "What makes you think I want to be part of a we?"

"I can explain." Jorgen held out his hands to calm her.

When she settled, he began his explanation. "Right before I met you at the brewery, I was in the bathroom."

Pam motioned to object, and Jorgen cut her off, "Don't worry. This story isn't going to be obscene. Anyway, this other guy was in there, which is no big deal. He does his thing I do mine. When out of nowhere, a woman's voice comes in through the door."

He changed the voice to sound like a woman. "Greg? Are you in there?"

"Now I'm thinking to myself this guy's got it bad. He can't have a minute to take care of his business."

Nancy walked into the room ready to talk. "You're not going to believe what happened in the park..." She stopped speaking when she saw Jorgen and Curtis standing on opposite sides of Pam. She back stepped out of the room, "I'll come talk to Pam a little later." When she had cleared the door, she made a pained face and hustled to the left

"Greg," Jorgen continued, "I'm on a first name basis with this guy, thanks to his wife. Anyway, Greg says yeah, I'm in here. But, he isn't bothered. Now me. I'm wondering if Greg's wife is going to see a little more of me than she expected."

Jorgen was such an easy storyteller; Pam forgot that she was supposed to be upset with him for what he did to her brother.

"This woman says, 'there's no toilet paper in the woman's bathroom. Can you bring some out with you when you're done?'"

Jorgen's eyes were wide, and he shook his head. "I was like wow! But Greg is smiling like a fox that caught a chicken. He says, 'That's my wife for you.' He washed his hands, unrolled a wad of toilet paper, and stuffed it in his jacket pocket. I can hear his wife through the door thanking him. And Greg. Greg is laughing with her over the whole thing. Anyway, I left that bathroom thinking, that's the kind of relationship I want."

He shoved his hands into his pockets. "I want to be the guy who has a wife bugging him in the bathroom for toilet paper. Well, right after I thought it, you sat beside me and started answering the questions. It was like you were the answer to my request. Then I asked you out, and you said that you just wanted to be friends. If you think about it that's what Greg had with his wife. I'm sure there's more to what they have. But I could tell in the bit of time I spent with them that they were good friends too. I knew it was only a matter of time before you and I were going to be close."

Jorgen turned to Curtis. "When you live in a small town, you're never really alone."

"Yeah," Nancy joined in. "We're more than friends. We're a family."

"That only happens in books and cheesy romance movies," Pam objected.

"Really?" Jorgen argued, "Who was out there like Dale Earnhardt Jr. when she heard that Claire was in the hospital?" He tucked his finger under her chin, "It's time for you to wake up and see that you are right where you belong."

"For the first time in my life, I'm going to have to say he's right," Nancy agreed.

77

HAPPILY EVER AFTER

"Pam, the family has spoken, and you need to come home." Curtis insisted.

Nancy cleared her throat. "I think I hear a cup of coffee calling your name." She hooked her elbow with Curtis's and guided him toward the door.

She was the disappointment, Curtis was the one who got it right. Her family had spoken, and they wanted her home. Pam imagined the digs they'd throw in conversations for the years to come.

Then again, there was one problem with Jorgen's plan. They didn't know each other well enough for Pam to feel comfortable staying at his house. For an overnight sure, but not for any amount of time longer than that. What if it was only the stress of the situation that made them get along so well? How would they react in the day to day pick up your socks and wash your dishes situations?

"Look I know this is sudden," Jorgen took both of her hands in his. "But I know this is right. We are supposed to be together."

His eyes implored her to agree with him. Pam opened her

mouth to answer his request. Moments prior, she had a list of reasons why it wouldn't work. She searched her mind for one of them. Nothing came to mind. With the absence of anything to say she closed her mouth.

"I promise we'll take it slow. I want to do this right. Court you, so you know that my intentions are sincere."

Pam had to say something. What it was eluded her? He was saying all the right things. The only thing she had to offer in the way of a rebuttal was they hadn't known each other long enough. Her family would think her a fool.

Jorgen tilted her chin, so they had direct eye contact. He leaned in shortening the distance between the two of them. His lips were mere inches away from hers. His voice was husky and daring. "What do you say?"

"I know what you're doing." She managed to speak barely above a whisper. His charm. He turned it on to disengage her resistance. Every fiber of her being wanted him to kiss her. Yet he had made his intention clear. Until she said what he wanted to hear, he was hands off.

He lowered his voice to match hers. Where hers issued an accusation, his offered an invitation. "Is it working?"

Pam swallowed. "Maybe."

"Maybe what?"

His grin. He knew she was caving.

Jorgen pulled away. "I was hoping for a yes."

Pam missed the closeness and whimpered inside. The man was using sexual tension as a weapon against her. It impressed and offended her that it was working.

Curtis burst into the room. "You can stay if you want!"

Pam startled. Jorgen lowered his hands to his side. Nothing had happened between them, yet Pam felt like she had been caught with her hand in the cookie jar.

"Nancy told me everything." He rushed to stand in front of

Jorgen and held out his hand for a handshake. "I had it all wrong."

Jorgen cautiously held out his hand. Curtis grabbed it and pumped his arm. "Welcome to the family."

"I didn't say I was staying." What did Nancy say to change her brother's mind?

"Don't listen to what I said earlier." Curtis sat in the chair beside the bed. "I was playing the part of the overprotective older brother." He spoke to Jorgen, "You'd be amazed at how many guys I had to chase away when she was younger."

"When are you planning on getting married? Once I have some facts mom and dad will be okay with everything."

Pam found her words. "Get married! We haven't gone on a date yet." A minute ago, she wished Jorgen was her happily ever after. Now she just wanted to be left alone.

"Curt, can I have a couple more minutes alone with Pam. We hadn't got all the details worked out yet."

"I hope I didn't cause a disagreement between you two." The troubled look on her brother's face said he knew he had. Curtis turned to leave. "I'll be in the cafeteria. Come get me when you're done." He closed the door behind him and opened it quickly. He held his hand to his mouth and used the back of it as a shield. With the other hand, he pointed in Jorgen's direction, He whispered to Pam, "Nancy told me he is loaded. You never told me that he owns close to three thousand acres of land." Curtis backed out of the room and quietly shut the door behind him.

"Look, I like you…" That was all Pam had the chance to say. The next thing she knew was the sensation of Jorgen's lips pressed up against hers. Her chest expanded in acceptance, and he pulled her toward him. A world of fireworks went off inside her chest. At the same time, she was a participant; she was an observer of all that was going on. She saw sweet smiles and passionate moments. There were some arguments and moments of reconciliation thrown in. She saw an older version of Jorgen and her playing with a baby. As the kiss softened the film reel of moments flickered until she was fully present. Pam blinked to test her reality. She had heard of people's lives flashing before their eyes when they died. Nobody told her it was possible to see the future in a kiss.

"I am in love with you. Tell me what I have to say. What do I have to do to convince you that we belong together? I will do it." The pleading from his eyes extended to his voice.

"You're in love with me?" Pam spoke barely above a whisper.

"I fell in love with you the moment you sat down beside me."

She grinned and recalled her thoughts before going to the bathroom. She was in love with a perfect stranger, and there was nothing anyone could do about it. And they had tried. Beginning with Nancy and Amanda telling her to forget about him, and nature creating all kinds of discord, to her brother insisting she go home to Oklahoma. Yet, there they were together—in love.

Pam smiled sweetly, "I'm in love with you too."

Jorgen threw his head back and exhaled in relief. He wrapped his arms around Pam and hugged her. "I feel like I just won the lottery."

78

WHERE IT ALL BEGAN

"This is where it all began," Jorgen wrapped his arm around Pam's shoulder and leaned down to kiss her forehead. "Three months ago, I was minding my own business. You appeared in the seat beside me, and my life has never been the same."

He opened the door to the brewery and stepped back to make room for her to walk through. The popcorn machine was to the left, the corridor to the general area was straight ahead. It all looked the same. The only difference was she was in love. While she remembered what life was like before Jorgen, she couldn't imagine what it would be like without him. Being with him was a joy.

Jorgen took Pam's hand in his and headed straight for the general area. She stopped short of the corridor. "Can we get some popcorn?"

Her request seemed to fluster Jorgen. He scanned the general area and turned back to answer her question. "Sure, but we have to hurry."

"The beer doesn't start to get warm until they pour it into

the mug." Pam rubbed the back of Jorgen's arm to sooth him. He had been on edge for the past couple days.

"No," he corrected, "It doesn't get warm until it passes through my lips." He nodded a hello to someone at the back of the room. "Nancy and Clark are here. They're sitting with Claire, Sam, and William."

Pam held out the two bowls of popcorn and motioned to step in the direction Jorgen headed. "Let me get that for you." Jorgen took the bowls and stepped away to make room for her to walk with the brace around her ankle. She limped in the direction he pointed.

Claire moved to make room for Jorgen and Pam to sit together at the table. The two had been roommates since the Claire was released from the hospital. After weeks of talking about it, Claire had finally agreed to venture out and visit the brewery. "You're right. This place is fun. I'll have to bring Darius here the next time he visits.

Stephanie, the waitress, placed the coaster on the table. "Are you going to have your usual?"

Familiar music from the sound system signaled the start of the next trivia game. "Yes, that'll be fine." Jorgen pulled out his phone in preparation to play.

The gesture caught Pam by surprise. Usually, he talked more. "I'll have a Blond Sunrise." Pam picked up his role of chatting with everyone they encountered. "How are you doing this week?"

"I'm doing well," Stephanie replied. "My son got first place in the track meet last week."

Pam was about to ask what event he ran when Jorgen broke into the conversation. "You're going to want to pay attention the game."

Stephanie smiled in amusement. Usually, Jorgen talked to everyone. Pam was taken back by his aloofness but didn't have time to question it. The first question came up. He read it aloud. "How many men did Elizabeth Taylor marry?"

"If she'd have married me, the answer'd be one," William joked.

"I know there were eight weddings," Claire answered.

"Seven!" Nancy exclaimed, "She married Richard Burton twice." When the answer was correct, Nancy elbowed Clark. "I know a thing or two about marriage." Clark who had been quiet just grinned.

Stephanie set the beers on the table. Pam decided to pick up Jorgen's social skills. She turned away from the game to give Stephanie her attention. "Thank you," The room fell silent, but Pam was committed to being friendly. Planning to pick up the conversation where they left off, Pam asked, "What event does your son run?"

"I think you want to pay attention to this question." Stephanie grinned.

Pam looked up at the screen. The silence made sense. The question read, "Pam, will you marry me?" The available answers were: A. yes, B. definitely yes, C. of course, and D. yes, yes, yes. A collective aww from the people around them pulled her attention from the screen to find Jorgen bent on one knee beside her chair. He held out a diamond engagement ring that glistened so bright she had to blink to make sure it was real. "Pam, you are the best friend I have been searching for, for my entire life. Talking to you is the highlight of my day. I wake in the morning wondering what we're going to do. When I rest my head on my pillow, my last thought is something you said, or we did together. The only way my life will be better is with you beside me for the rest of my life. Please say you'll marry me."

She gasped in response and covered her mouth with her hands. The swell of emotions stole her words. Her mind wandered back to the first day she met him, and his crooked grin caught her attention. Back then she mistook what she felt for him as the beginnings of a crush. Hindsight showed her it was love at first sight. The feelings hadn't changed, they only deepened. Like him, her only vision of the future included him. Still, at a loss for words, she nodded her answer.

A familiar voice from across the bar called out, "What was that? We didn't hear you from over here?"

Pam's eyes followed the sound. Her ears hadn't deceived her. It was Curtis. Her parents, who stood beside him, beamed with pride. Her mouth fell open, and she turned to regard Jorgen. She wondered why he was so intent on getting her to the table. He was keeping her focus away from the area where her family sat.

His smile widened. "What do you say?"

"I said, Yes." She opened her arms to pull him into a hug. "Yes, I'll marry you."

Another collective "awww" came from the brewery. This one had a happy note at the end of it.

Jorgen stood and held Pam's hands to help her rise. He gently slid the ring onto her finger. When it was in place, Pam set her hands on his chest and stood a little taller to kiss him. Right before their lips met, he said, "You have made me the happiest man in the world."

A flashback of the mind movie that played when he kissed her in the hospital came to her. She smiled in return. "I could say the same thing about you."

79

AUTHOR NOTES

This is a funny story. Well, a slightly funny story. Jorgen's story came to light in a unique situation. My friend, Kim, was not happy that he did not win the girl.

A lively discussion ensued where I defended the other guy by pointing out Jorgen's flaws. Kim wasn't having it. Jorgen deserved love. Sure he had his flaws, but there was something about him that made her think he deserved another chance.

Apparently, I wrote Jorgen as relatable and therefore redeemable. It took a while for me to figure out what it was that drew my friend to Jorgen. It was his tenacity. Our small town cutie did not give up. Once all that was sorted his story was easy to find. He had his second chance.

So, I hope you enjoyed reading the story as much as I enjoyed writing it.

And this is where I'll ask you to leave a review of *Just a Friend.* You can share what you like about the characters, plot, the friends of Ashbrook, or how the story made you feel. I read reviews to see if I'll like a story. So it would help others decide if they'd like this one.

Lastly, because I live in such a remote area, I am active on social media. I have a newsletter where I send out blog style stories every two weeks. My podcast Small Town Stories is available on anchor, the Google Store, Spotify, and the Apple Store. I also love to share on Facebook, Instagram, and Pinterest. All of the links are on the next page. So grab a cup of coffee or a glass of sweet tea and whichever way you choose you can get a huge dose of small town fun.

I'll close for now wishing you happy moments that you'll cherish for a lifetime.

Until the next book,

xoxoxo

Merri

80

KEEP IN TOUCH

You can keep in touch with me in any of the following ways:

TWITTER HTTPS://TWITTER.COM/MERRI_MAYWETHER

Facebook Merri Maywether https://www.facebook.com/merrimaywether/

Instagram https://instagram.com/merrimaywether/

Email. merri@merrimaywether.com

To sign up to my biweekly reader https://sendfox.com/lp/3zjn61

You can also follow my blog *Small Town Stories*

@ https://www.merrimaywether.com

81

WHAT'S NEXT

FROM FRIENDS TO FAMILY

Janine walked into the grocery with a list. A handsome businessman and his three lovable teens weren't on it.

Matthias and Janine have bumped into each other at the grocery store for weeks. His attraction to her is unavoidable, but he isn't looking for a relationship. He has his hands full with his three teenage children.

When Janine and Matthias meet at a high school community clean up, she decides avoiding him is the safest option. He sees that she is more than the cute woman who likes to eat steak for dinner, especially after Janine takes his handful of a daughter under her wing.

Matthias's three kids collaborate to prove Janine's feistiness is the perfect balance for Matthias's overly serious disposition.

And the plan would work if the adults would follow the script.

As Janine and Matthias work together to help his kids through their problems, they learn along with them that mistakes are meant to be forgiven; I'm sorry is as powerful as I love you, and second chances are just as fun as new beginnings.

From Friends to Family is a small-town, feel good, love story that will leave you with a smile long after you turn the last page.

Visit your favorite online retailer to get your copy of *From Friends to Family*.

82

VISIT ASHBROOK, MONTANA

Rule Number One

Chicken or steak? The cuts the butcher packaged of either meat were portioned too large for one person. Janine Darling envied older couples like the man and woman in front of her. The wife gripped the handle for balance while the husband showed her the different cuts of meat. After a couple of exchanges, they found something they agreed upon. She shuffled behind the cart, and he walked alongside her. *That's love.* Janine sighed her appreciation for the peek at the precious moment.

Hoping what she had in her cart would help with her decision, Janine took an inventory. She tapped a finger on the cart handle with each item. A six-pack of a microbrew, sanitary napkins that she concealed between a bag of barbecue chips, and a package of Oreos. *No help there.*

Whatever she chose would be her dinner for at least two and possibly three days. Janine bobbed her head like her ears were the trays of a scale weighing her options. It stopped on steak. Steak? Okay. Time to move on to the next item. What would she have for lunch tomorrow?

She gripped the red handle of her cart and turned it to the frozen food section. Except she didn't get too far. The body of a cute construction worker was in her way. If forced to guess, Janine would say that his ironed shirt and neatly pressed Wrangler jeans that he was the foreman. Janine tensed and pulled on the cart before it collided with his assets.

The measuring tape attached to his belt hook added a cute touch. *If I knew what he fixed, I'd go home and break it, so I'd have a reason to call him for help.* As quickly as the thought ran through her mind, Janine blushed. If the man she dubbed, Fix-It-Bob, had any inclination of what she thought about him, she would die of embarrassment. Janine recovered, backed away, and circled around the freezer that kept both of them contained to the small area.

Fix-It-Bob glanced up from the package of meat in his hands. Chocolate brown eyes and a polite smile rewarded her for not impaling him with her cart. When Fix-It-Bob directed his attention back to the package of meat in his hands, Janine decided the warm brown eyes with his closely shaved beard were a deadly combination. *Move quickly and don't look back.*

A gravelly drawl demanded Janine's attention. "Excuse me."

Janine halted. What could he want from her? She glanced toward the dangerously handsome man and her heart did a little flip-flop.

The wicked grin on his face betrayed him. Fix-It-Bob was aware of his effect on women and wasn't afraid to use it to his advantage. He probably broke more hearts than he fixed.

"I've never cooked salmon before. Do you have any recommendations on how I should prepare it?"

The drawl. Janine's heart whimpered. "Ah, well." She cleared her throat. "When in doubt, I go for the premade marinades." She could cook salmon using a variety of flavors and methods. She wasn't prepared to go into all the details with the handsome stranger.

The man tilted his head and peered into Janine's cart. "It looks like you and your husband are fixing to have a nice meal."

"No, it's just me." Janine's body warmed from the blush that began a little below her waist and rushed to her ears. It was the second time in less than five minutes. Her better judgment screamed to get away from the man who used his soft, you can trust me, grin to draw her in to the conversation.

Being single was one thing. Admitting it to a stranger opened the door to situations she'd rather not consider.

"Oh." He straightened. "I have a crazy idea. Do you want to hear it?"

"Ah, maybe." Janine's chirp gave away her loss of confidence.

"First, let me introduce myself. My name is Matthias Timmerman. I've seen you here for weeks. What's your name?"

"I'm Janine." There was something about associating a name with the face that made Matthias seem more approachable. Before she liked him because he was easy on the eyes. Now Janine found herself liking him because he seemed like an authentic person.

"I've seen you around for weeks. So, I'm not being impulsive." His smile asked her to trust him.

Janine spoke slowly hoping her effect would add levity to the discussion. "Okay, so you're trying to let me know you're not a serial killer."

"Exactly. My crazy idea–I've been wanting to visit the Hot Shot Grill for weeks. Would you want to join me?"

Janine's mouth fell open. Her heart screamed, *yes*. Her head warned her. *Your heart makes stupid decisions*. Her taste buds chimed in. Pan-seared steak always tasted better when somebody else was cooking it. She glanced down at her cart. Then her brain jumped in. There would be fresh vegetables. Steak and fresh vegetables were a better option than steak and barbecue chips. All of a sudden, her heart wasn't so stupid.

The air around Janine shifted. She blinked until the gray cloud that obscured her vision cleared. She knew something was a little out of focus. Her head, heart, and soul reached a firm decision. Later, when people asked her what it was that enticed her to run off with a complete stranger, she'd be candid and say *I forgot the first rule my mother taught me. Do not talk to strangers. Who cares how cute they are.*

MORE STORIES BY MERRI MAYWETHER

The Ashbrook, Montana Series

While navigating through real world problems, the friends and family in Ashbrook find second chances at love.

From Friends to Family

Let the Games Begin

A Chance to Win Her Heart

The Missing Piece of My Puzzle

Marry Me, Kate

Picture Perfect Romance

Same Wish Same Star

The Small-Town Stories Series

Light-hearted quick reads for characters within the Ashbrook and Three Creek's, Montana series.

Piece of Cake

Get Well Soon

Just A Friend

For a Visit

The Three Creeks, Montana Series

For a friends to happily ever after romance story, visit Three Creeks, Montana.

Welcome Home

Home Sweet Home

Honey, I'm Home

Home for Good

The Paradise Hills, Montana Series

In a cozy town nestled at the foothills of a mountain, love touches the heart of those who seek it.

Meet Me by the Christmas Tree

Paradise Hills Summer

Paradise Hills Trick or Treat

Paradise Hills Thanksgiving

Christmas Wishes

Made in the USA
Columbia, SC
30 November 2020